"TERRIFIC . . . A RACY, REALISTIC READ."—*New York Daily News*

"GERALD PETIEVICH IS AN ABLE THRILLER WRITER. . . . What raises the book above escapism is its tour of the Secret Service back shop: the advance teams that scrutinize every alley and overpass before a president's visit, the lines of defense within lines of defense ringing the White House. . . . Petievich delivers a persuasive and ironic critique of the craziness we take for granted."—*Newsweek*

"LIVELY, CREDIBLE SUSPENSE . . . informative about the workings of the Secret Service . . . twists and turns, coincidences and surprises keep the story spinning."—*New York Times*

"A TAUT STORY OF MURDER AND BETRAYAL . . . Captures the incestuous world of the Secret Service . . . the holes in the system . . . and the men who stop the bullets."
—*Chicago Tribune*

"ALL THE RIGHT ELEMENTS—ACTION, SUSPENSE, MURDER, LOVE, INTRIGUE!"—*West Coast Review of Books*

PARAMOUR

****

GERALD PETIEVICH

A SIGNET BOOK

SIGNET
Published by the Penguin Group
Penguin Books USA Inc., 375 Hudson Street,
New York, New York 10014, U.S.A.
Penguin Books Ltd, 27 Wrights Lane,
London W8 5TZ, England
Penguin Books Australia Ltd, Ringwood,
Victoria, Australia
Penguin Books Canada Ltd, 10 Alcorn Avenue,
Toronto, Ontario, Canada M4V 3B2
Penguin Books (N.Z.) Ltd, 182–190 Wairau Road,
Auckland 10, New Zealand

Penguin Books Ltd, Registered Offices:
Harmondsworth, Middlesex, England

Published by Signet, an imprint of New American Library, a
division of Penguin Books USA Inc. Previously published in a Dutton edition.

First Signet Printing, December, 1992
10 9 8 7 6 5 4 3 2 1

 REGISTERED TRADEMARK—MARCA REGISTRADA

PRINTED IN THE UNITED STATES OF AMERICA

PUBLISHER'S NOTE
This is a work of fiction. Names, characters, places, and incidents either
are the product of the author's imagination or are used fictitiously, and any
resemblance to actual persons, living or dead, events, or locales is entirely
coincidental.

For S/P4 John G. Petievich,
U.S. Army Military Police Corps

The position of Special Agent, U.S. Secret Service, requires that the incumbent cover designated security posts in connection with the protection of the President of the United States, whose safety is not only a matter of the utmost national concern but international in scope. If qualified, an agent may be assigned permanently as a member of the White House Presidential Protection Detail.

Special Agents so assigned may be exposed to physical combat, exchange of gunfire, and other hazards inherent with major protective assignments.

—*U.S. Secret Service Manual*, Sect. 402.56, para. 13

1

Outside, the White House night lights, though unobtrusive, kept the grounds well illuminated. Other than some midsummer traffic noise coming from Pennsylvania Avenue, there was only the muffled sound of two-way radios carried by the uniformed officers as they moved from post to post at half-hour intervals. Inside, the First Family was ensconced in the privacy of their second-floor living quarters. Other than the working shift of Secret Service agents and a few maintenance and communications employees, the White House halls were dim and hushed.

U.S. Secret Service Agent Ray Stryker, a lanky, thirty-nine-year-old man with weathered features, was trudging down a long cement corridor in the White House basement: a labyrinth of offices and security cubicles, storerooms . . . and a bomb shelter designed to withstand a nearly ground-zero blast. In obedience to a recently initiated security procedure, he was perfunctorily checking (he didn't want to say "shaking") doors. His shift of duty on the White House Presidential Protection Detail was nearly completed. In fact, he'd signed off on the command-post log a few minutes early to make the final security check: anything to shorten the drudging four-to-midnight shift.

Stryker's right knee was aching, as it had for the past three years—ever since the President's trip to Peshawar, Pakistan. There, Stryker had been "working the running board," as close-in presidential motorcade security duty was called in the Secret Service. Running alongside the left rear fender of 900X, the presidential limousine, keeping his eyes trained on the crowd line, he realized just an instant too late that the limousine had turned toward him slightly. He was helpless as the heavy, bulletproof tire rolled over his foot and wrenched his entire right leg in a clockwise motion upward into the wheel well. Though the multiple bone fractures, set by a turbaned Pakistani doctor, had healed in the normal time, the knee had never been the same. But what the hell. Though in motorcades he was now limited to driving the limo or being a "gun man" inside the car, he could still play soccer as goalie, and the injury, though leaving him with a dull, continuous ache, hadn't affected his seniority on the White House Detail.

At the White House Situation Room, where he remembered President Bush spending thirty-six straight hours during the 1991 Persian Gulf War, he tested the double-combination locks on the tall steel doors. Secure. Using a ballpoint pen attached to the wall with a short string, he wrote his initials and the date, 8/12/96, on the Secret Service Form 1632 Secure Area Log.

Moving door-to-door farther down the hallway, he felt the fatigue that comes from sheer boredom. During Stryker's entire tour of duty today, the President's only activity outside his private quarters had been to come downstairs to attend a black-tie dinner honoring the newly elected President of Zaire. All attendees, including both Presidents, the first ladies, and the other guests, had looked weary of the affair from beginning to end.

Stryker's mind was on his next three-day weekend. He would take care of some errands Friday at his Fairfax, Virginia, condominium. On Saturday he'd play soccer for the Fairfax Vikings, a team made up mostly of single government and military employees sponsored by Shaughnessy's Pub, where he spent a lot of time during off-hours. Sunday would be spent with his seven-year-old daughter Kelli, whom, per the divorce decree, he was allowed to visit twice each week. After taking Kelli home, if he felt like it he'd ask his next-door neighbor if she wanted to grab a pizza. Perhaps Flora would spend the night with him, as she often did whenever her steady boyfriend was at sea.

Passing the open door of the White House Communications Center, Stryker waved casually to Ed Sneed, a strapping, uniformed army major whose sole duty, in the imminence of nuclear war, was to rush upstairs and give the President the secret military code needed to launch missiles and thus blow up the world. Sneed, his teammate on the Fairfax Vikings, gave a little salute.

Farther down the hallway, Stryker checked a line of doors known as the Special Projects Office. The locks were secure. Per the Secret Service Standard Operating Procedure (SOP), he was required to check the safes inside.

Stryker took out a three-by-five card on which he'd noted the day's code. Referring to the note, he tapped three number combinations on a cipher lock and waited a moment. There was a *thud-click* as the lock came open. Stryker pulled the heavy steel door to enter. Inside, he flicked on the light.

There were two desks in the room, and the floor was covered with a utilitarian red carpet common to White House offices. The walls were covered with maps hidden by black CLASSIFIED drapes. To the right was a door to a small conference room. Both it and the room he was in were soundproof. Moving to a row of security document safes lining the facing wall, he checked the printed logs taped to the top front drawers. Today's date was written on the last line for each log, next to the initials *MK*. Starting at the left and moving right, he tugged at the drawer handles.

One wasn't locked.

Feeling his heart quicken, he pulled open the heavy drawer. It was full of hanging file folders.

There was the sound of the steel door clicking shut. Stryker whirled and saw a familiar face . . . and a gun being raised to the level of his head. "Don't," Stryker said, instinctively reaching for his own revolver.

With his breath at full stop, Stryker thought he heard a click, but he wasn't sure. Then there was a sudden excruciating stab of pain in his head, and the world turned bright white and exploded . . . into a devastating sense of peace.

2

A fetid breeze wafted from the Potomac River.

Special Agent Jack Powers, U.S. Secret Service, ended his daily five-mile jog at a sidewalk newspaper rack in front of the enormous Watergate apartment complex. He was wearing blue nylon jogging shorts, a white T-shirt, and a pair of Nike running shoes he'd purchased on sale at Woodward and Lothrup. Soaked in perspiration, he stood on the corner, arms akimbo, taking deep breaths. The workout had relaxed him, freed him from stress. Though the rest of his day would be planned and overseen by others, the early morning was his.

He tugged gently at the waistband of his shorts, picked change from a tiny waist pocket, and dropped the coins in the news rack's coin receptacle. He raised the clear plastic cover and took a copy of the *Washington Post*.

Looking both ways, he crossed Virginia Avenue with the green light. Heading slowly along New Hampshire, as was his custom after the morning run, he scanned the front page. The President was even (fifty-one percent to forty-nine percent) in a CBS campaign poll, and double-digit inflation and record high unemployment was continuing. The U.S. economy

15

continued to be outpaced by a booming, barrier-free Europe led by a reunified Germany. The President's popularity had dropped consistently, owing to his stumbling approach to foreign affairs in the Middle East. With the presidential election only three months away and the polls showing the President even with his challenger, the Chief Executive's job would be to maintain balance and avoid any last-minute glitches that could push him from power.

Powers turned the page. Having protected five different Presidents, he knew that though Presidents were invariably men of unbridled ego and ambition who thrived on adversity, they were equally invariably deeply pierced by criticism. As Powers could attest, the presidency ate some men alive.

At the second stoplight, Powers paused over an article headlined PRESIDENT TO ADDRESS FOREIGN POL-ICY CRITICISM. In it, presidential press secretary Richard Eggleston stated the President's intention to address the Los Angeles Chamber of Commerce on Friday of next week.

From rumors he'd heard recently while traveling with the President on the campaign trail, Powers surmised that since the speech was planned for a Friday, the President's real reason for traveling to the West Coast was to confer with the movie industry fat cats who financed his campaign, some of whom were rumored to be jumping ship. The entire trip, though undertaken for strictly partisan political purposes, would be paid for by the government, and the presidential party would probably spend the weekend at their usual lodging in southern California, the newly refurbished Breakwater Hotel in Santa Monica. Accordingly, since the shift change for the White House Detail was scheduled every other Friday, Powers would still be working the day shift on the West Coast—the same tour of duty as Louise Fisher, an attractive Santa Monica police officer whom he dated when in town.

But this presented a problem.

Though Louise was a veritable sexual athlete, she was incapable of making conversation about any topic except herself. Long ago, Powers had tired of her persecution stories—centering on a male-chauvinist patrol lieutenant she believed was out to get her—and of her incessant bragging about her prowess as starting center on the police volleyball team. For this reason, it was difficult to spend long periods of time with her.

Therefore, Powers decided to request a shift change to the 4 P.M. to midnight shift. This way, while in Santa Monica, he could enjoy sleeping with Louise at her beach condo after he got off work but avoid spending long stretches of off-duty time enduring her depressing stories. Instead, he'd have the daytime hours free to meet other women at the beach.

If nothing else, twenty-two years of being a member of the Secret Service's White House Detail had taught him the importance of conscientious advance planning.

Powers had been in charge of advance security arrangements for the last California trip. The advance man arranged security at each and every location on the President's California itinerary and bore the final responsibility for his safety, from the time the President arrived until Air Force One lifted wheels up on departure. Powers liked advance duties. In addition to the challenge, it was an easy way to make a lot of overtime pay.

By the time Powers reached Washington Circle he'd finished skimming the newspaper. At the entrance to the Georgetown Arms, a drab brick-front apartment building, like the others lining both sides of the street, he shoved the paper into a curbside trash can. Then he lifted a metal dog-tag chain from around his neck and used one of the two keys attached to it to open the front door. The foyer reeked with the odor of mildewed carpet. At the elevator, he pressed a button and waited.

Turning to a large mirror on the facing wall, he saw his reflection—five-foot-ten with height proportionate to weight, a full head of closely cropped dark hair flecked with gray, thick eyebrows, clean features, and, except for the premature wrinkles around his eyes from years of scanning thousands of faces in thousands of crowds looking for potential assassins—no distinguishing traits. Hell, he was just another forty-four-year-old jogger.

In his drab rent-by-the-week apartment (it didn't make sense to lease a D.C. residence when he was only in town a few days each month), he lifted his soaking T-shirt over his head and hung it over the bathroom shower rod. Pulling two Velcro fasteners open, he freed himself from a custom-made elastic holster wrapped tightly around his midsection like a rib brace. From a pocket in the holster, he slipped out a snub-nosed .38 revolver wrapped loosely in Saran Wrap as protection from jogging perspiration.

He'd developed this method of carrying the gun when he and the other agents on the White House Secret Service Detail were required to follow President Jimmy Carter on his daily jogs. After a couple of trials with other materials, Powers had determined that one thin layer of Saran Wrap kept the gun dry but didn't interfere with firing. To be sure, he'd tested the plastic-wrapped piece by firing more than a hundred rounds with it at the Secret Service firing range in Beltsville, Maryland.

Though the weapon was annoying during exercise and caused a slight abrasion where it rubbed against his waist, he carried it because he knew the odds were that in Washington, D.C., crime capital of the world, some armed robber would eventually, someday when he least expected it, accost him while he was jogging. If so, Powers would surprise him with the .38 and blow his head off.

After a long shower, Powers broke starch on a fresh white shirt. After pulling on his trousers and sturdy wing-tip shoes, he weighted his belt with his work equipment: revolver, handcuffs, a Motorola HL-20 radio receiver-transmitter keyed to the White House frequency, a small tear-gas canister, and a leather case containing an identification pin providing access to Location Rain City, a secret underground bomb shelter near the Pentagon where the President would be spirited to safety by the White House Detail in the event of nuclear war.

He shrugged on his conservative blue suit jacket, then checked the contents of his Secret Service—issue metal briefcase containing the other items he was required to have in his possession at all times when on-duty: his official passport, two pistol speed-loaders, a small flashlight, a book of government transportation requests good for flights on any airline in the world, an extra set of handcuffs, air force aviator sunglasses, and an extra pair of wing-tip shoes with the rubber nonslip soles required by Secret Service regulation. He checked to see that all faucets and appliances were off in the apartment and then headed downstairs to catch the Metro.

At the East Gate to the White House, Powers held up his Secret Service identification card to Betty Manning, the Secret Service Uniformed Division officer manning the guard booth. She had freckles, red hair drawn back tightly, and a white Secret Service uniform shirt tailored to accentuate her full figure. Once, during a presidential visit to Japan, he'd slept with her.

Rather than examining his ID card closely, she just smiled. "I thought you were gonna call me last weekend."

"Sorry, I got tied up," he said, moving quickly past.

She extended her middle finger and held it to the glass as he hurried through a doorway covered by a blue awning and into the White House basement.

Powers strolled down a wide marble walkway past the White House barbershop and the Travel Logistics Office, stopping at the nicely decorated Navy mess facility, the White House's restaurant.

He glanced both ways in the hall. There were no Secret Service supervisors in sight, so he went inside. Though, per the Secret Service White House operations manual, agents of the White House Detail were forbidden to use the mess with the White House staffers, general officers, and politicos, Powers had been eating there for years. After enjoying a breakfast of eggs and pancakes served to him by Ramon Valiente, a gray-haired Filipino mess steward whom he discreetly tipped to ensure being seated at a reserved table in the corner away from the door, Powers paid his bill and continued down the hall. Just past the White House photographer's office he stopped at a door marked w-16: the Secret Service White House command post. He used his own key in the lock.

Inside, a bank of black-and-white video screens lined the wall, focused on the on-duty Secret Service agents at their respective White House guard posts: mostly young, agile-looking men in Hong Kong suits similar to the one Powers was wearing, standing in hallways and corridors and in front of White House doors and windows—even on the roof—ready to defend the White House from an air attack with Redeye and Stinger hand-held surface-to-air-missiles.

On the other side of the room, fellow members of the oncoming day shift checked the duty board for messages, inspected revolvers, and inserted molded radio earpieces connected by a thin wire to the radios on their belts.

Special Agent John Alphonse Capizzi, a slack-jawed, olive-complexioned New Yorker with a pencil-thin mustache, was fastening his shoulder holster. His dark striped suit and styled ebony hair gave him the appearance of a Wall Street broker, or perhaps a dissipated Italian diplomat. The youthful Capizzi, a varsity-league ass-kisser and diligent student of the Secret Service promotion system (the "rabbi system"), which eschewed written or oral promotion tests for supervisory caprice, was, everyone on the detail said, destined to be Director someday.

Ken Landry, a tall, broad-shouldered African-American, was sitting in a high-backed chair in front of a cluttered radio console, busily making notes. A decorated Marine Corps veteran, Landry was the only agent assigned to the White House Detail longer than Powers (three months and thirteen days on the seniority list). Recently promoted to be shift leader, Landry had avoided the myriad cabals and alliances within the Secret Service bureaucracy because he recognized that, as a black man, he would suffer for being ambitious if such a coalition backfired. Instead, he had simply outlasted the White House Detail hotshots and, through seniority, moved slowly up the promotion ladder. At forty-nine, Landry still held the record for push-ups and chin-ups in the monthly Secret Service physical agility tests.

Powers liked and trusted him.

"Ken, since there's no travel on the schedule, how about putting me on the four-to-twelve shift for the next couple of weeks?" Powers said, keeping his voice down so others couldn't hear. "I have some things to take care of during the day."

Landry looked around to see that no one else was

listening. "My man," he said, without looking up from his paperwork, "may I ask you a question?"

"Sure."

"Are women all you ever think about?"

"What do you mean?"

"You've heard about the trip to California next week and you're trying to rearrange your schedule around pussy."

"If there's a problem . . ."

"Do you ever think about anything else? Like baseball. Do you ever think about baseball?" He looked up and winked. "Enjoy the beach, my man."

"Appreciate it."

Landry tore a page off his note pad and stood up to face the group of agents. "Listen up! The man will be staying in the House all day. He'll be having lunch in the Blue Room with Congressman Lyman from Pennsylvania, who happens to be on the Appropriations Committee. So if you're standing post when they walk by, look sharp: Lyman can cut the Secret Service budget. We're working on Whiskey frequency today."

He referred to his notes.

"Be advised that last night at twenty-three hundred hours a lunatic named Myron Foxbettor, fifty-one years old, approached the East Gate carrying a garden hoe and a box of Tide, which he was pouring over his head. He made verbal threats against the President and was committed to the psychiatric evaluation ward at St. Elizabeth Hospital. . . . An hour later one Richard Gastineau, thirty-three years old, also approached the gate. Gastineau, who was costumed like Charlie Chaplin, said he'd been hired to throw a lemon pie in the President's face. This whipdick was also committed to St. Elizabeth's. A search of his car revealed a lemon meringue pie, which is now being analyzed by Technical Security Division. That's all I have. Any questions?"

"Is it true we're going to Santa Monica next week?" Capizzi asked.

"There's no travel scheduled at this point. So those of you who are thinking about asking me to change your shifts in order to get beach time on the Coast can just forget it. Gentlemen, I spent five years on this detail before I dared ask my shift leader for so much as a sick day, much less a change to another shift. So a word to the wise should be sufficient." With a straight face, Landry glanced at his wristwatch. "It's about that time. Let's make the push."

There was some good-natured grumbling, and the agents filed out the door to man the interior guard posts. While the Secret Service Uniformed Division was responsible for manning the exterior posts, those visible from Pennsylvania Avenue and to visitors on the White House tour, the on-duty shift of plain-clothes special agents was responsible for the close-in posts. In the Secret Service manual for protective operations this system of guard posts was referred to as "the concentric theory of security," a meaningless term coined by the Director, Rexford J. Fogarty.

Powers took the stairs to the East Wing two at a time. Because of seniority, he relieved the agent standing outside the Oval Office.

For the rest of the day, at half-hour intervals, Powers and the other special agents on duty would move, in succession, from one guard post to another throughout the White House: from the door of the Cabinet Room to the door of the Oval Office, to the door leading to the President's study, and so on. Standing at these posts with arms either crossed on his chest or casually behind him or at his sides, shifting his weight now and then and balancing alternately on the balls of his feet to avoid fatigue, the agent would watch young White House staffers, Congressmen and Senators, generals, admirals, cabinet members, and members of the Vice-President's youthful staff rush in and out of various offices carrying papers and speaking fiercely in hushed tones.

White House staffers said little to Powers and the other on-duty Secret Service agents during the course of the average day. Powers had accepted his place in the hierarchy long ago: Inside the White House he was simply an observer, a symbol of security in a place already protected by spiked fences, electronic barriers, outside guard posts, and every type of alarm imaginable. Looking like gun-carrying cigar-store Indians, he and his colleagues would come to life only in the event someone already admitted through the elaborate screen of security tried to harm the President.

And Powers knew this was very unlikely.

In fact, the only action he'd seen while pushing post inside the White House was the time an insane army private, Leroy Mildebank, had stolen a helicopter from Fort Meade, Maryland, and tried to land it in the White House Rose Garden. Once it was established that the chopper was unauthorized, every special agent within range, including Powers, had emptied revolvers and Uzi submachine guns at it. Private Mildebank, uninjured because the military craft was bullet-resistant, had calmly turned off the chopper blades and surrendered outside the Oval Office.

Nevertheless, even though Powers kept vigilant because it was his job, he hated pushing post in the White House itself because, though his job certainly was necessary, it was monotonous. The only human contact he'd have all day, except for that with other special agents, was when some power-hungry politician or admiral asked him, with restrained condescension, where to find the nearest rest room.

When the President traveled, there was plenty of excitement. Powers had been one of the agents who wrestled the gun from John Hinckley's hands moments after Hinckley had shot President Reagan. He had also been standing two feet from President Ford when Sara Jane Moore opened fire. A bullet had whizzed so close to his face that the recurring memory, like the nightmares he'd experienced after returning from Vietnam, occasionally still woke him in the middle of the night.

Powers had just taken his post at the door of the Oval Office when there was the sound of static in his earpiece. He adjusted the squelch, to hear Landry inform him via radio that Chief of Staff David Morgan was headed for the Oval Office to see the President. Soon Morgan stepped off the nearby elevator. Fiftyish and with a receding hairline, the most visible member of the White House staff wore a pin-striped suit with a tight-fitting vest. Perpetually squinting because he was too vain to wear eyeglasses, he moved deliberately, ever conscious of maintaining an assured demeanor.

Powers nodded. Rather than ignoring him completely and entering the Oval Office, Morgan stopped.

"Good morning, Jack."

"Good morning, sir." And since you've taken the time to speak, you must be about to ask a favor.

"Jack, would you be good enough to check with your command post to find out if Dick Eggleston has arrived yet?"

"The President is alone, sir."

"I'm aware of that, Jack. I want to know if Eggleston has arrived."

"I'm not allowed to use my radio net for anything other than Secret Service official business," Powers said, in the impersonal but nonthreatening tone he'd developed over the years for dealing with "power freaks," as he called them. Powers believed Morgan just wanted to kill time because he was early for the meeting, and to remind Powers of Morgan's dominant position in the pecking order—something power freaks like to do.

Morgan—son of Durward V. Morgan, of the stock brokerage house of Morgan, Arbogast and Klingheim; author of the President's winning election ad campaign featuring well-known movie actors in folksy heart-to-heart television spots; graduate of the Fletcher School of Diplomacy and former U.S. Ambassador to the Soviet Union—gritted his teeth and looked momentarily at the ceiling.

Thriving on intrigue, Morgan, who'd been active in both political parties at one time or another before coming to the White House, spent most of his time shielding the President from ambitious staffers or military zealots attempting bureaucratic end runs. A genius at limiting political damage, he was the power behind the throne in the White House, and everyone knew crossing him meant a one-way ticket right out of the administration. But Powers felt there was little Morgan could do to him. The way he saw it, he'd been working in the White House before Morgan arrived, and he'd be there when Morgan was ushered out by the next administration.

A couple of minutes later Richard Eggleston, the hulking presidential Press Secretary, stepped off the elevator. Morgan immediately entered the Oval Office. Powers winked at Eggleston and touched his watch in a mock scolding manner as Eggleston reached the door. Eggleston smiled. In Powers's opinion, Eggleston was the hardest-working member of the staff. An easygoing former Yale journalism professor, Eggs had mastered the art of reinterpreting the President's controversial remarks for the press corps each time the President stepped on his dick during one of his infrequent press conferences. He had the unique ability to twist gaffes into something reasonable-sounding.

While Morgan and Eggleston were inside with the President, Powers could hear their voices clearly and was pleased he would have something to occupy his mind for the half hour until rotation, when, like a robot, he would move to the elevator post. He stepped a little closer to the door, permissible within the special orders of the Oval Office post.

They were talking about the Middle East again, in serious tones. From what he had learned inadvertently as a bystander during similar discussions and White House briefings, Powers had come to appreciate the President's dilemma. The incursion of American troops to stem the aggression of Iraq's ruler Saddam Hussein in the early nineties had backfired. Rather than produce a Pax Arabia, the Arab masses, fueled by the fires of Islamic fundamentalism and enraged by the sight of foreigners treading on the sacred soil of Islam, had risen up against their rulers. With new, radical regimes in Jordan and Lebanon, for the first time in modern history the Arabs were asserting their power as a coalition. With this worst-case political scenario now a reality, President Bush had been forced from office.

Syria, America's sworn enemy, had emerged as leader of the alliance. Taking advantage of the power vacuum caused by the destruction of the Iraqi war machine, Iran had promptly joined the new alliance. Forged by hatred of the infidel, and strengthened by a flood of arms from the Soviet Union, the Arabs had taken the first move toward reclaiming the glory of the Pharaohs, of Carthage and Babylon: the forming of a coalition. Syria's strongman Hafez al-Assad, champion of the dispossessed Palestinians and promulgator of worldwide terrorism, was now flag-bearer for most of the Arab world. And Syria believed there was only one more roadblock to reclaiming the glories of the distant past: Israel.

Whether the United States, with its continued dependence on Arab oil, would defend Israel against the new Syrian-led coalition, was the test of the administration. American public opinion was split over whether the United States should risk American lives in another war, one with much greater potential for loss of life, but there was no assurance that a general settlement of the Arab-Israeli conflict could be reached. The President, at his lowest point in the polls, had his political career riding on the issue of whether to risk American lives and fortune again by pledging unqualified United States support to Israel. During the discussion the President spoke softly, as was his habit, bluntly probing the others for their honest opinions.

Then the topic of conversation changed to the upcoming election debate.

"They're pushing for two hours," Morgan said.

"That's great if we're ahead," the President said. "But if things are rocky it could be a killer."

"We have great confidence in our President," Eggleston said, in the disarming, jocular fashion that made him well liked not only by the press but even by cynical Secret Service agents.

"We have to go with the assumption that I will be either slightly behind in the polls or even. With everything that has occurred, there's no way I'm going into this election as a sure winner," the President said. "They're going to hang the Middle East around my neck like a great big albatross."

"Good point," Morgan said.

"If we limit to an hour, we cut the risk potential," Eggleston said. "Anything can happen. Jesus, Nixon got hurt because of perspiration on his upper lip. I say we limit time, we limit risk."

"And if they're ahead and refuse to debate?" Morgan said. "What if they tell us to go pound sand up our ass?"

Straining to hear, Powers moved even closer to the door.

"Then you say I'll go to the American people and tell them presidential election debates are sacred," the President replied. "We've had them ever since Kennedy and Nixon, and we are prepared to debate anywhere on any date they choose. Tell them we'll screw them with that position every day until the end of the campaign. They'll debate, all right. Have no fear."

"Yes, sir," Morgan said.

"Mr. President, there is also the question of standing or sitting. You are taller, and we feel that if you are standing during the debate it will give you a psychological advantage. They of course want both candidates to be seated."

"I'll stand, and he can have a riser on the podium so we will appear to be the same height," the President snapped. "Next question."

"They're insisting on Philadelphia over San Antonio," Morgan said.

"Forget Philadelphia," the President said. "I want San Antonio."

There was the sound of the phone. One ring, then footsteps. A discussion ensued, but Powers couldn't make it out.

The door opened.

The eavesdropping Powers caught his breath. Stifling the urge to jump away from the door, he turned casually, as if to clear the doorway.

"The President has a question for you," Morgan said, holding an eyeglass front with lenses by the bridge. The temples probably had been removed, so they would fit nicely in Morgan's vest pocket without making an unsightly bulge in his tailored suit.

"Just a moment, sir."

Powers used his radio to notify Agent Bob Tomsic, manning the Cabinet Room post down the hall, that he would be entering the Oval Office. From Powers's earpiece receiver came the sound of two clicks, an informal acknowledgment of the message from Landry in the command post. Less than a minute later, Special Agent Tom Harrington, a sad-eyed man who looked older than his forty years, appeared from the stairwell.

"I'm working utility. What's up?" Harrington said.

"The man wants to talk to me."

"I'll cover the post."

Powers entered the Oval Office and Morgan closed the door behind him. The President was sitting behind an antique oak desk, on which were three telephones.

Without looking at Powers, the President continued his telephone conversation for a moment, then tapped the mute button. "Jack," the President said. "San Antonio. The Alamo. Is there any security reason why we can't hold an election debate there?"

"You should probably ask Director Fogarty. . . ."

"I'm asking you."

"No, sir. The streets can be blocked off, and a tent could be set up outside for the press."

"You're sure?"

"President Bush once spoke at a reception there, and I did the security advance. It was no problem."

The President winked a thanks and pressed the MUTE button on the phone again. "My Secret Service people tell me the Alamo is suitable," he said. "Tell them I said yes." The President mouthed the word "thanks" to Powers and continued his conversation. Eggleston gave Powers a little punch on the shoulder on his way out the door.

In the corridor, Powers whispered the President's question to Harrington so Harrington could relay it to Landry. Landry would pass it up the chain of command to Secret Service Director Fogarty. Fogarty, miffed at not being approached directly by the President with such a question, would in all probability try to contact the President to discuss the matter. But he would be rebuffed. Morgan considered him a dunce and preferred to deal with Deputy Director Peter Sullivan.

The sound of static came from Powers's earpiece. Powers used his sleeve microphone.

"Powers, this is Landry."

Powers pressed the TRANSMIT button on his radio. Had there been a tone of urgency in Landry's voice? "Powers. Go."

"Meet me at . . . the Special Projects Office."

3

Powers stepped off the elevator in the basement and hurried down a long shiny corridor, past the neatly labeled office doors. Landry was waiting in front of the steel security door of the Special Projects Office. His complexion was grayish, there was a mist of perspiration on his forehead, and . . . were tears welling in his eyes?

"Do you feel all right?"

"Ray Stryker's dead," Landry whispered.

Powers felt his stomach tighten. "What?"

Landry looked around and then opened the door. Powers followed him inside.

Landry pointed.

Ray Stryker was lying on his back. His head was turned and his legs were askew. There was a revolver in his right hand, a service-issue Smith and Wesson .357. His suit jacket was open, and the cross-draw holster on his belt was empty.

"Jesus Christ," Powers heard himself saying. He crept closer and knelt by the body. Stryker's mouth was open and his head was turned, as if twisted, to the left. There was a nearly bloodless entry wound at the right temple. The cranium at the left temple was open and distended—blown outward. Directly above the body, at head level, dried blood and brain matter were splattered across the word CLASSIFIED on a black drape covering a wall map. Powers, restraining a brief gag reflex, felt dizzy. "He must have been standing when he did it."

"He left a note," Landry said, his voice cracking.

A few inches from Stryker's left hand was a piece of unfolded government bond paper with typing on it. Powers moved close and knelt. The note read:

> TO WHOM IT MAY CONCERN:
> I'm sorry about the way things turned out, but I have never believed in looking back. Those of you who judge me certainly have that right, but I don't think what I did was so wrong. It was never my intention to harm the country in any way, shape, or form, and I apologize to my fellow agents for whatever embarrassment my death may cause. I accept full responsibility for my actions.
> To my Aunt Beatrice, my only living relative, and to everyone who wishes me well, I bid farewell. I guess I forfeited my life when I first violated my oath. I can only hope my years of loyal service and the fact that I always tried to be a good father to Kelli mean my life wasn't a complete waste. Goodbye, everyone. For me, it's wheels up for the last time.

The note was signed *Raymond Stryker*.

"Holy shit," Powers said.

"We'll have to handle this by the numbers," Landry said, his voice cracking with emotion.

"By the numbers" meant moving cautiously, getting the approval of the Secret Service chain of command. If the potential for embarrassment to the President was great enough, the White House Chief of Staff or perhaps even the President himself would be contacted before proceeding.

They stood there for a moment. Powers took out a handkerchief and wiped his eyes. Landry moved into the adjoining room and picked up a White House secure phone. Powers noticed his hand was shaking.

"This is Ken Landry. I need to speak with the Deputy Director, now. . . . Interrupt the meeting," he said. "Mr. Sullivan, Landry here. I'm going by the numbers in the Special Projects Office. We need you here, Code Three." He set the phone down and turned to Powers. "I was doing a security check. The door was locked," Landry said.

"Ray worked till midnight. I remember seeing his name on the duty roster," Powers said. Feeling a lump in his throat, he realized they were both avoiding looking at the body.

Five minutes later there was a knock on the door. Powers turned the handle. Sullivan, a well-built man of Powers's age, stepped inside. He had a powerful jaw and reddish cheeks. His black hair was parted neatly. Known for his expensive taste in clothes, he wore a starched white shirt, a Chanel necktie, and a well-tailored Brooks Brothers suit. Though at various times he'd sported a mustache, taking the time to trim it carefully as it grew in, at present he was clean-shaven. "What's up, gents?"

Powers stepped away so he could see. Sullivan blanched visibly, the edges of his lips turning white. "Jesus, Mary, and Joseph."

Slowly, almost reverently, he moved forward and knelt by the body. Craning his neck to read the suicide note without touching it, he grimaced and got to his feet. He stood there for a moment staring, then followed Powers and Landry into the adjoining room. Sullivan took a deep breath and let it out. "Who else knows about this?" he said, running his hands through his hair.

"No one," Landry said.

Sullivan picked up the telephone receiver and dialed a number. "Chief of Staff."

Before Chief of Staff David Morgan arrived, Powers, acting at Sullivan's direction, obtained Ray Stryker's personnel file from the Secret Service personnel division. The three of them reviewed the contents of the manila folder quickly. It revealed nothing Powers didn't already know: Stryker was a fourteen-year Secret Service veteran, had been a longtime member of the Secret Service soccer team, and was divorced. He'd never been the subject of any disciplinary action and had consistently received "satisfactory" on his yearly personal evaluations—always with an eighty-seven, the score secretly designated by the Director's staff as a code designating Stryker (and hundreds of other special agents who weren't counted among the Director's political allies) as someone who would never be promoted to supervisory rank.

There was a knock on the door. Sullivan opened it. Morgan sauntered confidently into the room and Powers closed the door behind him. "I hope this is a true emer—" His eyes widened as he saw the body, and he backed away slowly. "What the hell?"

"It looks like a suicide, sir," Sullivan said.

"Who is it?"

"Special Agent Ray Stryker."

Morgan reached behind him for the door handle.

"You'd better read the note, sir," Sullivan said.

Morgan looked at Powers and Landry. He moved forward, bent down to read the note, and returned to the door. Sullivan motioned him into the adjoining room. "It's probably best if we remain here until we decide what to do," Sullivan said.

"Yes, of course."

Morgan shrugged off his suit jacket and sat down. He wore plaid suspenders, a gift he and other members of the White House staff had received from the Prime Minister of Great Britain during a recent presidential trip to London. "How many people know?"

"Only those of us in this room," Sullivan said.

"No one heard the gunshot?"

"All rooms on this corridor are soundproof," Landry said.

Morgan cleared his throat. "Gentlemen, I have to make some very important decisions, and I want you to help me. First, is there any chance this is a murder and not a suicide? I want your frank opinions."

Sullivan rubbed his chin. "It sure as hell looks like a suicide. The gun's next to his hand and there are powder burns on his temple, which means the gun was fired at close range—not to mention the note."

"Do we have any reason to believe someone would want to kill him?" Morgan said. Adhering to protocol, he looked first at Sullivan.

"He had no enemies, as far as I know."

"He was well liked, got along with everyone," Powers said.

"If I was going to kill a man—a premeditated murder—I sure as hell wouldn't do it in the White House," Morgan said.

"On the other hand, Ray Stryker's not the kind of man to kill himself." Landry wiped perspiration from his upper lip and looked at it.

"Who the hell knows what kind of man would commit suicide?" Morgan said.

"You asked for opinions; that's mine," Landry said in his nonthreatening way.

"I spoke to Ray a couple of days ago. He didn't seem depressed," Powers said. "Not in the least." Nothing was said for a while. Powers shifted his weight from one foot to the other. He was fidgeting, like the others in the room. It was hot. He wondered if the air conditioning was on.

Morgan stood up. "That brings us to the next question," he said pensively. "If this is a simple suicide, as it appears to be, can we keep the lid on it?"

"If we handle this through normal channels, the cat's out of the bag," Sullivan said. "The wire services will have the story within minutes."

Morgan loosened his necktie—the first time Powers had ever seen him do so.

"By law we're required to notify the police," Landry said.

"And they notify the coroner," Powers added.

Morgan looked at Sullivan. "Am I safe in assuming the Secret Service has a contact on the D.C. police department who can be trusted to handle a hot potato?"

"Yes," Landry said. "But for special handling on something this sensitive, he'll need the backing of the Chief of Police."

Morgan nodded. "I need to make a phone call in private."

Powers, Sullivan, and Landry walked into the other room. Sullivan closed the door. Perhaps because they were all trying to hear what Morgan was saying in the next room, little was said for a few minutes. Sullivan, always the efficient planner, took out a small pad and pen and made notes.

Finally, Morgan called them back. "Gentlemen, I've just spoken with the President. He pointed out that we are nearing the end of a very close and difficult election campaign. The President wants to take the proper legal steps, but he asks that we do everything we can to keep the incident from the press. Are there any questions?"

Powers thought of a good one: Why are you such an imperious, insensitive prick? No one said anything.

Morgan shrugged on his jacket and strode out of the room.

"Who do we have at Metro Homicide?" Sullivan asked Landry.

"Art Lyons."

"Can he be trusted to keep his mouth shut?"

"He's solid," Powers said. Lyons, with whom he'd worked on other sensitive matters, including the investigation of several presidential threat cases, was a man who could keep his word. In any law-enforcement bureaucracy, where perfidy is frequently rewarded by promotion, such a man is hard to find.

"How do we get him assigned to the case?" Sullivan said.

"If we call the chief, he might assign someone we can't trust. The best way is to phone Lyons directly, bring him inside the tent, and then let him deal with his boss."

Landry phoned Art Lyons and asked him to come to the White House to discuss a "protective intelligence matter." No questions having been asked, Lyons arrived at the White House fifteen minutes later.

As Powers and Landry sat in desk chairs watching, Lyons, a diminutive, fortyish man with a heavily lined face and dark circles under his eyes, moved deliberately about the Special Projects Office, stopping now and then just to stare at things. Powers figured Lyons must have spent a full two minutes contemplating the bloodstain on the curtain. Once he had shed his jacket, they saw that his trousers and short-sleeved white shirt were baggy. His revolver, its butt wrapped neatly with black mechanics' tape, hung in a sweat-ringed leather shoulder holster. Powers had last spoken with Lyons at Lyons's watering hole, The English Grille in Georgetown. He remembered Lyons telling him he'd lost forty pounds in a month on a liquid protein weight-loss diet—stopping only when he'd been hospitalized with a mild heart attack.

Finally, Lyons stepped back from the body, lifted a package of Camels from his shirt pocket, and lit up. He coughed richly. "You said there was nothing in his behavior to indicate suicide?" he said, staring at the body.

"Nothing obvious," Powers said.

"Was he married?"

"Divorced."

Lyons nodded. "Heavy drinker?"

"He liked his suds. But there was never any drinking problem that I know of. At any rate, none that ever came to our attention," Landry said.

"Any ideas what it means in the note about 'violating his oath'?"

"Got me," Powers said.

"Sometimes something will set a man off . . . something no one knows about. Maybe his girlfriend telling him to get fucked." Holding his cigarette loosely between his fingers, Lyons took a double drag, then blew a heavy stream of smoke at the body. "A secret of some kind coming to light. I take it you checked the serial number of the gun?"

"We checked it in the files," Landry said. "It's his gun, all right."

Lyons squatted down next to the body. "In most suicides the hand is gripping the gun . . . a cadaveric spasm . . . the hand tightens involuntarily on the piece. But as you can see, the gun is just lying next to his hand."

"Does that mean . . . ?"

"It doesn't mean anything. I've handled suicides where the damn gun was thrown all the way across the room. . . . Hell, I had one where a guy shot himself twice. The first one was right into the nasal cavity.

If he didn't have a good reason for killing himself before, he certainly did after taking a red hot bullet right up the ol' schnozz."

"Do you see anything at all out of the ordinary with this suicide?" Powers said.

Lyons came to his feet. "He was standing up. . . . Most suicides like to lie down—or at least sit down, make themselves comfortable—before they pull the ol' plug. But some people do it standing up. Not often, but it happens. Hell, I had one where a guy killed himself while jerking off."

There was a knock on the door. It was Sullivan and Morgan. Landry introduced them to Lyons. They shook hands.

"How do you read this, Art?" Morgan said.

"It was his gun; there's a note matching the hand-writing in his personnel file. It looks like suicide to me."

Landry, who seldom smoked, asked Lyons for a cigarette. Lyons tossed him the pack and a plastic throwaway lighter. Landry lit a cigarette, perhaps to mask the odor of death in the room, which seemed to be getting stronger.

"I have to make a telephone call," Morgan said, on his way to the adjoining room. About fifteen minutes later, he opened the door and asked them to come inside. As they entered, Morgan handed the telephone receiver to Lyons. "Your chief."

Lyons set his cigarette in the ashtray.

"Yes, sir," Lyons said, holding the phone to his ear. "Yes. . . . That's right, sir. . . . I'll handle it. . . . Roger." He set the receiver down. "The chief received a call from the President. I'm to handle this any way you want."

"What about the coroner's office?" Landry said.

"The chief's already touched base with him," Lyons said, grinding his cigarette butt into a large glass ashtray. "He gave permission to handle this outside normal procedures."

Morgan turned to Sullivan. "You have your marching orders," he said. He left the room.

The others watched as Lyons took photos of the body and the room with a Kodak Instamatic camera he'd brought with him, made a rough pencil sketch of the room on a tablet, and recovered the spent bullet from the wall behind the curtain. He placed the round and the revolver in clear plastic evidence bags and dropped them in his briefcase.

Lyons shrugged. "You need me for anything else?"

"Thanks for coming over, Art."

Lyons said to call him if there was anything else he could do. He put on his jacket and left.

Landry shook his head slowly. "Hell, I still can't see Ray taking his own life. No way."

"We need to find out what Stryker meant in the note. 'Violating his oath' could mean anything," Sullivan said. "You'd better go search Stryker's place. I'll notify the next of kin."

"What about the body?" Powers said.

"We take it to a funeral home. There's no way we can hide the fact that he committed suicide, but we can keep the location a secret."

"There's no way to cover a body being taken out of the White House."

"We wait until after dark and use a tactical van. No one in the Press Room will think anything of that. In the meantime, we'll have briefed all three shifts not to discuss the matter."

"What exactly are you going to tell the press?" Powers said.

"That he committed suicide. . . . We'll just leave out where it happened. If they press for more, we tell 'em he was on extended sick leave for depression and killed himself at home. A suicide in the White House is a story. The newsies won't go with a sick man eating his gun at home. If one of 'em decides to try, the Press Secretary can have it quashed as an embarrassment to the Secret Service—and Stryker's next of kin." Sullivan ran his hands across his face and took a deep breath. "And even if one of the papers insists on writing the story, it would be nothing more than a one-inch column on the back page of the *Post*. . . ." His voice trailed off. He made eye contact with Powers, then Landry, noting their reaction. "Look, I know Ray was a good man. I don't like this any more than you do."

"We'll head for Stryker's place," Landry said.

"Keep me informed."

As Landry drove to Fairfax, Virginia, Powers kept reliving the sight of Ray's corpse. The effect of all that had happened seemed to sink in for the first time. He felt weary, and his vague foreboding reminded him of his first day in Vietnam.

Ray Stryker's two-bedroom condominium was wedged into a colorless six-block tract of similar dwellings. The entire development was surrounded by a six-foot concrete-block wall, and young trees had been planted at acceptable intervals along the parkways. There were neatly trimmed squares of recently planted grass sod, and wooden planter boxes with lines of drooping pansies, in front of each residence. Powers had once considered purchasing a similar townhouse but preferred his uncomfortable Georgetown Arms apartment to paying on a huge mortgage and living in such a sterile, lusterless suburb.

Landry parked at the curb. They climbed out and walked along a curving walkway to the door of Stryker's place. Powers knocked. There was no answer. After trying a few keys on Stryker's key ring, Landry unlocked the door and pushed it open.

"Anyone home?" Landry said.

They walked in cautiously and checked the bedroom and bath. No one was there. After a few words about how they should proceed with the search, Landry took the kitchen and Powers the bedroom.

In the bedroom, Powers not only searched the dresser drawers but methodically removed them from the cabinet and checked each bottom. He found nothing but socks and underwear. In the closet, he lifted each hangered piece of clothing and fingered every pocket. Finding a Santa Claus hat on one hanger he paused for a moment, remembering Stryker in the hat when tending bar at the White House Detail Christmas party. In a box of papers on the closet shelf were Stryker's U.S. Army discharge papers, a few Series E savings bonds all agents had to buy under the Secret Service payroll savings program, a Jimmy Carter tie clip, a few Ronald Reagan ballpoint pens, and some coupons for the Fairfax car wash.

In Stryker's nightstand Powers found a photo album with clear plastic pages. There were only a few photographs: Stryker at Yosemite with some other Secret Service agents . . . Stryker as a lanky child . . . Stryker as an army paratrooper . . . Stryker at the Secret Service firing range . . . an eight-by-ten of Stryker and some other agents and young women in Eastern European folk costumes. They were sitting around a long table in what Powers guessed was a beer tent. Powers remembered: the President's trip to Hungary. At the bottom of the box was a color shot of Stryker's ex-wife, Dora, a flight attendant, and his gangly, blue-eyed young daughter. The daughter, whose name he couldn't recall, looked to be about six years old and was wearing a dance leotard. Perhaps, thought Powers, the photo had been taken at a dance recital. He was suddenly thankful Sullivan hadn't assigned him to make the death notification to Stryker's family.

Under the bed was an Easy Glider fold-up walking exercise device, three pairs of soccer shoes, a Scrabble game, and a box of photos in cheap frames: some autographed black-and-whites of Presidents and foreign heads of state like those all Secret Service agents owned. Powers figured Stryker probably had had the photos hanging in a den or recreation room before his divorce. Though unaccustomed to introspection, it also occurred to Powers that Stryker had been much like himself: a man whose persona was formed almost entirely by his job.

In the other drawer in the nightstand, among some paperback Charles Willeford and James Jones novels, was a black patent-leather pocketbook. Powers picked it up and opened the clasp. As well as a lipstick, a compact, and a few hairpins, there was an outdated White House parking pass. The name on the pass read MARILYN KASINDORF.

"Ken," Powers said.

Landry entered the bedroom.

"Ever heard of a woman named Marilyn Kasindorf?" Powers handed him the pass.

Landry studied it and shook his head. "A Y pass," Landry said. "A civilian. Y usually means CIA."

Powers picked up the telephone on the nightstand and dialed Sullivan's direct number. "This is Jack Powers. We're inside. We found a White House pass."

Sullivan asked for the name.

"Marilyn Kasindorf."

"Hold the line. I'll check with pass section." A couple of minutes later the phone clicked. "It's a Y pass . . . current and in good standing. She works in the Special Projects Office. There's no supervisor listed, so she's probably CIA."

"Thanks," Powers said.

"Keep me informed," Sullivan said.

Powers set the receiver down. "She works in the basement—Special Projects."

"Spooks. I wonder what he's doing with her parking pass."

"Maybe they were dating."

"Could be."

"Maybe they had an argument and she killed him in her office, then put the gun in his hand to make it look like a suicide," Landry said.

Powers shrugged. The condo was giving him the creeps. He felt he was violating Ray Stryker's privacy. Even the dead should have privacy.

"There's nothing in the other rooms of any interest. Let's get out of here," Landry said.

4

When Powers and Landry returned to the White House, a copy of a Secret Service log entry recording Ray Stryker's death had already been posted on the bulletin board in W-16. Realizing there was no discreet way to move Stryker's body from the White House to a funeral home until after midnight, when the members of the White House press corps had gone home, Powers and Landry remained in W-16 filling out reports and enduring the expected questions about the death from shift agents coming on duty. Though naturally concerned and interested in further details, nearly everyone already knew of the suicide. With a telephone at every Secret Service post in the White House, news traveled fast. Powers assumed that within minutes of Sullivan's notification of Stryker's death, every Secret Service office in the world and every special agent, whether on- or off-duty, had been told of the suicide . . . or at least had a message concerning the incident left on his answering machine. Agents on every detail, from those assigned to the Vice-President or one of a number of foreign dignitaries visiting the United States, or to ex-Presidents, would have something to hash over during off-hours or between pushes. There would be theories and pronouncements of all kinds. With great relish, the usual Secret Service bullshitters would claim to have been Stryker's pals, and the Federal Law Enforcement Officers union representatives would jump at a chance to claim that job stress had driven Stryker to take his own life. In the incestuous world of the Secret Service, the carrion of death—as well as disciplinary proceedings, divorce, and other general gossip—was talked over, dissected, used, and consumed until nothing was left.

At three the next morning, having been notified by the agent posted nearest the White House newsroom that it was vacant, Powers pulled a large Secret Service tactical van up to the loading area at the rear of the Executive Office Building. He and Landry carried Stryker's body from the Special Projects Office down the hallway, through a passage leading past the White House bomb shelter, out a maintenance door, and loaded it into the cargo compartment of the van.

Driving the van out the east entrance, Powers felt begrimed by everything that had happened. Landry was in the passenger seat, staring blankly at the road ahead. The ordeal obviously was beginning to wear on him, too.

The funeral home, on the corner of a residential street two blocks south of the Washington Hilton, was a white, wood-shingled, two-story building, with a veranda and portico designed, Powers figured, to look homey for mourners. As Sullivan had instructed him earlier by phone, he swerved the van into the wide driveway and cruised slowly to the rear of the building. Waiting outside dimly lit double doors, looking nervous, was a wiry man in his fifties, dressed in a red cardigan sweater and Levi's. His gray crew cut and tanned features gave him the appearance of a tennis coach rather than a mortician.

Powers and Landry climbed out of the van.

"Agent Landry?"

Landry introduced Powers. The mortician said his name was Kimball.

"David Morgan phoned. He told me what to do. Please bring him inside."

Powers and Landry slid the body from the bed of the station wagon and carried it through the double doors. Inside a bare room reeking of mortuary chemicals, they lifted Stryker onto a metal table. The mortician searched his pockets and dumped the contents into a small brown paper bag.

"I'll handle everything from here, fellas," he said. "I've already been in touch with the next-of-kin. Your Mr. Sullivan located them."

He handed the bag to Powers, who left with Landry without another word.

For the rest of the night Powers slept fitfully, reliving the finding of the body. He woke the next morning with an unexplainable sense of guilt, which persisted as he climbed out of bed, showered, shaved, and headed for the White House.

On the bulletin board at W-16, a notice from Secret Service Chaplain Clint Howard announced a memorial service for Stryker to be held at Our Lady of Perpetual Help. By mid-morning, the agents would be tired of rehashing the Stryker incident and would return to the usual Secret Service topics of discussion during post-standing breaks: overtime pay and women. Powers was glancing at a *Runner's World* magazine before leaving to start his shift, when a telephone call came for him. It was the Chief of Staff. Morgan, understanding full well the speculation that would be caused among the other agents if anyone saw him talking to Powers, asked Powers to meet him immediately at the nearby Sheraton Hotel.

At the Sheraton, following Morgan's instructions, Powers moved through an ornate lobby to the registration desk. As Morgan had instructed him, he gave his name and asked for a key to Room 1202. He stepped onto the elevator and pushed the button for 12. At room 1202, he used the key to unlock the door.

Morgan was inside . . . standing at the window, staring out.

"Sorry about all the cloak-and-dagger," he said without turning around, "but I didn't want to start the rumor mill by calling you to my office."

He moved to a table.

"I want to thank you for the way you and Landry handled everything on the Stryker matter. It looks like the precautions worked. The press has missed what for them would have been a nice little news tidbit at Mr. Stryker's expense. I say fuck them."

"Yes, sir."

"Jack, let me get right to the point. I just received a call from the CIA—from Director Patterson himself, as a matter of fact. He tells me his people are working a defector operation: a Syrian colonel named"—Morgan took out a small leather pad, opened it, and flipped a couple of pages—"Terek Nassiri, a high-ranking officer in the Syrian Secret Service. He walks into our embassy in Paris early yesterday and defects. The Agency is skeptical at first, but verifies his bona fides. The balloon goes up. The CIA flies him out of Paris direct to Andrews Air Force Base. He's met by CIA interrogators and taken to a safe house and questioned all night. Well, he's singing like Pavarotti."

"Yes, sir?"

"Patterson says much of what he has provided has been verified," Morgan said, thumbing another page. "Early this morning, when their debriefing is nearly complete, Nassiri suddenly says he has another piece of information and insists on speaking to the President himself."

"He must be a mental case."

"That's the problem," Morgan said. "Patterson believes the man is sane."

"What kind of information?"

"He won't say exactly, just that it relates to the security of the President of the United States. The spooks told him no chance; no matter what he had, he couldn't give it to the man directly. So then he insists on speaking with a member of the White House Detail of the Secret Service. Obviously he doesn't trust the CIA."

"And you want me to hear what he has to say?"

"You got it, Jack. Any questions?"

"Why didn't Director Patterson go through normal liaison channels? It's not like we haven't handled situations like this before. Why go directly to the Chief of Staff?"

"Only he can answer that," Morgan said, shoving the note pad back into his inside jacket pocket. There was a thin briefcase resting on the table. He reached inside. "Maybe he wants to make sure the CIA gets credit as the original source of the information, rather than the Secret Service." He took out a sheet of paper and handed it to Powers. "I'm sure that kind of foolish bureaucratic rivalry doesn't surprise you."

"Not really," Powers said. *And since you happen to be the biggest showboat in the White House, I'm sure it doesn't surprise you either,* he thought.

"The safe house is at Rehoboth Beach. This is the address. I want you to go over there and find out what the good colonel has to say. Interview him alone, where you can't be overheard by the CIA people. Report to Sullivan when you return."

"The CIA people are going to want to know what he tells me," Powers said.

"Your orders are to report to Sullivan or to me before talking with anyone else."

Powers nodded. He wanted to ask a number of

questions, but settled for one. "Why are you sending *me* to handle this?"

"To be frank, if it turns out to have something to do with Ray Stryker's death, then we haven't had to let anyone else in."

"Does Landry know?"

"Landry is a supervisor, and he's tied up with the advance arrangements for the trip to the Coast. I suggested sending him, but Sullivan pointed out that if I pulled him off his regular duties at this point the other agents might suspect something was up. He knows how inquisitive you SS guys are. No disrespect intended."

"None taken." Prick.

As Powers drove across the Chesapeake Bay Bridge and onto the heavily wooded Highway 404, he went over what Morgan had told him. Morgan wouldn't have given him the assignment unless he thought it had the potential to be sensitive—more sensitive than just some defector trying to make points by getting the attention of the White House. Nor was it Powers's first sensitive assignment. Years ago, he'd been dispatched to cover the tracks of a President's daughter who'd spent a weekend with four Jamaican rock stars. And recently he'd been sent to interview one of the members of the President's kitchen cabinet, who was convincing rich foreign investors to buy gold from his brokerage house by telling them the President was suffering from a terminal illness. In both cases the more Powers learned, the less he wanted to know. But that was the way with political chores: molehills threatening to become mountains.

About an hour later, he turned south on US 1 and, minutes later, arrived in town. Checking his automobile club map for 1025 Seahorse Lane, the address Morgan had given him, he wound through narrow streets of beach cottages and residential homes hidden by pine trees to a beach boardwalk lined with shops, arcades, motels, and trendy restaurants. Near a miniature golf course, he spotted a street sign and turned right. Seahorse Lane, a cul-de-sac ending at the strand, was comprised of wood-frame one-story houses, many with FOR RENT signs—ideal for a safe house, because the neighbors would be used to seeing strangers. At the end of the street, Powers pulled up to the curb one door down from a two-story white clapboard house with dormers and a gray slate roof. Its number, 1025, was on the mailbox. Behind the house, sand dunes led to the boardwalk.

He climbed out of the car. At the trunk he leaned down, opened his briefcase, and took out a transistor radio he carried to listen to sporting events when on boring protection assignments. Dropping it in his jacket pocket, he made his way along a cracked, bumpy sidewalk toward a screened-in front porch. Inside, a husky young man dressed in a red Budweiser T-shirt and Bermuda shorts was sitting in a chair. Powers assumed he was the lookout.

"Jack Powers, U.S. Secret Service," Powers said, showing his badge and identification card. The man stepped forward. "I'm Dick Jones." He examined the identification, then reached down and knocked on the wall twice.

The door was opened by a tall, sandy-haired, freckled man of Powers's age. He was wearing a brown sport shirt with a button-down collar, pleated gabardine slacks, and utilitarian shoes. His eyeglasses had clear plastic frames, the kind perennially popular with Ivy Leaguers. His right hand was behind his back. Unlocking the screen door latch with his left hand, he allowed Powers inside.

Powers showed his identification again.

"I'm Bob Miller," the man said, closing the door.

"Jack Powers. Are you in charge here?"

"I guess you could say that."

Miller moved his hand from behind his back and shoved the Beretta he was holding into the front waistband of his trousers. "I guess you're here to talk with our guest."

To Powers's right, a short middle-aged man wearing Levi's and a polo shirt was standing behind the door holding a shiny Heckler and Koch submachine gun. He set the gun down on the sink and introduced himself as Tom Green. Powers figured CIA people preferred simple pseudonyms because they were easy to remember.

"What's he like?" Powers asked quietly, in case Nassiri was in a nearby room.

"Very confident, upbeat," Miller said. "My guess is that he's planned his defection for a long time. He doesn't seem to have any remorse."

"I understand he's been polygraphed?"

"Our best examiner administered four polygraph tests to him. He showed no signs of deception—but of course the Syrians are good at training disinformation agents to beat the lie detector."

Powers nodded. He had little faith in lie detector tests anyway. Unless the person undergoing the test broke down and confessed, nothing was proven other than that a person's heart rate and perspiration might increase when asked certain questions. "I understand you've verified his bona fides?"

"Our main file shows him as being in intelligence work since Hafez al-Assad came to power. In 1984, he was in Paris when a former Syrian prime minister was assassinated outside the Inter-Continental Hotel. We believe he was in command of the operation. He's been a case officer in London and Vienna under diplomatic cover. He's fluent in Russian and English."

"What kind of information has he given you?"

"He provided details of a new tank being used by Syrian forces, some valuable biographical information about the people he worked with, the name of a Syrian resident agent operating a network." He smiled condescendingly. "I hope you're not asking for specifics. That would be strictly need-to-know."

"I'm just trying to determine if the man is for real."

"We wouldn't have called you here if we didn't think he was for real."

"If they ask when I get back to the White House, may I mention your name?"

Miller bit his lip anxiously. "What you're asking is whether the information he provided is too valuable to be turned over as part of a disinformation operation. The answer is yes. It's too valuable, and we believe the man to be a genuine defector."

"Is there anything else you can tell me before I talk with him?"

"Only that he asked to speak with you alone," Miller said.

"I'm aware of that."

"You know how defectors are: masters of manipulation."

"Playing all sides against the middle," Green chimed in.

"I wouldn't trust a defector as far as I could throw him," Powers said.

"If you're ready, you may interview him in the back bedroom," Miller said.

"I prefer to interview him outside."

Miller shook his head. "No way."

"I'm not going to interview him in this house."

Miller and Green exchanged a look—a look that was too obvious to be genuine.

"He's a defector. And he's in our custody," Miller said. "If you want to interview him, you'll have to interview him here."

"I'm going to take a walk with him along the beach. We'll remain within your sight."

"No can do. This man is my responsibility."

"Perhaps we should phone the White House and have the Chief of Staff make the decision," Powers said.

The others just stood there as Powers moved to a telephone on a coffee table and picked up the receiver.

"There's no need for that," Miller said at last. "But if you try to walk more than a hundred yards away from this house, the interview is over."

Miller led him down a hallway and opened a door. Nassiri was lying on a bed covered with a blue chenille bedspread. There was nothing else in the room—no chest of drawers, nothing—and the window had been nailed over with thick plywood. Nassiri came to his feet, rubbing his eyes. A man in his fifties, about five feet, eight inches tall, he was wearing a wrinkled long-sleeved white shirt and an equally wrinkled pair of trousers. His black hair was thick and short, and he had a two-day growth of beard. His lips were thin and dark, and his shoulders were broad. He was unmistakably a soldier.

Powers introduced himself and showed Nassiri his badge and identification card. Nassiri studied both carefully. Finally, he nodded.

"Outside," Powers said. Miller stepped out of the bedroom doorway. Powers led Nassiri down the hall, through a small kitchen, and out the back door onto the dunes.

Walking without speaking, Powers led him past the boardwalk and onto the sand. At the edge of the wet sand, where the waves were breaking, Powers stopped and turned. There were solitary men about fifty yards in either direction on the beach. The curtains in two rooms of the beach house were pulled back slightly.

Powers assumed Miller and Green, probably using directional microphones, were prepared to eavesdrop on what Nassiri would tell him. But, as he'd learned from his pals in the Secret Service Technical Security Division, the crash of waves is one of the most effective audio interferences with the sounds of human speech.

To make doubly sure they couldn't be overheard, Powers took the transistor radio from his pocket and turned it on, adjusting the volume to a deafening high. Nassiri, as if he'd expected Powers to take such a precaution, cupped his hands and spoke into Powers's ear. "Very clever," he said.

"What did you want to tell me?"

"May I see your credentials again?"

Powers took out the case in his pocket and flipped it open. Nassiri studied it carefully.

"Who is the only French citizen employed by the U.S. Secret Service?"

"I didn't come here to answer questions."

"If you're really a U.S. Secret Service agent and not a CIA impostor, you'll know the answer to that question," Nassiri said.

"Pierre Le Denmat. He's the Special-Agent-in-Charge of the Secret Service liaison office in Paris."

Nassiri nodded. "I apologize for the little test."

"Fine. Now what is it you want to tell me?"

"I am a colonel in the Syrian intelligence service."

"I've been briefed on who you are."

"Of course. Then I'll get right to the point. Syrian intelligence has someone in the White House."

"How do you know this?"

"I was assigned to the intelligence briefing staff, and I saw copies of Presidential Eyes Only papers. We had them regularly."

"Describe these papers you're talking about."

Nassiri rubbed his eyes for a moment. "Bond paper marked TOP SECRET and OVAL OFFICE EYES ONLY—

PRESIDENT OF THE U.S. There was a presidential seal on the paper."

"What was their content?"

"Operation Desert Journey. The papers mentioned confidential U.S. sources in the Syrian, Jordanian, and Iranian governments."

"Was there a date on these papers?"

"The ones I saw were dated April sixteenth and May ninth of this year."

"Where was the date printed on the papers?" Powers said.

"The date was on the cover sheet only."

"The presidential scal—what color was it?"

"I was looking at black-and-white copies—made by a copying machine. I couldn't tell."

"Who stole the documents?" Powers asked. Nassiri was right about the placement of the date and, as far as Powers knew, no one other than the President and a few others would even know that sensitive presidential documents bore the Oval Office stamp. Such documents were hand-carried to him by high-level CIA briefers and picked up at the end of the day.

"A U.S. Secret Service agent attached to the White House Detail."

Powers felt the hair on the back of his neck tingle.

"Why didn't you want to tell the CIA about this?"

"I'm a career intelligence officer, and I've been sitting on the American desk for twelve years. I'm aware that Mr. Patterson, the Director of your CIA, is a politically ambitious man. I thought he might leak this information to the American press and harm your President. I don't want to tumble the walls of the house that takes me in. It's difficult enough just being a defector."

"What's the agent's name?"

"Pardon?"

"The special agent who you said stole the documents."

"Raymond Stryker."

Powers felt his stomach muscles tighten. "When was he recruited?"

"I'm not sure."

"What else do you know about this, Colonel?"

"Stryker may have had help from another White House employee, one with high access," Nassiri said. "The Stryker operation is known only to a few high-ranking officers in my service."

"Do you have any other information you want to give me?" Powers said coldly.

"If you check, you'll see what I am telling you is true."

"Is there anything else?"

"The rest I have given to the CIA people," Nassiri said, in his precise military manner.

Powers clicked off the transistor radio. His ears were ringing from its tinny sound as he shoved it back into his pocket. He and Nassiri walked across the sand to the beach house, and the men who'd been positioned on the beach followed.

Miller met them at the rear door and led them back to the bedroom. He unlocked the door and shoved it open. Nassiri nodded at Powers and, without offering his hand, entered the room. Miller closed the door and locked it.

Anxious to get back to D.C. and report what he'd learned, Powers moved down the hallway.

"What did he have to say?" Miller said, as if they were old friends.

"Nothing significant."

"May I offer you a drink, Jack?"

"Thanks anyway, but I have to be going."

"Is there some reason why you won't tell us what Colonel Nassiri said?"

"My orders were to interview him and report back to my own chain of command."

"I can understand your reluctance to share the information. But I'm sure you understand that eventually all intelligence information filters up the chain to us."

"Yes," Powers said, though it was common practice for both the CIA and the Secret Service to hold back sensitive White House information from each other. "But you understand I'd need authorization from my superiors to tell you anything at this point."

"Jack, I'm not trying to cause a big flap, but I'm sure you can understand that the information would help us get a better picture of the colonel. Like you, we're just trying to do a job."

"Sorry, but I can't help you."

Miller glared at him. "I understand your position," he said coldly. He turned to Green, who unfastened the latch and opened the front door.

Relieved the confrontation was over, Powers walked outside, imagining what the neighbors would think if they knew the house next door was filled with spies. He unlocked his car, climbed in behind the wheel, and started the engine. The air was still hot. He stopped at a traffic light. A tanned man and woman in swimsuits crossed the street in front of him. They were holding hands. Powers told himself that even with the West Coast trip coming up it was a good time for a beach vacation. But though he had the names of plenty of women in his black book who would gladly join him, there were none he liked well enough to spend a week at Rehoboth Beach with, holding hands. Nor was the idea of vacationing with the other bachelors on the detail—playing poker and carousing at beach singles bars to see how many women they could pick up and seduce—particularly appealing either. He decided to save his vacation days.

During the drive back to D.C., Powers reviewed his conversation with Nassiri. Overall, if he had to guess, he would say that Nassiri's information was too cut-and-dried. That wasn't to say it wasn't true, but there was a lot more he wasn't saying.

Secret Service headquarters was situated less than a block from the White House, on the top five floors of a modern office building that had a branch of the Maryland National Bank and a dingy snack shop on the first floor.

Powers stepped off the elevator on the eighth floor. A black Secret Service Uniformed Division officer sitting at a reception desk recognized him and pushed a button. There was the sound of a lock buzzing. Powers opened the door and headed down a long hallway, past office doors with plastic government-issue name tags:

> William J. Kelly, Vice-Presidential Protection Division, Agent-in-Charge
> Francis C. Donahue, Foreign Dignitary Protection Division, Agent-in-Charge
> Rexford J. Fogarty, Director, United States Secret Service

Though in recent years the Secret Service had been opened by government affirmative action programs to allow a few super-qualified blacks, Hispanics, and women into supervisory positions, the top slots were still held by a self-perpetuating hierarchy of New York Irish Catholics built by Director Fogarty, an obsequious bureaucrat who'd managed to hold his presidential appointment through four administrations.

Fogarty and his hand-picked aides were known as the "Potato Head family." Kelly, in fact, was related to Fogarty by marriage. And Donahue might as well have been; his wife owned the Century 21 franchise in Fairfax, Virginia (known to agents as "Fairfax Headquarters"), where Kelly's wife, Claudia, was employed. All Secret Service agents stationed in field offices outside the District of Columbia knew that receiving a Fairfax Century 21 brochure meant they would soon be receiving official orders transferring them to the White House Detail. Not surprisingly, eighty-seven percent of all Secret Service special agents used Claudia's services and lived in Fairfax.

Deputy Director Peter Sullivan's office was next to Fogarty's. The door was open, and Powers went in.

Lenore Shoequist, Sullivan's pert receptionist, greeted him. A fiftyish woman favoring high heels and tight skirts, she'd married and divorced three high-ranking special agents, none below the GS-15 supervisor classification, during her twenty-year Secret Service career. She was a notorious gossip, relishing the juicy morsels of information she gleaned from the Director's circle and sharing them whenever it benefited her personally. Powers often wondered how she would feel if she knew that her regular daytime trysts at the Mayflower Hotel with the Special-Agent-in-Charge of the Inspection Division, Elmer Cogswell, were common knowledge to everyone in the Secret Service.

She told him to go right in.

Powers entered Sullivan's inner office. Sullivan was sitting behind a wide desk covered with paperwork. There were bags under his eyes that reflected loss of sleep. Though jealous Secret Service pundits referred

to Sullivan as an "egotist," Powers respected his lead-
ership abilities. In fact, Sullivan was one of the clever-
est men he'd ever met. In the Secret Service Training
School where they'd been classmates, Sullivan had
maxed the final test. On the White House Detail, Sullivan had single-handedly revised the top-secret *Manual of Protective Operations*, thus gaining attention
from Director Fogarty. Fogarty, a former Boston tran-
sit policeman who had difficulty composing even a
simple government memorandum, always made a
point of appointing a good writer as his deputy. On
the Secret Service management fast track, Sullivan
was promoted rapidly. Assigned to Technical Security
Division as a first-level supervisor, he revamped the
entire White House electronic security system,
allowing the Director to take the credit. His latest
project was designing the security system for an international conference facility, under construction inside
the presidential retreat at Camp David.

Sullivan motioned for Powers to close the door.
Powers complied.

"Cup of coffee, Jack?"

"No thanks," Powers said. From the street below
came the sound of a distant siren.

"What does this defector look like?"

Careful not to omit any details, Powers related what
he'd learned from Nassiri, including the dates on the
documents Nassiri said he'd seen. Without a word,
Sullivan left his desk and moved to a large Diebold
safe in the corner of the room. He opened a drawer,
took out a folder, and thumbed the pages quickly.
"Was Nassiri sure about the dates?"

"He didn't hesitate."

"The shift reports show the President in residence
at Camp David on April sixteen and May nine," Sullivan said softly. He closed the file and slid it back in

the drawer. "What was the reaction of the spooks when you refused to tell them what Nassiri said?"

"Pissed off."

Sullivan returned to his desk. For a moment he just sat there, going over the notes he'd made as Powers briefed him. Finally, he swallowed. "Nassiri said Stryker may have had someone helping him, someone with high access?" he said, avoiding eye contact.

"Right."

"Maybe Marilyn Kasindorf."

"You know her?" Powers asked.

"The Special Projects Unit where she works is responsible for preparing intelligence summaries for the President, using information from the most sensitive CIA sources." He turned his swivel chair toward the window. "Was there anything else of hers in Stryker's place, anything other than the parking pass, that could tie him to her?"

"No. We checked everything."

"The kind of briefing documents Nassiri says he saw are stored in the Special Projects Office," Sullivan said numbly, as if traumatized. "Memoranda the President reads before every foreign policy meeting or visit by a head of state. National Security Council stuff. If this kind of information has been compromised, it could explain the failure of the last summit meeting. . . . For that matter, it could explain a lot of this administration's foreign policy problems in the Middle East."

Gloomily, Sullivan turned back to the desk and reached into his IN box for a folded copy of *Time* magazine. He handed it to Powers. On the "People on the Move" page, Sullivan's photo was in the upper-right-hand corner under the caption THE PRESIDENT'S MAN. "I'm the youngest Deputy Director in the history of the U.S. Secret Service," he said flatly. "I didn't get here by being out on the running board with you, Jack. I made compromises."

"Aren't you being a little harsh on yourself?" Powers wondered why Sullivan, a most direct man, was suddenly turning the subject to himself.

Sullivan picked up a half-empty coffee cup and studied it. "There are three types of agents in Uncle Sam's Secret Service. Those like you who work the White House, those who work field investigations, and power-seekers like me, who scrape and scratch their way up the promotion ladder." He took a sip of coffee and set the cup down. "As a supervisor, my duties have little to do with the Secret Service, really. Hell, I could be working for General Motors—or the post office, for that matter—managing people, putting out fires, catering to the people above me on the ladder. What I do has little relation to protecting the President. Sometimes I wish I had just remained on the detail as a working agent."

Powers fidgeted uncomfortably. He'd never heard Sullivan, a formal man, bare his feelings in this way.

Sullivan stood up and sauntered to a steel office door at his right. Stenciled on the door in red letters were the words SECURE FACILITY. He tapped numbers on a cipher lock above the doorknob. There was a *snap* as the bolt opened electronically. The door was the thickness of a bank safe's. With some effort, Sullivan pulled it open. He turned and motioned Powers to follow him inside.

In the soundproof twenty-by-twenty-foot room was a long conference table with a thick, see-through acrylic top and some clear plastic chairs. In the corner was a gray Diebold filing-cabinet safe. The walls, floor, and ceiling were covered with a silvery metallic cloth called an "ear blanket." The material had been invented after years of research conducted by the Secret Service Technical Security Division, to find a way of shielding the White House from intrusion by electronic eavesdropping. The fabric was reputed to be the ultimate protection from all known electronic eavesdropping equipment, transmitting on any frequency in the world.

Sullivan flipped a wall switch activating the air conditioning, pulled the heavy door closed, and turned a bar latch, locking them in.

The air conditioning came on in the room, and Powers felt a chill.

"Sorry about the air, but if I turn it off we'll suffocate in here," Sullivan said.

"No problem."

Sullivan rubbed his hands together briskly and looked up at the air-conditioning vent. "I've had GSA here to fix this air conditioning three times. They fiddle around with the thermostat for a while, then say it's fixed. But nothing changes." He coughed.

Seeking refuge from the air conditioner's direct breeze, Sullivan moved to the corner of the room and leaned back against the wall. "I want to thank you for the professional way you and Landry have been handling everything."

"No problem." *What the hell is going on?*

"I've been playing the political game in this town ever since I became an agent," Sullivan said. "Maneuvering, backstabbing, playing both sides of the fence, making deals to get ahead. Four years ago, I made a decision as to who I thought had the best chance of being elected President. I pulled some strings and got myself assigned as a supervisor on his campaign protective detail and made a point of ingratiating myself with the staff—with the hope that after the election I would be their Secret Service man. Well, it worked. Since the President was elected I've had the inside track. The White House staff has come to confide in me more than they do the Director."

For Powers, the room seemed to grow smaller.

"Last week David Morgan informed me that when Fogarty retires I'll get the Directorship," Sullivan continued.

"Congratulations," Powers said, wondering what Sullivan was leading up to.

"It's everything I ever wanted, the culmination of all my hopes." Sullivan looked Powers in the eye. "It also means I'll be promoting people I trust. Like a guy named Jack Powers."

"Pete . . ."

"I consider you the best protection man in the outfit, Jack."

"I don't know what to say."

Sullivan cleared his throat. "I guess what I'm saying is that the immediate future is extremely bright for both you and me. That is, if we can get past this obstacle."

"Obstacle?"

"Over the years, David Morgan has come to trust me completely," Sullivan said. "He calls on me to handle sensitive tasks he doesn't even entrust to the closest members of his White House staff." He picked up a pencil and tapped it rapidly on his desk blotter. "If I let you in on this, there's no way back. You understand?"

"You'll have to transmit that in the clear for me, Pete. Are we talking about something more than Stryker's suicide?"

"We're talking embarrassment to the President," Sullivan said. "Actually, maximum embarrassment. I need you to conduct an in-house investigation . . . a political chore. A varsity political chore so sensitive, that once I let you in the tent you have to stay in."

Powers's throat suddenly felt dry. "You're saying that if I allow you to tell me, there's no backing out?"

Sullivan nodded.

Powers swallowed. "Is what I'll be asked to do legal?" he said after a pause.

"The mission itself isn't covered under specific Secret Service jurisdictional authority, if that's what you mean. But I can assure you it's not illegal. It will have to be handled on a strict need-to-know basis, but there's no hidden agenda, no trapdoor waiting to spring open. And if the going gets tough, I promise you won't get dropped like a hot spud."

Powers had been in the Secret Service long enough to fear the potential mire accompanying all unofficial or quasi-official investigations. "You and I were still in Training School during Watergate, Pete," he said. "I don't want to get involved in anything political now."

"This has political ramifications, but it's a matter affecting the national security."

Powers trusted Sullivan. Besides, being promoted to Agent-in-Charge of the White House Detail would mean a raise, a government car with home-to-work driving privileges, and the opportunity to set his own work schedule. "I'll handle the assignment," Powers said.

Sullivan swallowed twice. "The President has been having an affair with Marilyn Kasindorf," he said, in a barely audible tone.

Powers felt utter astonishment. Like all Secret Service agents, he knew a wealth of inside information about the personal lives of the Presidents and Vice-Presidents and, for that matter, their wives and families and members of the cabinet and White House staff. Agents of the White House Detail discussed these tidbits among themselves, but never with anyone else. All special agents knew enough—hell, had forgotten enough—to fill any number of best-sellers with the details of White House behavior. But no agent had ever written a White House kiss-and-tell book.

The unwritten code inculcated in young Secret Service agents from the first day they came on duty was to listen a lot and say very little. In direct violation of civil service regulations, all talkers, egotists, and braggarts were quietly transferred out of the White House to field duties in order to preserve the integrity of the detail: secrets within secrets protected by the secret-keepers. But even on the scale of White House secrets, a presidential affair was a definite ten. Powers had never heard so much as a word about Marilyn Kasindorf or, for that matter, even any idle speculations about a presidential paramour. In fact, the President was known among the jaded detail agents as "Pa Kettle" because of his preference for family life over flashy social functions. Powers couldn't remember him even telling an off-color joke. A private man more similar in personality to Nixon and Carter than, for instance, to Reagan or Bush, the President bored easily and was in the habit of leaving official functions early, a trait that pleased Powers and the other members of the White House Detail. They could count on getting off on-time.

"Where?"

"Camp David."

How could the President manage an affair, when all cars entering Camp David, including those of cabinet members, were inspected by the shift agent posted at the front gate? "I've never even seen her."

"David Morgan gives me a time, and I arrange to be at the Camp David front gate when his limousine arrives. I wave him through. Even though the agent posted there is supposed to search all vehicles entering, he isn't going to countermand the Deputy Director."

Powers felt cold. "And she's behind smoked windows."

Sullivan nodded. "Right in the backseat. Morgan

has used me to arrange meetings between the President and this woman since shortly after the inauguration."

Powers's palms felt sweaty. He took a deep breath and let it out.

"Presidents can withstand rumors about their personal life, but balling a spy at Camp David? Jesus. Watergate and Irangate would be nothing compared to that," Sullivan said glumly. "We're talking resignation or impeachment. Aces and eights. The sewer. An absolute presidential tits-up." Sullivan was staring at him. "We need to put the lid on this, Jack. Lid on and screwed down tight. But at the same time we need to investigate—determine whether or not this woman is a spy. That'll be your job."

"How'd she meet the President?"

Sullivan sat back in his chair. "Morgan never told me, but I assume they've known each other since he was Director of the CIA," he said regretfully. "As you can imagine, I didn't grill Morgan as to the details of how the man and his girlfriend began their affair." He ran his hands through his hair.

"CIA employees are hidden in official records," Powers said. "If I conduct even routine records checks on her, the word will get back."

"I don't want you to do any records checks."

"How can I investigate her without doing background—"

Sullivan interrupted. "Surveillance. I want you to surveil her. It's not going to be easy to do alone, but this matter is too sensitive to bring in anyone else."

"And if I prove she's a spy, what then?"

Sullivan swallowed. "The President himself will have to make that decision."

Powers allowed his eyes to shut for a moment. He imagined himself saying, Pete, with all due respect, I'm afraid I have to decline this assignment after all.

It's a hot potato, and the risk of getting embroiled in a political adventure and ending up sitting in front of some hostile congressional investigating committee outweighs the lure of promotion. You can trust me not to say a word, but I'll just have to pass on this.

"Jack, I can tell by the look on your face this isn't an assignment you relish. I know the responsibility you must feel."

"Now that you mention it . . ."

Sullivan left the desk, adjusted the combination dial on the safe, and opened the heavy drawer. He took out a business-sized envelope and handed it to Powers. "Here's five thousand dollars to cover expenses. This is headquarters confidential fund money, so you don't have to keep receipts. If you need more, let me know."

Powers slipped the envelope into his inside jacket pocket. It felt heavy. "I've never seen this woman. How . . . ?"

"When the man wants to see her, he goes through Morgan. I'll have him set up a meeting and then cancel at the last minute. You can initiate the surveillance at that point. It won't alarm her. He's had to do this before when the President had a last-minute change in schedule. I'll phone you tomorrow at your apartment with the details."

"This whole thing could blow up in our faces, Pete," Powers said.

"We're not going to let that happen."

After the meeting, Powers took the elevator to the ground floor and walked out onto G Street. The air was oppressive. Standing there on the crowded sidewalk, his mind racing with what Sullivan had told him, he wished he could have asked more questions. But Sullivan had told him exactly what David Morgan had authorized him to say, and no more.

As he stood perspiring in the humidity, Powers considered going back up to Sullivan's office and begging off on the assignment. Then he took out a clean handkerchief, wiped his brow and neck, and headed down the street to his car.

6

Landry finished writing a duty roster for the following week and reviewing the stack of teletypes concerning security arrangements for the President's trip to California. There were long passages listing motorcade routes and hotel arrangements, police liaison problems, and the simple logistics of just getting off-duty shifts of agents from airport to hotels and from hotels to God knows where before the President arrived. Each teletype had been written by a different member of the Secret Service advance team. Landry could tell each agent was copying from the format of the previous presidential trip to Los Angeles and simply filling in the names of the different streets and locations. At the end of each teletype was the phrase POLICE LIAISON IS BEING MAINTAINED. Dozens of people were spending hundreds of man-hours making sure that manhole covers were welded shut and post office collection boxes were locked, that every room in every building the President was to visit would be checked by bomb experts, that all foods and beverages destined for his lips were analyzed beforehand by the Secret Service chemist (known as Dr. Death), that all service employees in hotels and restaurants, airports, and every other location the President would visit

73

would have their names checked against the master threat list on file in the Secret Service protective intelligence computer.

Since it appeared that the advance team had done its job properly and was ready to keep the President safe while he visited Los Angeles, Landry locked the paperwork in the W-16 safe. He hated paperwork, actually. Though attention to paperwork and the ability to write slick memos often helped agents to get ahead in the Secret Service, he considered ninety percent of it totally unnecessary. Hell, years ago one good advance man would have done the work of today's entire advance team, with all their laptop computers and endless teletypes. But in the old days, he told himself, a black man would never have been promoted to Agent-in-Charge of the White House Detail.

Having spun the dial on the safe, he signed off on the supervisor's log. He found Bob Tomsic, the on-duty shift leader, in the hallway briefing a new agent, and told him he was leaving for the day. Heading toward the EOB exit, Landry stopped for a moment. Something had been at the back of his mind all day. Though because of work he hadn't spent much time with his wife and kids lately, he now took time to move to a phone on a small table a few feet away and dial a number.

"Homicide."

Landry asked to speak with Lyons. The phone clicked, and Lyons gave his name.

"Landry here. I thought I'd stop by and pick up a copy of the Stryker report."

"I was just heading for the Grille. Feel like a drink?"

"Sounds good," Landry said, though he seldom drank alcoholic beverages.

"I'll run off a copy and bring it with me."

*   *   *

The English Grille in Georgetown was like a lot of other cop bars. Located near the university on a busy street lined with restaurants and shops, it had a small parking lot in back where detectives drinking on duty could hide their official cars from the view of passing police supervisors. Over the front door was a vertical neon sign with a martini-glass logo and the word EN-GLISH illuminated. The GRILLE part of the sign had never worked.

Inside, the fifteen bar stools and six booths in the dimly lit bar were filled with men in suits—mostly white men but a few blacks—and a couple of women who looked like police secretaries. There was a crude oil painting of a reclining Victorian nude above the bar. The bartender, a blotchy, red-faced man with a black toupee and dyed mustache, was busily pouring drinks.

Art Lyons waved at Landry from the end of the bar. He'd saved a stool. Landry joined him, and Lyons introduced him to the bartender and some of the regulars.

Landry shook hands a couple of times and ordered a light beer.

Lyons reached inside his jacket and gave Landry a folded police report. "You'll need this," he said, also handing him a small flashlight. Landry said thanks. The bartender set down a beer.

The homicide report, which listed Stryker's name and physical description, gave no address for the deceased. In the location box Lyons had written *Location #1—see Chief of Police log of this date* to hide the fact that the body had been discovered in the White House. Landry read further. "It says there was evidence of tattooing."

Lyons touched his temple. "Right inside the hair-line, near the wound. The pathologist noticed it during the autopsy. A little gunpowder embedded in the skin."

"What do you make of this, my man?"

Lyons twisted his wrist and demonstrated, as if aiming a gun at himself. "It's possible to shoot yourself like this. Uncommon, but certainly possible. See, most suicides have a contact wound. You touch the barrel right to the skin. This way, he fires while holding the piece a few inches away." He picked up his drink and took a sip. "It's possible that he was ready to do it, then just sort of halfway chickened out, pulling his hand away as he pulled the trigger. Only the Big Kahoona knows for sure."

Landry completed reading the report. There was nothing else in it that differed from what he had learned when Lyons had conducted his investigation in the Special Projects Office. He shoved the report in his inside coat pocket. "I'd like to ask you a hypothetical question."

"Shoot."

"Is it possible this could be a murder?"

"Anything is possible. The astronauts went to the moon."

"If this suicide was in fact a murder—and just pretend it was, for the time being—how could it have been done?"

"Someone would have to take Stryker's gun, shoot Stryker in the temple from close range, then find someone to forge Stryker's signature on a suicide note. Ridiculous."

Landry shook his head. "You said it was uncommon for a man to shoot himself while standing up."

"It is. Truthfully, that's the only thing I find out of the ordinary about the damn case. Other than the fact that you didn't have a hint of Stryker being depressed. A man doesn't kill himself on impulse. He thinks about it first. And to even consider the possibility,

there has to be something in his life making him believe he's up shit creek without a paddle."

"Ray Stryker worked for me. He wasn't the suicidal
type."

"I once worked with a guy in Vice who told me
over and over again how happy he was his wife had
left him. How overjoyed he was to finally get rid of
the bitch. One night he went to her apartment, kicked
the door down, and ate his lead right in front of the
ex-wife and her boyfriend. You just never know."

"I wouldn't have a man working for me in the
White House if I thought he had suicidal tendencies."

"You can't take this personal."

"I want you to test-fire the gun," Landry
interrupted.

Lyons finished his drink and spit some ice back into
the glass. "If it'll make you feel better, I'll take it
down to the lab and have it done tomorrow morning."

In the morning Powers rose early. He'd experienced
a fitful night's sleep, and felt as tired as he had when
he'd climbed into bed. While showering and dressing,
he still couldn't get the events of the previous day out
of his mind.

There was nothing in the refrigerator to eat for
breakfast, but rather than make a trip to the super-
market and chance missing Sullivan's call, he found a
Weight Watchers manicotti TV dinner in the back of
the freezer compartment and warmed it in the micro-
wave for breakfast.

To kill time, he filled in some Secret Service daily
report forms, a stack of which he kept in a kitchen
drawer. Every Secret Service agent was required to
complete a report for each day's work. After filling in
the top section, which listed his name, date of birth,
social security number, shift status, rank, and address
of permanent record, he filled in the narrative portion

under DAILY ACTIVITY. On each he wrote *Protective duties—POTUS*. POTUS, of course, was the Secret Service abbreviation for President of the United States. All special agents assigned to the White House Detail wrote the same vague phrase on their daily reports. Though filling in such meaningless memoranda had been a constant source of irritation to Powers for years, he had finally accepted the ritual as part of the job. As Landry always said, where else but in government service could one get paid to waste time filling in the same worthless form each day? In fact, recalled Powers, it was Ray Stryker who had used a calculator to figure that, over a thirty-year career, the average agent would spend two years and eleven months just filling in daily report forms.

By 5:30 P.M., Powers had not only caught up with the two months' worth of reports he was behind on but had completed enough reports for the next six months—which he would hand in, one each day, as required.

The phone rang.

He picked up the receiver. It was Sullivan.

"Do you know La Serre? The French restaurant?"

"Twenty-first and K Street?"

"That's the one. She'll be there at seven . . . at the counter. She's expecting Morgan to pick her up and drive her to meet the man, but he'll phone her at the last minute and cancel. She's yours from there on out."

The phone clicked.

Dressed casually, Powers left the apartment and took the Metro to the corner of 21st and K Street.

The restaurant faced north on K Street, raised from the sidewalk by about ten steps covered by a red awning on which was painted *La Serre*. He ambled along the sidewalks in the area for a while, checking entrances and exits to the place as well as any nearby

Metro stops and parking garages Marilyn might use. In a surveillance, such things could take on great importance. Then he checked his Rolex, inserted his flesh-colored Secret Service hearing aid-style radio receiver into his ear, plugged it into the HL-20 radio attached to his belt under his sport coat, adjusted the volume, and trudged up the steps. He was early, but arriving early was the custom in Secret Service work. Whether it was getting to the location of a presidential visit or going on surveillance, arriving late was considered an inexcusable mistake, one of the few infractions that could cause an agent to be transferred from the White House Detail. "The President of the United States," as the legendary Special Agent, Clint Hill of the Kennedy Detail, used to say, "doesn't like to wait."

Powers entered the restaurant. Inside were about twenty-five wooden tables, with checkered tablecloths and cane-backed chairs, and a butcher-block counter he guessed would seat ten or twelve. Less than half the tables and only three of the counter seats were occupied. The college-age waiters and waitresses wore white aprons and black pants. A chalkboard on the wall noted the daily specials: Algerian couscous and *fruits de mer*. Powers imagined the pseudo-cosmopolitan atmosphere would be popular with yuppies who'd once backpacked around Europe for a summer.

Powers chose his own table to get a good view of the door and sat down without waiting to be seated. A few minutes later a young waiter with a short greasy ponytail and fair features came over to the table. Telling himself that eating in a restaurant on a surveillance is the best way to appear inconspicuous, Powers ordered couscous. Then, recalling that Sullivan wasn't requiring him to furnish receipts for his expenditures, he also ordered the *fruits de mer* and a small bottle of wine.

With his earpiece receiver discreetly monitoring routine radio transmissions on the White House frequency, Powers finished his seashell of *fruits de mer* and set the plate on top of the empty couscous bowl. He still wasn't full. Because of nervous tension he had an urge to smoke a cigarette, but he had quit three years earlier after reading an article in *Reader's Digest* citing the fact that virtually all men suffering impotency were heavy smokers. He was determined never to smoke again.

He glanced at his wristwatch for what must have been the tenth time. It was 6:51 P.M. Was she going to be late?

A few moments later, the waiter finished a long conversation he'd been having with a waitress about backgammon and finally took the dirty dishes from his table.

Just then a woman came in the door.

She was in her thirties, willowy, and had long chestnut hair parted on the side. Her cheekbones were high, and she had full, sensuous lips, satiny red with a recent application of lipstick. Her eyes were brown, deep-set, and implied sophistication and perhaps even a certain world-weariness. She wore a maroon crocheted cardigan with wide sleeves, a black knit top, and tight-fitting black pants. Slung over her right shoulder was a large geometric-print leather bag.

Though Powers still thought it unfathomable that the President had risked his place in history by allowing himself to be compromised, now he understood: The strikingly attractive Marilyn Kasindorf was a woman no man could ignore. In a Secret Service hangout like Blackie's, agents would fight over her.

Marilyn set her bag on a chair at the counter and casually looked about. Powers pretended to review his bill to avoid eye contact with her.

She sat down and crossed her legs. There was a gold

anklet above her right foot. Was it a band of tiny hearts? She ordered coffee from the counter waiter, and he served her immediately.

Powers checked his wristwatch again. It was 7 P.M.: time for Morgan to make the call.

The phone rang. The waiter picked up the receiver. "I'll check, sir," he said after a moment, then scanned the customers. "Is there someone named Marilyn here?"

Poised, Marilyn came to her feet and moved to the end of the counter. The waiter stretched the expandable cord to hand her the phone, and she put the receiver to her ear. A moment later she spoke softly, just a few words, and then reached across the counter and set the receiver down.

There was the sound of five distinct transmitter clicks via the radio earpiece, Sullivan's prearranged signal that Morgan had phoned Marilyn and informed her the President had to cancel the meeting.

Without finishing her coffee, Marilyn took money from her leather bag and set it on the counter. She hoisted the bag and arranged its strap on her shoulder. Male customers turned their heads as she sauntered out the door.

Powers took out his wallet and left enough money on his table to cover the bill and a tip. Waiting until she had made her way to the bottom of the few steps leading to the pavement, he followed.

Marilyn walked along the sidewalk with the long strides of a fashion model, her leather bag moving to and fro. At the corner of Connecticut Avenue, she stopped and joined a crowd of pedestrians waiting for the light. Crossing the street with them, she strolled north for a block, stopping now and then to window-shop. At M Street, she glanced at her wristwatch, then suddenly turned to her right and entered the lobby of the Dupont Hotel.

Powers hurried inside. The hotel's expansive lobby, with its lush red carpet and highly polished antique furniture, was nearly empty. Walking briskly, he checked the registration area, the coffee shop, the elevator bank. She wasn't there. "Shit," he said out loud.

He moved quickly across the lobby and past a balustrade. In a wide hallway, he hurried past a Hertz rental car desk and an American Airlines ticketing counter. He checked the small gift shop and moved slowly along a bank of wooden telephone booths.

Marilyn was sitting in the booth on the end, with her leather bag propping the accordion door open. Was she waiting for a call?

Powers stepped into the gift shop and stood near the window. Marilyn glanced at her wristwatch, then leaned down, reached into her bag, and took out a filter-tip cigarette and a small gold lighter. She stepped out of the booth and lit the cigarette. Staying close to the phone she paced about, nervously changing the lighter from hand to hand.

Because the young man behind the counter in the gift shop was staring at him, Powers purchased a Snickers bar, which he figured would suffice for the rest of his dinner while on surveillance. He moved back near the window and thumbed through a magazine.

The phone rang once and stopped.

Marilyn slowly picked up her bag, stepped inside the phone booth, and pulled the door closed. With the light on inside the booth, she took change from her purse, lifted the receiver, and dropped the money into the slot. She dialed, then spoke quietly. For a moment she fumbled with her purse again, then took out a checkbook. With her head cocked to hold the telephone receiver, she made a note. Hanging the receiver back on the hook, she stuffed pen and checkbook back into her purse. Then she pulled open the door, stepped out, and headed toward the lobby.

The moment she was out of sight, Powers hurried to the telephone booth. Using a ballpoint pen he dug out of his shirt pocket, he wrote the telephone number on the back of his hand. Having been in charge of making advance security arrangements at the hotel a few months earlier, when the President had delivered a speech to a convention of religious broadcasters, Powers was familiar with the building's layout. He headed immediately through the hotel's busy restaurant and exited onto the sidewalk. He was fifty yards or so behind her. Perfect timing, he told himself.

Without looking back, she strode east past tall office buildings with first-floor retail businesses to Rhode Island Avenue, a wide thoroughfare lined with a mixture of multistoried apartment houses, hotels, retail outlets, and the Gramercy Park Hotel.

At Scott Circle, a convergence of six major streets with a circular traffic island guarded by a pigeon-stained statue of General Winfield Scott on horseback, she approached the glass door of an apartment house. The building was a ten-story upended brick rectangle, like the rest of the lodgings in the area. The number 1152 was affixed to the door in gold.

Using a key she took from her purse, Marilyn unlocked the front door and entered. She crossed a carpeted, well-lighted lobby and stepped into an elevator. The doors closed.

Powers moved to the door and pushed. It was locked. To the right was an intercom phone and a creased black-felt board, covered with glass and secured at the corner with a small lock. The names of the residents were affixed to the board in small white plastic letters. The name M. KASINDORF was listed for apartment 721. Checking carefully, he noted no video camera or other security device at the entrance or, as far as he could tell, inside the lobby. To the right, a wide entrance to the apartment house's underground garage was protected by an automatic steel gate.

Powers looked both ways and made his way across the street. He turned, looked up at the apartment house, and counted floors. On the seventh floor, the lights came on in the apartment second from the right. Powers walked to the corner and sat down on a bus bench.

Over the next few hours, the apartment house's front entrance was used infrequently: a man walking his miniature collie, two women arriving in a taxi and unloading groceries, a jogger (Powers thought his pace was particularly slow) doing his nightly mile.

The lights in Apartment 721 remained on until shortly after midnight. Powers, his clothing sticky from the humidity, hailed a cab.

At his apartment, Powers turned on the air conditioner. He picked up the phone and dialed Sullivan's number. The phone rang once and Sullivan answered.

"I think I've identified the residence," Powers said.

"Good."

"And there was a phone call made from a pay phone in the Dupont."

"What the hell was she doing there?"

"Looked like she just went in to use the phone. She waited at a booth. There was one ring, like a signal; then she made a call—a short one."

"Give me the number."

"Outgoing from 274-1169 at 1912 hours," Powers said, referring to the note on the back of his hand.

"I'll get the subscriber information."

Powers set the receiver down. He stripped off his damp clothing, took a quick shower, and dried off. In the bedroom, he turned out all the lights except his reading lamp and climbed into bed. Picking up a TV remote control from the nightstand, he turned on the television. Johnny Carson was interviewing a confused young blond starlet, who appeared to be under the influence of narcotics.

"I mean, like, I go, 'How do you expect me to sing if I'm supposed to be eating?' and he goes, 'I'm the director,' " she said. The audience laughed, then stopped abruptly. Johnny Carson made a face at the camera and straightened his necktie. There was another four-second burst of laughter.

Powers pressed the POWER button on the remote control. He reached to the nightstand, set the clock radio alarm for 4 A.M., and turned off the lamp. He wanted to be sure Marilyn didn't leave her apartment before he could follow her.

Lying in bed naked, covered only by a sheet, he relived Marilyn's walking into the restaurant and wondered what he would have done if he hadn't been on-duty. After some thought, he decided that, because of her aloofness, he would have hesitated to make a pass at her. She looked like the kind of woman who would coldly rebuff an advance.

He also decided that the President had good taste. Marilyn Kasindorf was one of the most beautiful women he'd ever seen. . . .

An electronic buzz sounded. Powers slapped the clock radio to shut it off and bounded out of bed. Marilyn was still on his mind as he shaved and dressed.

7

Darkness was turning to daylight on Rhode Island Avenue as Powers steered his Chevrolet into a parking space down the street from Marilyn's building. Using binoculars, he checked her apartment. The lights were still off. He leaned back in the seat. Over the next two hours, traffic slowly increased. A few early-bird bureaucrats walked briskly to work, sanitation trucks moved along both sides of the street, a few joggers and walkers hustled past. Washington, D.C.—city of power-brokers and street criminals; of shiny limousines transporting both Congressmen and dope dealers; of call girls, pages, lobbyists, diplomats, and spies; of multistory apartment houses occupied by single women working at Agriculture or Justice or HUD; of paper-shredders and empire-builders, idealists and greedy fixers; of the majesty of democracy and its delicate practice—came slowly alive.

By 6 A.M. he was tired of the morning news and weather on his radio and regretted having forgotten to pick up a newspaper before taking his surveillance position. By 7 A.M. his stomach was rumbling with hunger.

At 7:04 A.M. exactly, a light came on in Marilyn's

apartment. With the light from the rising sun, the drapes were only slightly illuminated.

During the next hour or so, residents of the apartment house began leaving. Most were on foot; a few left in automobiles from the underground garage. Powers used the binoculars to check if Marilyn was among them.

By 8:30 A.M., Powers became concerned he'd missed her. Could she have slipped away without his spotting her?

Less than a minute later, Marilyn came out the front door and walked to the corner. He left his car and followed. She crossed the street at the light and walked to M Street, where she followed the sidewalk to the Bentley Thompson Building, a modern multistory office structure. As she waited in a small crowd for an elevator, Powers checked the building registry. Every listing was for a U.S. government agency. Undoubtedly, one of them was a cover name for the CIA and she was going to work. . . .

At 5:30 P.M., Marilyn came out the front door of the building and retraced her morning route. She went directly to her apartment and remained there for the evening.

The next day, Saturday, Powers was sitting in his sedan in front of Marilyn's apartment house at dawn. Though it was not a workday, he'd arrived early anyway. At 9:47 A.M., as he considered leaving to phone Sullivan, Marilyn strolled out the front entrance. She was wearing a white shirt-dress, white tennis shoes, and a casual blue tunic. It was nice to see her in something other than her conservative CIA clothes. He had the urge—it sometimes happens on surveillance—to speak with her, perhaps tell her that he liked the outfit. Fantasy helped pass the time.

He started the engine.

Marilyn looked both ways, crossed the street, and walked along the sidewalk in his direction. Fearful of coming face-to-face with her, Powers pulled into traffic and drove past. At the corner, he turned right and sped up Fifteenth Street to the next block. For cover, he parked behind a truck. A minute or so later, she crossed the street. He quickly turned off the engine. Though his car was in a one-hour parking zone and would probably be towed away, he crossed the street and continued after her on foot.

At Sixteenth Street, a wide thoroughfare lined with retail businesses, she walked north, passing some clothing stores, a hotel, and a candy store. Stopping on the corner, she allowed other pedestrians to move past her in the crosswalk. Then, suddenly, she turned around and looked behind her.

To protect himself from her view, Powers stepped into the candy store. Marilyn looked up at the tall buildings, then at cars on the street, then at the other people on the sidewalk. This continued for what must have been three or four minutes. Then she headed back the way she'd come.

Powers felt his heart race.

"May I help you, sir?" said a youthful black woman standing behind the candy counter.

"No thanks," Powers said, hurrying out the door.

Marilyn continued to the end of the block, then stopped abruptly in front of Dorothy Bullitt's, a large women's clothing store. To keep from being seen, Powers stepped into an alcove in front of a leather goods establishment next door.

As if window-shopping, Marilyn moved slowly along the length of the display window, but without stopping to study any particular item. Then, suddenly picking up her pace, she turned, crossed to his side of the street, and entered a diminutive concern whose window was filled with travel posters. The sign above the door read THE TRAVEL BUREAU. Powers recognized it as a branch office of a nationwide chain of franchised travel agencies.

Marilyn came out of the place twelve minutes later and moved down the street.

Remaining behind at a discreet distance, Powers followed as she made her way back to her apartment house. Ignoring a black female mail carrier shoving mail into the receptacles in the joint mail collection box at the entrance, Marilyn used a key to unlock the front door and entered without looking back.

Powers hurried around the corner to his car. He climbed in, started the engine, and raced around the block. He pulled into a curbside parking space down the street from her apartment house. From the car he had a clear view of both the window of Marilyn's apartment and the apartment house entrance.

Thus ensconced, he leaned back in the seat, using the headrest to relax. Wondering what Marilyn was up to, he took deep breaths. Later, he turned on the radio and tuned it to a jazz station. Blossom Dearie, his favorite female vocalist, was singing a melancholy cabaret tune. Because of lack of sleep caused by the long hours of surveillance, his eyelids started to feel heavy. The morning passed.

Nothing else happened at the apartment house for the rest of the day.

By 7 P.M., he was starving.

In the Gramercy Park Hotel, he purchased three Snickers bars in the gift shop and hurried back outside. Behind the wheel again, he unwrapped one of the bars and ate it in three bites. Though it didn't fully satisfy his hunger, he dropped the other two bars in the glove box to save them for later, because he had no idea when he would get to eat a square meal again. Once, in Bangladesh, protecting Secretary of State Henry Kissinger, he'd lived on Snickers bars for three days. Though this was a source of mirth for the other special agents, when everyone else including Kissinger himself came down with a raging dysentery it was Powers who had the last laugh.

Later that evening, Powers headed across the street and entered the Gramercy Park Hotel. At a pay phone, he dropped change and dialed Sullivan's home number. Sullivan picked it up after the first ring.

"Sullivan here."

"She's in bed. Can we talk on this line?"

There was a pause. "No. Meet me at Blackie's."

Blackie's cocktail lounge, located on I Street around the corner from Secret Service headquarters, had become the Secret Service hangout after Powers and Ken Landry had rescued the owner, Blackie Horowitz. Headed home from working a night shift at the White House the previous summer, they happened upon Horowitz as he was being pistol-whipped by two armed robbers in front of the bar. In the running gun battle, one robber was stopped by a bullet piercing his buttocks laterally. The other, throwing his empty gun into a trash can so he too wouldn't be blown up, continued along Connecticut Avenue for more than a mile before he finally fell down in exhaustion.

After the shooting, Horowitz had invited Powers and Landry to the restaurant for dinner. They, in turn, had invited the entire seven-man White House Detail working shift. The grateful Horowitz had torn up both the bar and restaurant tabs for everyone, and the word spread quickly to other White House Detail shifts, groupies, and, eventually, headquarters divisions that Blackie's was the place to go. Blackie Horowitz not only earned the price of the shooting celebration back a thousandfold but became the permanent sponsor of the White House Detail softball team. In fact once, when faced with Happy Hour competition from the Dock, a secretary-loaded downtown bar that was the former Secret Service hangout, Blackie responded by offering Secret Service agents half price on all drinks any time, night or day. From then on, off-duty agents had never considered going anywhere else.

Powers pulled to curbside. Sullivan, dressed in slacks and a windbreaker, was waiting on the sidewalk in front. He pulled open the passenger door and climbed in.

"This morning she took a walk from her place to the District Mall," Powers said. "On the way she kept doubling back, checking window reflections. It looked like she was checking to see if she was under surveillance. The only place she stopped was a travel agency. She went inside for twelve minutes, then headed straight back to her apartment."

Sullivan reached into his windbreaker and took out a package of cigarettes. He lipped a cigarette from the pack and lit it with a disposable lighter. He took a puff and blew a sharp stream of smoke out the window. "Twelve minutes is long enough to pick up an airline ticket," he said ominously.

Powers nodded.

Sullivan took out a small note card. "The call she made Thursday night from the Dupont Hotel lists to a pay telephone located at 2711 Cumberland Avenue Northwest." He handed the card to Powers. The address was typed on it. "Calls from pay phones, street countersurveillance—people don't take these precautions unless they have something to hide."

Powers nodded gloomily. "I agree."

"But we're gonna need more than phone calls and a visit to a travel agent, a hell of a lot more." Sullivan dragged on his cigarette, then turned his palm and looked at it as smoke rose from his mouth. He rubbed his chin for a moment. "There are other ways to further an investigation."

Nothing was said for a while. A faint sound of music

came from the jukebox in Blackie's. Powers knew what Sullivan was getting at.

"The best evidence is physical evidence," Sullivan said, looking Powers directly in the eye.

Powers felt his face and hands flush. In Uncle Sam's Secret Service, the code words "best evidence" meant illegal entry.

"How hard would it be, Jack?"

Powers' throat suddenly felt dry. He swallowed. "It . . . uh . . . can be done."

"If she's involved in espionage there's a good chance you'll find something incriminating in her place. If so, the mission is accomplished. We'll have enough to convince the man. Even if the place isn't dirty, at least we'll have learned something about her to help in going forward with the investigation. Considering what we have to gain, I feel it's worth the risk."

Powers, remembering Watergate, knew he should refuse and walk out the door, no matter what the consequences. But he was a Secret Service agent who'd been asked to help the President. He couldn't walk away.

Powers cleared his throat. "I'll handle it. But I'll probably have to wait till Monday."

"Thanks, Jack," Sullivan said, looking him directly in the eye.

It was 1:15 A.M. by the time Powers arrived back at his apartment. He set his alarm clock for 5 A.M., stripped off his clothing, climbed into bed, and closed his eyes.

It seemed that the alarm went off only seconds later.

Powers dropped his feet to the floor. Drugged with exhaustion, he rubbed his eyes for a moment. Before rushing out of the apartment, he rummaged through a utility drawer in the kitchen and found a long screw-driver and the pair of rubber dishwashing gloves used by the Georgetown Arms cleaning lady during her once-a-week cleaning visit. Dropping the items into his briefcase, he hurried out the door.

As he drove toward Scott Circle, he considered the various ways to get into Marilyn's apartment. No matter how careful he was, no matter how carefully he planned the break-in, there was still an enormous risk. All it took was one neighbor getting suspicious and phoning the police or the building manager. If the police arrived, unless he could convince them he was on authorized government business, he would be arrested, handcuffed, and booked for burglary. Jack Powers, meet Howard Hunt.

"Shit," Powers said out loud.

8

****
****

Watching Marilyn's window from his car as the sun came up on Monday, Powers brooded over other sunrises he'd observed while on duty: sunrises in Palm Springs and Kennebunkport, Santa Barbara and Moscow, and at Jimmy Carter's retreat on St. Simon's Island. Because of a policy initiated by Director Fogarty ordering bachelor agents to work holidays in order to give married agents a chance to be with their families, a number of those sunrises were on Christmas, Easter, and Thanksgiving. Because his mother and father were both dead and his only relative was a younger sister, a real-estate agent living in Fresno, California, with whom he had never been particularly close, he'd always figured being on-duty was, under the circumstances, as good a way as any to spend the holidays. But now, with his career at midpoint, he had to admit he'd grown tired of being an observer, of living someone else's life, even if it was the President's—or the President's girlfriend.

But this sense of alienation was nothing to what he would feel if he ended up getting thrown in jail as a burglar.

Whether Marilyn was a spy or not, if he was caught

all bets were off. He would be tried and convicted of burglary and sent to prison, a scapegoat.

But a man was only as good as his word. He'd made the commitment to Sullivan, and he would go through with it.

It looked like Marilyn wasn't going to work today. And she had stayed indoors all day yesterday. What was going on?

At 9:30 A.M., a taxi pulled up in front of the apartment house. A minute or so later, Marilyn came out the front door and got in. The taxi pulled into traffic.

Powers started his engine and swerved into the street to follow. The taxi jogged through district streets to the corner of Twenty-first and K Street and pulled to the curb in front of a diminutive beauty shop, with a bay window. The sign read CURLS AND FURLS.

He slowed and pulled to the curb a few doors down the street. Marilyn paid the driver, climbed out of the taxi, and entered the beauty shop.

Powers left his car and hurried across the street. From there he had a clear view of the beauty shop window. Inside, Marilyn spoke briefly with a tall, platinum-haired female hairdresser wearing skintight black pants and an equally restrictive pink top. Then she sat down in a beauty chair near a sink. The hairdresser moved behind the chair and adjusted the chair back to rest Marilyn's neck on the edge of the sink, turned the water on, and began to wash Marilyn's hair.

The apartment was finally empty! Powers jogged across to his car and sped back to Scott Circle. Parking around the corner from Marilyn's building, he opened his briefcase and took out the screwdriver and gloves. Shoving one glove in each pocket of his sport jacket, he slid the screwdriver up the left sleeve and left the car. Walking around the corner to the apartment house, he held the screwdriver in place with his closed palm.

At the front entrance he looked around quickly, then allowed the screwdriver to drop into his hand. Slipping its tip between the jamb and the door, he gave a firm pull to the left. The lock snapped open. Without looking back, he slipped the screwdriver back up his sleeve and moved rapidly across the lobby. Inside the elevator, he pressed the button for 7.

At the seventh floor, he got off the elevator and counted doors down a hallway to Marilyn's apartment. He looked both ways, then got out the screwdriver.

From his right came the sound of a door opening. With his breathing at full stop, Powers shoved the screwdriver back up his sleeve and, without turning his head, knocked casually on Marilyn's door as a visitor would.

A short gray-haired woman carrying a large leather purse came out of the apartment next door and headed toward the elevator. Powers smiled as she walked past. Seemingly unalarmed, she smiled back. The woman stepped onto an elevator and turned to face the front. The doors closed.

Allowing himself to breathe again, Powers used the screwdriver to force the lock. The door wouldn't budge. He tried again, applying more power. There was a creaking sound. He stopped. He could hear himself breathing. Again he tried, applying even greater force. The doorjamb creaked loudly, and the lock snapped open. Powers pushed on the door and stepped inside.

He closed the door behind him gently, so as not to make noise. With the feeling that his heart was beating uncontrollably in his throat, he put his ear to the door and listened for a moment to determine if he'd alerted any neighbors. There was no sound in the hallway. He took a deep breath, let it out, and turned to

face the room. There was a faint smell of perfume
. . . a perfume, unless he was mistaken, different from
the brand he'd smelled when Marilyn had walked into
La Serre.

The living room was furnished neatly with a plaid
sofa and sectional, a wall lamp, and a tall bookcase.
On the walls were landscape prints: a waterfall gush-
ing into a lake, a forest near a stream. The furnishings
were the opposite of what he had expected. Perhaps
because of the trendy way she dressed, her confident
recherché gait, he would have guessed she would
choose Art Deco or Danish Modern rather than such
traditional furnishings. But, after knowing Senator
Victor Garland Danforth, a nattily dressed conservative former Republican presidential candidate Powers
had once been assigned to protect, he had learned
that image doesn't always fit with digs. Danforth lived
in a filthy three-bedroom house in Silver Springs,
Maryland, with a sloppy alcoholic wife and at least
twenty ringwormy cats and dogs.

Powers pulled the gloves from his pockets and put
them on.

In the bedroom, the fragrance of perfume was
stronger. On the facing wall, a large framed print of
Gainsborough's *Blue Boy* hung over a queen-sized bed
covered with a flowered print bedspread. The walnut
dresser was Queen Anne-style and had a tall oval-
shaped mirror. Women's toiletries were scattered
across the top of the dresser, including two small black
glass bottles of Passion perfume, sitting on a small
porcelain tray.

At the closet, he slid the door open. It was bursting
with women's clothes. On the floor, extending from
one side of the closet to the other, was a neat line of
paired women's shoes.

Moving quickly, he opened dresser drawers. The
top right-hand drawer was filled with scraps of paper:

laundry and credit card receipts, canceled checks, telephone bills bearing Marilyn's name, pens and pencils, and other miscellany. He checked the other drawers and the rest of the room and found nothing out of the ordinary.

In the living room, he removed the sofa cushions and checked them carefully, then turned the sofa upside down and checked underneath by running his gloved hand along the frame from end to end. There were no places where the covering had been altered. Turning the sofa upright again, he replaced the cushions. He checked the rest of the furniture in the room the same way.

Most of the books in the bookcase were on foreign affairs and international relations, though there were a few Raymond Carver short story collections. He began lifting books from the shelves one by one and flipping them open. Starting from the top, he completed the first, second, and third rows, replacing each book precisely where he had taken it. From the second-to-last row, he took out a Raymond Carver book titled *Fires* and fanned its pages quickly. Something heavy fell to the carpet. He knelt down and picked up a Minox miniature camera the size of a cigarette lighter. The pages of the book had been hollowed out to fit it. His breathing quickened as he checked the frame-counter window. There was no film in the camera.

Replacing the camera in the hollowed portion of the book, he set the book back on the shelf from where he'd taken it and checked the rest of the books on the shelves thoroughly. There was nothing in them except a few bookmarks from D.C. bookstores. His hands were sweating inside the gloves.

He checked the kitchen quickly, opening and closing drawers. There was little in the refrigerator: some soup in a Tupperware bowl, lunch meat in butcher paper, assorted jars of pickles and preserves. The freezer section was filled with stacks of TV dinners. Powers carefully opened a few of the packages at random—nothing. To cover the torn package ends, he restacked them facing the rear of the freezer.

On the kitchen table was a week-old *Washington Post*, a sealed box of shredded wheat, a *Vanity Fair* magazine, and a photograph of Marilyn standing alone in front of the domed colonnade of the Jefferson Memorial. It appeared to be dusk in the photo, and the looming statue behind her was lighted. Her arms were crossed and she was wearing a conservatively cut black business suit with a red scarf. Her expression—rather than playful or carefree, as in a shot taken by a friend or relative on holiday—was anxious, as if she might have been impatient with posing.

Also on the table was a *New York Times* newspaper clipping with a photo of an abstract brass sculpture that looked like a twisted leg. The article, about a West German art show, bore the headline DOCUMENTA: A SENSE OF THE ABSTRACT.

In the cupboard below the sink, behind some containers of dishwashing soap, scouring powder, and other kitchen supplies, was a cardboard box. Reaching inside, he lifted the box out of the cupboard and set it on the floor. Inside was a plastic photo developer pan, some bottles of developer solution, a light exposure meter, and two tiny film rolls for what he guessed was the miniature camera. The film magazines were empty. He lifted the box and set it back in the cupboard.

He tugged his sleeve and glanced at his wristwatch. He'd been inside the apartment for over twenty minutes. Other than tearing out the walls and ripping up the furniture piece by piece, there was nothing else to check.

Footsteps sounded in the hallway.

Electrified with fear, Powers moved to the front door. There was movement outside, a rattling of keys. He ripped off the gloves and dropped them to the floor.

Suddenly there was the sound of a baby crying. A door opened and closed, and the baby's crying became muffled. Powers felt himself breathing normally again. He grabbed the gloves and shoved one in his pocket. Using the other one to cover the doorknob, he turned it slowly, opened the door a couple of feet, and stepped into the hallway. Discreetly, he shoved the remaining glove into a pocket, then checked the lock carefully. Though there was a small indentation in the doorjamb from the screwdriver, it wasn't obvious. Using a handkerchief, he wiped the doorknob, closed the door gently, hurried to the elevator, and stepped on.

As the elevator door closed, he had the feeling he'd forgotten something—*the screwdriver!* He grabbed his sleeve. It was there.

Downstairs, he crossed the lobby and went out the front door.

From a pay phone at the Gramercy Park, he phoned Sullivan's private number. Sullivan answered on the first ring.

"It's done."

"Already?"

"She went to the beauty shop, so I figured it was as good a time as any," Powers said.

"Was there anything . . . ?"

"She keeps a Minox camera in a hollowed book. I checked. There's no film in it."

"Anything else?"

"The makings of a photo-developing kit, with a couple of empty Minox cartridges."

"What kind of a place is it, Jack?"

"Well kept, no expensive clothes or furniture. Nothing to show she's living over her head. If anything, the place was drab. Your average D.C. apartment."

"Any evidence of others living there?"

"None."

"Amateur photographers don't use miniature cameras. The Minox has to mean something."

"There's something else. The place didn't have the personal touch. I found only one photograph in the entire apartment, and there were no scrapbooks or diaries or letters—things women usually have."

"She works for the CIA. They don't allow people to keep diaries."

"It's not just that. There was nothing male in the place. No keepsake from a boyfriend, nothing. That's strange for a good-looking woman like her. There has to be someone."

"There is."

"I mean from before. Something didn't seem right to me."

"Frankly, I don't find this as strange as you do. She's a professional career type, not a bimbo. Did you have any problems getting in or out of the place?"

"None."

"Way to go, Jack. I owe you one. I mean that."

"A Minox would have been perfect to bring with her to . . . the camp," Powers said. Even over a secure line, he didn't want to risk mentioning Camp David.

"I agree. But, unfortunately, the fact that she owns a miniature camera doesn't add up to much. We need her to make some unmistakable move. You'd better stay on her."

"If I sit here on Scott Circle much longer, someone is going to get wise."

"For now, continue to march."

"You're the boss."

The phone clicked.

Powers set the receiver back on the hook and headed across the lobby to the entrance. He pulled open a glass door and exited.

A taxi had pulled up in front of the apartment house. Marilyn got out of the backseat and walked to the front door. Thank God he hadn't stayed inside the apartment any longer!

The rest of the day went by slowly, and Powers listened to talk radio: *The Brad Crocker Show*. The topic for the evening was Crocker's proposal that Congress allocate a portion of the New Mexico desert as a national penal colony to solve the D.C. prison shortage. Because Crocker decided which callers to put on the air, they all agreed with him.

Shortly after 10 P.M. a man wearing a suit walked across the street toward the apartment house from the direction of the Gramercy Hotel. As he crossed under the streetlight, Powers recognized him: CIA agent Bob Miller.

Miller walked past the front door of the apartment house and continued about fifty yards down the block. He stopped, returned to the entrance, and loitered about in front for a minute or so. Finally, he moved to the door and took a key ring from his pocket. He opened the door, entered the lobby, and stepped into an elevator.

Powers, sensing an increase in his own heart rate, noted the observation, and the time, in his log.

Nine minutes later, Miller walked out the front door of the apartment house and headed down the street.

At 11:30 P.M., a sedan pulled up behind Powers's car. The lights were turned off and the door opened. It was Landry. He walked to the passenger side and climbed in.

"What's up?" Landry said.

"Get this: One of the CIA agents I met at Rehoboth showed up here earlier. A guy named Miller."

"No shit."

"He goes in, stays nine minutes, and splits. I would have followed him inside, but I didn't want to chance burning the caper. He knows me."

"He was in there long enough to drop something off . . . or pick something up," Landry mused.

"On the other hand, maybe he knocked on her door and she refused to answer."

"Maybe Nassiri decided to tell the CIA about Stryker. Maybe they're conducting an investigation like we are."

"Did you find anything out at the House?" Powers asked.

Landry took out his reading glasses and some note cards. "Marilyn Kasindorf is a CIA employee assigned to the National Security Council as an analyst. The Special Projects unit is a National Security Council study group—high-level foreign strategy stuff. She's never married, has a master's degree in international relations, and plays on the CIA women's softball team. She uses a desk in the Special Projects Office when she comes to the White House but reports to a permanent office somewhere else—but not Langley. Her name is on the Oval Office log. The reason for her visits is always listed as 'briefing.' "

"Any CIA employee allowed to brief the President would be at staff level. Patterson must have picked her for the job himself."

"Patterson's known for dirty tricks."

Powers loosened his necktie. "He wouldn't have the guts to pull a honey-trap operation on the President himself."

Landry coughed. "You never know about those Agency eggheads. You're taking rich college kids, coming right off their mama's tit, and training them to lie and cheat."

"They're not that crazy, Ken."

"They start believing all that James Bond crap. It warps their minds and then they go out and pull some crazy shit."

"No. Somehow all this doesn't fit together."

"Then how do you read it, my man?"

"I don't know. But Ray Stryker committing suicide in the office of the President's main squeeze . . . there's something missing."

"Right on. Who stands to gain?"

"There's a lot going on . . . the Middle East . . . and because of the polls, the man's in trouble heading into the convention. That's the way Watergate happened. People were worried about the election and started doing crazy things."

"There's no way of knowing at this point. That's for damn sure."

Early the next morning, Powers gassed the car at the Secret Service garage and hurried to Scott Circle. The light in Marilyn's apartment was still off. At 6 A.M., he started the engine and sped to the McDonald's hamburger stand on Fourteenth Street. He ran inside and purchased two Egg McMuffin sandwiches and a large Styrofoam cup of coffee. He was parked in his surveillance position again within twelve minutes. He ate slowly, savoring each bite of the hot food and the Styrofoam-scented coffee as if it were French cuisine. The light came on around seven, but Marilyn never appeared.

Finally, in the mid-afternoon, a D.C. taxi pulled up in front of the apartment house. The cabdriver, a lanky black man wearing a baseball hat, climbed out and moved to the trunk.

Marilyn strolled through the front door carrying a large leather suitcase and a shoulder bag. Powers's heart jumped. She was leaving town!

9

Instinctively, Powers grabbed the microphone from the dashboard hook to contact Sullivan, but then he stopped himself. If he transmitted a message, even in a code only he and Sullivan would understand, everyone monitoring the White House Secret Service radio frequency would know something was up. GS-13 special agents just didn't contact the Deputy Director unless it was important official business.

The driver took the suitcase from Marilyn, unlocked the trunk, and set it inside. Closing the trunk, the driver opened the rear passenger door for Marilyn and she climbed in.

Powers turned the ignition key and started the engine.

The taxi pulled into traffic on Rhode Island Avenue.

Powers accelerated from the curb and followed the taxi as it maneuvered through city streets to the Theodore Roosevelt Bridge and onto the George Washington Memorial Parkway. Moving at about fifty miles an hour along the bank of the Potomac River, Powers passed the signs for Langley and was sure.

She was headed for Dulles International Airport.

A few minutes later the taxi left the highway at the

airport exit, cruised along a wide, curving ramp, and pulled to a stop in front of the departure terminal. The driver recovered the suitcase from the trunk. Marilyn stepped out, opened her purse, and paid him. A sky-cap lifted her luggage onto a metal cart and led her into the terminal.

Powers climbed out of his car and followed her inside.

At the American Airlines desk, Marilyn opened her purse and handed an airline ticket to a blond female ticket clerk. Marilyn lifted her suitcase onto the counter scale. The clerk tagged it with a yellow baggage tag, stapled the receipt to her ticket, and stuffed the ticket into a ticket folder. She handed the ticket back to Marilyn, then pointed toward the escalators leading up to the boarding gates on the second level. Marilyn headed toward the security checkpoint.

Powers moved closer to the counter and watched Marilyn's suitcase as it proceeded along a baggage conveyor belt behind the counter. The yellow tag on the suitcase read FFT. Frankfurt. She was going to Germany!

Powers joined a line of passengers leading to the American Airlines ticket counter. The line moved quickly, and at the counter he used a government transportation request to purchase a round-trip ticket to Frankfurt. The ticket clerk asked about his baggage. Because it would be suspicious to admit he was traveling without luggage, he told her his girlfriend had already checked it earlier. At the clerk's request, he opened his briefcase and showed his passport.

Finally, she handed him the ticket. "The flight will be boarding in half an hour, sir. Gate Twenty-three."

Powers headed for the security checkpoint and then stopped. He was wearing his gun, and thus would be required to identify himself to the security personnel. If he did, by federal aviation procedure they would, in turn, notify the crew of the aircraft. Because he couldn't take the chance some member of the crew (as had happened to him on flights in the past) might identify him in front of the other passengers, he turned and headed outside. He opened the trunk of his car and discreetly slipped his gun, bullet pouch, and handcuffs off his belt and hid them underneath the spare tire. There was no time to park the car in the long-term lot. He tossed the keys in the trunk and closed the lid.

Powers hurried back inside and spotted a bank of pay telephones. He dropped change and dialed the direct number to Sullivan's office. The phone rang ten times. He tapped the hook to obtain another dial tone and dialed Sullivan's home number. After two rings, Sullivan's answering machine recording came on the line. After the tone, Powers cleared his throat. "I tailed her to Dulles Airport. She checked a suitcase and boarded Flight One-oh-three to Frankfurt, Germany. I'm booked on the flight with her. My G-car is parked in front of the terminal with my issue equipment in the trunk."

He racked the phone. At the security checkpoint, he walked through the metal-detector to an escalator leading to the boarding gate area.

At the top of the landing he moved through the crowd, looking for Marilyn. She was in the gift shop, browsing. Finally, she carried a magazine to the cash register and paid. To camouflage himself as she made her way out of the shop, Powers joined some callers at a row of pay telephones and picked up a receiver. She moved past him without looking in his direction and headed for the American Airlines boarding area.

As she passed a group of blue-uniformed female flight attendants, one of them, an attractive redhead, turned and, excusing herself from the others, followed Marilyn, finally catching up with her near the boarding area. Powers moved closer. The flight attendant tapped Marilyn on the shoulder and said something. Marilyn seemed less than friendly, in fact somewhat anxious, as the woman spoke. From the redhead's body language, it seemed like nothing more than small talk, the way an acquaintance might spot someone in a public place and simply say hello. They held a brief conversation and then Marilyn touched her wrist-watch, as if to say she was in a hurry. The flight attendant said a few more words, then turned and left. She caught up with her colleagues as they were stepping on the down escalator.

Marilyn took a seat in the boarding area and thumbed the pages of her magazine. Powers wondered why she'd brushed off the flight attendant, but he didn't consider the contact sinister. He knew spies never passed messages face-to-face, but were trained to use clandestine forms of communication such as dead drops and accommodation addresses. Hell, maybe the woman was someone Marilyn simply didn't care for.

Sitting a few rows away from her, he took out his note pad and jotted down the time of the contact and the remark *Chance meeting; appears to be insignificant.* About forty minutes later, the agent announced the boarding call for the flight. He allowed Marilyn to board first. Finally, he stepped through a wide doorway onto a crowded people-mover bus.

Marilyn was sitting in a seat between a young uniformed soldier with a shaved head and an elderly black man wearing an African dashiki.

Later, over the Atlantic at thirty-one thousand feet, Powers imagined himself, as in a motion picture, strolling up the aisle, sitting in the empty seat next to Marilyn, and striking up a clever conversation. After a while she would leave her seat to go to the rest room and he would reach into her purse and find a secret code book.

Leaving that train of thought for a while, he pondered his own situation. He'd been assigned to the White House Detail long enough to know that secret presidential chores had a way of blowing up in one's face. He was following a White House employee into a foreign country where, as a federal agent, he had no real jurisdiction. He took a deep breath and let it out. Below, the clouds were inky black.

A flight attendant, a mature woman wearing a uniform slightly too small for her puffy body, served him a plastic tray containing a Salisbury steak covered with yellowish gravy, some noodles, and a salad with watery airplane dressing. Though just the thought of airplane food usually made him gag, this time his hunger overcame him and he wolfed down the meal, even finishing the dry roll, stale carrot cake, and lukewarm coffee.

His mind swirling with doubt, he tried to sleep during the flight but couldn't so much as close his eyes. Finally, daylight broke through the darkness and the land mass of Europe became visible. For a while the plane descended slowly; then, finally, a male flight attendant moved up the aisle and used a microphone to announce the landing.

Fearing he would be caught in the crush of disembarking passengers, Powers was out of his seat and heading down the aisle for the door the very moment the aircraft came to a stop. He hurried down the jetway into Frankfurt's large modern airport. Its air held the familiar lingering odor peculiar to European passenger terminals, a smell Powers remembered clearly from the thousands of hours he'd spent waiting for flights: a stale mixture of Gaulois smoke, rest-room disinfectant, and harried human beings. From the jetway, he ran to a *Geldwechsel* window near the baggage area and changed five hundred dollars into deutsche marks.

In the baggage area, he checked the American Airlines display board to determine the baggage carousel assigned to the flight, then positioned himself near it to wait for Marilyn.

She was among the first few passengers to arrive from the aircraft. She had applied fresh makeup, and her hair was pulled back into a ponytail. A few long strands had slipped out of her barrette and were hanging below her ear. Standing there, close to her but invisible among the sea of people now edging closer to the carousel, he had the inexplicable urge to reach out and brush the loose strands back . . . as one might with a female friend.

Feeling the effects of sleep loss since beginning the surveillance, Powers ran his hands over his face and took a couple of deep breaths. He wished he'd been able to sleep on the plane.

Luggage began to spill from a conveyor belt. Marilyn watched carefully, then stepped forward and retrieved her suitcase.

Outside the terminal, she went to an information booth and said something to the uniformed man inside. He pointed down the sidewalk. Marilyn picked up her suitcase and walked directly to a passenger bus parked curbside to the right of the terminal door. Setting her suitcase down in a row next to some other luggage being loaded by two baggage handlers, she joined a small line of passengers filing onto the bus.

Powers waited until a few people had queued behind her, and then he too joined the line.

On the bus Marilyn paid the driver, a balding, heavy-set German with a purplish nose, and took a seat in one of the middle rows on the right.

Because Powers had no idea of his destination and

thus the cost of the trip, he held out all the bills he'd obtained from the money-changer to the driver.

"Wir fahren nur zum Kassel, nicht Griechenland," the driver said condescendingly. He picked a couple of bills and handed Powers some change.

Rather than chance moving down the aisle and coming face-to-face with Marilyn, Powers sat in an empty seat directly behind the driver.

The driver closed the door and steered onto the autobahn, a modern, four-lanes-in-each-direction highway. Powers sat back in his seat as the bus, traveling north at what he guessed was more than seventy miles an hour, whipped past sterile rest stops and rolling green hills dotted with farmhouses. After little more than an hour or so, as they passed some signs for Bad Hersfeld, Marilyn left her seat and moved down the aisle to the driver.

"In Kassel," she said, *"wie weit von der Hauptstadt is das Hotel Zum Goldenen Hirsch?"*

"Nicht weit. Vielleicht fünf kilometer."

"Danke," she said and returned to her seat.

The bus passed a line of U.S. Army tanks, entering the main gate of an American army post protected by a high chain-link fence. The sign read: CAMP WILLIAM O. DARBY, 4TH ARMORED CAVALRY DIVISION, SIXTH ARMY. A few minutes later, the green landscape on the left side of the road changed to the outline of a city.

The bus slowed down, turned off the autobahn, and proceeded along a narrow road toward town. Kassel, a city hewn by the past, was a jumble of brownish tenements, apartment buildings, modern storefronts, wood-paneled taverns, and cobblestoned alleys. As in many German cities, a cathedral spire marked the center of town.

The bus pulled up at the train station and the driver made an announcement via the intercom. Powers made his way off the bus among other disembarking passengers and waited near a line of taxis in front of the station.

Marilyn waited until her suitcase had been off-loaded from the outside luggage compartment, then picked it up and moved to a taxi. The driver, who was standing on the sidewalk, took the suitcase from her and placed it on the front passenger seat. Marilyn climbed in the back.

Powers hurried to the taxi parked behind. The back-seat was filled with passengers. The last taxi in the line had no driver.

Marilyn's taxi pulled away from the curb and turned a corner.

Another taxi pulled up and Powers rushed to it. The driver was a young man with a crew cut and granny glasses. "Is there a hotel Golden Hirsch?" Powers said.

"Hotel Zum Goldenen Hirsch?"

"That's it, buddy," Powers said, climbing in.

The Zum Goldenen Hirsch was located outside the center of town, at the edge of a large public park. In the middle of the park was a modern building that looked like a museum, or perhaps an exhibition hall or convention center.

Powers paid the driver and hurried inside the hotel. Marilyn was at the reception desk.

Powers crossed the lobby and sat down on a sofa as she signed in. A bellman picked up her suitcase and started across the lobby. She stopped him and gave him a tip. As he headed toward the elevator with her luggage, Marilyn walked to a car rental desk near the front and exchanged a few words with a young, bespectacled female clerk wearing a dark suit. Marilyn said something in German. The clerk replied in English. Marilyn showed some identification and filled out a form. Finally, the clerk came from behind the counter and led Marilyn out the front door of the hotel.

Powers moved to a tall window providing a view of the front of the hotel and its parking lot. Outside, Marilyn followed the clerk to a line of cars parked near a tennis court. The clerk used a key to open the driver's door of a brown economy-model Mercedes-Benz and then pointed out some items in the interior. Marilyn nodded. The clerk locked the car again and handed the keys to Marilyn. Marilyn dropped the keys into her purse and they walked back inside, chatting amiably.

Powers took out a pen and noted the license number of the car on a matchbook.

Back in the hotel, Marilyn crossed the lobby to the elevator, waited until it arrived, and then stepped on. The doors closed.

At the registration desk Powers rented a room, listing his occupation in the required box of the registration card as an accountant for the firm of Sullivan and Company. He surrendered his passport to the clerk and told an inquiring bellman his luggage had been lost. He sauntered to the car rental desk and went through the same general procedure to rent a car that Marilyn had. In fact, the car he was assigned was an economy-model Mercedes-Benz just like the one she had rented.

Next he used a house phone to dial the hotel operator. Learning that Marilyn was in Room 202, he took the elevator to the second floor and checked the location of her room. Then, after inspecting the stairway exits and hallways, he returned to the lobby. There he examined the physical layout of the hotel, and determined that one could get from the guest rooms to the lobby by either the lobby elevator or one of two stairwells leading from the floors. Thus he would be able to monitor Marilyn's movements by sitting in the lobby.

If Marilyn decided to leave the hotel, however, he would be at a disadvantage, because he was alone and had no one to help him on the surveillance. If she walked through the lobby and headed for her rental car, it would be impossible to be discreet in rushing out of the hotel to jump in his own car before she drove away. But if he sat outside in his rental car prepared to follow her, he'd be unable to monitor her movements inside the hotel and might be sitting outside as she met with foreign agents. After some thought he concluded that, as sensitive as the investigation was, if he was to monitor her activities he'd need at least one other person to help him cover both the interior and the exterior of the hotel at the same time.

In his room, using direct dial, he phoned both Sullivan's office and his home number to request help, but both were busy. Frustrated, he racked the phone.

In the lobby, he took a seat on a sofa in the corner and took a few deep breaths. It was 1 P.M., according to the ornate clock on the wall above the elevator.

For the next seven hours, except for a quick trip down the corridor to the hotel's clothing store to purchase a change of clothes and some underwear he figured he would need, Powers didn't leave the lobby. Sitting with the clothing for a while, he finally tipped a bellman to take it to his room.

As the afternoon passed, he did nothing but move from sofa to sofa, exercise his legs by pacing about, and, every hour or so, try to reach Sullivan by phone.

At 10 P.M., Powers made a pretext call to the hotel kitchen and learned that Marilyn had taken dinner in her room.

10

During the flight to California on Air Force One, young White House staff members pestered Landry with questions about the L.A. presidential visit, using him to doublecheck possible glitches in the schedule. "Ken, do you know the arrival time at the museum? Ken, can you give me the number of cars in the motorcade at the City Hall stop?"

Landry, having learned many years ago that showing hostility was never a wise course in organizational culture, and, could in fact be career poison for a black man, calmly complied. Each time he would take out his copy of the Secret Service advance plan and provide the correct information. Sometimes he wished he had never worked so hard to get promoted. If he had remained just a working agent he'd be off-duty during the trip, sleeping or lounging in the Secret Service cabin shooting the bull with the guys. On the other hand, he had to admit he relished being not only the only Secret Service agent but the only black seated with the rich white boys in the Power Cabin. His dead father, a bricklayer who'd spent his life as the only "colored man" (his father's term) employed by the Colantonio Masonry Company of Baltimore, Maryland, would have been proud.

But even with the pester factor, the trip would have been relatively uneventful if he hadn't been seated next to Capizzi. The Secret Service White House Detail maxim was "There Is Always One"; no matter how cohesive a detail, no matter how well the agents worked together at all hours of the night and day, enduring inclement weather, dangerous assignments, and heavy stress, assigned to every shift was one agent the others would come to resent.

Capizzi was the one.

Known as "Easy Capizzi" in the small world of U.S. Secret Service agents, he was an opportunist whose only loyalties were to anyone above him in rank. Capizzi had managed to get himself promoted to Civil Service GS-13 rank by selling Amway products after work for Agent-in-Charge of the Secret Service Personnel Division Steve Garrison, one of the top Amway salesmen in the United States. Then, to curry favor with the Director's golfing partner, Agent-in-Charge of Inspection Division Elmer Cogswell, Capizzi reported Garrison for selling Amway soap from the trunk of his government car while on-duty. Assigned to work under Agent-in-Charge of Protective Research Division Todd Bundy, an alcoholic, Capizzi became a two-fisted drinker. Working in the Foreign Dignitary Division, Capizzi, though a baptized Roman Catholic, joined the Mormon church to impress his supervisor, Latter-day Saints Deacon Earl Borchard.

"My favorite actuh is Denzel Washington," Capizzi told Landry now, in his New York accent. "Always has been."

"I like him too."

"I heard there was a mix-up in the reservations at the hotel," Capizzi said, taking a shot at the agent handling the reservations, against whom Capizzi held a grudge. "If there aren't enough rooms, I'm willing to sleep in the command post."

"I'll keep that in mind," Landry said, wondering if Capizzi could feel his revulsion.

"I can sleep anywhere, after the Marines," Capizzi said, hoping Landry would assume he was a veteran like himself. But Landry had made a point of studying the background of every man assigned to the White House Detail, and he knew that Capizzi had served as a yeoman in the Navy reserve.

"Do you know any good soul food restaurants in L.A.? I love soul food."

"I'm afraid not," Landry said, dreading a possible invitation to dinner.

"If you want, I can drive the limo when we get to L.A. I know a lot of agents hate to be wheel-man, but it doesn't bother me at all. To me, it's just one more day toward twenty."

"Thanks for offering, but that slot is already filled," Landry said. Capizzi always volunteered for any duty that would put him near the President during a scheduled photo opportunity. Landry closed his eyes for a while and imagined Capizzi opening the aircraft door during flight and jumping out, never to be seen again.

As the aircraft descended, he wondered what would become the Problem of the Day. In the Secret Service there was always one of those. It could be anything from an assassination attempt to the presidential limousine breaking down in the middle of the motorcade. Because of the complicated aspects of the security net surrounding the President wherever he went, the sheer volume of interlocking security details, plans, procedures, and equipment, something was bound to go wrong. And Landry would bear the final responsibility. By the time the aircraft touched down, Landry had memorized the President's schedule. The only part that worried him was a short motorcade in downtown L.A. he'd been unable to talk the political advance men out of.

As the working shift of special agents moved up the aisle to the bulkhead door, Landry could hear the Los Angeles Secret Service radio traffic in his earpiece. As was the custom, the agents were first off the aircraft, hurrying down the ramp to take their assigned positions at the presidential limousine.

Landry stood at the bulkhead door and surveyed the area. Across the tarmac, on the roofs of airport buildings, agents with binoculars were posted at intervals. Below, the motorcade was in position, with the presidential limousine parked directly at the foot of the aircraft ramp. Shift leader Bob Tomsic had taken his position in the elevated rear command seat of the "Queen Mary," the Secret Service's Cadillac. The other shift agents, like linemen waiting for the ball to be hiked, surrounded the limo in Secret Service formation.

Landry made eye contact with Tomsic. Tomsic gave the thumbs-up gesture. All was ready.

Landry turned, motioned to the Secret Service press agent at the rear of the aircraft, and stepped out of the way as the White House pool reporters and photographers rushed up the aisle, elbowing and shoving one another like schoolchildren rushing to recess. Believing as he did that most reporters secretly lust for an assassination attempt—or better yet, a successful assassination—to further their careers, Landry distrusted them. After the last reporter had climbed onto the press bus, Landry knocked on the door of the President's private compartment in the aft cabin. "We're ready when you are, Mr. President."

Moments later the President came out, moved to the bulkhead door, and waved to the crowd gathered below. Landry followed him closely as he moved down the ramp. At the limousine, Landry kept his eyes on the crowd as he opened the right rear door. The President gave another wave to the cheering crowd and climbed in. Landry shut the door, then took his position in the right front seat. He picked up the microphone on the dashboard and pressed the transmit button. "This is Landry. Let's move."

The pilot car, a marked LAPD black-and-white with red lights flashing, accelerated, and the motorcade followed.

"What happens first?" the President said, studying his schedule.

"We stop in front of City Hall. Four minutes to shake hands with Mayor Molina and the members of the city council. Brief photo opportunity, then an open-top motorcade down First Street for about a mile."

"There's a city councilman named Brown. . . ."

"Yes, sir. I know who he is."

"If he tries to get in the limo, tell him there's not enough room. The Mayor and the other council members are okay. Just not him."

"Yes, sir."

During the remainder of the trip to City Hall, the President went over the rest of the stops on the schedule the same way, informing Landry of various similar specific political requests. Landry memorized the instructions without making notes. At City Hall he would relay this daily "menu" to Tomsic. Tomsic, in turn, would pass it on to the agents.

During the motorcade, the President stood with his head and shoulders protruding from the limousine's bubble top. Landry, hidden behind the smoked windows, was poised just below the level of the bubble, with his right hand under the President's suit jacket at the small of his back. Holding the President's belt tightly, he was prepared to yank him down into the safety of the glass bubble at the first utterance of the day's Secret Service code word, "Drumbeat"—which would mean that an agent posted along the route somewhere had spotted imminent danger. Though he felt somewhat foolish in this position, particularly balanced between three L.A. city councilmen crowded into the rear seat (Tomsic had led Councilman Brown to a staff car before departure), he knew he would feel much more foolish sitting in front of a congressional committee after an assassination.

Three agents were running on either side of the limousine, and close to the end of the motorcade, Landry could hear the sound of their cap-toed Bostonians slapping the pavement. Rounding the corner onto Sixth Street, there was the sound of a transmitter being activated, then a heaving breathing sound. One of the running agents had pressed his transmitter. . . .

"Drumbeat!"

To the right, a man was running toward the limousine holding something in both hands. Harrington broke into a sprint. Landry pulled the President down.

Aiming low, Harrington tackled the running man.

"Just flowers. It's okay!" shouted Tomsic through radio static.

"Clear! Clear!" Harrington shouted, out of breath, as the motorcade left him behind with the flower man. "They're just flowers."

Landry helped the President back into position. "Sorry, sir. Just some posies."

As if his dipping inside the limousine had been unrelated to the running man, the President popped up again and resumed his waving to the crowd. Over the course of the day, the President never mentioned the incident to Landry. Similar things had happened before and would happen again, and the President, whom Landry respected, was smart enough to know that criticism of any security precaution taken by the White House Secret Service Detail was a rock thrown from a glass house.

Arriving at the Breakwater Hotel in Santa Monica

later that afternoon, Landry escorted the President to his penthouse suite. Having checked the posts, including those on the roof, in the basement, and in the lobby, which were manned whenever the President was in residence at the hotel, Landry made his way to the room down the hall from the presidential suite—the Secret Service command post. He quickly wrote a short report about the running man incident, the Problem of the Day, and entered the paragraph in the Secret Service daily log. From the radio traffic, Landry discerned that David Morgan had been admitted to the presidential suite. It seemed that Morgan was with the President almost every minute of the day lately. Something big must be going on.

That evening the President had dinner at Mistral with "The Three Musketeers." Dubbed this by someone in the White House press corps, they were the President's closest, most trusted advisers: philanthropist Milo Dimkich, restaurateur Arnold Stone, and entertainment attorney Anthony Chan, all powerful, politically active multimillionaires he'd known since his days as a Congressman. The President consulted with them during every crisis. Though cynics accused the three of secretly running the country, Landry knew that every President, at least every one he'd protected since becoming a Secret Service agent, had such a group with whom he consulted. To Landry, these fat cats from either political party were interchangeable: They not only lived in the same places (Beverly Hills and Manhattan) but, to him, somehow even managed to look alike. All were golfers, had beautiful wives, and were members of San Francisco's elite Bohemian Club. All supported charities, and all contributed heavily to both political parties to ensure their place in the kitchen cabinet—*any* kitchen cabinet.

Returning to the hotel late that night, Landry

checked the posts. With everything in order, he turned over the command post to Bob Tomsic, ate a peaceful dinner alone in the hotel coffee shop, walked around the block a few times whistling the Marine hymn, and retired to his room. Picking up the phone, he dialed the D.C. homicide squad room. Art Lyons answered.

"Landry here. Did you get the results to that test?"

"They just finished test-firing Stryker's gun this afternoon. The bullet I took out of the wall, the one that passed through Stryker's head, was fired from his gun."

"Thanks," Landry said after a moment. "I appreciate your taking the trouble."

"I hope that clears up any doubts you have about the suicide."

"I still can't see the man doing himself, Art. I picked him for the White House Detail because he was steady as a rock. But thanks again. We'll talk when I get back."

Lyons said good night and Landry set the phone down for a moment. Then he dialed his home number. Doris answered. "I hope I didn't wake you," he said.

"You can wake me any time, handsome."

"How are Reggie and Tisha?"

"They had one of their usual scraps after dinner, but report cards are in and Reggie came up in both English and math."

"Good for him. I knew he could do it."

"You sound kinda down, handsome."

"I don't know. I guess I've been thinking about Ray Stryker."

"You shouldn't dwell on that kind of thing."

"Can't help it."

"He's in the hands of the Lord."

"I'll call Reggie in the morning before he goes to school, dear. Sorry I woke you up."

"Are you all right tonight, handsome?"

"Sure. You go back to sleep now."

"I love you."

"And I love you."

It was morning, and Powers was still sitting on an overstuffed sofa in the lobby of the Zum Goldenen Hirsch. He was pleased when a new shift of hotel employees entered one by one and began taking up their assigned duties. During the early morning hours, he'd overheard bellmen and desk clerks commenting to one another about his constant presence in the lobby. If he was lucky, it would be some hours before those on the new shift noticed his loitering.

At 10 A.M., Marilyn left the elevator and strolled across the lobby. Powers followed her outside into the park and stayed behind her at a discreet distance as she moved along a path leading across a small bridge and under the shade of some trees. Emerging into the sunlight again, she made her way to the exhibition hall. At a booth near the front entrance she stood in a short line for a minute or so, purchased a ticket, and entered the hall.

Because he could see that the front entrance was, with the exception of the fire exits, the only way out of the place, Powers decided to wait outside rather than follow her inside and risk being spotted. For the next two hours he lingered about, keeping a watchful eye on the door. At about noon a man set up a frankfurter cart nearby, so he was able to eat lunch without taking his eyes off the place. As far as surveillances go, the opportunity to eat made it a good day. After eating, Powers took out his wallet and removed a lot of unnecessary papers that had been piling up, like credit card receipts and business cards. Inside a compartment was a folded paper with a list of names and phone numbers of women whom he dated: his little black book.

This list, like that of many other bachelor agents, contained the names of scores of women: mostly airline flight attendants and hotel employees, because they were the ones with whom Secret Service agents most frequently came in contact, but also cocktail waitresses and secretaries, hairdressers and schoolteachers: women of all races, classes, and political affiliations, including some whom he probably never would have met if it hadn't been for the fact he carried a Secret Service badge.

The very nature of a Secret Service agent's duties provides opportunities for sexual contact afforded by few other occupations. It's as though being within arm's reach of the President at all times and thus constantly bathed in the light of news cameras, agents are somehow irradiated with power . . . or dominance . . . or whatever primal longing it is that draws women to men. Powers found that women from all walks of life, not just the usual nymphomaniacs and other women of low self-esteem who are police groupies, were eager to live out their fantasy of having an affair with a clean-cut, honest-to-God presidential bodyguard.

A realist, Powers was aware that most of the women were as taken with his status as a presidential bodyguard as they were with him. On the other hand, though he'd never admitted it to anyone, for the last couple of years he'd grown weary—not bored, but simply weary—of living like a legionnaire. Frankly, he longed for a permanent relationship—even if it meant tossing his little black book.

At 4 P.M. Marilyn Kasindorf came out and headed back across the park. Powers followed her back to the hotel. There she stepped on the elevator and the door closed.

Powers went into the lobby. Since he was maintaining the surveillance alone, he checked the hotel to find the rooms with the best view of the corridor leading from Marilyn's room. Then, because he thought it more discreet than contacting the hotel security man, he gave the head bellman a substantial tip to arrange moving him into one of those rooms. This way, during the night he would be able to monitor Marilyn's movements outside her room without sitting in the lobby all night looking like a hotel burglar.

As this matter was being taken care of, he lounged about the lobby keeping an eye on the elevators. Later, the bellman slipped him a key to his new room and informed him he'd moved his few belongings into it. Powers gave him another tip.

Shortly after 9 P.M., just as Powers was beginning to think Marilyn was going to remain in her room as she had the previous evening, the elevator door opened and she emerged. She was wearing a jacquard dress in pink and gray, and long, dangling silver earrings.

Bellmen turned their heads as she walked to the dining room.

There the maître d', a short, well-fed man wearing a snug-fitting tuxedo, greeted her warmly. He had rosy cheeks, a full head of gelled hair combed straight back to the collar, and a smile revealing a gold incisor. Snatching a menu from a shelf under the podium, he led her inside.

Powers considered waiting in the lobby until she had finished dinner, but decided against it because he'd be unable to see if she met anyone inside. Besides he was starving, and the dining room was so big that she'd probably never even notice him.

Feeling conspicuous because of a day's growth of beard, Powers hurried to his room and shaved quickly. He put on the clothes he'd purchased at the gift shop and headed back to the entrance to the dining room.

Marilyn was sitting at a table near the window.

"Will you be dining alone, sir?" the maître d' asked in a heavy German accent.

"Yes. I'd prefer not to sit by the window," Powers said.

"Certainly."

The maître d' led him inside. The tables in the immense, well-lit chamber were covered with starched white linen and anchored with tiny vases containing a single pink carnation. The thick wall-to-wall carpet was dark blue, and the only sounds in the room were of silverware touching dinner plates and subdued conversations in German.

The maître d' seated Powers at a table in the corner, handed him a menu, and headed back toward the doorway.

Marilyn was on the opposite side of the room, still studying the menu. Setting it down, she stared out the window, as if in deep thought. A young waiter approached and spoke briefly with her. He wrote down her order and moved to a nearby table.

A few minutes later another waiter, a lanky, middle-aged man with a high forehead, came to Powers's table. Powers ordered the dinner special—wild boar with spaetzle—a salad, and, since Uncle Sam was picking up the bill, a full bottle of expensive Piesporter Goldtröpfchen wine. The waiter left the table and returned shortly. He uncorked a bottle and poured a little wine in a glass. Powers tasted the chilled, fruity wine and nodded. The waiter withdrew.

Marilyn had turned in her seat and was looking in his direction.

Powers felt naked. Rather than return her stare, he set the wineglass down and fiddled with the menu. Finally, she turned away. Powers had been on enough surveillances to know that people looking—even staring—at others wasn't all that uncommon, and the feeling that the subject of a surveillance was aware of the surveillant was a common one.

Nevertheless, Powers was concerned. He considered canceling his order and leaving the dining room, but figured if she was suspicious of him he would only be drawing attention to himself. Waiting for his meal to be served, he avoided looking directly at her.

A few minutes later Marilyn's waiter served her meal and, after wiping the mouth of the bottle with a linen towel, carefully filled her wineglass.

She turned in Powers's direction again—just a glance. And it was a glance. Her attention was drawn to him. Then she turned away, ignoring him as she ate.

Powers felt like crawling under the table. Finally, the waiter brought his plate. It was filled with a generous portion of the dark boar meat, which had a pungent, rich taste, and a large helping of spaetzle: strings of dumpling soaked in butter. He ate heartily, promising himself he'd jog extra miles to make up for the excess calories.

Marilyn, though having finished nearly half the bottle of wine on her table, seemed to be only pushing food about on her plate. Again, she glanced in his direction. Powers prayed she was only looking for her waiter rather than staring at him. She waved to get the waiter's attention and he came to her table. They exchanged a few words and he took a bill from his inside pocket. Setting it on the table in front of her, he handed her a pen. She was going to leave.

Powers breathed a sigh of relief. He decided to wait in the dining room until she'd left the room before trying to follow her.

She signed the check. The waiter picked it up and left the table. Then, in a deliberate fashion, Marilyn took her napkin from her lap and set it on the table next to her plate. She pushed her chair back and got to her feet.

Figuring she was heading for the door, Powers kept his eyes on his plate to avoid eye contact. Then he heard her footsteps on the carpet. Were they coming closer? The footsteps stopped. He looked up and caught his breath.

"May I join you?" Marilyn said. She was standing in front of his table. Her cheeks were slightly flushed, perhaps from the wine she'd been drinking. "Since you're following me, it'll make things easier for you."

Powers felt his stomach muscles tighten. His temples throbbed, and his mouth felt dry. As he saw it, he had three choices: He could remain mute, lie and hope she would believe him, or, accepting the fact that he'd blown the surveillance, simply get up and leave the table. But from the look in her eye and the confidence in her voice he could tell it would do no good. The cat was out of the bag. Damn!

He cleared his throat. "I'm sorry, but I don't know what you're talking about." It sounded lame the moment the words were out of his mouth.

"I said, may I join you?"

He found himself standing and pulling a chair back for her.

She sat down. "I first spotted you on Scott Circle near my apartment," she said as Powers returned to his seat. "I could tell you were watching someone who lived in the apartment house. Then I walked out to go shopping and there you were, right behind me."

Powers's face and hands were tingling with chagrin.

Marilyn eyed the wine.

Taking the hint, he slid an empty wineglass in front of her and, hoping she didn't notice the nervous tremor in his hand as he poured, filled it nearly full.

"I want to compliment you on your surveillance abilities. Very professional."

"Obviously not professional enough."

She picked up the glass. "I ran the license plate of your car and found out it registers to the Library of Congress. A friend in the FBI told me Secret Service uses the library as a cover registration for its vehicles. I was relieved." She sipped the wine.

As the full impact of what was happening hit him, the dining room suddenly seemed bigger and colder. He was sitting across a table from the target of his surveillance. His mission had failed. He was burned, made; the case was over.

"Relieved?"

"I was relieved to learn you weren't a foreign spy or a sex fiend."

She ran her finger around the rim of her wineglass, and it made a squeaking sound. "Someone ordered you to follow me . . . to investigate me. Well, what could be better than getting the information direct from the source? Go ahead. Ask me any question you want. I have nothing to hide."

They stared at each other for what must have been half a minute.

"Look, it's inappropriate for me to talk with you," Powers said.

"But it's not inappropriate for you to surveil me twenty-four hours a day?" she said angrily. "To follow me halfway around the world? Look, fella, I have a top-secret clearance just like you." There was a tear welling at the corner of her right eye. She brushed it away with the back of her hand and glared at him. "Don't just sit there and act like you don't know what's going on." Her chin quivered, but she controlled herself quickly. Wiping at another tear, she opened her purse and foraged for a handkerchief. "If you won't admit who you are, I'm going to get up right now and make a telephone call to the Director of the United States Secret Service."

"Okay." Powers reached into his inside jacket pocket for a clean handkerchief. "I'm a Secret Service agent assigned to the White House Detail," he said, feeling off-balance. He handed the handkerchief to her.

She hesitated for a moment and then accepted it. "I'm usually not emotional, but I've been under a lot of pressure recently," she said, dabbing at her eyes. "That's why I had to get away from D.C." She opened the handkerchief and blew her nose.

"I'm just doing a job."

"I knew working in the White House meant being under a lot of scrutiny, but I didn't think it would go so far as actual surveillance."

She picked up her wineglass.

"They must have given you some reason for following me. What did they tell you, that I was a potential presidential assassin?"

"No. Actually . . . it's just a routine surveillance. Everyone working in the White House is surveilled now and then."

"I've never heard that."

"Even the White House barber is tailed now and then," Powers lied. "But you're the first one to have left the country."

She gazed at him with a puzzled expression. "I guess that would look suspicious."

Powers sipped some wine and set the glass down on the table, trying to hide his nervousness. "Why did you fly here?"

"I'm interested in art. . . . Look. Lately the stress of working in the White House has been getting to me. I began losing sleep . . . and weight."

"I guess that would be a cause for some concern," Powers said, trying to lighten the conversation.

"So I requested two weeks' vacation. It was routinely approved. The first day of my vacation I realized I was under surveillance. Don't blame yourself. You did an excellent job, but I make a habit of looking for it."

"Just some free Secret Service protection."

"What's your name? Forgive me for being inquisitive, but you know my name. I'd like to know yours."

"Jack. Jack Powers."

"Jack. I really did think you were a hostile intelligence agent of some kind."

"So you decided to save yourself from the hostile intelligence operative following you and fly to Germany," he said.

"I'd always wanted to attend the Documenta. Documenta is the art show you followed me to today. I just went down to a travel agency and purchased a ticket."

"A spur-of-the-moment decision?" he said sarcastically.

"Though it's really none of your business, I'll be happy to explain: Like all us government drones, I don't make a lot of money. I had talked myself out of going to the Documenta three years in a row because of the cost. The spur-of-the-moment decision was to spend the money. I just said the hell with what it cost and put it on my credit card. So here I am."

"Unauthorized foreign travel is in violation of the rules of your agency."

"If I had submitted an amended leave form requesting travel to a foreign country it would have taken two weeks to get the trip approved. By then my annual leave would have expired."

"You could have speeded up the process," Powers said.

"The first rule of the CIA is to avoid drawing attention to oneself. It may be difficult for you glory boys in the Secret Service to understand, but it's a fact of life in the Agency. One doesn't ask for a vacation trip to Germany or any other foreign country without expecting the in-house people to start asking questions."

"Are you saying Agency personnel never travel to foreign countries on vacation?"

"My request to travel to Germany would have been immediately referred to the security section, and I would have become the subject of an investigation."

"Do you have something to hide?" Powers said.

"No," she said, glaring at him. "But in-house investigations in the CIA give rise to rumors. And rumors cause people to lose chances for promotions. You know how it is in government: Appearance is more important than reality."

Powers wished he hadn't been so assertive. "I understand," he said.

"May I have a little more wine?"

He filled her glass and motioned to the waiter for another bottle.

"You probably think I'm crazy for confronting you like this."

"Not at all," he said. She wasn't the power-seeker type he'd learned to recognize in D.C., women who always seem to show up at every party, every gathering where one might gain exposure to the White House circle: the fast talkers, masters of flirtation and currying favor, cultivators of Boston or Southern accents able to discuss any subject and take any side, to lobby any cause serving their interest, to conquer men of power. Also, she wasn't at all like the depressive Secret Service groupies he'd known. She was different.

He liked her.

The waiter came with the wine. There was an uncomfortable silence at the table as he took his time opening the bottle. Finally he popped the cork, filled their glasses, and hurried away. They both sipped uncomfortably.

"I'm on vacation, and I'm not going to let the fact that I'm under surveillance bother me one bit. And because I know none of this is your doing, you needn't get in trouble by telling whoever sent you here that I burned you. I don't intend to tell anyone about this. Ever. Thanks for the wine." She got up and headed toward the door. As she passed the maître d', he made a little bow and gave her an admiring glance. She turned left and headed toward the elevator.

Powers signed his bill quickly and hurried out of the dining room.

Marilyn stepped on the elevator and the doors closed. Powers moved through the lobby and into the garden. He looked up. The light in her room came on.

In his room, Powers dialed the White House operator and asked for Sullivan. Sullivan answered on the first ring.

"That person we're interested in. She went up against me. It's a burn."

"Shit," Sullivan said bitterly.

"There was nothing I could do."

"It's not your fault," Sullivan said after a long silence.

"What should I do now?"

"Stay on her."

"Stay on her even after she faced me off?"

"I'll talk to the powers that be, but we can't walk away. We need to know what she's doing over there," Sullivan said.

"This could get sticky."

"Just do your best to stay on her, until I see how the interested party wants to handle it from here. Look, I understand the position you're in, and I sympathize."

"That's a Roger."

"And one more thing, Jack. No more phone calls. It's too risky. Good luck."

The phone clicked.

Powers stood there for a moment, then set the receiver down. He turned off the light. In darkness, he moved to the window and tugged the curtain back a few inches. The light in Marilyn's room was now off. To the right was a glass-enclosed second-floor walkway, the only way to reach the lobby or the outside from her room. Even if she was clever enough to slip out of her room without turning on the light, he would see her when she crossed the walkway.

Powers arranged a chair in front of the window and folded the curtain back a few inches. Sitting there, invisible in the darkness and with exhaustion from the long days of surveillance weighting his eyelids, he relived his conversation with her, concentrating on her expressions, her hand movements. What she had said made sense, all right, but she was nervous—holding something back. Of course everyone in the world is holding something back, he told himself, and who wouldn't be nervous under the same circumstances? He alternated between sitting, standing, and pacing at the window for the rest of the hours of darkness.

As the sun came up he allowed himself a quick shower; then, headachy from lack of sleep, he trudged down to the lobby where he'd be able to follow her if she left the hotel.

Because of the morning rush of guests checking out at the registration desk, and bellmen carrying luggage here and there, no one seemed to notice him wandering about the lobby. Shortly after 9 A.M., Marilyn stepped off the elevator dressed in a tank top and fluffy shirt of Madras plaid. Powers stepped behind a pillar to hide from her view.

She crossed the lobby and went out the front door.

Powers followed at a discreet distance. She continued across the park and followed a gravel path leading to a small wooden bridge. After crossing the bridge, she entered the cover of some trees at the edge of the grounds of the exhibition hall.

She was out of sight, so Powers picked up his pace. Hurrying along the path with the sound of the gravel crunching, he felt the full weight of his fatigue. On the art gallery side of the bridge, the path between the trees leading to the gallery was empty. Powers broke into a jog toward the exhibition hall.

"Obviously you've been told to continue the surveillance," Marilyn said.

Powers stopped and turned.

Marilyn stepped from behind a tree. "Do you like contemporary art?"

"Pardon me?"

"Do you like contemporary art?"

He realized he was slightly out of breath. "Not particularly."

"Well, that's what I'm going to do for the rest of the day: wander around the gallery and the grounds enjoying the show. There's no need for you to be discreet any longer. I know you're following me and I accept it. Now that you know my itinerary, you can go back to the hotel and relax. As a matter of fact, you look like you could use some rest."

"I have to stay with you."

"Get serious. What kind of surveillance is it when the subject knows you're watching?"

"A useless surveillance. But be that as it may, where you go, I have to go."

"It's unnerving."

"Just ignore me. I won't bother you."

"Look, goddammit, I'm not going to have someone creeping around after me for the entire week I'm here."

"Sorry, but I have my instructions."

"The President's man, eh? Following orders whether they make sense or not. How typical of you Secret Service types. Glorified door-shakers. A bunch of second-rate presidential bellhop G-men. That's what you are."

"We're not smart enough to get involved in LSD experiments or plan Bay of Pigs invasions, like you Agency geeks."

She glared at him. Then, as if coming to a decision, she bit her lip. "I'm sorry," she said regretfully. "I didn't mean that. I know you're just doing your job."

"And I apologize for the geek remark."

"If we're going to be stuck together, let's cut the intrigue. I'm here to see an art show, and I don't want someone shadowing me all day."

"I don't think—"

"It's foolish for you to follow fifty feet behind. If we're stuck together, so be it. Can't we just cut the cat-and-mouse act?" She stood there for a moment, staring at him. Finally, she shook her head in frustration, turned, and headed toward the exhibition hall.

Play It by Ear, Powers told himself, is the unofficial motto of the Secret Service. The phrase implies that no two situations are alike. On a given day, an agent might be required to tackle and handcuff a screeching, biting lunatic on his way over the White House fence . . . and an hour later diplomatically escort a drunk United States Senator out of a White House cocktail party. Rather than pass the buck, like the law-enforcement bureaucrats of the FBI and CIA, who were guided by the dictum Cover Your Ass, the culture of the Secret Service was for operatives to act independently to accomplish the mission. This stemmed from the incontrovertible fact that if the President was assassinated, no plea or explanation in all the world would suffice for the agent who had failed in his assigned mission. He or she would enter the enduring annals of American history as the man who had allowed the President to get killed.

Playing it by ear, Powers joined Marilyn, and they walked the rest of the way to the exhibition hall without saying a word to each other. At the door, they both bought tickets and went in.

Inside the carpeted auditorium, which Powers estimated as the size of two football fields, the crowd was heavy. A maze of room dividers, on which paintings of all sizes were displayed, covered the entire hall. He realized it would have been nearly impossible to follow her all day in such a crowd.

"Do you know much about contemporary art?" she said.

"Never thought much about it."

"Then you can learn something today."

After moving along a line of canvases bearing only slashes and spots of color, Marilyn stopped for a minute or so in front of a five-foot-square white canvas. There was nothing on it other than a spot of yellow directly in its middle, as if the artist had touched the canvas only once with a loaded brush.

"What do you think?" she asked.

He shrugged.

"Seriously, what do you think?"

"Spare. Very spare."

"You think this is nothing, don't you? A sham."

"Now that you mention it, yes. I don't consider a dab of paint on a canvas to be anything but just that. This work could be the result of the artist dropping his brush."

She shook her head. "It all depends on what we see," she said.

"I see a glob of yellow on a blank canvas."

"The artist sees something else."

"I'll tell you what he sees. Dollar signs."

TOWER BOOKS

All locations open 9 a.m. to midnight everyday
3 Bay Area Locations

San Mateo 2727 El Camino Real (415) 570-7444
Concord 1280 Willow Pass Road (510) 827-2920
Mountain View 630 San Antonio Road (415) 941-7300

She shook her head for a moment. She tried not to smile, then gave up and began to chuckle. There was a devilish sparkle in her eye. They both laughed.

For the next couple of hours he accompanied her from exhibit to exhibit, past mobiles fashioned from nuts and bolts and birds, collages of matchbook covers and ice cream sticks pasted onto newspaper, pseudo-primitive nudes carved with oversized genitals, canvases of formless color, uneven geometric design, slashes, marks, spots, and stains—shapes Powers considered, at best, hasty projects of the uncreative and, at worst, factory-line pseudo-art bullshit. But as the hours passed and he could see her continued deep fascination with the exhibits, the strain between them lessened.

In the middle of the day, they took a table at an outdoor café overlooking the park which was adjacent to the gallery. It felt good to sit down.

"You must be exhausted from the surveillance," she said matter-of-factly, as the waiter served them plates of sauerkraut and a thick white sausage called *weisswurst*. "I know how it is to follow someone."

"Do you often vacation alone?" he said, to change the subject.

"I've had tours of duty in Moscow, Berlin, and Sofia. Being under diplomatic cover, I wasn't allowed to date any locals, and since the only men hanging around American embassies are horny eighteen-year-old Marine guards, yes, I did get used to being alone. Alone is a way of life for those of us in the Agency."

"I'm not trying to interrogate you."

"I know you're not."

Lingering after the meal, they chatted for a while and she seemed to relax. Avoiding the uncomfortable discussion of why they found themselves together, they chatted instead about Washington apartments, intelligence bureaucracies, art, and food. As they finally headed back into the exhibit hall, it occurred to Powers that they'd both gone out of their way to be considerate to each other. Taken with her grace and poise, he also realized that under other circumstances he would have made a full play for her. Not only was she attractive and intelligent, there was a wholesomeness, a feminine vulnerability about her, he found compelling.

Crossing under the trees on their way back to the hotel, Marilyn talked about her love for contemporary art. Listening without disagreeing, he had the strange, fleeting sensation that the two of them were completely alone in the world. He wondered if she felt the same way.

They entered the hotel lobby and crossed to the elevator.

"I'm going to change, then have dinner downtown at the Heilige Geist restaurant," she said as the elevator arrived. "I'll be leaving in about an hour." She stepped onto the elevator, turned to face the door, and winked at him: not a condescending wink, but the gesture of a fellow professional who understood his position and sympathized.

He winked back. The elevator door closed.

Powers hurried to the hotel courtyard. A minute or so later, the light in her room went on and there was movement behind the sheer curtains. Thus verifying that she'd actually gone to her room, he headed to his own room.

Powers needed a change of clothes. Figuring he could easily be back in the lobby before she left the hotel, he hurried to his room. Having shaved and showered at double-time, as he used to do in army basic training at Fort Ord before the morning company formation, or when trying to make the early baggage call when traveling with the President, he checked the window again. There was still movement behind the curtains in Marilyn's room.

He slapped on some after-shave lotion to refresh himself, and dressed quickly. Pleased that the clothing he'd purchased—a white shirt and pleated trousers, shorts, T-shirt, and socks—fit well, he stood in front of the dresser mirror and combed his hair. He shrugged on his sport coat and stepped to the window.

The light in Marilyn's room was off.

He ran from his room and raced down the hall. Rather than wait for an elevator, he used the fire exit and descended three flights of steps two at a time to the lobby. She wasn't there. He raced outside. Her rental car was still there.

Back in the lobby, he made another check: the dining room, bar, and gift shop. At a phone near the registration desk, he dialed her room number. It rang one, two, three, four times. His face felt flushed, and a feeling of utter helplessness came over him as he realized that somehow she'd gotten away from him.

The elevator door opened. Marilyn stepped out.

He racked the phone and rushed to her.

"Where were you?" he said, regretting the words the moment they came out.

"I couldn't find you in the lobby, so I went to your room," she said diffidently.

"Uh . . . we must have missed each other."

"You thought I ran away, didn't you?" she said with an amused smile.

"Now that you mention it, I did get a little shaky there for a minute."

"Jack, you may not have an eye for art, but I take back what I said earlier. You do have an imagination." She laughed as they walked out of the hotel.

12

The phone rang.

Landry reached automatically for the nightstand as he struggled to come awake. "Landry."

"This is Sullivan. Meet me at room 5412."

"Now?"

"I'll explain when you get here."

"Room 5412," Landry said, still fighting the effects of slumber. "That's a Roger." He climbed out of bed, dressed quickly, and, because he never left it in a hotel room, strapped on his gun.

Landry stepped off the elevator. Room 5412 was to the right. There was a uniformed Santa Monica policeman posted in the hallway, and yellow evidence tape extended across the hall. Landry's heart beat faster. He showed his Secret Service badge.

Sullivan came out of the room and ushered him inside. The body of a man was lying on the carpet just outside the bathroom. He was wearing a pin-striped sport shirt, navy blue shorts, and sneakers. There were two bloody spots in the middle of his chest. The rest of the room was a shambles, with dresser drawers overturned and the contents of a leather suitcase strewn about. In the bathroom, the contents of a leather toilet kit had been turned out onto the tile floor. There was the smell of men's cologne. On top of the dresser were a pipe and plastic tobacco pouch, a penknife, a pack of Breakwater Hotel matches, and a well-worn cross-draw pistol holster that looked like it might fit a .38 snub-nosed revolver.

A stocky, crew-cut Oriental man holding a metal clipboard was standing over the body. Sullivan introduced him as Detective Fukuhara, Santa Monica Police.

"You recognize this guy?"

Landry leaned closer. The dead man's eyes were open. "Never seen him before in my life."

Fukuhara motioned to the holster. "With the President staying here at the hotel, I figured he might be one of your people."

Sullivan cleared his throat. "The hotel manager is pulling the registration card."

"He checked in this afternoon: a Reston, Virginia, address. The name is Miller, Robert Miller. Name ring a bell?" Fukuhara said.

"Not with me," Sullivan said.

Miller, the CIA man Powers had told him about. Landry shook his head. "Never heard of him.

"What do you think happened?" Landry said.

"Looks like the victim walked in on a hot prowl. There's a vacant room directly above this one on the floor above. I think the prowler dropped down onto the balcony and jimmied the sliding glass door. From the ransacking, it looks like he was in the act when the victim came back to the room. His valuables—wallet, gun, and wristwatch—are gone."

"Sorry we can't be of any help," Sullivan said.

"Sorry to wake you up."

Landry followed Sullivan out of the room. They ducked under the evidence tape and stepped onto the elevator. Sullivan pushed the button, and a car arrived about a minute later. They stepped inside and the doors closed.

Sullivan was staring at the carpeted floor. "Powers said there was a Bob Miller on the CIA debriefing team at Rehoboth Beach."

"That was the name, all right. Bob Miller," Landry agreed.

"What the hell is a CIA agent doing here at this hotel?"

"Powers told me Miller had been nosing around at Marilyn Kasindorf's apartment."

"Something is going on at CIA," Sullivan said. "Something major."

"And my bet is Stryker's death has something to do with it."

"That remains to be seen. But I want you to maintain contact with Santa Monica PD on this homicide. Have someone from Protective Research follow up with the detective, stay on the case with him."

"Will do."

The elevator came to a stop. The door opened and they stepped out.

"And there's something else I want you to do, Ken. This has to be on the QT. Have our agents keep their ears open around the House for any staff talk about what's going on in CIA, particularly any mention of the Special Projects Office. I want to know anything they hear."

Landry felt his heart quicken. He took a deep breath before speaking, to mollify his tone. "We're playing with fire to start spying around the House."

"This isn't spying. This is gathering intelligence of what we hear during the normal routine of the day. There are strange things going on, and I want to know what the story is."

"It's going to be pretty hard for me to go to the men and ask them to start carrying tales, after I've warned them all personally about talking out of turn about what they learn on the job."

"Look, goddammit, I'm just trying to protect the Service—to have some advance warning if something is coming our way. I don't need a lecture on what's in the White House Detail operations manual."

Landry nodded. "Are you going to brief the President?"

Sullivan rubbed his hands roughly over his face. "Yes," he said, letting his breath out. "And he's going to ask me what's going on. And I'm going to have to tell him I have no goddamn idea."

"I wouldn't put anything past the CIA."

"On the other hand, we shouldn't jump to conclusions. Maybe Miller had a legitimate reason for being here, and maybe he *was* just killed by a hotel burglar. After all, this is L.A. Things happen. Hell, maybe the dead guy isn't the CIA Miller. Maybe he's some fucking shoe salesman from Kansas City."

"You don't believe that, and neither do I," Landry said.

Sullivan nodded. "I'll phone Powers and fill him in."

The Heilige Geist restaurant, located on a crowded cobblestone alley at the center of town near the Kassel train station, was sandwiched between a small bakery and a cutlery shop. The sign above its door was hand-carved on a wooden plaque.

The interior of the place was lit by candles on tables, and the walls were crowded with shelves of steins, beer mugs, wood carvings, clocks, and other German kitsch. There were about twenty tables, only half of them occupied. A waiter who spoke fluent English led them to a table in the corner. After they were seated, Marilyn told him the place was listed in

Peter Wesselink's Travel Guide to Germany as the best for the money in Kassel.

During dinner Marilyn talked of her childhood: moving from one army post to another. Her father had been a career army officer, and in the course of frequent military transfers she discovered an aptitude for learning foreign languages. When she graduated from Princeton, she was recruited for the CIA by one of her professors.

Powers found himself talking about his early years in the Secret Service, his assignments with Presidents Carter and Ford.

"Did you volunteer for this assignment?" she said.

"I guess you could say that."

"Funny. You don't seem like a climber."

"What's that supposed to mean?"

"In the CIA, agents used for off-the-wall assignments are usually people on the verge of being promoted. Those who know a refusal might mean treading water for the remainder of one's career."

"How did you end up working in the White House?" Powers asked.

"There you go again."

"Pardon?"

"Turning the question back to me. I'm getting tired of doing all the talking, Jack."

"I'm not trying to make this difficult."

"You're on-duty, and getting paid to be here. That's not difficult. Difficult isn't even being followed everywhere I go on vacation by a Secret Service agent. Difficult is having dinner with someone who won't talk."

"There is one benefit," Powers said in a mock-serious tone. "Uncle Sam is picking up the tab."

She returned his smile and shook her head. "How generous."

The waiter came to the table and refilled their glasses. The bottle empty, Powers ordered another.

"Will you answer one question for me?" she said, picking up her wineglass.

"Probably."

"Did you search my apartment?"

"Why do you ask?"

"If I'd been instructed to find out whether someone was a security risk, the first thing I'd do would be to see the way he or she lived."

He took a big gulp. "Great wine, isn't it?"

"That means you did search my place, and you probably found the Minox camera I keep hidden in a hollowed book. If that's the reason you are so suspicious of me, perhaps you should know the camera is CIA property and I was issued it as part of an Agency photography course. I keep it in the bookshelf hiding place because, like everyone else who lives in D.C., I'm worried about burglars."

"Thanks for clearing that up."

"I just hope my apartment was decent when you conducted the search."

"Spotless."

"You know a lot about me," she said, "but I know absolutely nothing about you."

"I've been on the White House Detail since—"

"Are you married, Jack?"

Powers shook his head.

"Why not?" she said softly.

"Never got around to it, I guess."

"Or never *wanted* to get around to it?"

"Actually, I've never met a woman with whom I wanted to spend the rest of my life."

She obviously was amused. "That's a nice way of saying you're a confirmed bachelor. I know about you guys on the White House Detail. A bunch of rakes."

"Actually a group of sensitive, caring chaps."

"I understand most of the secretaries on the White House staff have been cared for rather well."

They both laughed.

As they chatted, Powers found himself talking about the army and about working on his father's fishing boat. Marilyn talked warmly about her years at Princeton. Though they both avoided any discussion of the present, for the first time since they'd met Powers thought the ice actually had been broken. She was articulate and clever, and he found himself taken with her. It was midnight when he realized the place was closing.

"We'd better go," she said.

Powers paid the bill, and she gathered her purse and coat. Outside, though it had been warm all day, it had turned cold. As they walked down the sidewalk toward his rental car, they passed an orange neon sign over a door. It read TANZ CLUB TANGERINE. A young, modish couple was entering, and the sound of rock music came from inside.

Powers nodded toward the place. "How about one for the road?"

"Why not?"

He took her by the arm and, opening the door, entered a cauldron of sound. A young, well-dressed crowd was milling around the bar, and the cocktail tables were filled. The dance floor was full, and against the facing wall a disk jockey with blond spiked hair stood behind a record turntable and an array of stereo sound equipment. In the corner, a few younger men with short hair, who Powers thought looked like off-duty American soldiers, were huddled around a table.

A tall lady wearing skintight black pants, a red pullover sweater, and a stiff German push-up bra took their drink orders. Marilyn stared at the crowded dance floor as the woman prepared the drinks.

"Do you think I'm a security risk?" she said, turning to him.

"Frankly, I wish I hadn't accepted this assignment. I feel like some sleazy private eye."

"You didn't answer my question."

"No," he said after a while.

The bartender brought drinks. Marilyn picked up a glass, drank, and set it down on the bar carefully, as if it contained something valuable. "I don't believe you, but I want you to know I still think you're a nice guy. I mean that."

Powers felt chastened and small.

Marilyn turned toward the dance floor. "I haven't danced in years," she said. "Will you dance with me?"

"I'm not a very good dancer."

"I won't tell."

Deciding dancing with her was no more sinister than having dinner with her, Powers took her hand and, weaving through cocktail tables, led her to the dance floor. A romantic tune was playing, one he'd heard a thousand times, but what was its title?

She held herself politely away from him as they danced, as if to tell him in a nice way that her invitation to dance was nothing more than that. "Thank you for dancing with me. I expected you to refuse," she said as they moved to the music.

"My pleasure."

"I'm going to resign from the Agency when I get back," she said.

Powers sensed the tension in her. "You're foolish to give up your career just because you're the subject of a security investigation."

"I'm tired of the bureaucratic intrigue, of living in a pecking order. I want to do something on my own—something in the field of art, hopefully."

"There won't be any record of this investigation, if that's what's bothering you."

"Are you really concerned about me?" she said, tilting her head back to look him in the eye.

"I don't want to be the reason someone gave up a career."

She stopped dancing. "I hope you're not trying to convince me you actually give a damn about what I do."

"Maybe it'd be better if I just drove you back to the hotel."

Her eyes flashed. "Maybe it'd be better if you went straight to hell. I didn't ask you to follow me here," she said angrily. Her lip quivered for a moment, and she dropped her head and broke into tears. Embarrassed, she covered her face quickly. They stood there for a moment, and Powers realized others on the dance floor were looking at them. Marilyn suddenly seemed embarrassed.

He stepped closer, slipped his arm around her waist, and took her arm. She tried to pull away but he led her, moving to the music.

"Let me go."

"I thought you wanted to dance."

She wiped tears away with her hand. "I'm sorry about that, but in the last few months I've been working a lot and . . . my personal life has gotten somewhat complicated. And now . . . people watching me . . ."

"Forget about that."

"I've used some very bad judgment."

They continued to dance. When the tune ended, they remained on the dance floor and danced again to the next one. Back at the bar, avoiding the topic of her proposed resignation, they talked about everything under the sun. They danced again and again, and Powers lost count of the drinks. Finally, at 2 A.M., she suggested they leave.

Outside the bar, the cold night air slapped them and

brought them back to reality. On the way back to the hotel in the rental car they spoke very little. Powers found himself wishing she had chosen to sit close to him.

In the deserted hotel lobby a sleepy-looking desk clerk was shining the registration counter with a dirty cloth. He ignored them as they stepped on the elevator. The door closed.

Marilyn pushed the button for her floor, then his. The car ascended and the doors opened. She stepped out into the hallway.

"I'll walk you to your room," he said, following her out of the elevator.

"That's not necessary," she said, without looking at him.

Ignoring her protest, he accompanied her to the door of her room. She reached into her purse, took out the room key, and slid it into the lock.

"I know you were sticking your neck out by inviting me for a drink," she said, without looking at him. "Thanks. You have my word no one will know."

"I enjoyed myself."

"I'd almost forgotten what it was like to have a date. Not that we're on a date, but . . . well, you know what I mean."

"I know what you mean."

Opening the door, she stepped inside the room. "Good night, Jack," she said, looking more alluring than ever.

He reached out to take her in his arms.

"I think we've both had too much to drink," she said, resisting him.

His lips found hers. Her arms slid up his back. Suddenly he realized what he was doing, and released her. "I'd better not make things more complicated than they are," he said, stepping back.

They stood there looking into each other's eyes. "Good night," she said softly.

Powers closed the door slowly. Standing alone in the hallway, flushed, with the taste of her lipstick on his lips, he wanted to hold her, to take her, to be close to her, to bring his lips to hers, to have her under him, to have her on top of him, to please her, to bring her to ecstasy, to own her as much as a man can own a woman: to conquer and unite with her.

But she was the subject of an investigation, and an affair with her would be the kiss of death to his career. When they were back in Washington and the investigation was over and she was cleared, he could date her without risk.

The problem was, he didn't want to wait.

Imagining her arms around him, he returned to his room. Inside, leaving the lights out, he opened the curtain a few inches. Marilyn was standing on her balcony. Her arms were crossed and she was gazing, as if transfixed, in the direction of the exhibition hall. Powers stepped back from the window to hide himself from her view. After a while, Marilyn rubbed her arms as if she were cold and stepped inside her room. The curtains closed. For the next few minutes her shadow moved intermittently behind the curtains, and he imagined her getting ready for bed. Then, finally, the light in her room went out.

And, though he'd had his doubts since she'd first confronted him in the hotel dining room, at that moment Powers decided she wasn't a spy. There was no way to articulate his conclusion, but the fact was he had watched her, searched her apartment, talked with her . . . and kissed her. She wasn't a spy. Her affair with the President was unsettling to her, all right, but Powers was convinced she wasn't working for the Germans or anyone else.

He paced the room for a while, then finally kicked

off his shoes and lay down on the bed. But he didn't feel sleepy. Lying there in the darkness, he admitted to himself he was infatuated with her. Unable to sleep, he left the bed and returned to the window. He imagined the smell of her perfume, her hair brushing his cheek as they'd kissed. He wanted her. And he could tell when they'd kissed that she wanted him.

There was the sound of two soft knocks on his door.

Startled, he reached to his waistband. But his gun was in the trunk of his car in D.C. He moved across the room and stepped to the side of the door, in case someone shot through it. For the first time, he realized there was no peephole.

"Who's there?" he said.

"It's me," Marilyn said.

He turned on the light and opened the door. She had combed her hair and applied fresh lipstick. Their eyes met. He just stood there for a moment. Then he took her in his arms and covered her mouth with his. Their tongues met. Feeling the length of her body against his own, her arms around him tightly, he pulled her inside and slammed the door.

They undressed each other feverishly, and Powers's breathing quickened. Marilyn shrugged from her brassiere. There was a small scar on her shoulder.

"I didn't want to be alone tonight," she whispered.

"You shouldn't have come here," he said between kisses.

Naked, he picked her up and carried her to the bed. They kissed and he touched the softness between her legs. She moaned as he massaged her gently. Her nipples became erect.

Suddenly, she guided him into her warmth. Fingernails were in his shoulders and he gave himself to her unregenerately, helplessly, absolutely, and her legs raised to accept him. Her eyes were closed, and she moaned. Both of them locked in this rhythm for a long time, her hands reached up to his face and he realized he was perspiring—perspiring and breathing hard. Transported in rapture, they clung to one another, then changed positions hurriedly, as if stealing pleasure. Then she was under him again.

"Don't stop," she said. "Please. Don't stop."

He didn't. In fact, he couldn't. Her hands took his waist and he was lost in the timeless cadence of sex. Her nails dug into his buttocks. Captured and held, he could hold back no longer. From deep inside, he released himself and became, in flashes of surging whiteness and pink surrender, all men with all women since the beginning of time.

Then, lying on their sides with their arms around each other, they stayed there for a while, neither saying a word. He could feel her abdomen touch his with each breath. He felt comfortable, unburdened with her, as if they'd been sexual partners and friends for a long time.

Powers realized they hadn't even taken the time to turn off the light. "How'd you get that scar on your shoulder?" he said.

"Fell off a bike when I was in college."

He kissed her, and nothing was said for a long time. She twisted and turned off the light. In the darkness, she snuggled into his arms. Feeling one with her, he closed his eyes.

"You're so quiet," he said.

"I wish we had never met," she said sadly.

"That's a funny thing to say."

"I mean it." She lifted her head from his shoulder. She kissed his cheeks, his mouth, his chest, biting kisses, sucking kisses everywhere, and soon, to his own surprise, he felt a new stirring. She grasped him firmly, ministering to him, her head moving up and down on him. He opened his palms and allowed her lifting and falling hair to touch them lightly. Erect again, he took her under him, abandoning himself. After a long, long time, he closed his eyes and came.

Lying there on his back, feeling depleted and drained, he sensed the tingle of perspiration evaporating from his chest and legs.

Marilyn climbed out of bed and went into the bathroom. She returned with a white, fluffy towel and used it to dry him.

Allowing himself to breathe deeply, Powers finally felt the effects of his loss of sleep over the past days. The deep, paralyzing fatigue that makes eyelids weigh twenty pounds took him.

"What time is it?" he said.

She pulled the covers up and snuggled next to him. "Four-thirty."

Powers closed his eyes.

"You're wonderful, Jack."

"I like you, too."

"Get some sleep," she whispered, resting her head on his shoulder.

For a moment he thought he felt Marilyn shudder, as if she might be stifling tears.

"What's wrong?" he said.

"I wish we could have met under other circumstances."

"I don't understand."

Her fingers touched his lips. "Go to sleep," she whispered. "We can talk in the morning."

Her arms held him tightly. Slipping comfortably into sleep's blackness, he saw her walking into the restaurant in Washington. She stopped and looked around, then sat down. Silently, as if transformed into a cloud, Powers imagined himself moving to her. Her back was to him and, standing behind her, he was unable to see her face. He reached out and touched her hair. She didn't acknowledge him. "Marilyn," he said, and the others in the restaurant turned to look, but she ignored him. . . .

The phone was ringing. Powers opened his eyes. He was on his stomach, and his left arm was asleep. There was a wide break in the curtain, and a shaft of morning light trailed across the bed. Powers grabbed the receiver and said hello.

"This is me." It was Sullivan.

"Yes," Powers said, coming awake. "I read your voice."

"One of the men you met at the beach was found dead in a hotel room at the Breakwater during the visit."

Powers rubbed his face to come fully awake. "Sounds spooky."

"I thought you should know. How is everything going?"

"I'm hanging in." Powers suddenly realized he was alone in the room. He sat up. Was she in the bathroom?

"Has the other person made any contacts over there?"

Only one. "None."

"Keep me advised," Sullivan said. The phone clicked.

"Marilyn . . . ?"

13

Powers reached to the nightstand for his wristwatch. It was 7 A.M. He felt a sense of uneasiness coming over him as he picked up the phone receiver.

"Miss Kasindorf's room, please."

"Moment, bitte," the operator said. The phone clicked and there was a ring, then another and another. Powers dropped the receiver on the cradle and climbed out of bed. Quickly, he pulled his clothes on and hurried to the ground floor. He checked the restaurant, the lobby, and the gift shop, but she wasn't there. Then he ran past the reception desk and out the front door. Her rental car, the brown Mercedes-Benz, was gone.

At her room, he knocked loudly on the door. There was no answer. Without hesitation, he stepped back and, holding his arms out to his sides to maintain balance, lifted his right foot and kicked. The door snapped open.

Inside, the bed was unmade. With hands flying, he opened drawers. They were empty. Her suitcase was on a stand next to the bathroom door. He opened it. Nothing but clothes. Her purse was nowhere in the room. Closing the suitcase, Powers noticed a small wooden wastebasket with a white plastic liner. Even

157

it had been emptied. Powers shut his eyes and covered them with his hands for a moment. His mind raced with the events of the night before. He felt like screaming, crying, perhaps vomiting in frustration and anger.

Rather than wait for the elevator, Powers hurried to the stairwell and descended the steps two at a time into the lobby. He checked with the desk clerk and the doorman. Neither had noticed Marilyn leave.

Powers left the hotel and ran outside to his rental car. He climbed in, started the engine, and sped out of the drive down the highway to Camp Darby. It took him about ten minutes.

The guard booth at the front gate, and the tall chain-link fence surrounding the post itself, were illuminated by security lights on tall metal poles. On top of the fence, razor-sharp concertina wire glimmered in the morning light. He pulled up to the guard booth and a uniformed military policeman, a tall young man with a regulation-trimmed mustache, stepped outside warily.

"Yes, sir?" the MP said, eying him suspiciously.

Powers took out a black leather case containing his Secret Service identification card and badge and held it open. The MP studied it closely.

"Secret Service?"

"Special Agent Powers, White House Detail. Is there an intelligence officer assigned here?"

"The only spook we have on this post is Sergeant Fuller. You can find him in the headquarters building Monday morning at oh-eight hundred."

"It's an emergency. Call him and ask him to meet me here."

"May I see that identification again, sir?"

Powers complied.

"Thank you, sir." The MP stepped into his guard booth and grabbed a phone.

About ten minutes later, a black Ford sedan sped up to the guard booth. The driver, a rangy man a few years older than Powers, stepped out. He had a ruddy outdoorsman's complexion and wore a blue sport coat, gray dress slacks, and a white shirt open at the collar. His brown hair was just long enough to comb. He was wearing a snub-nosed .38 in a waist holster, a garish silver-eagle belt buckle, and shiny army-issue "low-quarter" dress shoes.

"Special Agent Charles Fuller," he said in a Southern accent. "Army Intelligence."

Powers showed his badge and introduced himself.

Fuller studied the identification, holding it up to the light, and nodded. "Is the President coming here?"

"No. I'm on a special assignment, a surveillance of a U.S. civilian. I need your help."

"Sir, I can't give you any help unless I have authorization from my group headquarters."

From a pocket in his commission book, Powers slipped out a laminated plastic card all Secret Service agents carry and handed it to Fuller.

"This is a copy of the Presidential Executive Order 1976, stating that any officer of the Military Services shall assist an agent of the United States Secret Service in the performance of his duties by providing service, equipment, and facilities whenever officially requested by any Secret Service special agent," Powers said.

Fuller studied the card for about a minute. "That's what it says, all right," he mused. "Come to think of it, I remember learning about the order in intelligence school."

"I'm officially requesting your immediate assistance under this lawful order from the Commander in Chief."

Fuller stood there for a moment biting his lip. He turned, picked up a metal clipboard from the front

seat of his jeep, and handed it to Powers with a pen.
"I want that in writing."

Without hesitation, Powers wrote the following:

> *August 24, 1996: I, Special Agent Jack Powers,*
> *U.S. Secret Service (badge #364), hereby request*
> *the assistance of Sergeant Fuller, U.S. Army Intelli-*
> *gence, under Executive Order 1976.*

Powers signed his name and handed the clipboard
back. Fuller's lips moved as he read it carefully. He
handed it to the MP. "You are my witness," he said.
"Please initial this." The MP signed, then handed the
pen and the clipboard back to Fuller.

"The subject of the surveillance is a woman, a U.S.
government employee with a Top Secret Security
Clearance, and I have to find her," Powers said. "She
left the Zum Goldenen Hirsch hotel within the last
couple of hours. She's driving a rented brown Mercedes-Benz." Powers reached into his shirt pocket for
the matchbook on which he'd noted the car's license
number and handed it to Fuller. "Here's the license
number."

Fuller stepped into the guard booth and picked up
the phone. "This is Fuller. I'm calling a Blue Light
alert. That's right, a full alert. I read: Delta, Foxtrot,
and Whisky. Roger. Notify the colonel, and stand by
to monitor Romeo frequency. Out." He slammed the
phone down.

"We'll take my car," he said.

Powers hurried to the passenger side and climbed
in.

Fuller drove as they searched the vicinity of Kassel.
The radio crackled with Southern and New York accents, as military policemen exchanged information
about the description and license number of Marilyn's

car and gave instructions in military jargon. Occasionally, American military helicopters taking part in the search passed overhead. During the first hour or so, Fuller, after exchanging radio messages, met up with military police units and gave orders about the search. By the third hour, Powers had lost hope and was thinking about what he was going to tell Sullivan when he returned to D.C.

While they were driving back and forth through the city and countryside black clouds had grown, and now the smell of rain filled the air. As the first raindrops started to fall, they were cruising along a winding road in the vicinity of the old Iron Curtain, the dividing line between East and West Germany before reunification. Like most of the rest of Germany it was comprised of fertile, rolling hills and thick forests. For a moment, the horrid thought occurred to him that she might have defected—gone across the border into East Germany—but of course there was no East Germany and no more Iron Curtain.

The sound of static came from the radio. "Foxtrot King, this is Blue Light."

Fuller grabbed the microphone. "Go, Blue Light."

"Niner Delta reports they have your brown Mercedes parked at 1532 Erlangen Strasse."

"Have them stand by. Repeat. Stand by."

Fuller executed a U-turn, nearly tipping the car over, and stepped on the gas. They raced through a section of highway shaded by tall birches, leaning inward and creating a tunnel-like effect.

"Erlangen Strasse is by the City Hall," Fuller said.

Powers, consumed by the thought that his ability to judge people had failed him, kept his eyes on the road.

Fuller drove recklessly at what must have been about a hundred miles an hour during the short drive into town. Turning sharply near the railroad station, he wound through a mixture of cobblestoned and modern streets. At Erlangen Strasse, he slowed down to look for numbers. A Volkswagen bus with U.S. Military Police markings was parked at the curb behind the brown Mercedes-Benz. Fuller stepped on the brakes and Powers grabbed the dashboard to steady himself. "Whoa, Nellie!" Fuller shouted.

Powers and Fuller stepped out of the car. The doors of the Volkswagen bus opened and two tall young MPs in full dress uniform climbed out. There was a violent crack of thunder and it began to rain lightly.

Fuller showed a badge. "Nice going, gentlemen."

As Fuller spoke with the MPs, Powers moved closer to the car. His stomach churning nervously, he touched the hood. It was cold. The windows were rolled up, and there was nothing on either the front or back seats. "I'd like to know what's around here," Powers said, staring at the car.

"Roger that."

As Fuller gave instructions to the military cops, Powers tested the driver's door lock, opened the door, and slid behind the wheel. There was the faint smell of Marilyn's perfume. He checked under the seat and in the glove compartment. Nothing but rental and insurance forms, maps, and a screwdriver. He compared the odometer reading to the rental form and shoved the form back in the glove compartment. He stepped out of the car. The trunk was locked. He went back inside the car for the screwdriver, and after a few tries he was able to pop the trunk open.

It was empty.

Feeling castrated, Powers ran his hands through his hair. The rain tickled his face as he looked around and considered the possibilities. If she'd gotten help from someone, she wouldn't have picked a residential street lined with windows to transfer to another vehicle. But if she was on the run, she might have considered her head start her only advantage and thus thrown caution to the winds.

Fuller walked across the cobblestoned street to join him.

"There's nothing in the car."

"Those are all apartment houses across the street. If you think it'll do any good, we can go to the resident registration office and get the name of every occupant of every apartment."

"Wouldn't tell us anything."

The MPs came out of the building adjacent to the Mercedes-Benz.

"Sir, that's a commercial building. The first floor is a German *Versicherung*. I think that means an insurance company. The second floor is the Syrian trade mission."

"What's that?"

"The Syrian trade mission. We knocked on the doors. There's no one at either place. Of course, it's Saturday."

Powers felt his stomach begin to churn. He felt warm.

"Sir? Do you need us for anything else? We're scheduled to go off-duty." Powers said no and thanked the MPs.

"No problem, sir," said the taller officer.

"The woman who rented the car. Was she someone you knew?" Fuller inquired, as the MPs climbed into their Volkswagen and drove away.

"Not very well," Powers said after a while. How was he going to be able to explain?

"No use standing here in the rain," Fuller said, moving to his sedan. "Jack . . ."

Powers turned and walked numbly to the car. Reaching down, he opened the passenger door and climbed in. The rain was machine-gunning the roof and windshield, and he realized he was soaked.

Fuller took out a clean handkerchief and dried his face and the top of his head. "I'll need the woman's name for my report," he said.

"Just write that I asked for assistance under Section Six in finding a female civilian employee of the U.S. Government. Your report should be classified Top Secret, with limited distribution."

"Where's the rest of your surveillance team?" he said.

"I'm it."

"Kind of strange."

"What's kind of strange?"

"Following someone from Washington, D.C. to Germany, alone . . . without a surveillance team," he said, smiling wryly.

"I'm not going to bullshit you. We both know a one-man surveillance means the people upstairs want minimum exposure. In fact, they probably won't like the idea of my asking the army for help."

Fuller took out a package of Kools and lifted a cigarette from the pack with his teeth. He flamed the cigarette with a Zippo lighter and lowered the driver's window about an inch for air circulation.

"I can relate to that," he said, emphasizing the *re* in *relate*. "Damned if you do and damned if you don't."

"In the Secret Service it's called 'Playing It by Ear.' "

Fuller nodded. "You ever heard tell of a pfffft bird?"

"Can't say I have."

"Rather than flying straight like the other birds, the pffft bird flies in ever-decreasing circles until finally— *pffft!* It flies right up its own asshole. Same thing can happen during an investigation. Everything seems to be going right; then, all of a sudden, *pffft!* You're in a world of hurt."

"You've got that one right," Powers said. The rain came down in sheets, swirling back and forth across the road.

During the flight back to Washington, his mind awash in guilt, anger, and humiliation, Powers neither ate, drank, read, nor watched the movie. Leaning back in the seat with his eyes half closed, he relived the details of every moment he'd been with Marilyn, including the time they'd spent together in bed. Still in this state of self-absorption as the aircraft began its final descent, he'd convinced himself that the best thing to do was simply tell Sullivan the truth: Marilyn had convinced him she wasn't a spy, they'd slept together, and she'd given him the slip. But Marilyn was the President's girlfriend. . . .

Airplane wheels shrieked as they touched tarmac at Dulles Airport. The weather was still gray, as if, Powers thought in his state of depression, a storm were covering the earth itself. As the aircraft taxied toward the terminal area, Powers finally decided how he would play it with Sullivan. Because he'd been instructed to surveil Marilyn single-handedly, and thus couldn't be held accountable if she were to slip away, he'd simply tell the truth about everything in Germany—except, of course, that he'd slept with her.

At Secret Service headquarters, Powers felt the tension building as he walked down the long hallway toward Sullivan's office. He stopped in front of the door, took a deep breath, and entered. Lenore Shoequist stopped filing her long red nails and showed him into Sullivan's inner office.

Sullivan, looking drawn and pale as if he hadn't slept, got to his feet. "No calls," he said.

Lenore Shoequist smiled perfunctorily and pulled the door shut.

Powers cleared his throat. "She—"

Sullivan put a finger to his lips and led Powers to the security room. Inside, he flipped on the light and the air-conditioner switches and bolted the door. The room was stuffy and overheated, and Powers felt his knees actually shaking.

"She gave me the slip."

"I already know what happened," Sullivan interrupted.

"How . . . how did you find out?"

Sullivan turned away from him and worked the combination dial on the safe. Finally, the lock clicked and he pulled open the heavy steel drawer. He took out a green folder marked TOP SECRET and returned to the table. From the folder he removed a document. "Director Patterson called me to CIA headquarters this morning," he said, handing the document to Powers. It looked like a teletype message. "He gave me this."

The message read as follows:

TOP SECRET—NO FORN

BEGIN MESSAGE
FLASH—USAREUR COMMAND (NATO)
ARMY INTELLIGENCE COLLECTION COMMAND REPORTS IN AREA FOXTROT ONE US SECRET SERVICE AGENT POWERS ACTING UNDER AUTHORITY OF THE PRESIDENTIAL EXECUTIVE ORDER

1976 REQUESTED ASSISTANCE IN SEARCHING FOR
POSSIBLE MISSING CIVILIAN EMPLOYEE US GOVT.
(NFI) REPEAT CIVILIAN EMPLOYEE US GOVT. (NFI)
    SUBJECT'S RENTED VEHICLE FOUND IN DOWN-
TOWN KASSEL. SECRET SERVICE AGENT POWERS
REQUEST LIMITED DISTRIBUTION ON THIS MES-
SAGE. (NFI)
    END MESSAGE

                TOP SECRET—NO FORN

Sullivan sat down at the table and took out a pen.
"Start at the beginning," he said, turning the page of
a yellow legal tablet.

Powers sat across from him. For the next hour or
so, he related the events of the surveillance from the
time he'd arrived in Germany to the finding of Marilyn's car. He included all the pertinent details, esti-
mating times for his observations of Marilyn's actions
as he went along. Sullivan took copious notes as he
spoke. When he reached the part where Marilyn had
first confronted him in the hotel restaurant, he was
puzzled when Sullivan didn't flinch.

"The next day I followed her out of the hotel and
she confronted me again," Powers said reticently.
"She told me she was going to an art show, and suggested I accompany her. I figured that under the circumstances, since she was already aware of the
surveillance, I might as well."

"I would have probably made the same decision
under the circumstances," Sullivan said, making a
note.

"That night I accompanied her to a restaurant, a
place called the Heilige Geist."

"Did you sit together?"

"Yes."

"What did she talk about at dinner?" Sullivan
asked.

"Casual conversation, nothing significant."

"Then what?"

Powers felt his stomach muscles tighten involuntarily. "We stopped for a drink after dinner."

"Where?"

"I think the place was called the Tanz Bar."

"How long did you stay there?"

"We had a couple of drinks."

Sullivan set his pen down. "Then what?"

"We returned to the hotel."

"What happened then?"

"You mean after we arrived at the hotel?"

"Yes."

Powers coughed dryly. "She went to her room and I went to mine."

"How were you able to keep an eye on her?"

"There was a bank of windows. . . . From my room I was able to keep an eye on her door."

"So you watched her room all night to see if she left the hotel?"

"I admit to catching a few winks. I hadn't slept since beginning the surveillance."

"I understand," Sullivan said in a fatherly tone. "When did you notice her missing?"

"In the morning."

"You went to her room?"

"I called her room and there was no answer."

"How do you think she got out of the hotel without you seeing her?" Sullivan said. There was a definite tinge of hostility in his words.

I shouldn't have lied. I just should have told the truth, faced the music. Now I'm locked into the story. "I'm not sure," Powers said mournfully. "I must have nodded off for a few minutes."

Sullivan gave him an icy stare. "It's just you and me in this room, Jack. I have to know everything. This is too important not to know everything."

Powers felt perspiration running down the middle of his back. "I've told you everything."

Sullivan checked his notes. "Tanz Bar. *Tanz* means dance, doesn't it?"

"Yes."

"Did you dance?"

Powers felt blood rushing to his face. "I don't recall."

"It's me, Jack. There's no one else in this room."

"Come to think of it, we might have danced."

"Did you or didn't you?"

"I didn't see any big deal in—"

"You danced with her. Then what?" Sullivan said, staring at him.

"You mean when we left the bar?"

Expressionless and maintaining direct eye contact, Sullivan nodded. Just one nod. "When you left the bar."

Powers wished he could disappear, or that he could wake up and have it all be a dream. "Like I said, we returned to the hotel."

Sullivan made a note on the pad. "Go ahead."

"That's about it. We went back to the hotel."

"She's a very attractive woman, isn't she? A ten on the ten scale."

"I guess you could say that."

"It must have been a strange feeling, being over there alone with this beautiful woman. Just you and her."

Powers ran his hands through his hair. There was no use lying anymore. "She spent the night in my room," he said quietly. "I woke up in the morning and she was gone. . . . I'm sorry."

Sullivan's face turned red.

Powers heard his own heart beating.

Sullivan slid the TOP SECRET folder across the table.

Powers opened it. In it was a piece of bond paper without letterhead. It read as follows:

TOP SECRET
CONTACT REPORT

Source 2048LKA, during a routine contact, stated substantially as follows:

During the last twenty-four hours an American double agent, a woman, possibly an employee of the CIA named *Kasindorf*, first name *Mary* or *Marilyn*, traveled to Damascus, Syria, via Paris and Ankara where she was met by Syrian Secret Service officials (nfi). Her travel is believed to have been part of an escape plan effected from Kassel, FRG, where she recognized an American surveillance and initiated escape plan. Syrian agents, operating under cover of the Syrian trade mission in Kassel, provided her with a forged Turkish passport (nfi). This information is believed to be reliable and is classified R-1.

TOP SECRET
END OF MESSAGE

Powers felt nauseated: nauseated, chastened, and helpless.

"I guess that answers the question whether Marilyn Kasindorf was a spy," Sullivan said.

"Are you going to tell the President?"

"I'm afraid so," Sullivan said apologetically.

"Will you have to tell him everything . . . ? I mean, about her and me?"

"I'm not going to volunteer anything. But if he asks, I'm not going to lie."

"I understand. I'd do the same thing."

Sullivan rubbed his hands together. "Patterson made an issue about following her without telling him. I covered it by saying the President told me to handle it, and he backed off. But he knows something's up. He'll be putting feelers out at the White House to find out what the hell is going on. The problem is he knows what the President thinks of him, and how he's out of a job after the election. I'm afraid if he finds out about Marilyn and the President . . ."

"He'll leak," Powers said, thinking out loud.

"Good chance. Leak to cut some kind of deal with the other campaign, allowing him to stay at CIA during the next administration. But it's a big step for him to make. He's probably the only guy in this town with more political enemies than the President."

Powers shook his head for a moment.

"Jack, I know the train seems out of control for the moment, but we just have to take it one step at a time."

"What happens now?"

"The Senate Intelligence Oversight Committee is always briefed on American defectors within forty-eight hours. You'll be the main witness."

"How do I . . . ?"

"Jack," Sullivan interrupted, "this was a White House security problem, and I enlisted your help in handling it. I'll have plenty of plausible reasons for why I chose to handle it this way. And Jack Powers, as far as I'm concerned, acted properly, professionally."

"If Patterson finds out about Marilyn and the President, and wants to make his play, the perfect scenario would be to leak to a member of the Oversight Committee. They'd ask me the question under oath—make me the fall guy."

"I'm not trying to minimize, but we have a lot going for us. The President has friends on the committee. If they are properly primed and if Patterson doesn't throw his spear, you should be able to slide through without a lot of hostile questions."

"One of them could drop the zinger, ask me point-blank about the President and Marilyn."

"The way you answer could change the course of American history," Sullivan said hoarsely. He coughed. "The Chairman is Senator Eastland. He and the President were roommates at Yale. If Eastland can be convinced to limit the questioning, we're home-free."

"And if he doesn't, or if Patterson starts pulling strings, the President gets impeached." Powers put his head in his hands. "She knew she couldn't get out of the hotel without me seeing her, so she conned me—reeled me in like a fish!" he cried.

"It's not going to be easy to get out of this mess," Sullivan said. "It may call for some sacrifices."

Powers sat up. "I'm a Secret Service agent, and I'll do what needs to be done," he said, feeling as embarrassed as he ever had in his life.

Sullivan walked to the safe and replaced the folder. He shoved the heavy drawer closed and spun the combination dial. "Unfortunately, the hardest part is yet to come," he said somberly.

"The President."

"That's right, Jack. He has questions."

"Does he suspect something?"

"When I briefed him and Morgan on the defection, he kept asking for specifics: how she got away from the hotel without you seeing her. I went through a song-and-dance about how difficult it was for you—following her alone and all—but he wasn't satisfied."

"You mean I have to brief him in person?"

Sullivan nodded.

"Can't you answer his questions for me?" Powers pleaded.

"The President is a former prosecutor. He likes to hear things from the horse's mouth," Sullivan said.

"What if he gets specific?"

"Then you'll have to . . . handle it."

"I mean what if he gets *specific*?"

"You'll have to do what you have to do, Jack."

"I can't lie to the President. Jesus H. Christ."

"Then tell him the truth."

"If I tell him the truth about Marilyn, my career is ended." Frustrated, Powers let out his breath. "Shit!" he said angrily. "Shit."

"Or I could tell him for you. It would be easier if it comes from me."

"Either way, I get fired."

"Don't forget: The President is twisting in the wind *with* you. She was *his* girlfriend. I'm going to do everything in my power to sweep this thing under the rug and keep you from getting hurt. You just have to trust me until we see which way the wind is blowing."

Powers felt reassured. Sullivan was a master at power games, a politician in his own right. He would take his advice.

"I'll phone you after I talk with the man. In the meantime, don't report back for duty. If anyone asks, you're extending your vacation to take care of some personal errands."

15

Outside Secret Service headquarters, Sullivan offered Powers a ride. Powers declined, preferring to walk and give himself time to get his thoughts together.

Sullivan climbed in his car, started the engine, and pulled away from the curb.

Standing there with a warm, humid breeze at his back, Powers suddenly felt as alone as he ever had in his entire life: alone and burdened with a sense of guilt and foreboding. Absorbed in this state of depression, he began walking slowly, aimlessly, in the general direction of the White House. Though fretting over his personal situation, he found himself thinking about Marilyn—and, again and again, reliving the time he'd spent with her.

In Lafayette Park, a diminutive patch of lawn and trees across Pennsylvania Avenue from the White House, he sat down on a bench and stared blankly at the tourists as they moved along the sidewalk and through the park. Though he wasn't counting, he spotted three women during the next hour or so who he thought looked like Marilyn.

Finally, Powers stood up from the bench and headed down Pennsylvania Avenue. At the Georgetown Arms Apartments, he knocked on the manager's door. From inside came the sound of a TV commercial jingle. Mrs. Hammerstrom let him in. Her hair was wrapped in a dye-spotted towel. She was barefoot and wearing a tattered pink housecoat. He greeted her and asked for his mail and the key to a vacant apartment.

Without saying anything, she plodded to a Formica-topped dinette table in the middle of her living room. Keeping her eyes on the television so she wouldn't miss any of the show, she dug into a cardboard box and took out a four-inch stack of letters fastened with a rubber band. Then, from a small board on top of the television, she lifted a set of keys. She handed the items to Powers, and he thanked her.

"I still have your application and your deposit from the last time," she said, hypnotized by a couple kissing on the television screen. "You're in 412. It's the only vacancy."

He took the elevator to the cluttered basement. He found a Safeway grocery cart in the corner near the furnace and loaded his footlockers in it. And figuring the apartment would need cleaning, like the others he'd rented at the Georgetown Arms over the years, he set the apartment house's upright vacuum on the bottom rack of the cart. Then he rolled the cart to apartment 412.

Unlike the other apartments he'd had, which had a view of the street, all that could be seen from the window of 412 was the pigeon-stained roof of the three-story apartment house next door. And the place was filthy: the brown wall-to-wall carpet was dotted with dustballs, which for some reason had been missed by the apartment-cleaning crew Mrs. Hammerstrom hired to clean vacant apartments. On the other hand, he was pleased the walls and the bathroom and kitchen sinks had been washed down adequately.

Having carefully vacuumed the entire apartment, Powers arranged his toilet articles on the edge of the bathroom sink and unpacked his belongings. By 5 P.M., he'd returned the shopping cart and vacuum to the basement and was fully moved in.

He dug a bottle of Chivas Regal Scotch whisky from a footlocker. The bottle had been a gift to each member of the Secret Service protective detail from the Prime Minister of Canada after a three-day D.C. stay. At the kitchen sink, he rinsed out one of the six glasses he owned and poured himself a stiff drink. Then he walked to the window and stood there for a long time, sipping Scotch and opening his mail—all advertisements—and stared anxiously at the roof next door.

He couldn't get Marilyn out of his mind.

Leaving the apartment an hour or so later, he headed for Blackie's.

There, Powers moved through the restaurant portion of the establishment, a few cramped booths with red checkered tablecloths, to the entrance of a dimly lit, red leather-upholstered barroom indistinguishable from a million other bars in D.C. If the lights were ever to be turned on so that one could inspect them, Powers imagined that the furniture and carpeting in both the restaurant and the bar would be filthy.

At the end of the bar, Capizzi was leaning across the bar kissing Tiffany Kilgore, a peroxide-blond bartender known to be Blackie Horowitz's private stock.

Powers turned to leave, but he was too late. Capizzi had already seen him.

"Hey, Jackie boy!" Capizzi called out. "I thought you were on vacation."

"Just got back."

"Where were you, Bangladesh?" he said, winking at Tiffany.

"What's that supposed to mean?"

"You look like shit."

"Thanks."

Rather than giving Capizzi the satisfaction of running him off, Powers climbed onto a bar stool. He would have one drink and leave.

Tiffany slid a cocktail napkin in front of him. He ordered a drink and she mixed his usual: Scotch on the rocks, which, because Tiffany was making it, was mostly rocks. Though Tiffany was unable to make a decent drink for the life of her, her oversized breasts and outgoing personality kept agents—and the few neighborhood customers whose business supported the place when the detail was traveling with the President—from complaining.

Predictably, Capizzi left his stool and seated himself on another next to Powers.

Tiffany moved farther down the bar to wash dishes.

Powers sipped his drink.

"Santa Monica was great," Capizzi said. "You missed a good trip."

Powers nodded. He would finish his drink quickly and leave.

"A Santa Monica police officer was waiting in the command post when we arrived. Louise Fisher, I think her name was. She asked about you."

"Is that right."

"She looked disappointed when I told her you were on vacation."

"Nice person, Louise."

"Heard the rumor?" Capizzi said, changing the subject.

Powers shook his head.

"The man is gonna bounce Fogarty and move Sullivan in as Director. That means promotions right up the chain."

"Don't you ever get tired of trying to figure out who's gonna get promoted?" Powers said.

"If Landry gets bumped up to Assistant Director, I see you as the logical one to take his place."

"That's because Lenore Shoequist told you she saw me in Sullivan's office the day before I went on vacation."

"Did he offer you a promotion?" Capizzi said hungrily. "You can tell me. I swear I'll never tell anyone."

Powers looked Capizzi in the eye. "No," he said coldly.

Capizzi smiled. "Then why'd he call you in?"

"Just some campaign paperwork."

Seeing he wasn't getting anywhere, Capizzi slid off his stool. "The beach was great," he said, moving down the bar to Tiffany. "I got in a lot of exercise."

Landry came in a few minutes after 4 P.M., the end of the day shift. Ignoring Capizzi, he joined Powers.

"Sullivan told me about what happened. It's not your fault," he said, keeping his voice down.

"Yes it is," Powers said gloomily.

"On a surveillance, there's only so much a man can do working alone. You shouldn't blame yourself."

"Is the lid still on everything?" Powers said, being careful to lower his voice so Capizzi couldn't overhear.

"As far as I know. But I don't know what to make of Miller getting killed."

"He could have surprised a burglar, but what the hell was he doing at the Breakwater in the first place?"

"Nosing around."

"We'll never know now, that's for sure."

"The man has been having some late-night meetings in the Oval Office."

"With who?"

"Morgan. And when we were on the West Coast, he had dinner with The Three Musketeers—a long session."

"Maybe he's talking to them about . . . this mess."

Landry finished his drink. "He doesn't trust anybody enough to tell 'em that."

Powers rubbed his eyes. He was tired.

Landry waved at Tiffany.

"What are you drinking?"

For the thousandth time, Landry told Tiffany he drank rum and Coke and Powers told her he drank Scotch on the rocks. Tiffany scooped ice into glasses.

"By the way, when we were in Santa Monica, Capizzi hit on your girlfriend, Louise Fisher," Landry said. "He invited her to go jogging and ended up fucking her on the beach . . . or at least that's what he told everyone who'd listen to him."

"Figures."

Landry laughed. "The man threw you a cockblock."

Powers shrugged.

Tiffany served their drinks. Landry sipped, then held up his glass. "I said rum, not bourbon, Tiff."

Tiffany took the glass. "Picky picky picky," she said, moving to the other end of the bar.

Powers arrived at his apartment shortly after midnight. Though he hadn't eaten all day, and had consumed probably eight or nine Scotches at Blackie's over the course of the late afternoon and evening, he felt simply depressed rather than drunk.

The telephone rang.

He picked up the receiver. It was Sullivan.

"I've been trying to call you all evening," Sullivan said balefully.

"I was at Blackie's."

"Meet me at Twelfth and Constitution in fifteen minutes."

"I'll be there."

*   *   *

As Powers's taxi pulled up at Twelfth and Constitution Avenue, Sullivan was standing on the corner. The humidity was oppressive, and the air was rich with the smell of new-mown grass. Because of the hour, the wide sidewalks lining Constitution were deserted and eerie.

Sullivan, looking ill at ease even from a distance, was wearing a wrinkled suit jacket and a dress shirt open at the collar. In his right hand he was holding a thin black attaché case.

It was the first time in years Powers had seen him without a necktie.

Powers paid the taxi driver, a black man with dreadlocks, and climbed out of the taxi. Without saying anything, Sullivan began walking. Powers fell into step next to him. To the right, the Museum of Natural History, an urban mountain, loomed darkly. The building's well-lit glass-front entrance framed, almost like one of the modern paintings Powers had seen at the art show in Kassel, an unmoving black uniformed guard sitting behind a small desk.

"I ran into Capizzi tonight. He knew about my visit to your office already," Powers said.

"Lenore Shoequist, shooting off her mouth as usual," Sullivan said.

They continued to walk. Other than intermittent traffic noise, there was only the sound of their footsteps. Powers could tell Sullivan had something important to tell him.

"Back when you and I were in Secret Service School," Sullivan said, "there were no two young men more idealistic. Not naïve by any means—we could see through the smoke and mirrors—but we really believed in what we were doing: protecting the life of the President of the United States. Uncle Sam was lucky to have people like us. I really believe that."

Powers suddenly had a sinking feeling. It wasn't so

much what Sullivan was saying as the tone of finality in his voice.

"Through the years you and I have watched the politicians come and go," Sullivan continued. "The staff men, the sharpies, the bag men, the political pimps. We outlast them because we're better than them, Jack. We didn't come to this town for the power. And we've never been government leeches like Senator Eastland—or Capizzi, for that matter. We came here as true believers." His voice cracked. "I'd tell anyone that." He stopped walking.

"You talked to the President."

Sullivan stared at the sidewalk. "Yes."

"What did he say?"

Sullivan continued to stare. "He was interested in the details of your surveillance in Germany. I gave them to him . . . being evasive about the last day, of course."

"Did you—"

"The President isn't a dumb man, Jack. It became obvious to me that he smelled a rat. Finally, he looked me in the eye and asked the direct question."

"About Marilyn and me?"

Sullivan nodded.

"Shit."

"You said you couldn't lie to the man. Well, when it came right down to it, neither could I. Funny, isn't it? Every politician, every power-broker, every fucking lobbyist and lawyer and straphanger in this town cultivates the art of lying, and you and I bite our tongues even when it comes to . . . survival." He looked up.

"What did he . . . ?" Powers said.

"He didn't take it well, Jack."

Powers felt perspiration at his temples and under his arms. He wished there were a bench nearby so he could sit down. But there wasn't. "Go ahead, say it."

"The President doesn't want you in the White House ever again."

Powers suddenly felt light-headed.

"I explained to him that you were second in seniority on the detail, and it would cause disruption to transfer you," Sullivan said flatly. "But he said if I didn't remove you he'd go straight to Director Fogarty. You and I both know what would happen when Fogarty got a request from the President for an agent to be removed from the White House Detail. He'd be doing somersaults to please him."

"I don't want a transfer," Powers said.

"Even if you were willing to take a transfer from the White House Detail, it wouldn't end there. Fogarty would put you on the wheel: Fresno today, Detroit tomorrow, Newark next week. He's done this to every agent who leaves under a cloud. He'd hammer you within civil service guidelines."

"I don't understand."

"The President is well aware of how Fogarty overdoes things. He told me he didn't want to see this happen."

"You're telling me I'm . . . ?" Powers said.

Sullivan cleared his throat sharply. "The President asked about your eligibility for retirement."

Powers felt a lump in his throat. He swallowed. "When it came right down to the wire you bailed out on me, Pete. You hung me out to dry."

"If you were to request retirement, it's within my purview to approve—"

"No."

"Let me finish, Jack. Please. I can get David Crumpmaster or one of the President's other big-money supporters to give you a good job in private industry, paying more than your government salary. Taking a higher-paying job would stop speculation about why you left."

Powers felt weak in the knees.

"Hell, in the long run you'd be better off," Sullivan said. "You could buy a condo. I'm sorry. Goddamn, I'm sorry. . . ." Sullivan's voice trailed off.

A taxi, grinding its gears, sped past. Powers followed it with his eyes as it hurtled down Constitution Avenue. "Would it do any good now if I talked with the President?" he said.

"You know how the man is once he's made a decision," Sullivan said. "This whole thing is all my fault. I got you in, and now I can't get you out."

Powers's career was ended. He'd seen it happen before: agents who'd been injured on-duty and were no longer able to meet the stringent physical requirements of the Secret Service, or who'd been involved in scandal of one kind or another or had displeased some member of the White House staff or the First Family; the few alcoholics, the two agents who got into a fistfight in the Lincoln Room over a bet on a Redskins game, the agent who came to believe his wristwatch was ordering him to do strange things and was committed to St. Elizabeth's in a straitjacket. Now it was his turn.

"I have no one to blame but myself," Powers said under his breath.

Sullivan unzipped the attaché case and took out a piece of paper. He set it on the flat side of the case and handed it to Powers. "This is a Form 1094 retirement request. I'll let it be known this was the reason you came to my office before you took the vacation days—you'd had a big offer from a private firm and wanted to keep it quiet." He was avoiding eye contact. "You'll be on salary for the next three months until your annual leave time is used up."

From his shirt pocket, he took out a pen and offered it to Powers.

Powers stood there, feeling slightly nauseated. "She just didn't seem like a spy," he said.

"I understand, Jack."

Powers accepted the pen. Using the attaché case to support the printed form, he signed his name.

"You know I'd give anything to be able to change this," Sullivan said, shoving the document back into the attaché case.

"I don't want to go to the House and lie to everyone about why I'm leaving."

"No need. I'll tell Landry. Just send him a note that you wanted to double your salary, and had to take the position when it was offered. No one will question it."

Powers nodded.

They stood there for a moment in uncomfortable silence.

"Do you . . . uh . . . want to go have a drink?" Sullivan said weakly.

Powers shook his head. "No, thanks."

"I'll let you know tomorrow about the new job."

Powers nodded.

Sullivan suddenly reached out and gave Powers an *abrazo*. "I'm sorry, Jack. Sorry about everything." He picked up the case and walked across the street to his car.

Powers, overwhelmed by a feeling of profound guilt and loss, walked aimlessly for what must have been an hour or more. He'd often wondered about how the others who'd been forced to leave the spotlight of the White House had felt, and now he knew. The loss was personal: the death of self-image. *Humiliation* was the word—and a sense of twisted awe, perhaps, that all the years of long hours, of missing meals and standing post in the rain and snow and waiting in the follow-up car and changing shifts at midnight and working sick and dragging his suitcase all over the world to be

somewhere on time . . . of standing for long periods
in backyards and front yards and service entrances and
alleys and outside ten thousand doors in ten thousand
hotel hallways throughout the world, had been for
nothing. No longer, working as a team with the other
members of the shift, would he lead the President
through a thousand crowds made up of a million faces,
hoping to live if he had to take a bullet for the man.
At the next inauguration a President would be in the
presidential limousine, and the President's follow-up
car would be manned in the running-board position,
with his pals alert and ready to leap into danger, to
fire accurately to save the President.

But he wouldn't be there.

His years of slogging up and down the stairs in the
White House had been ended forever by one mistake.
The invisible Secret Service wash line had been
stretched tight, and it was Jack Powers's turn to dan-
gle in the wind.

16

★★★★★★★★★★
★★★★★★★★★★

At his apartment, Powers went to the closet and took out an empty shoe box. He placed his Secret Service badge and credential, his holstered revolver and handcuffs, and his secret identification pins into it.

At the kitchen table, he wrote the following letter on government stationery:

Special-Agent-in-Charge Kenneth Landry
White House Detail, USSS
The White House

Dear Ken:
I'm sorry I didn't have time to stop by the House before I left, but by now I'm sure Sullivan has told you about the job offer I accepted. Forgive the abrupt departure, but I have a lot of things to take care of before I assume the new position and I really don't feel like going through either a retirement party or an endless round of goodbyes. You know how it is. Nevertheless, please give my best to everyone on the detail—except Capizzi, of course.
I'll drop you a line soon and fill you in on the details of my new job.

All the best,
Jack

Powers dropped the letter into the shoe box and closed it. Using tape and string, he wrapped the box securely; then, numb from the events of the evening, he sat on the sofa and, without changing channels, stared at television until about 4 A.M.

Finally, he staggered in to bed and dropped into fitful sleep.

He awoke at 6 A.M., thinking about Marilyn. Having showered and shaved, he left the apartment carrying the shoe box and took the Metro to Secret Service headquarters. In the mail room, he used a magic marker to label the shoe box with Landry's name. Then he shoved it into a canvas classified message bin marked IMMEDIATE DELIVERY and hurried out of the building to avoid contact with anyone.

On the way back to his apartment, he stopped at Long's Cafeteria and ordered bacon and eggs. He ate a few bites of the meal, realized he wasn't hungry, and left.

He spent the rest of the day lounging about the apartment, just worrying about what it was going to be like to start a new career.

Sullivan phoned him that evening and gave him instructions: a job had been arranged by David Crumpmaster, president of Highland Oil and Gas of Arlington, Virginia. Crumpmaster, the President's former law partner, was the chief political fixer and point man for the administration and, for all intents and purposes, wielded more actual power than any officer of the government. In every administration, there was always at least one Crumpmaster. During presidential campaigns, Secret Service agents, like political reporters, made a game of figuring out who would fill this secret position.

The next day Jack Powers reported to work at the security department of Highland Oil and Gas. The building was located in the heart of the Arlington business area, in a modern four-story pillar of tinted glass.

He was shown into the office of the Highland vice-president in charge of security, Casimir Novatny. Novatny was in his fifties, overweight, and wore a dark, linty blue suit and an ill-fitting hairpiece.

Powers remembered him from the last presidential campaign. Novatny had been a political advance man for the President, organizing rallies in the Midwest, mostly Chicago. Though he always introduced himself as a former FBI agent, his FBI experience had come more than twenty years ago and he'd been an agent for less than a year, which Powers knew meant he'd been terminated even before achieving probationary status. Powers disliked him immediately.

"You'll be making a salary almost twice what you were making as a Secret Service agent," Novatny said in a heavy New York accent. "That includes a company car and an expense account. How's that sound?"

"Great," Powers said, forcing a smile.

"Occasionally you'll be a troubleshooter," Novatny said. "If one of our employees steps on his dick, then we conduct an investigation. You report to me, and I decide what to do with the information. You don't do anything on your own. You understand that?"

Powers nodded, realizing the source of the faint clacking sound as Novatny spoke. He had false teeth.

"And with your Secret Service experience, I plan on using you for executive protection. Now and then Mr. Crumpmaster and the Board of Directors like to have someone around when golfing or taking vacations, and you'll be in charge of seeing to it that the alarm systems on their homes are in working order." He pronounced order as *awdah*.

Novatny left his chair and closed the door. "It's not so much actual security work; having bodyguards makes them look important to their customers and social contacts," he said, returning to his seat. "That means if you're on the golf course with one of the members of the Board and he asks you to carry golf clubs, you carry the golf clubs. But this sort of work will be only a small part of your duties. Okay so far?"

Powers nodded.

"Let's take a look at your office," Novatny said, coming to his feet.

Powers followed him down a hallway to another office. Novatny allowed him to enter first. As in Novatny's office, the facing wall was of tinted glass and provided a view of a similar office building across the street. The only furnishings in the room were a blue synthetic-fabric chair and a medium-sized veneer desk. There was nothing on the desk but plastic trays labeled IN and OUT. In the IN tray was a stack of printed health insurance forms.

Novatny picked up the printed forms and clacked some instructions about filling them out. Powers only half listened.

"All set to this point?" Novatny said.

"Yes, I think so."

"How do you like your office?"

"Fine."

Novatny sat down on a chair in front of the desk. He pointed to the framed emblem on the wall, an alert American eagle superimposed on an oil derrick. "N.H.A.H.," he said. "This is what will take up most of your time here at Highland."

"Pardon?"

"The Never High at Highland program. This is the company's drug-resistance effort. It's the man's pet project." Novatny leaned back in his chair, his wig lifting slightly from his forehead. "The man—that's Mr. Crumpmaster. Those of us in Security call him the man."

"What kind of drug program is it?"

Novatny opened a file cabinet desk drawer and removed a thick binder titled "Highland Oil and Gas Security Manual." He slid it across the desk. "Your duties are all explained in here. Mr. Crumpmaster is determined to have a drug-free environment at Highland."

"What exactly do I have to do?"

"Your actual title will be Compliance Officer. You have the full responsibility, and no one will get in your way as long as the compliance requirements are met."

Powers had a sinking feeling. "Compliance? Are we talking drug-testing?"

"Yes, regular supervised testing of all employees is part and parcel of the program. I take it you do agree with the concept of a drug-free workplace?"

"Of course," Powers said after a moment.

"All the equipment you need is in this file cabinet . . . including the master schedule of when employees are due."

"Due?"

"Due to give you a urine sample."

"I'm in charge of seeing to it that people piss?"

"That's one way to put it," Novatny said warily. "Any other questions?"

Powers shook his head.

Novatny winked at him insincerely and left the room.

Powers sat down at the desk. Telling himself that, as in the Secret Service, new employees were always given the most disagreeable tasks, and that in time he'd be promoted to a better position in the company, Powers opened the security manual and spent the next couple of hours thumbing pages. But his mind was on Marilyn, and for the life of him he couldn't concentrate. Over and over, he remembered waking in the hotel room in Kassel to find her gone. Somehow, sitting in the sterile office, he had the feeling that nothing had changed, and he was only on another Secret Service temporary assignment: that any minute he would be headed to Andrews Air Force Base to board Air Force One. . . .

Later in the day Novatny led Powers around the office, introducing him ("This is our new Compliance Officer, Jack Powers") to the other members of the security staff, most of whom were ex-policemen or federal agents. Though mortified because he figured they knew he was the new piss monitor, Powers smiled and shook hands with everyone. Back in his office, Powers realized that out of all the people he'd met he couldn't recall a single name.

After work, Powers purchased a quart of Chivas Regal at a liquor store.

At his apartment the red light on his answering machine was blinking. He pressed REWIND, then the PLAY button. The messages were as follows:

1. Landry telling him he'd received his letter and asking him to call.

2. Louise Fisher asking him not to believe the things Capizzi was saying about her.

3. Mrs. Hammerstrom informing him that he wouldn't be able to leave his footlockers in the storeroom during future trips because she was going to rent the storeroom itself to the Georgetown Arms cleanup crew, who were all Colombians and needed a place to stay.

4. Sharon Fantozzi, an aggressive telephone company security agent whom he dated occasionally, telling him she was horny and asking him to call.

Powers pressed the ERASE button.

As with all Secret Service agents, his career, though unique and challenging in its own way, had not prepared him for any other occupation. Unlike others in law-enforcement work who easily fit into the corporate-security field upon retirement, leaving the White

House was, by any and all standards, an unequivocal step down. At forty-four years old he was now a has-been working for a never-been, Casimir Novatny—a President's man ending up as a piss monitor at an oil company.

In bed, he told himself he would just have to accept it. But he couldn't sleep.

The next morning, Powers showed up a few minutes late for the Highland Oil and Gas security department daily staff meeting, and listened as Casimir Novatny read a security bulletin concerning the theft of six hundred and fourteen dollars in company imprest funds. Then he gave a short lecture on how to examine employee expense vouchers in order to detect cheating. When the meeting was over Powers returned to his desk, to avoid chatting with the other members of the security staff.

At about 10 A.M., a paunchy, middle-aged man in horn-rimmed eyeglasses with thick lenses came into Powers's office. He was wearing slacks and a short-sleeved white shirt, with a pocket sagging with pens and mechanical pencils.

"Roy Hawkins, from the engineering department," he said gruffly. "I'm here for my yearly test."

"I see," Powers said. He stood up and introduced himself. Hawkins accepted his handshake reticently. Recalling the procedure as outlined in the security manual, Powers opened the file drawer and took out a small glass specimen bottle. Avoiding eye contact, he handed the bottle to Hawkins.

"How about a paper cup."

"Excuse me?"

"The last guy that had your job gave out a Dixie cup with the jar," Hawkins said. "In the bathroom, it's easier to piss into the cup, then pour the piss into the glass bottle. Otherwise you have to aim."

"I'm sorry. I don't have any cups."

Hawkins shrugged. He moved to the door and stopped, as if waiting for Powers to follow. "Well, aren't you coming?"

"Coming where?"

"Coming in the bathroom to watch me piss. That's what the other guy always did. He said the security manual said he had to watch, so if a person had been using narcotics they couldn't substitute another person's piss and beat the test."

"That's okay. I trust you," Powers said.

Hawkins gave him a puzzled expression and left the room. There was the sound of his footsteps in the hall and the door of the men's rest room opening and shutting.

Powers moved to the window. In the distance was the Washington monument and, just beyond it, the White House.

He felt like punching his fist through the glass.

Hawkins returned a few minutes later and set his urine-filled bottle on the desk. It was wet, and moisture dampened the ink blotter.

"There she be," Hawkins said, wiping his hands on his trousers. He left the room.

Powers was still standing at the window a few minutes later when Novatny came in the room.

"I just spoke with Roy Hawkins from engineering," Novatny said, ignoring the urine sample on the desk. "He mentioned that you didn't monitor the taking of the sample."

"That's right," Powers said without turning around.

"The security manual calls for monitoring. You have to stand right there when the sample is given. This is to ensure that—"

"How long has Hawkins worked here?" Powers broke in.

"Over twenty years."

"Do you suspect him of using narcotics?"

Novatny crossed his arms across his chest and smiled sardonically. "Of course not. But that doesn't change the fact that people have to obey rules."

Powers just shook his head.

"Does this mean you are refusing an order?" Novatny said.

Powers walked past Novatny and out the door.

"Where are you going?"

Powers headed down the hallway and descended the stairs. Novatny was behind him.

Powers reached the ground floor lobby and headed toward the front door.

"You're fired!" Novatny shouted after him.

17

Landry leaned back in his chair and stretched. It had been a busy day at the White House—and any day when the President did something other than remain inside the Oval Office was a good day. Landry preferred activity, any activity, over sitting at the radio console monitoring radio transmissions as agents moved from post to post in the White House rotation. *Post thirteen requesting a push. . . . Post nine has a visitor who's lost his pass. . . .* He heard the damn radio in his sleep.

At 8 A.M., Landry had led the President from the Oval Office to the White House briefing room for a press conference: thirty-six minutes of the man evading questions about the U.S. loss of influence in the Middle East.

Later, Landry had accompanied the President to the D.C. Marriott Hotel, where the President was scheduled to give a speech to the Veterans of Foreign Wars convention. Riding in the right front passenger seat of the presidential limousine, Landry bore overall Secret Service responsibility for the trip. But as Agent-in-Charge, his only required duty per the Secret Service *Manual of Protective Operations* was to stay within arm's reach of the President at all times and ceremoni-

196

ously open the limo door for him upon arrival and
departure. Of course, in the event of an assassination
attempt, Landry knew he would be required to shield
the President with his own body—to "draw fire" and
probably get killed.

The speech went well, Landry recognizing it as the
same one the President always gave to veterans
groups. The working phrase was "I stand with you; I
salute you," repeated for emotional effect. The President was a relatively dull speaker but, since he'd
served in the Marine Corps like Landry, Landry considered his remarks unfeigned and heartfelt—in con-
trast to the patriotic speeches of former Secretary of
Defense Richard Cheney and former Vice-President
Dan Quayle, who were Vietnam-era draft dodgers.

After the speech, as the President was walking in a
hallway from the convention meeting room toward the
exit, Capizzi roughly frisked a hotel bellman who he
said had a bulge under his coat. This caused a stir
among the White House press pool reporters tagging
along: Problem of the Day.

Returning to W-16, Landry was besieged by reporters wanting to know more about the incident. He told
them Capizzi's action had been justified, in that he'd
seen what he believed might have been a weapon,
although actually Landry suspected Capizzi was only
showing off for Chief of Staff David Morgan and a
couple of other high-ranking White House staffers
who were standing nearby. Capizzi was frequently
good for *causing* the Problem of the Day.

But Landry chose to complain neither to Sullivan
nor to the Director about Capizzi, realizing that if he
did Capizzi would probably file a complaint with the
Secret Service Inspection Division. This would result
in an investigation directed by Chief Inspector Elmer
Cogswell, an Alabama hillbilly. Cogswell, who secretly hated blacks, had been passed over for promo-

tion many times, and was desperate to move up a rung in the Secret Service pecking order. Using his team of hand-picked incompetents, he would conduct endless interviews and reinterviews and then finally sign off on a lengthy, overwrought inspection report, finding fault not only with Capizzi but with Landry himself and everyone else assigned to the White House Detail—thus hoping to force Landry's removal as Agent-in-Charge and thus put Cogswell in line for the job.

Therefore, thought Landry, it's better to tolerate Capizzi's showboating.

Landry picked up the receiver and dialed Powers's number. Busy again. He'd been trying to reach Powers for days and had left numerous messages since Powers had resigned, but he'd received no answer. It was totally out of character for Powers not to return his calls.

Leaving the White House that evening on his way home, Landry stopped by the dry cleaners on G Street and picked up some white shirts. On the way out the door he almost bumped into Ed Sneed, a tall army major in uniform—one tailored to fit his V-shaped weightlifter's physique.

"Say, Ken, where've you been hiding?"

"On the day shift, my man."

"I'm still working nights. Been doing it for so many years I'm used to it. By the way, I just heard about Powers quitting. I don't believe that crap about finding a better job at Highland. There has to have been something else."

Landry shrugged. "Who knows?"

"At first I thought it had something to do with Operation Fencing Master."

Landry nodded and smiled wryly. The first thing he'd learned in the Secret Service was never to let on when you didn't know what someone was talking about. "Hard to say."

"After all that went down, I thought somebody was going to be rolled up for sure."

"You off-duty?" Landry said.

Sneed nodded. "Till tomorrow at sixteen hundred hours."

"Feel like a drink?"

"You talked me into it."

At Blackie's, Landry phoned Doris and told her he wouldn't be home for dinner. He spent the rest of the evening in conversation with Sneed. Sneed was drinking bourbon on the rocks, and as the evening wore on he became less and less inhibited.

As they talked and drank, Landry would leave his glass half-full as it was replaced by Tiffany the bartender, to avoid becoming inebriated. Conversely, Sneed would jiggle ice and down what was left in his glass whenever Tiffany got around to refilling drinks. By 11 P.M. Sneed was drunk, and complaining bitterly about how he hadn't been promoted to lieutenant colonel—while of course not mentioning that he'd passed up more than one opportunity at a regular field command leading to promotion in order to stay in his comfortable White House job.

At midnight Sneed checked his watch, the first time he'd done so all evening.

Fearing that Sneed would leave and he'd have wasted the entire evening, Landry decided to wait no longer. "Operation Fencing Master," Landry said. "How did you know about it?"

"Shit fire. There ain't no secrets in this man's army," Sneed said, lifting his glass.

Landry considered a follow-up question, but held back. If he said the wrong thing, Sneed would realize he was probing for information.

Sneed finished his drink and set the glass down. "I knew it was something big. They don't roll out every examiner at Fort McClellan and send them to D.C. just for the fuck of it."

"They sure as hell don't," Landry said. *Examiners?*

"One of the examiners they sent up here is an old friend from the five-eleventh. He said they did everyone simultaneously on a Sunday—at their homes."

"Lucky the word never got out," Landry said. *What the hell is he talking about?*

Sneed chuckled. "Hell, the *Washington Post* would have had a damn field day. Headline: 'Cabinet and highest White House staff made to sit down on lie box.' "

"You can say that again," Landry said. *Lie detector tests!*

"Did you get tested?"

"Me? No. No one in Secret Service was tested, as far as I know," Landry said.

"As I understand it, they only asked one question: 'Are you now working, or have you ever worked, for a hostile intelligence agency?' Is it true Morgan told everyone if they refused the test, it would be considered a resignation?"

"I heard a rumor to that effect," Landry said, feeling he had to answer.

Sneed looked him in the eye. "You sure you knew about this in the first place? I don't want to be talking out of turn."

Landry sipped his drink. "Nothing happens at the House without the Secret Service knowing about it."

Sneed slapped Landry on the shoulder and checked his watch again. "I'd better be going," he said, climbing off his bar stool. He headed for the door.

Landry remained at the bar after Sneed had left, his mind swirling with what he'd learned. *The entire cabinet forced to take lie detector tests? Ray Stryker killing himself? A CIA agent getting killed during a presidential visit? Powers quitting his job suddenly?*

Coming to a decision, he left the bar and returned to the White House.

At the East Gate, Landry stopped at the guard booth. Howard Singer, the uniformed officer on-duty, came to his feet.

"How you doin', my man?"

"Fine, Mr. Landry. Working late tonight?"

"I just thought I'd stop by to see how things are going on the night shift. Any suggestions on how we can increase security—make things better?"

"No, sir. Things seem fine to me."

"That's good, Howard," Landry said. He turned and entered the White House itself. Once inside, he stepped into the logistics office. From the window, he had a view of the guard booth. Singer was on the phone, making one quick call after another, informing all guard posts that Landry was present conducting an unannounced inspection—exactly what Landry wanted him to do. Inspecting posts was a legitimate reason for the Agent-in-Charge of the presidential detail to be in the White House after midnight.

At the upstairs elevator bank, Landry stopped and made small talk with Agent Jim Anderson, the only other black on the White House Secret Service Detail. Anderson told him that Singer had, as Landry had suspected, notified everyone that the Agent-in-Charge was in the White House.

Landry continued down the hall to Morgan's office. Using the White House master key he kept on his key chain, he opened the door and entered, closing the door behind him.

Recalling the safe diagrams kept on file in W-16, he surmised that Morgan kept his private papers in the Diebold safe against the facing wall. The number 8336 was stenciled on the top of the safe. Memorizing the number, he left the office and continued down the hallway. At the end of the hall, he took the stairs down to W-16. Agent Harrington, the acting shift leader, had his suit coat on and his tie straightened. Landry told him he'd forgotten a phone number, then opened the file cabinet next to the radio console. He thumbed through files until Harrington was busy answering a radio call, then reached to the back of the drawer for the safe combination file. Quickly, he found the combination for number 8336, repeated it three times to himself, then shoved the file back into its place.

"Can I help you find anything?" Harrington said.

"I was just looking for my shift report. I had some more calls from the press about Capizzi and his little act today."

"Capizzi is a deluxe, grade-A, tournament-class pain in the ass. An asshole's asshole."

"He is that," Landry said. "But look at it this way: He probably can't help the way he is. His mom and dad may have been assholes."

"You have a point," Harrington said, as Landry left the room.

"I'm going to make one more run through the House before I go," Landry said, because he knew Harrington would follow him on the closed-circuit camera. "Have a good night."

"You too, Ken."

Landry checked the outside posts, chatting amiably with each of the agents on-duty, then made his way back into the House through the bowling alley. He returned upstairs to Morgan's office. Thankful there was no closed-circuit camera on this floor, again he used the key to enter Morgan's office. Inside, he closed the door gently and ran to the safe. He dialed the combination as fast as he could, yanked open the top drawer, and quickly checked file tabs. While in the second drawer, flipping through tabs, he became concerned that Harrington, wondering what he was doing upstairs for so long, might investigate. He could hear himself breathing.

He found the file. The tab was marked FENCING MASTER. He opened it. There were only two pages. He ran to the copying machine on the other side of the room. Thankfully someone had left it on, so he didn't have to wait for it to warm up. He copied the two memos, shoved the copies in his jacket pocket, and rushed back to the safe to return the originals. He closed the drawers, locked the safe, and ran to the door.

Taking a deep breath, he stepped into the hallway and pulled the door closed behind him. He walked briskly down the hall, his heart beating wildly. Taking the elevator to the first floor, he made his way out of the White House and walked along G Street. Passing Secret Service headquarters, he had the terrible feeling that at any moment someone might rush up, arrest him, and yank the stolen memos from his pocket. He entered the four-story parking garage at Nineteenth and G Street, where he rented a space by the month, then stopped and looked behind him. Seeing there was no one on the street, he let out his breath and loosened his necktie. Still not taking any chances, he didn't so much as take the memos from his pocket until he was safely inside his automobile.

At the Georgetown Arms, Powers had changed clothes, unplugged his telephone, closed the curtains, and lain down on the sofa. Hell, he needed time to think.

The living room was decorated with impersonal Georgetown Arms furnishings: a thin-cushioned sofa, a small veneer coffee table, an oversized commercial oil painting of a sailing ship on an indigo sea. Though the room looked like a hotel cubicle as much as a rented flat, the place had suited him perfectly—when he was a Secret Service agent. In fact, the sum total of his belongings—out-of-season clothes, a tennis racket, a baseball mitt, some books (biographies mostly, because he didn't care much for fiction), a few marksmanship trophies, and a couple of shoe boxes containing such items as his army discharge papers and a framed Secret Service commendation awarded by Director Fogarty for his actions during the attempt on President Ford's life—fit nicely into two army footlockers. This lack of possessions had made it convenient for him to abandon the apartment at a moment's notice when sent on long-term Secret Service protection assignments.

For a moment Powers considered phoning Sullivan and telling him about what had happened at Highland. But Sullivan had lined up the job in the first place, and Powers would rather die than ask him for the same favor again. Besides, Powers told himself, he could always get a job. There were any number of bodyguard services in D.C., most of them run by retired Secret Service agents. The problem was he'd been a security agent for the President of the United States, and he didn't relish the idea of being a bodyguard for some alcoholic businessman with a Lear jet, or a twenty-two-year-old Saudi prince on vacation. Still, he had to find a way to earn a living soon, because he had only two thousand dollars in savings. He went into the kitchen and made another drink.

At about 1 A.M., dizzy-drunk and sick of both liquor and the sight and sound of television, he went in the bathroom and vomited into the toilet. Cupping his hands under the tap, he washed his mouth out with water, then staggered into the bedroom and stretched out on the bed.

Lying on his back with the room spinning, he found himself dwelling on Ray Stryker and the bloodstained drape in the Special Projects conference room. He still considered the act of suicide cowardly and foolish, but thinking about it over and over made it seem somehow no longer repulsive . . . a legitimate consideration for human beings, perhaps. Who was to say suicide was right or wrong? He breathed deeply a few times. Thankfully, blackness took him. . . .

Marilyn, dressed the way she'd been the first day he'd seen her, was running away from him through the exhibit hall at the art show. He tried to run after her, but his clothes were made of lead and he couldn't keep up. He was out of breath as he continued after her, knocking down the paintings and sculptures in his way. She stopped and looked back at him, then continued on. For the life of him, he couldn't catch up.

The door buzzer sounded.

Powers awoke. Figuring that whoever it was would eventually go away, he didn't move. The buzzer continued for a while, then finally stopped. He closed his eyes again. Peace.

A few minutes later, there was the sound of a key being slipped into the front door lock. Powers sat upright.

"Jack . . . ?" It was Landry. Powers said nothing.

There was the sound of footsteps. Landry stood in the bedroom doorway. "Jack? You okay?"

"Fine."

"Why haven't you been answering your telephone?"

"How did you get in here?" Powers said.

"I talked Mrs. Hammerstrom out of a key." Landry flicked the bedroom light switch, and Powers covered his eyes. "I've been trying to reach you, my man."

"Whataya want?"

"I came here to talk."

"What about?"

"Why don't you get up?"

"Because I don't feel like getting up."

Landry came to the bedside. "You sick?"

"No. I just want some peace and quiet."

"Jack, I'm your friend. Talk to me."

Powers closed his eyes and rolled over onto his stomach. "I don't feel like talking."

"Get up," Landry said.

"Fuck you."

Suddenly Powers felt the mattress rise, and he was thrown out of bed onto the hardwood floor. Furious, he came to his feet ready to fight. Landry didn't raise his hands to defend himself. He just stood there staring at him.

Powers stopped.

"Put your clothes on, my man," Landry said softly. Then he turned and left the room.

Powers angrily threw on a pair of jeans and a T-shirt and went to the living room. Landry had thrown open the windows. He was standing in front of the refrigerator taking out lunch meat and bread.

"What are you doing?" Powers said.

Landry ripped open the plastic wrap covering some sliced bologna. "I didn't eat dinner tonight."

Powers sat down on the sofa. Nothing was said as Landry finished making a sandwich.

Having put the fixings back in the refrigerator, Landry popped open a can of Pepsi and sat down at the kitchen table. "Someday you're going to talk about the real reason why you resigned," Landry said as he ate. "Someday you'll do just that." He took a bite of the sandwich. "There comes a time when a man needs to share what's bothering him. Otherwise he might eat himself alive."

Powers rubbed his eyes.

Nothing was said as Landry slowly finished the sandwich. Finally he wiped his mouth with a paper towel and drank some Pepsi. "You and I both know

Jack Powers would never voluntarily leave the Secret Service," Landry said without looking at him.

"I was offered a job with higher pay."

Landry came to his feet and brushed crumbs off his pants. "I've been standing post in the White House since I was twenty-three years old," he said. "I can sense when something is out of kilter . . . like before the Watergate and Irangate crises. There's tension in the air, my man."

He stood there for a moment, then shrugged and walked to the apartment door.

"The man wanted me out of the White House," Powers heard himself saying. "I chose to resign rather than take a transfer."

Landry shoved the door closed gently. He took off his suit jacket, hung it neatly on a dinette chair, and sat down on the sofa.

Powers told him about meeting Sullivan in front of the Museum of Natural History and signing the resignation. Landry, as was his habit, showed no emotion.

"So now you know," Powers said. Suddenly thirsty, he stood up and went to the sink. He ran the faucet, drank water, and set the glass down.

Landry left the sofa and stood at the window with his thumbs hooked in the thick, diamond-weave leather belt that held his revolver and other Secret Service equipment. "It's a funny thing in this town. Nobody, I mean nobody, ever gets the full story. Ever think about that?"

"What are you driving at?"

"Take Watergate, for instance. Everyone went to jail and Nixon went down the political drain, but still, to this very day, no one for sure knows the real reason for the burglary. There's a lot of speculation—for that matter, a lot of damn good reasons—yet no one has yet established beyond doubt why the break-in was planned in the first place. There's always more than meets the eye, my man."

"I don't see the point."

Landry cleared his throat. "About a year ago Capizzi called in one of his phony sick days, and I was filling in on the rotation. The President and Morgan were playing chess in the Lincoln Room."

"Post twelve."

Landry nodded. "The door was cracked a few inches. They were talking about the President's foreign policy failures—the way the Syrians have out-negotiated us time after time, as if they knew our next move. Morgan said he thought the reason the administration had been doing so badly was that there was a leak in the White House."

"I never heard anything like that."

"Then tonight I ran across Ed Sneed. He mentioned something called 'Operation Fencing Master.' Ever heard of it?"

"No."

"Well, get this, my man. The entire cabinet and the ranking members of the White House staff were forced to take lie detector tests—administered by army polygraph examiners."

"Bullshit."

"That's what I thought. So I went back to the White House and checked Morgan's safe."

"You actually went into his safe?"

"Let's just say I conducted an after-hours security check and found something in plain sight—a file titled 'Fencing Master.' " He reached inside his jacket, took out a piece of paper, and handed it to Powers. "In the file were two memos: a Top Secret addressed to the Provost Marshal of the Army, requesting a platoon of polygraph examiners, and this."

Powers examined the photocopied memo. It was a list of the cabinet and staff members' home addresses.

There were check marks by all the names except 'Russel Patterson.' Next to his name the word *refused* had been scribbled in what looked like Morgan's handwriting.

"Everyone takes the test except Patterson," Powers said. "A defector is interviewed by the Director of the CIA. Ray Stryker's body is found in a CIA office. Marilyn Kasindorf works for the CIA, and one of Patterson's CIA shine boys shows up at her apartment, then ends up dead."

"Patterson . . . the man who would be King," Landry said facetiously.

"But does he want the Presidency bad enough to burn down the White House?"

"The President has been cutting back the CIA since the Russians folded their tent. It's possible that Patterson would love nothing more than to embarrass the man. He figures passing a few goodies out to the other side to screw the man helps the country in the long run. Some Ollie North–style thinking. Besides, I've heard Patterson and the President go way back in hating each other."

"Then you and I are right in the middle of a great big bag of worms," Powers said meditatively.

Landry checked his watch. "It's late. Come over to my place tomorrow." Landry walked to the door. "We'll talk after dinner. Just wear a pair of Levi's. I'll expect you about six." He turned the doorknob and left.

In the kitchen, Powers dropped ice in a glass and poured himself a stiff drink. He lifted the glass to his lips, then stopped himself and dumped the contents of the glass into the sink.

18

Powers awoke with a painful hangover. In a fury he threw out trash, including a nearly full bottle of Scotch, and washed the dishes in the sink. In the bathroom, he shaved and then showered for a long time, as if to cleanse the poison from his body. Finally he dressed in a suit and tie, slipped a screwdriver in his inside coat pocket, and headed down the street to the All-American Cafeteria.

Moving along a buffet line, he filled a plastic tray with enough food for two breakfasts. At a table in the corner he ate slowly, sipping coffee and reading a newspaper for a long time, concentrating on an article with the headline PRESIDENT TRAILS IN POLL, analyzing the President's failure to surge ahead in the polls even after his latest campaign swing. By the time Powers had finished eating, he felt better than he had in days.

Outside the cafeteria, he shoved the newspaper in a trash receptacle and headed down the street toward Scott Circle.

At Marilyn's apartment house, Powers took out the screwdriver and jimmied the front door. Entering the lobby, he checked the mail: rows of small brass-plated boxes with slits, so no one could see if there was anything inside. There was mail in box 721, Marilyn's apartment. Obviously it had been piling up since her defection.

On the seventh floor, Powers stepped out of the elevator and walked down the carpeted hallway to Marilyn's apartment. Having familiarized himself with the lock the first time he'd broken in, he jimmied it easily and opened the door on the first try. He stepped inside the apartment. The living room was vacant, and there were indentations in the carpeting where the furniture had been. He walked slowly across the room and toured the apartment. There was no furniture of any kind in the bedroom or in the bathroom. All drawers and closets, including the medicine chest, were empty. Seeing the barren apartment reminded him that he would never see her again.

Powers returned to the living room. For a moment, it occurred to him that he might like to take something of Marilyn's with him as a keepsake.

In front of the bay window was a short length of telephone cord, left where the telephone had been. He surmised that the CIA had searched the apartment once they'd learned of Marilyn's defection, but why would they remove the furniture and the telephone?

On the wall under the living room window a faceplate was missing from an electrical outlet. He moved closer to inspect. A small trail of paint dust led along the baseboard, leading him to believe the baseboard might have been removed and replaced since the last time the apartment had been painted.

Powers dropped to his knees and tugged on the baseboard. It was loose, and came away from the wall easily. There was an inch-long length of thin black insulating wire near the electrical outlet, the kind of wire used as an antenna for an eavesdropping transmitter designed to draw power from an electrical socket. This kind of device was known as a "hard-wire rig." Though unsophisticated by today's eaves-dropping standards, it was extremely effective. With a good receiver, it could pick up all the sounds not only in the living room but throughout the entire apartment.

Powers picked up the tiny length of wire and dropped it in his shirt pocket.

"May I help you?" a woman said. Powers started.

Marilyn's clear-eyed elderly neighbor, the one who'd walked past him when he had broken in the first time, was standing in the doorway. She was wearing a matronly blue suit and a designer scarf.

"The door was open," Powers said, standing up. "I'm a friend of Marilyn's."

"She doesn't live here anymore. What are you doing here?"

"Looking for Marilyn."

"Did you think you'd find her on the floor?"

"I'm sorry to alarm you," Powers said, smiling obsequiously. "But the door was open."

"No, it wasn't. You get out of here, or I'm going to call the police."

Powers came to his feet. "There's no need for that, ma'am. You can see I've stolen nothing."

"That's only because there's nothing to steal."

Powers moved past the woman and down the hallway. She stood in the hallway watching, as he waited for the elevator. At least she hadn't called the police.

Downstairs, Powers stepped off the elevator and stopped again at Marilyn's mailbox. He looked around to see that no one was watching, then used the screwdriver he'd brought with him to snap the mailbox's small lock. He grabbed the envelopes and shoved them in his coat pocket.

There was the sound of footsteps.

"You don't live here," a voice said.

Powers whirled. A young woman in a red dress was standing a few feet away from him, holding a bag of groceries.

"I forgot my key," Powers said. He turned and walked briskly toward the door.

"You put that mail back right now!" the woman shouted. "Stop!"

He pulled open the door and broke into a run.

The woman ran after him, dropping her grocery sack. "Help, police! Help!"

At the corner, Powers entered the Metro entrance and ran down the stairs. At the first landing, he hurried to a ticket machine and purchased a subway ticket. Stepping onto a down escalator, he jogged right and left as he moved past other passengers. Reaching the lobby below, he turned and glanced toward the top of the escalator.

The woman in the red dress and two tall D.C. policemen were standing looking down, scanning the lobby crowd. Powers turned away and felt his breath quicken. He strolled over to three businessmen chatting near the rest room. Standing near them with his back toward the escalators, he hoped he would look like part of the group. After a minute or two, one of the men stopped chatting, looked at him strangely, and nodded to the others. They turned to look at him. Powers gave a wan smile and moved on.

Moving quickly, but not so fast as to draw attention to himself, Powers walked to the rest room entrance and pushed through the swinging door. Stepping into one of the twenty toilet stalls, he pulled the letters from his pocket and sorted through them. They were all mail advertisements, except for Marilyn Kasindorf's August telephone bill. He shoved the bill into his trouser pocket, tore the ad mail into small pieces, and flushed them down the toilet.

Shrugging off his jacket and removing his tie, he

checked to make sure there were no laundry tags. Then he stepped out of the stall. There was no one else in the rest room. He shoved the jacket and tie into the trash can. The woman and the cops wouldn't be looking for a man wearing an open-collared white shirt. Quickly surveying the room, he could see that the mirror over the sinks provided a view of the entrance door. By standing at a sink he would be shielded from the view of anyone entering, at least until they turned past the metal partition between the door and the sinks.

At a sink, he turned on a faucet. Using the mirror to keep an eye on the door while listening intently for the sound of an arriving train, he rubbed his hands together under running water to avoid being conspicuous to the passengers moving in and out of the rest room. One of the policemen entered through the swinging door. Without drying his hands, Powers moved directly out the exit swinging door. The woman from the apartment house was standing just outside the rest room, and he almost walked into her. Keeping out of her line of sight, Powers walked the opposite way, back toward the escalator. Powers considered making a run for the escalator but decided against it, figuring the other cop was waiting at the top of the landing in case he doubled back.

There was the sound of a train in the tunnel. Powers hurried to the platform. He looked back.

The policeman came out of the bathroom and spoke with the woman. She made shrugging motions, probably to say she couldn't imagine where Powers had gone.

The train slowed as it approached the platform. He turned away to avoid being seen.

Powers knew that if he didn't make it onto the car, there would be no way to avoid being discovered when the train departed and the train platform and lobby cleared.

Someone touched his shoulder. Powers felt a cold shudder pass through his body. He turned. It was an elderly black man carrying a shopping bag. Powers let out his breath.

"Spare some change?"

Powers reached in his pocket and handed over his change. The man moved away.

The train car pulled to a stop at the platform. Its doors opened. The officer and the woman walked onto the train platform. Believing there was nothing else he could do, Powers joined the crowd of passengers hurrying toward the platform. His heart was beating wildly. Though he didn't turn his head to look, he had the feeling that he might have actually bumped into the policeman as he edged his way through the crowd and into the train. The woman and the policeman were still looking about. *What's holding up this goddamn train?*

The woman was looking in his direction. She pointed and said something to the policeman. The policeman headed toward the car.

The doors of the subway car closed. As the train pulled away from the platform, the cop pulled his radio from his belt and transmitted. Because Powers knew policemen weren't stationed at every subway stop, when the train car came to a halt at the next stop he ran out the door and across the lobby. Breathing hard, he ran up the moving escalator, bumping past passengers. At the street, he shouted down a taxi and climbed in. He was back at his apartment a few minutes later.

Sitting at the dinette table in his apartment, Powers unfolded Marilyn's telephone bill. Though there were nineteen calls listed on the bill, there were only eight different telephone numbers dialed. Of these calls only one, which had been called four times, bore a long-distance prefix. Though the billing period covered the entire month of August, there were no calls made after 7 A.M. Monday, August 12.

Since Powers knew that government employees made most of their personal telephone calls and certainly all of their long-distance calls while at work from a government phone, he didn't consider the paucity of calls on the bill unusual. Civil service workers considered the use of the government phone lines while at work an added perk. One by one, Powers dialed the numbers. By the way the phones were answered or by asking a few brief questions he determined the numbers were registered as follows: 1) CIA Headquarters, 2) the White House, 3) La Serre restaurant, and 4) a French laundry located near Scott Circle.

The one long-distance number was 415-926-8319. If he remembered correctly, 415 was the area code for San Francisco. Checking the dates on a calendar, he determined that all four calls had been made after 7:30 P.M. on weeknights.

Powers dialed the number. It rang twelve times. He set the receiver down.

He considered phoning someone at the Secret Service field office in San Francisco and asking them to check the number in a reverse telephone directory, but he was no longer a Secret Service agent.

So he phoned Sharon Fantozzi. She answered on the second ring.

"It's Jack," he said. "I just got your message."

"You're such a liar, Jack."

"I've been out of town. Didn't you get my postcard?"

"I love the way you lie. I think it's cute. Where were you—or is that some deep dark secret?"

"Europe."

"That narrows it down to a continent, anyway."

"How are things at the phone company?" Powers asked.

"Boring. Why don't you come over and cheer me up?"

"I need a favor, Sharon."

"You know I'm always good for a . . . favor."

"Seriously. I need subscriber information on a San Francisco number."

"I could lose my job giving out subscriber information."

"I'm involved in something very important and I need this."

"You sound uptight, Jack. Is everything okay?"

"Of course. It's just that I'm working on an investigation that doesn't allow me to go through regular channels."

"I guess I should have figured you weren't calling to take me out to dinner."

"As soon as the case is over I'll take you to Duke Zeibert's . . . or anywhere you name."

"I'd settle for having you over here to jump my skinny little bones."

"Do you have a pencil handy?"

"Okay, smooth talker," Sharon said sarcastically.

Powers read off the number and she read it back.

"I'll see what I can do," she said.

The backyard of Landry's newly built home in Fairfax, Virginia, a patch of grass surrounded by a neat grape-stake fence, was like all the others on the block. The development was called Keyboard Estates, and the signboard advertising the tract depicted a piano-keyboard street between palatial homes.

Powers, wearing jeans and a T-shirt, sipped a beer as Landry tended his homemade barbecue, a hundred-gallon steel drum on welded steel legs. Wearing a butcher's apron, Landry turned barbecued sides of rib with a long fork. His six-year-old-son, Reggie, wearing a soccer uniform, stood next to him, dutifully extinguishing flames when needed with a clear-plastic squirt gun.

"In her apartment there was an electrical outlet with the faceplate removed," Powers said.

Landry hung the fork on a hook on the side of the barbecue. "Reggie, why don't you see what you can do to help your mom? If there are any more fires, I'll let you know."

"Okay, Dad," Reggie said. He rushed toward the house.

"The CIA probably rented the apartment for her while she was assigned to the White House," Landry said, using a basting brush to apply barbecue sauce to the meat. "When she defected, they sent some cleanup folks to make sure there was nothing of theirs left in her apartment."

Powers reached into his pocket for the tiny length of insulated wire he'd found in Marilyn's apartment. "What about this?"

Landry examined the wire closely. "Antenna wire. Patterson might have suspected her of working for the other side and had the apartment bugged."

"The CIA suspects her of espionage and continues to allow her access to top-secret papers? I just can't see it."

"Maybe he gave her access to planted papers . . . a disinformation operation. Patterson loves that kind of double-think bullshit. Or maybe he was just trying to record some sweet talk between her and the man: political blackmail. Maybe he's waiting to leak the story to the press. A Director of the CIA who wants to make the President look bad might do anything."

Powers nodded. "Ken, you should have been a politician."

At dinner, Doris Landry, a pixieish woman with light brown skin and shiny corn-rowed hair, was overly solicitous to Powers. A former career-minded Secret Service headquarters secretary who understood the politics of the Secret Service as well as anyone, she had opted for being a full-time housewife after her marriage to Landry. Though she frequently spoke disparagingly of the Director and his staff of "Beltway bandits," as she called them, during dinner she'd been careful not to touch on anything that would lead to the topic of Powers's resignation or even the general subject of the Secret Service. This made Powers uncomfortable.

With the meal finished and Reggie and seven-year-old Tisha having cleaned off the table, Doris brought out coffee and filled cups. She sat down next to Powers and took his hand. Landry met her eyes with a frown.

"Ken isn't going to like me saying this, but I believe in speaking my mind. As far as I'm concerned, you're one of the best Secret Service agents ever."

"Thanks, Doris, but you don't have to—"

"Ken isn't very good at expressing his deepest feelings, because men are just that way," she said, with tears in her eyes, "but both of us want you to know that you've always been a fine friend and a wonderful man . . . and I think you got screwed by the President. I would tell him that to his face."

Powers put his arm around her. "Thanks, Doris," he said, feeling a lump in his throat.

Landry turned away and wiped his eyes. He grabbed his cup and saucer and took them to the sink.

With the tension broken, the rest of the evening proceeded cordially, as had so many others he'd spent with them, usually accompanied by a date to whom he'd invariably have to explain the Secret Service inside jokes.

Later, as Doris put the children to bed, Powers and Landry sat down with more coffee in the kitchen. Using the wall phone, Powers dialed Sharon Fantozzi.

"I phoned your apartment. Where are you, out dipping your wick?"

"Just having dinner with a pal."

"A likely story. The San Francisco number you gave me is for the San Francisco Public Library. It's not a listed number but a direct dial—probably a number they don't want tied up by people calling in."

He thanked her and said he would call her soon. She said she wouldn't hold her breath. He set the receiver down, took out a small notebook he'd brought with him, and made a note.

"Marilyn calls the San Francisco Public Library at night," he said.

"That might be a winner," Landry said, stirring sugar into his coffee.

"Marilyn is the key to everything," Powers said.

He rubbed his chin. "The day she left for Germany, the twentieth, she stopped at a beauty shop. And at Dulles she spoke with a United Airlines flight attendant. Those were her only contacts during the entire surveillance."

"I'll handle the beauty shop," Landry said.

"Then I'll take the airport and the San Francisco lead."

"In the meantime, I'll do some more nosing around at the House," Landry said.

"Should we tell Sullivan about all this?"

"My man, what would you do if two agents came to you and said they believed the Director of the CIA was involved in some kind of plot to undermine the President of the United States?"

"You're right. We'd better have some hard evidence before going to him or anyone else," Powers said.

"If the CIA is up to something, you'd better watch your back. Things could get real nasty, my man."

19

The next morning in the White House Rose Garden, the President was handing out plaques to a line of rosy-cheeked Future Farmers of America. Per protocol, Landry, preoccupied with what he'd discussed with Powers the night before, stood a few feet behind him to remain out of photo opportunity.

Later, sitting at the radio console in W-16, he found it difficult to concentrate on even the mundane tasks of preparing a duty roster and completing the previous day's shift report.

At noon, Landry was relieved for lunch by Bob Tomsic and went to the pass section, on the first floor of the Executive Office Building adjacent to the White House. He made small talk with a secretary as he opened a file safe and thumbed through it until he came to Marilyn Kasindorf's file. Inside were a couple of forms requesting White House clearance and listing her payroll address as CIA, Langley, Virginia. Also in the file were two wallet-sized, face-only photographs. He palmed one of the photos and replaced the file in the safe, then pulled out a couple of other files at random to make it look like he was doing nothing more than checking files routinely.

Drawing a car from the Secret Service motor pool,

Landry drove to the Curls and Furls beauty shop and parked in a red zone in front.

Inside, he was met by a din of radios tuned to rock stations and a powerful odor of permanent-wave solution. Four modish female hair stylists were working on women customers. Everyone in the place turned to look at him as he walked in.

A tall red-haired stylist was leaning against a counter reading a *Sex Forum* magazine. She was about forty years old and wore a pink tank top and slick, black leather pants, so tight they showed her sharp pelvic bones. Her face and arms were covered with a spray of tiny freckles, and she had long curving red fingernails. Her bright red hair was cut garishly short and styled high in front to give her . . . well, a Woody Woodpecker look. She put the magazine down.

"We don't do men's hair."

Landry took out his Secret Service badge and credential and held them out. "I just need some information."

"Secret Service?" the woman said.

Her eyes grew hooded, and she glanced suspiciously at a young hairdresser working at the closest chair. Her hair was styled in what Powers would describe as a crew cut: white-walled sides, and a level landing strip of black hair on top of her head. She wore heavy dangling silver earrings.

Landry reached into his jacket pocket and took out the pass-section photograph of Marilyn Kasindorf. "Do you remember doing this woman's hair? She came in here August nineteenth."

She looked at him sternly for a moment, then at the photo. "The nineteenth . . . Oh, yes. I remember her."

"Can you tell me anything about her?"

She handed the photograph back to him. "What did she do?"

"It's a confidential inquiry."

"I shouldn't really be talking about a customer."

"She's a forger, ma'am. Social Security checks."

Her eyes widened. "God, I hope I didn't take a check from her." She reached under the counter, pulled out a metal box, and thumbed through some papers for a moment. The other stylists had lowered radio volumes and silenced hair dryers to eavesdrop. "No," she said finally. "I have six checks and twelve credit card drafts listed for the nineteenth, but I know all the customers. She must have paid in cash."

"Lucky for you," Landry said. "Do you remember anything about her?"

"Lemme see the photograph again."

He handed her the photo.

"This isn't a very good picture of her," she said. "Nice person, friendly. It was the first time she'd been in here."

"What did she talk about?"

"Art. I think she mentioned something about an art show. God, I wonder if she buys paintings by forging checks. I saw a TV show one time about people who did that kind of thing."

"This woman's name is Marilyn. Marilyn Kasindorf. Does that ring a bell?"

"Forgers use different names, don't they?"

"Usually," Landry said. "Are you sure she'd never been in here before?"

She nodded. "I know every regular customer."

Landry shrugged. "Thanks for the help."

"What should I do if she comes in here again?" the woman asked.

"She won't be back," Landry said on his way to the door.

Powers used one of his free airline travel coupons for the trip to San Francisco. Though tired, he was unable to sleep during the flight. He couldn't get Marilyn off his mind.

The weather was clear and sunny, much cooler than Washington, as Powers stepped off the airplane. At the terminal gift shop he purchased a map of the city and took a bus to the Summit Hotel on Post Street.

Powers had stayed at the Summit on numerous Secret Service protection assignments. It was a modest place, a remodeled fleabag catering to civil servants, trial witnesses, and tourists trying to save a buck. Just as he'd figured, the Samoan room clerk, who'd come to recognize him over the years, assigned him a room at the government discount without asking to see his Secret Service identification. With the savings on the room, Powers would be able to pay for taxis and meals.

The San Francisco Library, a massive gray-stone edifice with ten Corinthian columns, was located on Larkin Street across from the modern federal building. Powers entered through the glass double doors. He made his way past a large book-return desk manned by two young women, each of whom had a telephone on her desk. He noted the library hours, which were posted on a sign at the desk, and strolled past the stacks to the other side of the library. There was another telephone on a small desk in the children's section and one on a wall in periodicals.

At a bank of pay telephones in the children's section, he dropped change and dialed the library number from Marilyn's phone bill. It began to ring. Allowing the receiver to hang from its cord rather than setting it back on the hook, he stepped out of the booth. There was no sound of ringing, and none of the employees within his sight on the first floor answered a phone. Quickly, he moved up the stairs to the general reference area. An elderly gray-haired woman wearing an earth-mother dress moved from her desk to one in the corner and picked up the receiver. She said hello a couple of times, then set the receiver back on the cradle and returned to her desk.

Powers wandered around for a while until the woman had left her desk to assist a customer, then hurried to the desk in the corner and checked the number on the telephone. It was the one he'd dialed.

He left the library and took a long walk to his favorite restaurant, the Via Reggio on Lombard Street. Though the place was busy, the owner, Bill Smith, a slim, curly-haired young Irishman, greeted him warmly and showed him to a seat. Powers ordered and ate a leisurely lunch of fried squid and pasta, refusing wine because he didn't feel like drinking. Smith joined him and they chatted about the time President Reagan had lunched at the restaurant, and the Secret Service agents had lined up an off-duty party with the lady gym instructors at the classy Fog City Health Club down the street.

After lunch, Powers killed the rest of the day and early evening as a tourist strolling along Fisherman's Wharf.

At 6 P.M. he took a cable car to the Hertz rental car office on Montgomery Street. There he rented a compact car and drove it to the library. He found a parking place across the street.

In the library, there was a man sitting at the desk in the corner on the second level. He was about twenty-five, of medium height, and had a thick dishwater beard. His hair was shoulder-length and drawn back into a ponytail, and he was wearing Levi's, a SAVE THE WHALES T-shirt, and granny glasses. Powers returned to the car and waited.

At 9 P.M. a security guard in a khaki uniform came to the front door and opened it for each of the last few remaining library customers. Then the lights, upstairs first, then downstairs, were dimmed. A few minutes later, the guard opened the front door from the inside and several employees, including the man with the ponytail, came out the front door. They walked together, chatting amiably, to the corner of McAllister and Larkin, and then went in different directions.

Powers started the engine and drove slowly to the corner. The man with the ponytail moved briskly down the street. In the middle of the block he entered a well-lit parking lot and climbed into a primer-gray Volkswagen beetle. He backed out of the parking space and drove out of the driveway onto McAllister. Powers accelerated and followed him through downtown to the Mission district. On a street of two-story Victorian-style houses, he pulled into an alley and parked the Volkswagen. He climbed out, locked the car, and entered the front door of the house without using a key.

Powers found a parking space for his car around the corner. Returning to the house, he opened the door and climbed a steep flight of stairs to a landing. There were four closed doors lining a hallway that extended to the end of the building. To Powers, it looked like a private residence whose bedrooms had been converted to rentals.

He knocked on the closest door.

"Yes?" a woman said.

"I'm looking for the man who works at the library," he said.

"End of the hall on your right," she said.

Powers moved to the door and knocked. The man opened the door almost immediately.

"My name is Jack Powers. Forgive me for bothering you at this late hour, but I'm conducting an investigation. May I step in?"

"Is this some kind of sales pitch?"

"I assure you it's not. May I come in where we can talk without being overheard?"

"I guess so," the man said after a moment. "But only because I'm curious."

Powers stepped in, and the man closed the door behind him. The room had a marred wood floor and was small and well-lit. In front of the window was an artist's easel, which held a nearly finished oil painting of a red-haired young girl standing behind the counter in a flower shop. A spattered canvas drop cloth covered half the floor, and artist's brushes and tubes of oil paint, filled and half-filled canvases, and cans of turpentine covered a small dining table. The walls, from floor to ceiling, were covered with oil paintings of differing sizes: realistic portraits of men, women, and children, all done in subdued pastels like the painting on the easel. On the other side of the room, on the floor, were a mattress and a clock radio. The room smelled like turpentine, oil paint, and marijuana.

"I served in the U.S. Secret Service for over twenty years, but I'm here unofficially."

"So what's this all about?"

"Do you know Marilyn Kasindorf?"

"I don't know anyone by that name."

On the wall to Powers's right was an oil painting of a woman standing near a motorcycle on a dark street, an impressionistic work with slashing lines of dark reds and grays, plus the yellowish glimmer of a streetlight. The woman looked like Marilyn Kasindorf. Powers raised his eyebrows.

The artist's face turned red. "Marilyn's my step-sister," he said warily.

"Are you aware she defected?"

"I was told."

"By whom?"

"The people she works for informed me," the young man said.

"Look. I was assigned to investigate her. We met

and became . . . friends, and then suddenly she defected. Now I'm trying to figure out what happened."

"Some CIA people came here a few days ago."

"What did they say?"

"Just that she'd defected. I couldn't believe it, but they showed me a teletype about her defection. I felt like I'd been slammed in the stomach with a baseball bat. They said the furniture in Marilyn's apartment belonged to the CIA, and it wouldn't be necessary for me to travel to Washington to dispose of it."

"Sounds a little strange."

"Not really. Marilyn told me when she moved into the place a few months ago it was being furnished by the Company. She said her assignment would only last a few months. She sold her own furniture when she went to Saudi Arabia. That was her last job before Washington—the American Embassy in Riyadh."

"What about her personal effects?" Powers asked.

"In the other room. They just arrived this morning. I don't really understand who you are or why you are here."

"I've been assigned to determine why a longtime government employee would defect," Powers said. "May I ask your name?"

"Jim Chilcott."

"Mr. Chilcott, I have a job to do. I'm only here to see if you can throw some light on what happened."

"I don't believe she defected! I say it's bullshit!" Chilcott said angrily. "I should be the one conducting the fucking investigation."

"I'm sorry."

"Lemme tell you something. My sister was—is—a flag-waver. She gave the patriotic speech in high school." He turned his head. "She didn't defect. She must be on some kind of a mission. She would never voluntarily defect. Give up everything."

"Did she mention to you that she was going to Europe a couple of weeks ago?" Powers said.

"She hadn't called me for a while. She used to phone me at the library because I don't have a telephone here. It disturbs my work."

"If she was going to Europe on a vacation," Powers interrupted, "would she have told you?"

"Absolutely. That's why this whole thing is so strange. Marilyn and I both attended art school," he said, his voice cracking. "My mother wanted us to be artists, but Marilyn went her own way. She wanted to do something different." Chilcott made his way into the tiny kitchen area, ran water, and splashed it on his face. He tore a paper towel from a holder and dried himself.

"Did she ever mention an art exhibition in Kassel, Germany—the Documenta?"

"It's a well-known contemporary art exhibition, but I don't remember ever discussing it with her."

"How did she sound the last time you spoke with her?"

"Fine. Just like always."

"What did you talk about?"

"She asked about my work. We always discuss art," Chilcott said.

"I'd like you to think back. Was there anything she mentioned the last few times you spoke with her that you thought out of the ordinary?"

Chilcott stood for a moment, rubbing his chin. "Nothing," he said finally. "That's what I find so strange. We shared everything. It was just the two of us in the family, and we shared everything. She told me about who she was dating. We held nothing back. If she had been in some kind of trouble she would have told me. Even . . . even if she'd been doing something illegal, she'd have told me."

Powers moved to a shelf near the window and

picked up a small framed, slightly out-of-focus baseball team photograph. Marilyn was standing third from the right in a group of women wearing Levi's, shorts, and T-shirts with *Langley Kittens* scrawled across the front. She had a softball in her right hand and her arm was drawn back, ready to throw.

"Marilyn plays on a CIA softball team," Chilcott said.

"Can you think of any reason why she would defect?" Powers said, staring at the photo.

Chilcott shook his head. "I'll never believe she's a traitor."

"May I take this photograph? I'll return it to you."

"I guess."

Powers slipped the photograph into his shirt pocket and walked to the door.

"The last coupla times we spoke I got the impression that she'd been dating. She said he was older than her. Other than that there was absolutely nothing out of the ordinary in what she told me, what we talked about."

"What's his name?"

"I never asked."

"Did she mention anything specific about him?" Powers said.

"She didn't go into much detail . . . as if she didn't want to talk about him. I assumed it was because he was married, so I didn't press the issue. Oh, yeah. She mentioned something about him having a very important job."

"By the way," Powers, said opening the door. "The Agency. With whom did you speak?"

"Green and Jones. They said they were from Langley."

Downstairs, Powers walked across the street, unlocked the rental car, and climbed in behind the wheel. Leaning back in the seat, he pondered: If Marilyn was so close to her brother, wouldn't she have wanted to speak to him one last time before she defected? He took out the baseball team photograph and turned on the dome light. In the photo, Marilyn's hair was pulled back and she was wearing a baseball hat cocked to one side. She looked different, the way people do in photographs, particularly poor-quality Polaroids. It occurred to him, as some thought buried and suddenly coming into his consciousness, that he would never see her again. And he had the familiar feeling of having forgotten something . . . a name-on-the-tip-of-one's-tongue sensation. Hell, maybe he was going crazy. He might as well. Everything else in his life seemed to have turned to shit.

Powers looked up at the house. Chilcott was standing at the window looking down at him. Suddenly uncomfortable, Powers shoved the photograph back in his shirt pocket, started the engine, and drove away, telling himself that the trip to San Francisco had been for nothing.

At the corner, Powers turned onto Mission Street to head back to the hotel. He drove for a mile or so to Market Street in the direction of the bay. At a traffic light he checked the rearview mirror. There was a compact car behind him. Unless he was mistaken, the same car had been behind him on Mission.

Powers cruised through a yellow light. The car sped up, drove through the intersection on the red light, and accelerated past him, its single occupant staring straight ahead. It was a gray Toyota. At the next corner, it turned off—just what an experienced surveillant would do if he found himself too close to his prey. Powers took his foot off the accelerator. As his car slowed, a black van about a quarter block ahead of him pulled into the right lane and slowed down too.

Powers changed lanes, accelerated past the van, and turned right. He moderated his speed and kept his eye on the rearview mirror. A block behind, the Toyota pulled out from a side street and turned in his direction, then turned off again as the van came into view. Powers felt his breath quicken. He was being followed—by professionals, he guessed, because of the street-paralleling technique.

Powers's mind raced. During a security advance he'd done for President Reagan's visit to the San Francisco convention center, a Secret Service tech man had informed him that the area across the street from the center was a communications "dead spot." Radios could neither transmit nor receive because of the unique geography of the location, and special transmitting equipment had to be set up to ensure that the presidential party had reliable communications. Powers made his decision. Turning south, he made his way to the convention center and pulled into an alley next to a brownstone building over whose entrance was a neon sign, *Ted Duffy's Grill*. He climbed out of the car and hurried down the alley. Entering the rear entrance to the tavern, he knew that whoever was following him would be unable to communicate with the other cars on the surveillance.

Inside, the two customers at the bar, both elderly men wearing Giants baseball hats, were talking with the bartender, a tall man with wavy hair combed straight back. Powers sat down on a bar stool close to the door. The bartender set a cocktail napkin in front of him. "What'll ya have, sport?"

"Scotch and water."

"You got it."

As the bartender mixed the drink, Powers surveyed the bar. The bartender set the drink down, collected money, and returned to the other customers. Powers picked up the drink and moved to a cocktail table next to the window. Because of the bar's darkness, he could look out to the street without fear of being seen by anyone outside.

For the next two hours, as customers came and went, the van and the Toyota alternately cruised past the bar every few minutes, checking, as Powers surmised, to see if his car was still parked in the alley. It would only be a matter of time before whoever was in charge of the surveillance felt it was necessary to verify he was inside and hadn't slipped away unnoticed.

A half hour later, an athletic-looking man wearing a windbreaker entered by the front door. He had a well-trimmed mustache and closely cropped hair that gave him a military appearance. At any rate, he didn't look like he belonged in a neighborhood bar. As Powers would have done under the same circumstances, the man was careful not to make eye contact. Without so much as looking in Powers's direction, he walked directly past the bar to the rest room. After an appropriate amount of time he came out, walked out the door, and moved past the window to Powers's right.

Powers left the table and hurried out the rear door. The man continued on the sidewalk, passing the mouth of the alley. Powers turned right and, breaking into a jog, made his way along a rutted sluiceway at the rear of the businesses. He stopped at a driveway crossing the sidewalk. There was a gray Toyota like the one the man had been driving parked two doors down, toward Market Street. Powers ducked back from the sidewalk and stepped behind an industrial trash receptacle.

There was the sound of footsteps on the sidewalk, and Powers peered out to see the man stop at the edge of the driveway, check the sluiceway for traffic, and continue on to the Toyota.

Powers stepped from the shadow of the building. Lunging from behind, he threw his right arm around the man's neck and pulled him backward. Using his knee as a lever in the small of the man's back, he broke his balance and pulled him down and backward, arms flailing, toward the alley, back into the shadow of the building. The man grunted and kicked wildly.

"Take it easy, clown, or I'll break your neck," Powers said as the man struggled. Without loosening his grip, Powers frisked him quickly. On the man's left side was a gun in an inside-the-belt holster. Powers yanked the gun out and shoved the barrel to the man's left temple. He stopped flailing.

"Who are you working for?" Powers said.

"I don't know what you are talking about, sir," the man said with a slight accent.

Powers whirled the man around and shoved him against the wall. "Drag out some ID."

"I . . . I don't have any."

Powers aimed the gun at his face. "Empty your pockets, fucker. Turn 'em inside out."

The man complied. From his right pocket he pulled out a large wad of cash and dropped it to the pavement. He pulled the pocket inside out. The same with the left pocket. Only car keys. He turned, showed Powers his rear pockets. Nothing. Suddenly, Powers felt a chill. There was only one reason for a surveillant to carry no identification: if his mission was to kill. If arrested, he'd have nothing to tie him to a motive for the murder. The cash would facilitate an untraceable escape.

"If I knew for sure you'd been sent to waste me, I'd put a bullet in your brain right here and now, but since I don't, tell whoever you work for I'm gonna find out who they are. And then I'm gonna pull the plug on 'em."

There was a squeal of brakes in the street.

The black van came to a stop. The man broke into a run toward it. Powers moved to chase him, then stopped as the van suddenly reversed—and sped directly toward him. Powers had the near-death sensation that some Secret Service agents refer to as "the edge." It was a feeling he'd experienced first in Vietnam, when his barracks was mortared the day he arrived in-country. The edge manifested itself in the feeling of senses instantaneously becoming acute, the tooth-baring, muscle-tightening, fight-or-flight frozen-in-time response human beings probably first experienced stepping outside the primordial cave and finding a sabertooth tiger, the same adrenaline rush Powers had felt when shots rang out during the assassination attempts on Presidents Ford and Reagan.

He aimed instinctively and fired: one, two, three rounds. The shots echoed between the buildings.

The van, still coming in his direction, sideswiped the wall. Powers was brushed by the bumper and thrown violently backward; the force of the impact caused him to pull the trigger again.

He came to his feet and ran to the end of the sluiceway. Heart pounding, he ran across the street. Hoping to lose anyone else who might be following him, he jogged for blocks, moving in and out of department stores, taking elevators and escalators and back alleys, then doubling back. At Market Street, still not convinced he'd eluded the surveillance, he entered Macy's and broke into a run. At the rear of the store, he ran through a storage area past shocked employees and out the back.

Up the street, he rushed into Clancy's, a spacious, dimly lit restaurant with a cafeteria-style steam table in the center. He hurried past some elderly customers lining up for corned beef and cabbage and found a pay telephone. He picked up the receiver and phoned the San Francisco airport. After reserving a seat on a red-eye to D.C. under a phony name, he used his telephone credit card to call the White House and asked for the Secret Service command post.

"W-16. Landry."

"I'm in San Francisco. Things are getting nasty."

"What happened?"

"We'd better not talk on the phone. Get Sullivan and meet me at Emerson's at 0900."

Powers racked the phone. Fearing that the surveillants might be staked out on the Summit Hotel, Powers chose to leave the few items of clothing he'd brought with him and return to D.C. immediately. At San Francisco International Airport, Powers purchased an inexpensive flight bag. In a restroom, he unloaded the remaining two rounds from the revolver. There was a grayish line on the butt of the revolver where the serial number had been removed—permanently—by what he surmised was acid. The bullets were hollow-point rounds, the kind used to achieve maximum killing power. Wrapping the gun and bullets in newspaper so they wouldn't bounce around, he put them in the bag. At the ticket counter, he purchased a ticket. Avoiding security procedures, he checked the bag through to Washington, D.C.

20

★★★★★★★★★★★★★★★★
★★★★★★★★★★★★★★★★

The morning was muggy, and during the drive downtown from National Airport Powers sensed electricity in the air—as if at any moment there might be an uncontrollable cloudburst.

Emerson's, a large coffee shop on M Street, was a place Powers and Landry had frequented when first assigned to the White House Detail. One of the thirty or more comfortable leather booths in the always crowded room was the perfect place to discuss secrets. Powers arrived a few minutes early, carrying the flight bag. Landry and Sullivan were waiting in a booth at the corner.

"What the hell is going on?" Sullivan said sternly as Powers sat down.

Powers recounted tracing the telephone call, interviewing Jim Chilcott, and spotting the surveillance. "At least two one-man cars," Powers said. "I did a double-back and went up against one of 'em. A young guy, a military type with a slight accent. I took his piece away from him."

"He was carrying?" Sullivan said incredulously.

Powers tapped the flight bag. "A Smith and Wesson thirty-eight four-inch, loaded with hollow points. The serial number looks like it's been worked on with acid."

"CIA agents don't carry guns on surveillance," Landry said.

"Not unless they're going to kill someone."

Sullivan ran his hands through his hair and let out his breath. "This is *un-fucking-believable*."

"What happened at the beauty shop?" Powers said.

"They said Marilyn was a first-time customer." Landry said. "She talked about art. That's about it. You look like you could use a square meal, my man."

"I'm starving."

Sullivan motioned to the waitress. "This one's on me," he said.

For the next half hour or so, they rehashed the details. They ate and talked and talked, as if the act of talking itself might somehow solve the enigma.

"Marilyn Kasindorf's White House pass shows her coming to the House only once or twice a month carrying top-secret documents," Landry said. "She would sign in at the gate and go to the Special Projects Office. Morgan would go to the office, pick up the documents from her, and take them to the President for the briefing session. Twice, the upstairs log shows her accompanying Morgan into the Oval Office while the President was there. The visits were short, one about ten and the other about fifteen minutes. The last date she appears on the log is August twelfth."

"Sounds like they might have had a question on the briefing papers," Sullivan said.

"And they called her in to clear it up," Powers said.

Landry sipped his drink and set down the glass. From his jacket pocket he took out a small clear-plastic bag and set it on the table in front of Powers.

Powers picked it up. In the bag was a round telephone transmitter, the part of a telephone fitting inside the mouthpiece. It was one of the most common listening devices, easily installed by simply replacing the genuine transmitter with an electronic bugging device shaped like it.

"The telephone on Marilyn's desk in the Special Projects Office was bugged."

It was common knowledge at the White House that Secret Service Technical Security specialists searched the White House regularly for electronic eavesdropping devices. Though no listening devices had been uncovered for years, a "find"—as the uncovering of such a device was called in Secret Service vernacular—would be treated as a major security breach and would immediately be brought to the attention of the President as well as the National Security Council. An intelligence damage assessment investigation (IDAI) would be launched, one involving the use of lie detector tests for everyone with access to the area where the bug was found.

"I'll be damned," Powers said.

Sullivan cleared his throat. "Whoever planted that bug is someone with unlimited White House clearance: a staff or cabinet member, a member of the National Security Council. . . ."

"None of this makes any sense to me," Powers said.

"If the CIA is making a move, they're sure stepping on their dicks," Landry said.

"Maybe there's more to this than just her," Powers said. "Maybe there's a whole ring of spies in the White House."

"But why would that make the Syrians want to kill you?" Sullivan said.

Powers furrowed his brow and shrugged. He didn't know either.

"I say it's Patterson," Landry said. "Patterson and his CIA pointy-heads."

"Were there any witnesses to what happened to you in San Francisco?" Sullivan asked.

"No."

After another forty minutes or so of rehashing the same ground and asking the same questions, they were talked out. "I guess we don't have a hell of a lot," Sullivan said. "And frankly, I don't know where to go from here. But as of now, we have to go on war footing. Keep in touch daily. Before I go to the President with this, I want our ducks in a row. Jack, in the meantime you'll have to take precautions."

"I will."

Sullivan left, after leaving money for the bill. Powers had a coffee refill for the road and realized he was exhausted, bone-weary from all that had happened.

Finally, they walked outside and climbed in Landry's sedan.

"You'd better watch yourself, my man," Landry said on the way to the Georgetown Arms.

"I'll take precautions."

At his apartment, Powers stood at the window for a while as a light, warm breeze caused the curtains to billow. He couldn't get Marilyn off his mind.

In his bedroom, Powers opened the nightstand drawer and took out his own gun, a .38-caliber Smith and Wesson snub-nosed revolver he used to carry when off-duty. He flipped open the cylinder to check rounds. With a flick of the wrist, he snapped the cylinder shut. He set the gun on the nightstand, where it would be within reach in case the CIA or whoever it was decided to try to kill him, then undressed and climbed into bed. There was traffic noise rising from the street, and he lay there for a long time, unable to get to sleep.

After dropping off Powers at the Georgetown Arms, Landry drove to the Secret Service garage and parked the car in its assigned space. He waved at the attendant in the booth and walked out the street entrance. There was a time when he would have driven the Secret Service car home, but with Elmer Cogswell in charge of Inspection Division, he knew even a minor traffic accident on the way to or from work could destroy his career. All traffic accidents in official Secret Service cars were investigated by the Inspection Division—giving Agent-in-Charge Elmer Cogswell a chance to twist the facts and, by innuendo, allege negligence on Landry's part no matter what the facts. Therefore, Landry had decided that it was better to pay an exorbitant monthly parking fee in a private garage to park his own car rather than use a government car for home-to-work driving and risk being sandbagged.

Moving down G Street, Landry hummed the U.S. Marine Corps hymn, his favorite tune. Crossing the street, he passed a blue Chevrolet with two men sitting in it.

Farther down the street, at the Nineteenth and G Street parking garage, a three-story garage with open bays, he entered by way of the driveway. It was dimly lit inside as he walked toward the far corner where his Ford was parked. Outside, a blue Chevrolet drove past with its lights out. Was it the same car that had been parked in front of the headquarters garage? Because of the darkness it was hard to tell. He stopped walking. There was silence.

Instinctively sensing danger, he unfastened the button of his jacket to allow better access to his gun and continued along the shiny garage floor toward his car. Moving cautiously, he realized that the wide cement pillars in the garage were the most likely places for a robber—or perhaps one of the men who'd been following Powers—to lie in wait.

There was an echoing sound of footsteps moving on cement. Landry stopped. The footsteps stopped.

Unable to determine from what direction the sound had come, he unholstered his revolver.

Holding the gun at his side with the barrel pointed down, he moved nimbly, ready for action. Near a pillar adjacent to the spot where his car was parked there was movement. Was someone hiding? Landry raised his weapon.

"Federal officer, motherfucker. Come on out!" Landry called.

He wished to hell he had a flashlight.

"I'm only going to say it once more, slick. Raise your hands and stand up. Don't make me shoot you."

The man moved closer. His hands were on his head. He was wearing a dark suit.

"Keep the hands up and turn around!" Landry shouted. His heart was beating wildly, and he could hear the sound of his own breathing. As the man complied, Landry, using his left hand, touched his waist, checking for handcuffs. Slipping them from his belt, he moved slowly forward.

Realizing that the man hadn't actually violated any law, he hoped that when he searched him he at least had some kind of weapon. If not, Elmer Cogswell would have a field day with the subsequent investigation for false arrest. On the other hand, he remembered the Secret Service School graduation address given by former Secret Service Director Robert Powis. "Gentlemen, during your careers you'll be required to make many crisis decisions. But I want you always to remember that, in making those decisions, it's infinitely better to be tried by twelve than carried by six."

There was the sound of running.

Landry, raising his gun, wheeled to his right. The figure of a man came from behind a pillar to his right. There was a popping sound, like that of the air gun Landry had played soldier with as a child in Chicago. With the sound, a powerful force lifted Landry and slammed him down. Instinctively, he fired his revolver, but more impacts pounded his body. Then, as if in a dream, he was lying on his back angrily trying to pull the trigger of his Secret Service revolver . . . but he couldn't move. In fact he couldn't even breathe, and just as he had in Vietnam when he'd been shot he wondered, God only knows why, whether the bullets had remained inside or passed through his body. But it was different this time. This time he was going to be carried by six. "Doris . . ." Landry said, and then a wave of pain and freezing cold overtook and suffocated him.

21

★★★★★★★★★★★
★★★★★★★★★★★

There was a violent pounding on the door of Powers's apartment.

Powers rolled over, struggling to emerge from the paralysis of sleep.

The pounding continued. "Police officers! Open up!"

Powers turned to the clock radio on the nightstand. It was 4 A.M. He swung his feet to the floor and threw on jeans and a T-shirt. He made his way to the front door and used the peephole. There were two uniformed policemen standing in the hallway: a young man with glasses, and a heavyset African-American woman whose uniform cap was set back high on her forehead.

Powers opened the door.

"Sorry to wake you, sir, but we're investigating a street robbery," the male cop said. "The robbers took everything from the victim except his appointment book." He held up a copy of a photocopied page from a tiny government appointment book. On the page was the notation *510–4521*, scribbled in a barely legible handwriting that looked familiar.

"Is that your telephone number?"

"Yes," Powers said.

245

Then, in a sudden wave of trepidation that made him feel weak at the knees, he recognized the handwriting. "The victim," Powers said, steadying himself. "Is he a tall black man with short gray hair?"

The female officer averted her eyes from Powers. "Yes, sir," she said somberly. "Do you know him?"

Powers felt as if he had fallen and landed on cement. "Ken Landry. He's a friend."

"We'd like you to accompany us back to the scene of the robbery."

Powers cleared his throat. "The victim—what's the condition of the victim?"

"I'm sorry, sir. He was pronounced dead at the scene."

Flashing police emergency lights gave Nineteenth Street near G an eerie intermittent glow. The avenue, a short commercial block near the White House, had been shut off by a combination of police cars and yellow evidence tape extending from curb to curb and across the driveway of a parking garage—where, because he had driven to and from work with Landry many times, Powers knew Landry always parked his car.

The officers led Powers under a boundary of yellow tape and up the ramp of the garage. In the dim fluorescent dusk of the first level, uniformed policemen and detectives milling about glanced coldly at Powers, an outsider. In the corner of the building, Landry's car was parked facing the wall.

Landry's body was lying next to the driver's side of the car. He was flat on his back about ten feet from the door, his arms at his sides, his lifeless palms upturned. His shirt was soaked with blood. His necktie and suit jacket were askew, and every pocket in his clothing had been turned inside out. His eyes and mouth were closed. There was a murmur among the other policemen standing nearby.

"Oh, God . . ."

"Do you know him?"

"I want you to call Art Lyons at homicide," Powers said to the male cop, as he stared at the body.

"Homicide is already—"

"Lyons knows the victim."

"Yes, sir."

Powers turned away, wiping his eyes.

Art Lyons was located at home and arrived shortly. He blanched visibly when he saw the body.

For the next hour or so, Powers, seething with anger, watched as Lyons moved about the crime scene. Finally, Lyons joined him.

"How do you read it?" Powers said, gathering himself.

"At this point it looks like someone—there may have been more than one suspect—tried to rob him, and he shot it out rather than turn over his money. Ken got off two wild shots. When he was down, they rifled his pockets and took his wallet, wristwatch, gun, and cuffs. A cold son of a bitch did this one."

"You think they shot him first, then took his money."

"There are no signs of a struggle, no defensive wounds—scratches, bruises—but we'll have to wait for the autopsy before—"

"Are there any witnesses?" Powers interrupted.

"We're doing a neighborhood canvass, but so far no one saw or heard anything."

"So there's nothing to go on."

"Not a hell of a lot. Just a street robbery."

"Or at least that's what it looks like."

Lyons reached inside his jacket for smokes. He lit up.

"Landry didn't believe Stryker's death was a suicide. I don't believe this is a robbery," Powers said.

Lyons blew some smoke. "In this town, a street robbery would be a good way to cover up a murder. The next question is, who has a motive for killing him?"

"I'm not sure yet, Art, but one way or the other I'm going to find out. In the meantime I'd appreciate it if you would keep what we just talked about between the two of us."

"Are you saying this has something to do with Stryker's death?"

"I'll know more soon."

"I'll keep my mouth shut and investigate this case for the time being, but if you or anybody else tries to lock me out, to keep me from finding who killed him, I'll go public and blow this thing out of the water. What I'm saying is that Ken Landry was my friend. Fuck the White House and the cloak-and-dagger bullshit."

"When that time comes, I'll be right there with you."

"Get a sheet," Lyons said to a uniformed officer standing nearby. The officer stepped to a police car and opened the trunk. He took out a sheet, and Powers helped him cover Landry's body.

Sullivan, dressed in a sport coat and an open-collar shirt, hurried into the garage and approached the body. "What happened?"

"A robbery," Powers said.

"Is there anything to go on?"

Powers shook his head. "I'll notify the family," he said, blinking back tears.

At the Landry house in Keyboard Estates, Powers, summoning all his strength to maintain composure, told Doris gently that her husband was dead. She cried hysterically in his arms at first, then retired to a bedroom with Reggie and Tisha. When relatives arrived and Powers was sure the family was in good hands, he left.

At his apartment there were numerous messages on his answering machine—White House Detail agents and Blackie Horowitz informing him of Landry's murder—but he didn't feel like returning any calls. Overwhelmed by loss and anger, he sat down on the sofa, cupped his face in his hands, and wept bitterly. Then, after a while, he came to his feet and washed his face at the kitchen sink. And suddenly he was overwhelmed by anger—calculating, eye-darting, combat anger.

Powers picked up the telephone receiver and dialed Dulles International Airport. After being transferred a few times, he reached Scott Settle, an FBI agent stationed permanently at the Dulles FBI office. They chatted briefly, Powers praying Settle hadn't heard about his resignation from the Secret Service. Settle mentioned he'd seen the news and asked if Powers knew Landry.

"Yes, I knew him," Powers muttered. He cleared his throat. "United Airlines," he said. "I'm trying to identify a flight attendant I saw meet with a suspect during a surveillance."

"I'll make the arrangements," Settle said.

At the United Airlines office at Dulles, Powers flipped quickly through a series of binders containing color photographs of all male and female flight attendants as Settle, a tall, former All-American football player, wandered about the office.

Finally, he found a photo of the redhead who'd spoken with Marilyn shortly before she boarded the flight to Germany. Below the photo was an employee identification number and a name and address: ALBERTS,

WINONA, 13293 GRISHOLM, MCLEAN, VIRGINIA. Fearing Settle would write an FBI contact report about assisting him and list the name of the flight attendant, Powers repeated the name and address to himself several times to commit them to memory. Then he turned a few more pages and closed the book.

"Find who you're looking for?"

"Afraid not."

"Sure you're not just looking for some fine piece of tail you saw on a flight?" Settle said.

Powers shook his head and smiled. "Thanks for the help."

In McLean, Virginia, a high-income community of private family dwellings, condominiums, and shopping malls that looked like all the other suburbs in the greater D.C. area, Powers used an automobile club map to find Winona Alberts's address. Her condominium was in the middle of a bank of stucco condos, all of which were facing other condos.

He knocked on the front door. Through the frosted glass panes he could see movement inside. A young woman opened the door. Her red hair was wrapped in a scarf, and she wore a yellow T-shirt and blue jeans.

"Miss Alberts? I'm Jack Powers. I have a few questions for you. May I step in?"

"Questions about what?" she said cautiously.

"About someone you were seen with at Dulles Airport."

"Who— Are you a policeman?"

"I'm acting on behalf of the U.S. government."

"Who is it I was seen with?"

Powers took out the baseball team photograph and pointed to Marilyn. "This woman."

"That isn't a very good photograph."

"August twentieth. You spoke with her briefly at Dulles Airport."

"I don't think I . . . the twentieth. Yes, I had just come in on a flight."

"How long have you known her?"

"Is she in some kind of trouble?"

"She's missing."

"Missing?"

"Anything you can tell me about her would be helpful."

"I met her at Heathrow about a year or so ago. We were both stranded by fog and stuck in the waiting area all night, and we just struck up a conversation. That was the first and only time I saw her. But even with the change in hair color I remembered her, because . . . we were chatting all night."

"What color was her hair when you met her?"

"Blond. I think she looked better as a blonde."

"What did she tell you about herself?"

"She talked a lot about art. Susan was interested in art."

"Susan?"

"Yes. I never asked her last name."

"Are you sure that was the name she gave you?"

"Positive. Susan."

"Are you sure the woman you spoke with at Dulles is the Susan you met?"

"When I approached her at Dulles, at first I thought I might have made a mistake; she was standoffish. But that was because she was in a hurry to catch a flight. I never forget a face. And her voice. It was her, all right. I'm positive."

"That night at Heathrow. Did she mention anything about what she did for a living?"

"I'm afraid I don't remember. I did most of the talking that evening. I'd just broken up with a guy, and I couldn't stop talking about it. Emotional release."

"What was her destination?" Powers said.

"Good question. She said she'd been on vacation in England and was headed home. That's all I remember. . . . You haven't even shown me any identification."

"Just let me ask—"

"How do I know you're really a policeman?"

"This is a matter of national security. I have just one more question: The night you met her at Heathrow, what was her destination?"

"Germany."

"Where in Germany?"

"Frankfurt, I think. I'm sorry. I'm not going to answer any more questions unless you show me some identification."

"Just one more?"

She shook her head, stepped back, and shut the door in his face.

That Labor Day evening, the Homicide Squad room at D.C. Police Headquarters was deserted. The long rows of dingy desks were empty, and the walls were littered with wanted posters and composite drawings of black victims and murder suspects, plus a few mimeographed invitations to a police retirement party for a detective named Leroy Caradine. In the corner of the room next to Lyons's desk was a map with ten or twelve red dots at various D.C. locations and the heading BLUE CHEVY TASK FORCE.

Only one secretary was there, an attractive young woman with garishly short hair and a low-cut summer dress revealing caked talcum powder between her cleavage. She was sitting at a desk near the door, reading.

Powers asked about Lyons, and she told him he was

at the morgue and would be in shortly. He stepped into the hallway and purchased coffee from a vending machine, still picturing Landry's body lying on the garage floor.

Lyons came in a few minutes later. His eyes were baggy, red-rimmed slits. He looked surprised to see Powers.

"Have you developed any leads?" Powers said.

Lyons shook his head. "Nothing so far. By the way, thanks for notifying Landry's family."

Powers nodded. "What were the results of the autopsy?"

"The rounds were thirty-eight caliber—three, all in or near the heart. Even singly, any one of the wounds could have been mortal. The trajectories showed that he was twisting to the right when he was hit from behind."

"How do the rounds look?"

Lyons opened a three-ringed notebook on his desk. He turned pages to some blown-up color photographs of the three bullet rounds. "As you can see, two of the rounds are misshapen, but this one is in good enough condition to tie to a weapon, if we ever find it."

The phone rang. Lyons picked it up. "Yes, sir." He racked the receiver. "I have to brief the captain. It'll only take a few minutes, so make yourself at home."

"Thanks," Powers said.

Lyons crossed the room and went out the door.

Powers sat down at Lyons's desk. The secretary looked up from her reading. He smiled. She smiled back, turned a page.

He opened the binder and took out one of the copies of the photograph of the bullet round recovered during the autopsy. With one movement, he slipped it inside his jacket and under his arm. Then he stood up and walked directly past the secretary and out of the room.

*   *   *

In Fairfax, Virginia, about thirty minutes out of D.C., Powers slowed down and left the highway at Butler Road. Traffic on the opposite side of the highway had been bumper-to-bumper all the way.

Passing through the center of well-manicured suburban Fairfax, he took a right on Fargo Way, a two-lane, tree-lined road leading past a series of residential cul-de-sacs that all looked the same. After a mile or so, he turned left and climbed a slight grade. Twelve cookie-cutter two-story houses lined a short keyhole-shaped street. The garage door of the third house on the right was up. Herb Kugler was using a table saw.

Powers pulled into the wide driveway, parked, and climbed out of the car carrying an 8 × 11 manila envelope. Kugler, a youthful-looking man of sixty, brushed the OFF switch on the saw and pulled off his glasses.

"Well, look who's here," he said, coming from the garage.

They shook hands warmly. Kugler, a man of medium height, had curly gray hair, trimmed short. Though he'd been Chief of the Secret Service Forensics Division for more than thirty years, he looked more like a fit old soldier than a technician, researcher, and author of *The Guide to Modern Police Handguns*. After the assassination of President Kennedy, Kugler, at the behest of the Warren Commission, had been charged with determining whether Oswald, or anyone else, for that matter, could have fired from the window of the Dallas School Book Depository and scored two hits on a passenger seated in a moving convertible limousine.

The meticulous Kugler, enlisting the aid of medical doctors and a famous sculptor, personally constructed a mannequin out of various materials including rubber, soft plastic, and animal bones to the exact size, weight, and anatomical specifications, including brain and tissue density, of President Kennedy.

Re-creating the events of the assassination even down to using the same Secret Service driver who'd driven Kennedy on the day of the assassination, Kugler had positioned himself at the window in the book depository and fired Lee Harvey Oswald's Mannlicher Carcano rifle at the mannequin as the presidential limousine rounded the corner.

The fifty-page article he'd written for the Warren Commission, outlining his experiment and showing the similarity of Kennedy's wounds to those of the mannequin, was considered by the Commission the most telling evidence that Oswald had not only been the assassin but had acted alone.

"I heard about Ken Landry on television," Kugler said. "What happened?"

"Street robbery."

"Ken always carried his piece off-duty. I wonder if he got a chance to—"

"He got off a couple of shots, but it didn't do him any good."

"Damn. God damn. His wife and family . . . ?"

"Actually, that's why I'm here, Herb. I'd like you to take a look at some evidence."

"Certainly."

Kugler put his arm around Powers's shoulders and took him through the garage entrance to the kitchen. He led him to a dining room table and turned on a light. Powers took the photo of the spent bullet round from his inside jacket pocket and handed it to Kugler. They sat down and Kugler studied the photograph for a long time.

"How's retirement treating you, Herb?"

"I miss the Secret Service, but not some of the people in it," he said, without taking his eyes off the photograph. "Used to be every man in the outfit was on a first-name basis. The politicians respected us. The Service was an elite group. But Director Fogarty is nothing but a damn stooge for the President—any President. And for that matter, any First Lady. The man was born to bow and scrape. I'll bet he's eaten ten thousand miles of shit during his career." He smiled. "It feels good to say that without fear of being transferred to Newark."

Kugler left the table and went to the garage. He returned immediately with a Sherlock Holmes–style magnifying glass. Using the glass, he turned the photograph upside down, then sideways, holding it at arm's length.

Finally he set the photo down on the table.

"Is there anything you can tell me, other than it's a thirty-eight?" Powers said.

"I'd have to look at the round itself, of course, but from what I can tell by this photo, it looks like there's grating." He pointed. "See here? It looks like the striations have been shaved around the sides a little."

"What could cause that?"

"Shaving is usually evidence of a suppressor of some kind," he said ominously.

"A silencer."

"I'm not positive, but that's what it looks like. Is the Service handling the investigation?"

Powers shook his head. "Metro. It's being handled as a street robbery. That's why I wanted someone else to take a look at the evidence."

"This is something a criminalist might not notice right off the bat. What did Secret Service Forensics Division have to say?"

"I didn't show it to anyone there. Actually I'm no longer an agent, Herb. I took retirement."

"You what?"

"I decided to go out in the big world and try to make some real bucks."

Kugler studied him. "I always figured you for a thirty-year man," he said cautiously.

"I'm involved in this investigation because Ken was my friend."

Kugler's eyes met his. "What's going on, Jack?"

"I don't know exactly," Powers said, reaching into the flight bag. He took out the revolver and removed the newspaper covering it. "I need to know everything you can tell me about this."

Kugler rubbed his thumb across the defaced serial number. "I'll see what I can do."

"This is a . . , political chore relating to the man. So I'd rather you didn't mention—"

"No one will ever know," Kugler said, studying him.

"Thanks, friend," Powers said, coming to his feet.

"Are you in some kind of trouble, Jack?"

"I'm not sure."

"I've never heard of a street robber using a pistol silencer."

"Neither have I," Powers said. Though silencers are frequently evident in television and in motion pictures, they are seldom used in real life.

"Even the Mafia doesn't use them," Kugler said ominously.

"The silencer was invented by the CIA, wasn't it, Herb?"

"It sure as hell was."

22

At his apartment that night, Powers sat at his kitchen table and pondered what he knew. Doodling, he wrote the words *Susan* and *Frankfurt* on his note pad. Though there was a possibility Winona Alberts had been mistaken when she'd approached Marilyn at the airport, something, perhaps her levelheaded demeanor, told him to believe her. He took out the baseball team photograph James Chilcott had given him and stared at it for a long time. Having made a decision, he rummaged through a kitchen drawer until he found his American Airlines Advantage Club mileage record. Checking, he saw that he had more than enough mileage left for a free round trip to Europe.

He phoned for an airline reservation.

There was a flight leaving in two hours.

Powers arrived in Frankfurt at 10 A.M. the following day. Though there were dark clouds forming to the west, it was warm and the sun was out. During the flight he'd tried to read a newspaper and a *Time* magazine he'd purchased at the airport gift shop, but couldn't keep his concentration.

The aircraft taxied down the runway and came to a stop at the terminal. He waited until all the passen-

258

gers, tired and grouchy from the long flight, had pushed and shoved their way into the jetway. With the aisles clear, he came to his feet and followed them, moving slowly in the crowds through lines at both the customs and the immigration control points. After perfunctory questions by uniformed officials, he was allowed to pass.

At the Hertz desk he rented a car and, using a city map he found in the glove compartment, maneuvered his way to the autobahn. There he headed north, moving to the right lane frequently as speeding Mercedes-Benzes and BMWs, as if to point out he was a foreigner and unaccustomed to traveling at dangerous speeds, pulled up precariously within inches of his rear bumper and blinked headlights for him to clear the way.

At Camp Darby, he pulled up to the guard gate and showed his passport to the military policeman on duty. After the MP on duty had issued him a visitor's pass, he phoned the camp's G-2 office and determined that Sergeant Fuller had just left for lunch at the post exchange cafeteria.

Powers parked his car in the large parking lot in front of the supermarket-sized post exchange and went in. The cafeteria was inside the front door to the right. The place was filled with clusters of enlisted men in camouflage fatigue uniforms and homely, overweight women with young children and babies sitting at Formica-topped tables. The tables were set with plastic flowers, plastic ashtrays, and plastic salt and pepper shakers. And, probably because an army special order had been issued stating that the walls of all post exchange food facilities must be decorated, framed photographs of out-of-date Indianapolis race cars were hanging here and there. The place was a bedlam of mixed conversations, crying babies, and the rattle of dishes and trays. Entering, Powers wondered for a moment why soldiers would prefer to eat in such a place, as opposed to getting a free meal in a quiet company mess hall. But, as an army veteran, he knew that to soldiers any change in routine was better than an established practice.

Fuller, wearing slacks and a cheap-looking brown corduroy sport coat with an open-collar shirt, was sitting alone at a corner table smoking a filter-tipped cigarette and reading a copy of *Overseas Weekly*.

As Powers approached, Fuller came to his feet to shake hands. "What brings you back here?" he said amiably, raising his voice to be heard over the din.

"A couple of loose ends concerning that missing government employee." Powers and Fuller sat down at the table.

"Must be a flap of major proportions," Fuller said.

"What makes you say that?"

"Because you're not the first to do a follow-up," he said with a wry grin. "A few days after I helped you, I was called into the CO's office. He introduces me to Mr. Green and Mr. Jones from Berlin Station, a coupla guys who looked like they just came from a sale at Brooks Brothers," Fuller said facetiously.

"CIA."

"You got that one right, Kemo Sabe," Fuller said.

"What did they want?"

"They questioned me about helping you. At first I thought it was just a routine follow-up, but they were too cagey for it to be routine. If I asked them a question, they would turn it back to me—as if they didn't want to let some big fuggin' cat out of the bag. They were particularly interested in your executive order authority and all that. It was definitely unusual."

"Most CIA people are unusual."

"I hear you," Fuller said. He took a big drag to finish his smoke, then stubbed it in the plastic ashtray.

"A bunch of goddamn eggheads. What the hell is going on?"

"I'm not sure, but I need your help."

"You name it."

"You mentioned something about German intelligence keeping an eye on the Syrian trade mission building. Can you tell me more about that?"

"I've heard the German LfV—that's *Landesamt für Verfassungschutz*, the German equivalent of our FBI—has a permanent observation post near the trade mission. They film everybody going in or out and keep the members of the mission under surveillance, all four of them, twenty-four hours a day. We share information about what the ragheads are up to."

"Did they report any of them helping a woman?"

"They told me three of the four were out of town at the time she would have parked her car there. The fourth was home with the flu."

"Thanks, Charlie," Powers said, coming to his feet.

"This is more than just a routine White House security investigation, isn't it?"

Powers nodded and walked out to his car.

On the way to Frankfurt, Powers listened to a manic army disk jockey play popular music on the American Armed Forces Network. At the northern edge of Frankfurt, he pulled off the highway and wound through the city's eclectic mixture of wide and narrow streets, modern and ancient buildings.

The Frankfurt *Einwohnermeldeamt* was situated in the top three floors of a modern five-story building near the train station. As Powers had learned from working with the German security forces during presidential visits, every city in Germany has an *Einwohnermeldeamt*—a resident registration office. Every person in the country is required by law to register at the office, and unlike the United States, where some people even balk at answering questions for the national census, virtually everyone complies. There is such an office in each city, and the records contain limited information on every person living in every city residence.

Inside the polished first-floor lobby, Powers crossed a hallway and entered through glass doors. A line of clerks stood behind a long counter. There were short lines at each of the counter stations. Powers made a few inquiries in broken German and was referred to the clerk at the end of the counter. Powers approached the rotund woman. She was wearing a gray skirt and sweater, and her dishwater-blond hair was wrapped tightly in a bun. Powers used his broken high school German to ask about obtaining information.

"I speak English," she said officiously. There was a computer screen to her right.

"Is it possible to obtain a list of all Americans living in Frankfurt with the first name Susan?"

"Is it possible? Yes. This information it is possible to come from the computer. There will be too many names, but it is possible."

"May I—"

"Are you German?"

"No."

"It is not allowed for you."

"Do you have the information available?" Powers asked.

"Such information is available in the computer. But you are not a policeman. And you are not German. You are an *Ausländer*. This information is restricted to you."

"I'm just trying to determine if such information is available in your computer. If it is, I will go through the proper police channels to request it."

She turned and punched up the name SUSAN and, if he was right, the letters ADK and a control key. Straining his neck slightly, Powers could see the computer screen. It was filled with columns of the name SUSAN.

"Yes. There are many Susans."

"Thank you." Powers moved away, and the next person in line moved to the counter. Loitering at the other end of the lobby, he watched the other clerks as they used their computers, trying to decipher the keys that activated the print function. When he thought he had the procedure down, he left through the glass doors.

Outside, he repositioned his car three blocks away at the edge of a small park, then walked back to the *Einwohnermeldeamt* and went inside. In a hallway just outside the office itself, he sat down on a bench facing glass doors leading into the service lobby.

An hour and twenty minutes later, the woman he'd spoken with left her position. Powers stood up and went back inside. Without hesitation, he walked across the lobby to the end of the counter, stepped over the wooden gate, and punched keys on the computer. The name SUSAN appeared on the screen, then columns of full names with addresses. He punched the print key. The printer activated and began to print. Employees were staring at him. A young man with thick glasses asked in German what he was doing. Powers just stared at the man as the printed paper reached the floor. The man picked up a telephone and made a call. Finally, the machine stopped printing. The man grabbed him by the arm as if to usher him out of the work area. Powers resisted. The woman clerk hurried from across the lobby. She screamed something in German and shouted, "You go away!" over and over again, as if Powers were deaf.

Powers shoved the man aside and tore the long page from the printer. The woman and the man both tried to grab the paper out of his hands as Powers backed away. Then he turned and ran out the door. Outside, he ran around the corner and down an alley. Coming to the next street, he stopped running and walked briskly to avoid calling attention to himself on his way to the park. There, he looked around carefully to make sure no one was following him and climbed into his car.

Powers drove a few blocks and parked near a sidewalk café. He took out the list. There were more than two hundred names, each listed with a date of birth, occupation, and physical description including height, weight, and color of eyes, and a Frankfurt address.

Checking the date-of-birth column, Powers drew lines through more than three-fourths of the names. Of the remaining ones, he was able to eliminate about half by height and weight, omitting color of hair and eyes because he knew women often changed the color of their hair and that eye color was often wrong on official documents.

Finally, there were thirty-seven names remaining. For the rest of the day, using a map he purchased at a bookstore, he made his way from one location to another. He was able to eliminate the first ten locations he went to. Either the Susan was home and he would politely tell her he had the wrong address and excuse himself or, if she wasn't, he'd show the Polaroid photograph of Marilyn Kasindorf to a neighbor.

No one recognized her.

By 9 P.M. his feet and back hurt, and he was starting to have doubts about the entire endeavor. After all, he was following up a bit of information that could be totally meaningless. The name Susan was probably just a cover name Marilyn had given Winona Alberts. Or maybe Susan was a second name . . . or God only knew.

One of the last fifteen names on the list, Susan Brewster, was listed as living in apartment 403 at 8 Kohlengasse, a side street joining the wide Mainzer

Landstrasse. Kohlengasse 8 was a modern, ten-story gray-stone building, each apartment in which had its own sliding glass door leading onto a narrow balcony.

The front door of the building was open, and he entered a large lobby whose brown utilitarian carpeting he imagined had been chosen because it would easily hide winter mud stains. The walls were undecorated, and there was the strong odor of fresh paint. It was a busy place, and a steady stream of people were entering the building: a young German man, an older couple, a couple of East Indians whom Powers guessed to be university students, a tanned young German army lieutenant in dress uniform.

On the fourth floor, Powers stepped out of the elevator and moved down the hallway. At apartment 403, he touched his ear to the door. There was the sound of music coming from inside—vocalist Matt Monro singing "My Kind of Girl"—and someone was moving about, perhaps in the kitchen.

He knocked. There was the sound of footsteps.

"Wer ist da?" a woman said.

"Susan Brewster?"

The lock turned and a young woman wearing a loose-fitting purple Adidas jogging suit opened the chain-locked door a few inches. Her platinum-blond hair was in a pixie cut, and she was wearing eyeglasses with European designer frames. There was something familiar about her.

"Are you Susan Brewster?"

Because of the chain the door was only open a few inches, and she remained half-hidden. "Yes," she said.

"I'm Jack Powers. I'd like to ask you a few questions. May I come in?"

"No."

"I've come here from Washington, D.C., and I need to speak with you."

"I don't allow strangers in my apartment," she said. There was a thick nervousness in her voice. Was it Marilyn's voice? Powers's breathing quickened, and he had a sudden unexplainable sense of anxiety, an excitement he felt deep in his loins. Was it the smell of Marilyn's perfume?

"Do you know Marilyn Kasindorf?"

"No," she said quietly. "Is there anything else?" *It was Marilyn's voice.*

"Marilyn?" he said, studying her features closely.

"There is no Marilyn here." She slammed the door.

Powers, feeling heat rush to his face and limbs, stepped back and kicked the door handle powerfully. The door flew open. He stepped inside.

She was standing in the middle of the living room, her hands covering her mouth.

The facial structure, the complexion . . . "I know it's you, Marilyn."

"I don't know what you're talking about."

"You made a fool of me. You played me for a sucker."

"I don't know who you think I am, but you're wrong. Please go away."

The living room was furnished with a white Danish-modern sofa with overstuffed pillows, a lounge chair, and a wide glass coffee table. On a tile-topped island separating the kitchen from the living room was a large bowl of papier-mâché fruit in garish, almost fluorescent colors. On the wall was a large abstract tapestry: a rectangle of black and green splashes surrounded by a thick border of iridescent red.

She backed away from him fearfully. At the coffee table, she turned and grabbed a telephone receiver. "I'm going to call the police."

"Go ahead. Tell 'em you're an American CIA agent who staged her own defection and is living here under an assumed name."

"I have no idea what you're talking about. Please leave me alone. You have the wrong person."

"Do you actually think that because you've cut and dyed your hair I wouldn't know it was you?"

"Who do you think I am?"

"Marilyn Kasindorf."

"My name is Susan Brewster."

"Why aren't you dialing the police?"

She set the receiver down. "You've made a mistake. If you leave right now, I won't call the police."

He grabbed her and tore open her blouse. The scar was there on her shoulder. "A scar is a bad thing for a spy to have."

Covering herself, she pulled away from him. There was a long silence.

"What do you want from me?" she said finally, her voice cracking.

"An explanation."

"There's nothing to say."

"I fell for you, and you humiliated me."

"Please go away."

"I was forced to resign from my job."

"I'm sorry about everything," she said stiffly.

"I'm not leaving until you give it to me by the numbers," Powers said. "The whole story from beginning to end."

She cleared her throat. "Anything I say is only going to get me in trouble."

"Now. Tell me right now. I want to know exactly what the hell is going on."

"Everything I did was authorized by—"

"What's that supposed to mean?" he interrupted. "What the hell are you talking about?"

"By the . . . U.S. government. What I did was official business. That's all I'm going to say."

"Are you telling me someone ordered you to stage your own defection?"

"Yes. I'm sorry you . . . got caught up in all this. I mean that." There were tears in her eyes.

"Bullshit."

"Look, I don't know. All I was told was that I was to go to Kassel and you would be following me."

"*Why?*"

She pulled away from him, and involuntarily he drew back his fist.

"I don't *know* why!" she cried.

"Then who the hell put you up to it?"

"I can't answer that question either. You worked for the government. You should know why I can't answer."

He released her. His temples were throbbing. "Do you actually think I'm going to accept that and walk out of here?"

"No, I guess not," she said, after a long silence.

They stood there staring at each other. Finally, she sat down warily on the sofa. Powers, regretting having torn her blouse, closed the apartment door. After a while she got to her feet and headed toward the bedroom.

"Where are you going?"

"To change my blouse."

Though his first instinct was to follow proper arrest procedure and follow her into the bedroom to ensure she didn't arm herself, he just sat there. Perhaps he didn't really care if she came back with a gun and killed him.

She came back a few minutes later—without a gun but with a new blouse on—and sat down in an uphol- stered chair across from him.

"I was told you were suspected of being a spy," she said, without looking him in the eye. "That there was a leak in the White House Secret Service Detail and they were testing you by having you follow me—to see if you reported the details of your mission to the other side. Now you know what happened."

He studied her. She appeared to be telling the truth. However, he'd believed she was telling the truth in Kassel, too.

For the first time, she looked directly at him. "Would you like a glass of wine?"

He nodded.

She moved into the kitchen, opened a small refrigerator, and took out a bottle of German white wine. He watched as she pulled open a drawer and took out a corkscrew. Holding the neck of the bottle in her right hand, she turned the corkscrew into the cork and removed it from the bottle. She took two wineglasses from a cupboard and filled them. She set the bottle down on the counter and carried the glasses into the living room.

"You mean they thought I was a mole," he said.

"Yes."

"It doesn't make any sense."

"I can't help that," she said. "I just do as I'm told."

Along with the thrill of having found her, Powers was feeling a sense of dizzying confusion as his mind whirled with the possibilities. Then, almost as an involuntary reflex, he reached into his suit jacket pocket and pulled out the baseball team photograph James Chilcott had given him. He stared at it for a moment without saying anything.

"What's that?"

"Your step-brother gave it to me."

Her brow furrowed.

"Your step-brother Jim Chilcott, who lives in San Francisco." Powers leaned across the coffee table and handed her the photo.

Her expression didn't change as she examined it.

"There was something about it that's been bothering me," he continued. "And now I realize what it is. In the picture you're ready to throw the baseball with your right hand . . . but *you're* left-handed. You're not Marilyn Kasindorf!"

She set the photograph down on the coffee table. Then she removed her eyeglasses and wiped her eyes.

"You resemble her, and when your hair is dyed and you're made up like her it's hard to tell the difference, but *you're not her.*"

She turned away.

"Who are you?"

"Susan Brewster is my real name."

"Where is Marilyn Kasindorf?"

"I have no idea."

23

Powers's heart was pounding heavily.

"You've never met her?"

"Never."

Powers let out his breath. "Well, I'll be goddamned."

"I thought there was something wrong with the mission from the beginning," Susan said. "It sounded too complicated."

"The mission . . . ?"

"I signed a paper years ago promising to never reveal operational facts," she told him. "They said I could be prosecuted."

"The only way I'm going to be able to figure out what the hell is going on is if you tell me what you know."

"I'm a flight attendant," she said softly. "A few years ago I was recruited by a pilot to help the CIA with a few small intelligence chores. It sounded exciting and I agreed. I was given some training, the usual trade craft. My first assignments were simple ones: to mail letters from certain cities I fly to, or rent apartments here and there and mail the keys to an accommodation address. I never knew the ramifications of any of this and I never asked. I liked the extra money and, besides, I thought I was doing something worthwhile for the country."

Amazed, Powers sat back. "Who assigned you the missions?"

"Different CIA people. I never knew their real names. After a couple of years I was told that my name was being put in the Inter-Agency Source Index. I filled out a detailed questionnaire and took some photos for the computer, so that any government agency could use me according to the needs of a particular mission. From then on I never met anyone. I would get the mission by phone. Once the FBI asked me to stop by a gallery in Amsterdam and inquire about a painting they thought had been stolen from the Metropolitan Museum of Art."

"How did you get the assignment to impersonate Marilyn Kasindorf?"

"On August twelfth I flew into Dulles Airport from London on a Lufthansa flight. There was a message waiting for me at the flight desk to call 'Cousin Sandy' at a local number. 'Cousin Sandy' was the code that someone had a mission for me. I phoned the number and a man told me I'd been picked from the Inter-Agency Source Index because I had a close physical resemblance to a CIA agent named Marilyn Kasindorf. Also, I had a working knowledge of art, a subject she was familiar with. I was directed to an airport rental locker. In it was a color photograph of Kasindorf and some biographical information. I was told to dye my hair and make myself up like her, then check in at the Dupont Hotel and wait for further instructions. Over the next few days, he would call and tell me to go places: the French restaurant La Serre, the apartment house on Scott Circle, some buildings with government offices. I spotted you following me."

"You weren't living in the apartment on Scott Circle?"

She shook her head. "No. Sometimes he instructed me to go in the front and out the back, other times to come in the back and out the front. I never went into any apartment."

Powers ran a hand through his hair. "The lights in the apartment must have been on a timer," he ruminated.

"In Germany I followed the scenario he gave me the same way."

"And he told you to compromise me."

"He said you were suspected of working for hostile intelligence, and the purpose of the mission was to test your loyalty. What happened between us started as an act, a mission. Then, I don't know exactly why or how, but I could tell you weren't a spy. I liked you. . . . I hope you can understand what I'm trying to say. . . . Oh, hell." She covered her eyes with her hands.

Powers drained his glass.

"The morning you left?"

"I was told to park my rental car in front of a building on Erlangen Strasse and then walk to my apartment. That's what I did."

"Slick."

"Look, I'm really sorry for the problems this caused you," she said. "I know now that the suspicions they had about you were wrong."

"How did you verify that you were being activated by the proper people?" he asked.

"There's a code, a series of numbers they read off when they call. . . . Why are you asking me this? You must know how the Source Index works. You don't believe a word I'm saying, do you?"

He returned her stare.

"I guess I can't blame you for that," Susan said. She got to her feet and moved onto the balcony. He followed her. "When I was first recruited it was thrilling—leading a secret life, and all that." She put her hands on the balcony rail. "I never thought I'd be ashamed. But I am."

"Both of us were used," he said quietly.

She turned to him. "What did all this accomplish? Who benefited?"

"I have a better question," Powers said. "Where is the real Marilyn Kasindorf?"

"I don't know." She paused. "What are you going to do now?"

He shrugged.

She wiped her eyes. "Would you like another glass of wine?"

He nodded.

Susan picked up the bottle from the kitchen counter and poured.

"If you'd like, I can fix dinner while we talk," she said, avoiding eye contact.

"Okay."

For the next hour or so, as she moved around the kitchen preparing dinner, he sat at the table asking questions and making notes. The note-taking continued through a dinner of *Zigeuner schnitzel*—a sweet-and-sour red cabbage—and warm potato salad. By dessert—apple strudel, with a thick whipped cream she called *Schlag*—he finally understood exactly how the defection had been staged. But in the Byzantium that was Washington, Powers understood that knowing *what* had happened was only the beginning. It was always the *why* rather than the *how* that mattered. After all, they'd both been acting on orders. They'd both been used. In fact, she hadn't betrayed him—or the country or anyone else, for that matter. Like him, she'd simply been carrying out a mission.

Somehow, during the course of the meal, though he felt drained and confused, he came to terms with what she had done.

After dinner Susan busied herself in the kitchen, perhaps to avoid him, and Powers strolled out onto the balcony. The traffic noise had subsided and, below, Frankfurt had become a tapestry of blacks and grays held together by dots of light. From the east came the distant sound of a jet. He'd found her, and she wasn't Marilyn Kasindorf. But she was still the woman he'd fallen in love with.

Later, he smelled her perfume as she joined him on the balcony.

"I guess I should be going," he said, without looking at her.

"I never thought I'd see you again, Jack."

"I haven't been able to get you off my mind," he said with difficulty.

He felt her hand touch his. He turned and took her in his arms, and they embraced. She met his lips forcefully.

In bed, they made love for a long time.

Afterward they lay in each other's arms, talking quietly for what must have been hours. Finally, there were no more secrets between them. When he finally closed his eyes and dropped off to sleep, she was in his arms.

Powers woke about nine the next morning, feeling more rested and refreshed than he had in months. He realized he was alone in bed and sat up quickly. He climbed out of bed and moved to the bedroom door. The smell of coffee was coming from the kitchen, and Susan (he almost thought "Marilyn") was standing at the stove cooking breakfast. Relieved, he let out his breath.

In the bathroom he showered, shaved, and dressed. In the kitchen, he put his arms around her waist and kissed her neck.

"You were talking in your sleep," she said.

"What did I say?"

"You said 'Watch out!' as if you were warning someone."

During breakfast they chatted amiably, avoiding any discussion of what had happened in Kassel, and he found himself becoming relaxed and at ease with her again. Finally the small talk was over, and there was an uncomfortable silence.

"What is this all about?" she asked. "What is this really all about?"

"As I see it, either Marilyn Kasindorf used you to stage her own defection, or the CIA engineered the disappearance as part of . . . some bigger plan."

"Why a staged defection?"

"To cover up for something—a smokescreen, perhaps. I'll find out. This is some kind of renegade operation."

"How can you tell?"

"I'm privy to certain things," Powers said.

"I never thought I'd be involved in— What are you going to do?"

"I want you to come back to Washington with me."

"Jack, I signed a secrecy oath."

"I think someone is trying to destroy the President," Powers said, looking her in the eye. "I need you to help me prove it."

"I had a feeling about this mission," she said, after a while. "When I met you, I could see you weren't up to anything. You were just doing your job."

After breakfast, Powers phoned the Frankfurt airport and reserved two seats on a flight to Washington departing at 2 P.M. Because they had a little time to kill, at Susan's suggestion they left the apartment house and took a short walk. Though Powers was tense and preoccupied, he found comfort in talking and holding hands. On the way back to Susan's place, Powers admitted to himself a feeling he'd never had with any woman in his life before: He never wanted to be without her again.

Arriving at the apartment, Powers sauntered onto the balcony. It was a sunny day, and the air was filled with the sound of traffic rising from the street below. Across the street a hefty middle-aged woman was standing at a streetcar stop. She was wearing a scarf and a faded, long-sleeved flower-print dress. In her left hand she was holding a fishnet shopping bag by the handle. She raised a handkerchief to her nose and mouth, then lowered it.

Down a few doors on the east side of the street was a green BMW sedan, parked at the curb. A man with slick black hair was sitting behind the wheel. In the opposite direction on the south side of the street was another sedan, with a single male occupant.

A streetcar arrived at the stop. Its doors opened, and a few passengers climbed off and moved along the sidewalk in various directions. The doors closed; the *Strassenbahn* pulled away and continued down the street.

The woman was still there.

A few minutes later, Susan joined him on the balcony. "You're so quiet."

The woman lifted the handkerchief to her lips. Her mouth moved. Her hand returned to her pocket.

"Go inside and get me a drink, then come back out here and hand it to me," he said, without taking his eyes off the street.

"Is something wrong?"

"I'm not sure."

She gave him a puzzled expression and left the balcony.

The woman lifted the handkerchief to her face, then put it down.

Another streetcar arrived and left and the woman was still standing there.

Susan returned to the balcony with a glass of wine and handed it to Powers. The woman on the street lifted her handkerchief.

Powers put his arm around Susan and turned her to him. "That woman is using a hand-held microphone," he said, smiling in case any of the surveillants was using binoculars. "We're under surveillance." He led her inside and pulled the curtains closed.

24

Who do you think it is?" she said fearfully.

"I don't know, but we're not safe here. Pack a bag."

In the bedroom, as Susan shoved some clothes into a blue Lufthansa suitcase and filled a makeup case, Powers unplugged the lamps on either side of the dressing table and removed the shades. To the harp of one lamp he attached a round Styrofoam wig-holder he found in the closet. To the other, he wrapped a bed sheet into a human head-sized ball. Foraging through drawers in the bedroom and the kitchen, he found some yellow yarn, a feather duster, and some household glue. Using generous amounts of the glue, he pasted the yarn on top of one lamp and feathers from the duster on the other.

"What are you doing?" she said.

"Buying time."

He carried the lamps into the living room and set them on the sofa side by side, so that just an inch or two of the camouflage hair showed over the backrest. He turned on the television, and adjusted the dimmer switch on the living room lamp to its minimum. With the back of the sofa facing the balcony as it was, from outside he hoped the dummies would, given the dimness of the room, look like silhouettes of him and Susan sitting on the sofa watching television.

He led Susan out the door into the hallway.

He moved to the curtain, pulled the cord to fully open it, and walked quickly in front of the sofa. Lowering himself down below the level of the backrest, where he knew he was out of sight of anyone watching him, he low-crawled out the door.

She touched his arm. "Who are they? Who's watching us?"

"We'll find out in D.C." He picked up her suitcase. "Do you have a car?"

"No."

"Is there a rear exit to this building?"

"Only a fire door in the underground garage."

He led her to the elevator.

At the apartment house's rear exit, they followed an alley for the entire length of the block. They entered the rear of another apartment house, hurried through a storage and heating room, a dingy lobby, and onto a cobblestoned street lined with small shops. Walking briskly along back alleys and through parking lots, Susan led him to the Frankfurt train station.

Inside the terminal, Powers checked the train schedule. It was fifteen minutes before the next train to the airport. He purchased two tickets, and they sat down on a bench near the door to catch their breath.

Susan pointed. "Look," she said, indicating the entrance.

The woman wearing the scarf who'd been standing across from the apartment was now standing inside the door, looking about for them while cleverly obscuring herself among a bustling crowd of passengers. An obvious professional, Powers guessed that she worked for an intelligence rather than a law enforcement agency.

"Damn," he said.

"What are we going to do?" Susan said.

The woman, having spotted them, sat down dispassionately on a bench.

A train pulled into the station. The sign on the side read WÜRZBURG/BAYREUTH/BAD NEUSTADT.

The train announcer said something in German, in French, and then in broken English. "The fast train to Würzburg is departing from track nine. All aboard, please."

"I don't see anyone else. If she's part of a surveillance team, they probably haven't caught up to her yet," Powers said. He picked up the luggage. "Follow me."

"Our train isn't here yet," she said, following him toward the Würzburg train.

He helped her onto the train. They entered the first empty compartment and set the luggage down.

The woman with the scarf hurried toward the train and joined the crowd funneling into the aft car door. The moment she had stepped inside, Powers grabbed Susan's hand and pulled her out of the car.

"Take a taxi to the airport and meet me at the American Airlines ticket counter," he said. "Go."

She backed away a couple of steps and hurried into the crowd. Powers stepped back onto the train.

Peeking through the window in the interior door, Powers could see the broad-shouldered woman moving up and down the aisle, searching. She spotted the suitcases in the compartment and, shoving her way past passengers, moved frantically down the aisle in his direction.

The ten-second warning buzzer sounded. Powers stepped off the train. The train's hydraulic brakes hissed and the train began to move.

The woman burst from the interior door to disembark.

Using a straight-arm, Powers shoved her back inside. The doors closed, and he jumped back. The train pulled away. Powers ran past train platforms and out the door. For a few minutes, he waited nervously in a taxi line.

At Frankfurt International Airport, Susan was waiting for him at the airport ticket counter. Before they boarded the aircraft, Powers phoned Herb Kugler and asked him to meet them on arrival.

The flight from Frankfurt to Dulles Airport was only half-full. They talked nonstop through the airplane movie: a comedy about a rich Wall Street broker who drinks a magic potion and becomes a southern plantation slave.

"I've lived in Germany for the last ten years," she said. "I majored in art at the Anton Feder Institute. It's a big art school here. Being a flight attendant was perfect for me. I'd fly for a few days and have a week to paint."

Powers found himself telling her about his childhood in Monterey, California—how during the summers he worked on his father's fishing boat. In high school, he'd been a member of both the cross-country and the gymnastics teams, and had had little interest in scholarly endeavors. In 1970, rather than flee to Canada or hide from the Vietnam draft by joining the National Guard as a lot of his pals on the gymnastics team had done, he'd quit his criminology classes at Pacific Grove Community College and enlisted in the army. After a combat tour in Vietnam as an infantryman, he completed a bachelor's degree in Law Enforcement at San Francisco State College.

"The classes were boring," he said. "Studying police administrative procedures and law of evidence. Because there is no way you can actually teach someone to be a law-enforcement officer, all the classes repeated themselves. It was like studying for four years on how to be a mail carrier."

"I can see you in college in those days," she said sarcastically.

"I didn't care much for the hippies," he said. "But who was I to fight the Age of Aquarius?"

Powers woke up as the aircraft touched down at Dulles Airport. In the early dark, a pall of rain-filled clouds hugged the countryside.

Powers and Susan had their passports stamped and passed the customs-control point. Herb Kugler was waiting in the baggage area. Powers introduced him to Susan.

"You can talk freely," Powers said to the reticent Kugler.

"I was able to raise a serial number on the gun. The trace shows it was purchased from a sporting goods store in San Francisco about a year ago by someone named Daniel McVey. I ran his driver's license number and it comes back to a mail drop, an accommodation address. McVey has no criminal or credit history. He doesn't exist."

"Sounds like whoever purchased the gun was using a phony license."

"That's the way I see it."

"CIA?"

"The serial numbers of all their guns usually trace to gun stores in Indiana, for some reason. If anyone checks, the trail dies then and there. But for what it's worth, I remember a political assassination that occurred in the Caribbean a few years ago. A gun was recovered and, unless I'm mistaken, it had been purchased in a similar way in San Francisco. It was traced to a Syrian military attaché assigned to the San Francisco consulate."

"Thanks, Herb. I appreciate the help."

"By the way," Kugler said. "I know of cases where the CIA has obtained weapons using methods that would throw suspicion on other intelligence services. They're into all that sleight-of-hand Yale-and-Harvard crapola."

Powers nodded.

"Can I give you two a ride somewhere?"

"No thanks, Herb."

"You know where to reach me," Kugler said. He told Susan it was nice to meet her and walked away into the crowd.

Powers dropped change into a pay phone and dialed.

"White House Signal," the operator said.

"This is Jack Powers. Please connect me with Deputy Director Sullivan."

"He's at the White House. I'll connect you." The line clicked twice.

The line clicked three times and Sullivan came on the line. "We need to talk," Powers said.

"What is it, Jack?" Sullivan said warily.

"I want you to meet someone. That's all I can say over the phone."

There was a pause.

"I can't get away for an hour. Say eight P.M., at The Rustic Inn?"

"See you there," Powers said. He set the receiver down.

"Where are we going?" Susan asked.

"To rent a car and meet Sullivan."

"Who's Sullivan?"

"The Deputy Director of the Secret Service."

About fifteen minutes out of Washington, near Great Falls Park, Powers pulled off Highway 190 onto a wooded road following the Potomac River. After a half mile or so, he reached a large wooden sign that read THE RUSTIC INN. Powers made a sharp turn and pulled into a rectangle-shaped parking lot filled with cars.

Powers and Susan climbed out of the car. It was a warm night, with a smell of rain in the air. They followed some garden lights to a path that ascended some inlaid rock steps and wound up at the restaurant itself. Only the muffled restaurant sounds, gaining in intensity as they continued upward, could be heard.

The restaurant, a one-story, half-timbered traditional structure, was situated in a natural clearing. Inside, the walls were covered with antique kitsch and there were potbellied stoves and false-front fireplaces here and there for decoration. One of a nationwide chain of restaurants, it was neither genuinely rustic (the potbellied stoves being only for decoration) nor an inn.

Most of the forty or so tables were filled—a middle-class family crowd. Few men wore neckties. Powers figured Sullivan had picked the place because it was out of the circle of D.C. places frequented by Secret Service agents.

A sallow young woman wearing a gingham uniform dress greeted them at the door and showed them to a booth in the corner. She took drink orders and left.

At eight-thirty Sullivan came in the door. Spotting them immediately, he moved to the table. Powers introduced him to Susan. Sullivan sat down. There was a mist of perspiration across his upper lip. "Sorry I'm late," he said, staring at Susan.

"I'd like you to meet Susan Brewster," Powers said.

"How do you do," Sullivan said warily.

"Susan is the woman I knew as Marilyn Kasindorf," Powers said.

"I'm afraid I don't—"

"Susan is the woman I followed to Kassel. She was impersonating Marilyn Kasindorf."

"You mean . . . ?"

"I've been an agency asset for years. I'm a flight attendant, and I've been called on for a lot of routine chores."

"She's activated by a phone cut-out."

"The Inter-Agency Source Index," Sullivan said.

"Exactly."

"And your handler asked you to impersonate Marilyn Kasindorf?"

"Sent me the money and faxed me a photograph of her, so I could make myself up to look like her."

"Jesus," Sullivan said. "Jesus, Mary, and Joseph . . . Who . . . who gave you the assignment?"

"I don't know," she said. "I've never known the identity of my handlers."

"I've been through everything with her," Powers said. "She was given the assignment by phone, and has no idea who activated her for the mission."

The waitress came to the table and Sullivan ordered a drink. She left.

Powers cleared his throat. "And there's something else. The bullets found in Ken Landry's body had been fired through a silencer."

"Who said that?"

"Herb Kugler," Powers said. "Landry was killed by a professional."

"Why . . . why would someone want to kill Landry?"

"Ken found a bug in the White House Special Projects Office. Someone—a White House insider—was keeping tabs on Marilyn Kasindorf's activities; I found a bug in her apartment. And something else: We've been followed by a professional surveillance team. I think they're CIA."

Sullivan started to speak but, looking at Susan, stopped abruptly.

"You can talk in front of Susan," Powers said. "She was used just like we were."

Sullivan wiped moisture from his upper lip. "I guess that brings us to the big question: What the hell do we do now?"

"I know what I would do. I'd walk right into the Oval Office."

Sullivan nodded. "I know this President. The first thing he's gonna do is ask, 'What's the bottom line? What the hell is it all about?' Can you give him an answer?"

Powers shook his head.

"Neither can I," Sullivan said. He inhaled and let out his breath. "The President is going to Camp David tonight and will remain there preparing for the election debates. He knows—everybody knows—that if the boat gets rocked even a little at this point he'll lose the election." Sullivan's face was stony. "We're talking a possible coup."

"What are you going to do?" Powers said.

"Brief the President. The problem is, I'm not sure he'll buy what I tell him. He'll ask me for proof, and there is none."

"Landry is proof."

"As far as the police are concerned, Landry was killed in a street robbery," Sullivan said. "The President might think I'm lying . . . or crazy."

"You have us as witnesses."

"I'll need you two somewhere where I can reach you," Sullivan said.

"It's too dangerous to go back to my apartment. I'll register at the Ramada," Powers said.

"I'll contact you there," Sullivan said. He shook hands with Susan, then offered his hand to Powers.

"Good luck," Powers said.

"I'll need it."

They shook hands tightly; Powers sensed the tension. Sullivan pushed his chair back and left the restaurant.

"I sense something terrible," Susan said. "I can feel it."

"My guess is we're going to be called into the President's office and asked to explain what we know," Powers said. "We have to keep our heads."

She nodded. He kissed her on the cheek. They chatted nervously for the next few minutes and Powers, aware that the President thrived on facts and hated supposition, advised her not to volunteer any theories when he questioned her. Powers checked his watch.

"Let's go," he said.

With Susan at his side, Powers walked past tables and booths. As they reached the doorway, a strapping man with the build of a heavyweight wrestler and a tall, broad-shouldered woman with dark eyes stood up from their seats at a table in the corner. The man had a dark trimmed beard and mustache and was dressed in Levi's and a loose-flowing plaid shirt. He had a dark olive complexion—Italian or possibly Lebanese. The woman, whose hair was wrapped in a bun, wore a green blouse and a pleated skirt with embroidered trim. She was carrying a leather purse with a long shoulder strap. If Powers recalled correctly, the couple had entered the restaurant shortly after he and Susan had arrived.

As Powers paid the bill, the couple took their time at the door. Were they stalling to allow him to leave first?

Powers knew a number of things about people who are carrying concealed weapons. Even with those who are accustomed to being armed, a certain self-consciousness invariably evidences itself. With those who carry weapons at the waist it's a way of walking that favors the opposite side from the gun, and a frequent touching of one's coat or jacket to sense if the gun is protruding indiscreetly. With women who carry a gun in a purse, it's the way the hand grips the strap, always where it attaches to the purse, to steady it from tilting from the weight of the gun. Though Powers admitted it might be his imagination, he believed the man and woman were armed.

Without being obvious, Powers reached for the door handle and pulled. He stopped Susan, smiled, and held the door open wide for the couple. Exiting, the man forced a smile. The woman followed, holding her arm crooked, grasping the purse strap.

In the darkness outside, Powers took Susan's arm and they began slowly descending the path toward the parking lot. A light mist of rain was filtering from the darkness, and the branches of the tall trees spanning the path were dripping.

The only sound was footsteps. The couple was about thirty yards ahead of them, descending the steps. Powers felt something cold land on the back of his neck: rain dripping from a tree branch.

At about the midpoint between the restaurant and the parking lot, there was no light other than the bulbs illuminating the footpath. The sound of the footsteps stopped. Powers stopped too, grasping Susan's arm firmly.

"What's wrong?"

Powers touched a finger to her lips.

Snap-click.

The sound had come from below—unmistakably the slide of an automatic pistol being pulled back to chamber a round. Another *snap-click*. There were two guns.

25

Powers pulled Susan off the path and into the forest. Moving in total darkness, with his right hand in front of him to keep from running into a tree trunk, he headed away from the path.

"Stand here and don't move," he whispered, shoving her behind a tree.

"What's happening?"

"Just don't move," he whispered. "No matter what happens, stay right here." Powers moved away from her and took a position behind another tree. He remembered his Secret Service training: *If you wait for them to come get you, you're finished. If the protectee is secure, attack the danger.* Unfortunately, the instructor hadn't told them how to do this when unarmed.

In the weak illumination provided by the footlights along the path, two shadows moved up the steps. Suddenly a flashlight beam pierced the forest in their direction. Powers tensed, and for a moment he asked himself what had brought him here. Why had he joined the army and then the Secret Service, instead of becoming a fisherman in Monterey with his dad? But he'd always drawn himself into harm's way. The path of his life had led him to be standing in the woods near The Rustic Inn, waiting to get killed. For a split second, rather than seeing his life flash before him as people often say who know nothing about it, Powers saw what he'd seen before, in Vietnam and other times he'd been shot at: his death. Then suddenly, in a warm wave of self-mastery reminding him of the first day he'd been shot at in Vietnam, the emotions of fear and rage and revenge, the urge to protect and the urge to kill and control, meshed with the locus of his reasoning. Fear and doubt were supplanted by eye-darting, muscle-tensing, primal anger, that peculiar vision-sharpening, adrenaline-pumping, last-stand acuity that comes when life is threatened: when one must kill or be killed.

"Powers, where are you?" the man with the flashlight said, moving in their direction. The woman was walking behind him. She too had a flashlight. They knew that Powers, having come through airport security checks, was unarmed. Staying behind the tree to remain hidden from view, Powers dropped to his knees.

The man's flashlight beam moved from side to side on the ground, coming in his direction.

In the darkness, Powers patted the leaf-covered ground frantically. His hand hit something hard. A rock. A sharp rock the size of a baseball. Using both hands, and praying they wouldn't hear him, he freed it from the earth and stood up.

The flashlights were moving closer.

"Powers, we need to talk with you," the man said. "We're friends."

Powers's eyes were darting . . . and for a second, perhaps just a split second, the woman's flashlight passed over the right hand of the man in front of her.

The man was holding an automatic in the combat-ready position. He was about thirty feet away. Confident that the darkness would hide him, Powers moved toward him. As the flashlight beam neared his feet, he sprang forward and, with all the force he could muster, brought the rock down on the man's head. *Thwack!* The man shrieked. Powers yanked the gun from his hand. It fired; there was a fire flash past his face. Powers dove instinctively for the ground with the gun in his hand, rolled, and stopped. He held his breath.

"Nicky?" the woman called.

Powers took cover behind a tree. The man's flashlight was lying beside him, its beam shining only a few feet to the trunk of a tree.

"He has my gun!" Nicky moaned.

The woman's flashlight went out immediately. She hadn't panicked and fired into the darkness. Clearly, she was military-trained. With the tree cover acting as a roof, there was total blackness except for Nicky's flashlight. Powers dropped to the ground and began low-crawling toward the flashlight. Without it, he'd never have the advantage. There was a sound of crunching leaves. Powers figured the woman was probably taking cover behind a tree. In the darkness, his fingers sought the outline of the gun. It was a Colt .45. He could tell it was cocked. The slide had been pulled and it was ready to fire. Holding the gun in his right hand, and surmising that she wouldn't risk using her flashlight again, Powers low-crawled slowly from behind the tree to within a foot or two of the flashlight. He took a deep breath and snatched the flashlight from the ground. A shot rang out as he dove behind a tree, fumbling frantically to find the OFF switch on the flashlight. Another shot thudded into the trunk. Finally, he clicked off the light.

"Jack!" Susan cried out fearfully.

"Stay where you are!" he shouted.

A shot rang out, and there was another *thump* as the round slammed into the tree. Figuring her partner was on the ground, the woman had fired at torso level to get Powers to move . . . so she could line him up in a flashlight beam for the kill.

Nicky moaned. There was the sound of leaves rustling. Nicky was coming to his feet, staggering. "Where are you?" he said groggily.

Seeing his opportunity, Powers ducked low. Moving from tree to tree to maintain cover, Powers followed the sound of Nicky's footsteps. Creeping on the balls of his feet to catch up, Powers maneuvered to a position directly behind him.

"Don't shoot!" Powers shouted, shoving Nicky violently forward toward her and diving to the right.

Rapid-fire gunshots lit the woman's silhouette as she fired. There was a wet sound as Nicky was slammed backward and down, as if punched in the stomach with a sledgehammer.

Now Powers knew where she was.

"Nicky, I got him."

Maintaining his cover behind a tree, Powers readied his finger on the flashlight's ON switch and aimed the automatic in the direction of the woman. He flipped on the switch, and the flashlight beam found her. Aiming instinctively at center body mass as he'd been taught at the training academy, Powers fired twice. The woman flipped backward.

His ears were ringing.

Keeping the flashlight beam on her, Powers moved forward cautiously and aimed the light. Her eyes and mouth were open in death. He moved the beam of the light around quickly, focusing on the male lying in the fetal position, unmoving. His head was bloody, and there was white foam at his mouth. He too was dead.

Powers moved to him and, steadying the flashlight under his arm, searched him. There was no pocket litter of any kind. The woman's purse was lying nearby. Powers opened it. It contained only cash, about a hundred dollars.

Using the flashlight to guide him, Powers hurried back to Susan. She threw her arms around him.

"It's okay," Powers said, pulling her with him back through the forest toward the footpath.

At the steps, he paused for a moment to see if anyone in the restaurant had heard the shots. There was no movement near the restaurant, and only the sound of music. He flicked the safety lever on the automatic and shoved it in his waistband. Still carrying the flashlight, he grasped Susan's hand tightly and hurried down the steps.

"Where are we going?"

"Away from here."

"What about the police?"

"I just killed two people. If I tell the truth, the President is finished. If I lie, I'll get booked for murder. It'd be weeks before I could explain what happened."

In the car, they were both out of breath. Powers started the engine and sped out of the lot onto the highway.

26

In Washington the streets were wet with rain. Powers pulled into the parking lot of the Decatur Hotel.

"I thought we were going to the Ramada."

"*I'm* going to the Ramada. You're staying here."

"You don't trust Sullivan?"

"At this point I don't trust anybody."

The lobby of the Decatur was furnished with well-used leather sofas and polished wood, like some venerable men's club. Powers entered arm-in-arm with Susan and crossed the lobby to a reception desk. In the adjacent bar area, a well-dressed, gray-haired man was playing Chopin on a baby grand piano.

"Do you have a double room available?" Powers said to a well-groomed young man wearing a dark tailored suit.

"Certainly," he said, sliding a registration card across the counter.

Powers signed *John and Kathy Ames* and listed a phony Montreal, Canada, address.

"How was the weather in Montreal?" the clerk said.

"We've been having a nice summer."

"Have you any luggage?"

"Unfortunately, it was stolen at Dulles Airport."

"I'm sorry to hear that."

Powers smiled pleasantly. The man smiled back, reached into a drawer, and handed Powers a large brass key.

A young olive-skinned bellman led them to their room. Powers tipped him. The bellman left.

"You and I are the only ones who know about this place, so you should be safe here."

"Where are you going?"

"To wait for Sullivan." Powers pulled the gun from his belt and handed it to her. "Stay in the room. And don't be afraid to use this if you have to."

They embraced and she held him tightly. "Please be careful, Jack."

The Farragut Ramada, a modern three-story rectangle of glass and steel, was located three blocks away from the Decatur. Set back from the roadway on well-manicured grounds, it could just as easily have been the Marriott in Cleveland or the Sheraton in Los Angeles. Powers had spent lots of time guarding various foreign dignitaries who stayed there, and knew the layout of the interior and the exterior in detail.

At the registration desk, Powers informed the clerk he was expecting a call. For the next half hour he lounged about the lobby, moving from the bar to the coffee shop to the lobby and restaurant to kill time. Finally, at 10 P.M., he walked to a bank of pay phones in the corner of the lobby. Picking up a receiver, he dialed a number he knew by heart.

"White House Signal."

"Deputy Director Peter Sullivan," Powers said to the operator.

"Mr. Sullivan is on sick leave."

"Pardon me?"

"Someone came and signed him out a couple of hours ago."

"Are you absolutely sure he's nowhere in the House?" Powers said.

"Positive, sir."

Powers, feeling slightly dizzy, set the receiver on its hook for a moment.

Referring to an emergency phone number card he kept in his wallet, Powers phoned Sullivan's Fairfax residence. There was no answer. Then he phoned the Secret Service headquarters. An operator informed him that Sullivan's name wasn't on the locator board—which meant he wasn't on-duty. Powers, feeling both stunned and angry, set the receiver down. Consciously restraining his emotions, he analyzed the situation: Sullivan, the most meticulous man he'd ever known, would have phoned him—unless something was wrong. For all Powers knew, there had been other assassins outside The Rustic Inn waiting for Sullivan. Or, God only knew, perhaps Sullivan had been hiding something from him all along.

Powers moved deliberately across the lobby to the front door.

A group of Japanese tourists were climbing off a bus. Powers walked outside and stepped to the left of the doorway. A balding man wearing a nylon baseball jacket—the below-the-waist length favored by police detectives and others who carry guns—came out the door and looked about. Spotting Powers, he busied himself and checked his watch, then returned inside.

Across the street, a brown BMW was parked in front of a dry cleaner. There were two men sitting in it.

Powers stood there for what must have been a full minute. He swallowed twice and took a deep breath. He knew what he had to do.

Steeling himself, Powers turned and walked back into the lobby. Formulating his plan as he walked, he headed into an open elevator car. The door closed. He pressed the first-floor button and the car ascended. The elevator door opened and he stepped into a hallway lined with guest rooms. Powers broke into a full run. At the far end of the hallway, he burst through the fire exit door and hurried down the steps three at a time. At the lobby floor, breathing hard, he peeked out the door. The man in the baseball jacket was stepping onto the elevator.

Powers sprinted along a service corridor and into the hotel kitchen. Continuing past three chefs working at a metal table, he ran out the back door into a small parking lot and vaulted over a wall. Making his way across three commercial dumpsters, he jumped down and made his way to the next street.

Using alleys and avoiding sidewalks to keep hidden from the street, he wound a circuitous route to M Street. Across from the Finnish Embassy, he pushed open the heavy wooden door of Mistral, an exclusive French restaurant. In every presidential administration, at least one French restaurant becomes known as the "in" place for key members of the White House staff. In the current administration, it was Mistral. Its latticework hand-embroidered tablecloths and gold-plated silverware had become familiar layouts in more than one major magazine.

The tuxedoed maître d', Roget Lorraine, a lanky Frenchman with deep-set eyes and a pencil-thin mustache, was at the desk.

"Agent Powers. Is the President . . . ?"

"No, I'm looking for the Press Secretary."

He pointed to the corner table. "Mr. Eggleston has almost finished his dinner. He's at his usual table."

Powers moved past a long, well-stocked bar and black leather booths filled with well-dressed men and women. The walls were covered with flower prints.

Richard Eggleston, in an unwrinkled suit and tie, was sitting in the second booth from the window between two conservatively dressed women who were his secretaries. The women greeted Powers as he approached the table. Eggleston seemed suddenly ill at ease.

"Jack. I didn't get a chance to wish you well before you . . . uh . . . retired."

"I'm sorry to interrupt your dinner, but I need to speak with you in private."

Eggleston excused himself from the table and followed Powers to the front door.

"Where are we going?"

"Would you mind if we talk outside?"

"This must be a real doosie."

Eggleston followed him out the door cautiously. "What's up, Jack?"

"I need a meeting with the President," Powers said, looking Eggleston in the eye.

Eggleston started to smile, then stopped when he saw Powers wasn't joking. "What about?"

"About the national security."

"Jack, you've been around long enough to know it'll take more than that to get a meeting with the man."

"I know this is going to sound crazy, but I have good reason to believe there is a plot to undermine the President."

"By whom?"

"By someone with high access."

"Can you give me a name?"

"I don't know who, but I think the President will figure it out once I tell him what I know."

"You know how this works, Jack. The Chief of Staff is the only one who can set up the meeting you want."

"I'm asking you to set up a meeting without going through Morgan. I have to speak with the President one-on-one."

"I can't do that."

"Look. You've known me since this administration

came to the White House. I'm not crazy and I'm not an alarmist," Powers said.

Eggleston realized he was holding a cloth napkin and shoved it in his suit coat pocket. "The President is headed for Camp David to prepare for the election debates, and you expect me to go rushing in to him with something I don't understand?"

"I need to speak with the President on a matter affecting the national security," Powers said, gritting his teeth. "Do you understand that?"

"Jack, you're not a special agent any longer. Can't you just tell me and I'll relay it, word-for-word? I promise."

"No. It's too sensitive."

"Then you can write it down and I'll take the note straight to him."

"Listen to me," Powers interrupted. "I took care of a political chore for the President, and now someone is trying to kill me and Pete Sullivan is missing. If you don't let me talk to him you'll be responsible when everything blows up in his face."

"You say someone is trying to kill you?"

"Yes. And Sullivan may be in danger."

"I see."

"Don't look at me like I'm some goddamn lunatic. There's nothing wrong with me. I'm not crazy. Just phone the President. He'll know what I'm talking about. If you tell him exactly what I've said, I know he'll agree to see me."

Eggleston rubbed his chin for a moment.

"Look at me," Powers said. "I'm not crazy."

Eggleston looked him in the eyes. "I'll make the call," he said finally.

Eggleston went back inside the restaurant. Powers paced back and forth on the sidewalk for what must have been ten minutes. Finally, he said to himself, the nightmare will be over. The President will provide the missing facts, and everything will make sense.

The door swooshed open with a blast of restaurant air. Eggleston stepped out cautiously, looking up and down.

"What did he say?" Powers said.

"I have a pool car picking us up," he said, without looking Powers in the eye. "We're going to Camp David."

"I'd like to meet him without the Secret Service working shift finding out," Powers said.

"I can have him come to my quarters. No one from the working shift would enter my private office," Eggleston said matter-of-factly.

Powers, like everyone who's ever been a law-enforcement officer, had developed a radar for detecting lies. Was it a change in Eggleston's tone of voice since making the call?

"Who's picking us up?"

Eggleston was staring down the street. "One of the military drivers," he said, looking down the street.

Powers suddenly realized something was wrong.

"I asked you what the man said, but you didn't answer my question."

Eggleston turned to him. "Jack, the President said he didn't know what I was talking about."

Powers felt a chill on his neck.

A black Chevrolet sedan sped through the red light at the corner and, with brakes squealing, came to a stop at the curb in front of them.

The front passenger door flew open and Special Agent John Capizzi jumped out, aiming his revolver at Powers. "Jack Powers, you are under arrest on suspicion of threatening the life of the President of the United States!"

A police car sped around the corner and pulled up.

Two uniformed D.C. policemen burst from the car, pointing guns.

Powers raised his hands.

"I'm sorry, Jack," Eggleston said. "But you'll be able to get some help now."

One of the police officers shoved him roughly against the sedan and frisked him. As he was handcuffed, Capizzi, in his heavy New York accent, was reading him his Miranda rights from a card. Restaurant customers were coming out to watch.

"We'll take it from here, Mr. Eggleston," Capizzi said.

"Get him out of here before the press gets wind of this," Eggleston said.

"I haven't done anything," Powers said to Capizzi. "This is a setup."

"Relax. Everything's going to be okay."

"Can't you see I'm not crazy, you dumb son of a bitch?" Powers shouted.

A policeman grabbed Powers's arm and shoved him into the backseat of the sedan. As he leaned forward with his arms shackled tightly behind him, the cops climbed in on either side and pulled the doors closed.

At Secret Service headquarters, Powers was seated at a small wooden table in an interview room reeking of cigarette residue. The walls were pale green, the ceiling yellowish, and a small ashtray formed out of aluminum foil decorated the table.

Powers's right hand, tightly handcuffed to a reinforced eyebolt protruding from the table, was starting to get numb. He'd been ensconced in the room immediately upon arrival, probably so that Capizzi could phone the Protective Research Section and take credit for the big arrest.

The door handle turned and Capizzi came into the room and sat down at the table.

"How do you feel, Jack?"

"What the hell is going on?"

"I just need to ask you a few questions," Capizzi said condescendingly. "What's all this about having to see the President?"

"Let's get something straight: I'm not crazy," Powers said. "But I did ask to see the President."

"What about?"

"I'm not at liberty to say."

"Jack, you can level with me. I'm your friend."

"Capizzi. For once, please try to pull your head out of your ass."

"I'm someone you can confide in, Jack. We used to work together."

"Capizzi, you're not the kind of guy anyone should confide in. That's why I'm guessing you're an unwitting participant in this. And even if I were guilty of something, I'd die before I'd confess it to an asshole like you."

"We're going to get you some help."

"Please, just shut your mouth for a minute and let me talk."

"Sure, Jack."

"I'm not crazy. I haven't made any threats. Whoever told you that is lying. I was on-duty at the White House less than three weeks ago. Did I look like I was crazy then?"

"No one is saying you're crazy."

Powers felt his face flush with anger and frustration. He took a deep breath to regain his composure. "I need to talk to the President because someone tried to kill me tonight, and it relates to a political chore I handled for him."

"What chore is this?"

"I can't tell you."

"Those people who tried to kill you . . . do you think they are still out there?"

Powers's mind raced. There was no other option. "I killed them first," he said.

"Can't blame you for defending yourself," Capizzi said, as if conversing with a child.

"If you were telling me this I might not believe you either," Powers said, baring his teeth. "But so help me God, it's true. This is why I need to talk with the President before it's too late."

Capizzi opened his notebook and began filling out what Powers knew was a mental evaluation form. Per standard Secret Service procedure in presidential threat cases, he was going to commit Powers to a mental institution for a three-day psychiatric evaluation.

"If you take me to The Rustic Inn in Great Falls, I'll point out the bodies."

"You're telling me you killed two people?" Capizzi said, without looking up from the paperwork.

"A man and a woman armed with Berettas. It was self-defense."

"How did you kill them?"

"With one of their own guns."

Capizzi nodded. "Where is the gun?"

"I prefer not to tell you at this point," Powers said, realizing that if he told him about Susan it might endanger her. "Don't sit there treating me like some presidential threat case. There's nothing wrong with me. Acting in self-defense, I had to kill two people."

Capizzi stopped writing, stood up, and left the room. He came back a few minutes later. "There were no murders reported tonight."

"Take me there and I'll point out the bodies to you. You'll see what I'm telling you is the truth. I'm asking you, man-to-man, to take me there."

"How do I know you're not going to try and get away?"

"Bring ten agents along with us. Chain my feet. No

one could ever criticize you for following up on what I'm telling you. You're covered."

Capizzi stood there for a moment. "Okay." He left the room and returned in a few minutes with four young special agents from the Protective Research Section responsible for investigating those who threaten the President. They led him down a hallway and took an elevator to the underground garage. Capizzi led him to a sedan and opened the door for him. He sat in the backseat with Powers, and one of the agents climbed behind the wheel.

A police radio car containing two uniformed policemen and two detectives followed them to The Rustic Inn parking lot.

Before Capizzi allowed Powers to leave the sedan, one of the uniformed policemen brought leg shackles to the car and affixed them to Powers's legs. Tripping now and then on the leg chain, Powers led the group of cops up the steps. There was the sound of leaves underfoot as the group, surrounding him in case he tried to run, moved into the forest.

The bodies weren't there.

This is where it happened," Powers said. "Someone must have moved the bodies."

The cops and agents exchanged "told you so" glances with one another. The plainclothesmen turned to Capizzi.

"Check the trees," Powers said. "I know at least one of the slugs hit a tree."

"Sure," Capizzi said, taking him by the arm.

Powers pulled away from his grasp. "I need to talk to the President."

Capizzi grabbed his arm again. "C'mon, Jack. We have to go back now."

"The President is in danger!" Powers shouted. "You've got to tell him! Listen to me, goddammit!"

The cops and agents moved closer.

"Take him!" Capizzi shouted. From behind, a policeman's arm slid around Powers's neck and he was pulled backward off his feet. He was being choked. Then his feet were lifted and the group carried him roughly down the steps to the car. Someone opened the trunk of the radio car and took something out.

Powers was forced facedown on the hood of the sedan. With each arm and leg secured firmly by a policeman, he felt his handcuffs being unfastened. He was pulled upright. His arms were forcibly extended and shoved into canvas sleeves . . . a straitjacket! With a mighty effort, he freed his right arm and punched Capizzi squarely in the jaw. Then he himself was being punched and kicked. His wind was knocked out, and as he tried to catch his breath he was manipulated into the straitjacket. It was pulled closed, restricting his arms tightly across his chest.

Someone opened the back door of the sedan, and he felt himself being lifted, then tossed into the backseat, hitting his head sharply against the opposite door. He saw black for a moment, and felt a twinge of nausea as the front doors were opened and men climbed inside.

He sat up on the seat as the car was pulling out of the parking lot. There was reinforced steel mesh extending from the front seat backrest to the roof. Capizzi was sitting in the passenger seat.

"Where are we going?" Powers said, leaning forward in the seat. No answer.

Capizzi ignored him during the trip back to D.C. Powers began to suspect where they were taking him as they drove past the downtown area. And he knew for sure as they reached the southeast. Passing blocks of brick-front row houses, the driver steered into the driveway of St. Elizabeth's Hospital, a large mental health facility operated by the District of Columbia Department of Health and Human Services. They pulled up to the John Howard Pavilion, situated in the heart of the compound. The only maximum-security section of the hospital, it was where the "White House cases," lunatics arrested at the White House, were taken. Powers knew that the man who'd shot President Reagan was housed on the seventh floor.

"Who told you to do this?" Powers said angrily. "I'm not crazy, and you're not going to commit me!"

The policeman at the wheel showed something to

the uniformed guard at the gate and the gate opened electronically. Its rollers grated loudly on the asphalt. The driver pulled up to the front of the John Howard Pavilion and he and Capizzi climbed out. Capizzi opened the rear passenger door and he and the policeman pulled Powers from the car. Capizzi had a swollen lip, which pleased Powers. They led him up the steps.

Inside, Powers was met by the strong, warm odor of mental illness. Though there was no way to quantify such a smell, or to determine whether it actually existed, among themselves all Secret Service agents acknowledged it. Over the years, when investigating persons making threats against the life of the President, Powers had searched hundreds of motel rooms, cars, houses, and trailers looking for weapons and other evidence. Though some places were more pungent than others, each had at least a hint of the scent . . . once described by Ken Landry as a combination of nervous perspiration and dead human skin: the odor of schizophrenia.

Capizzi led him to a reception counter. A hulking, blotchy-faced young man standing behind the counter handed them some forms, and Capizzi filled them out.

When he was finished, a Filipino attendant rose from a desk and examined the completed forms. He asked Capizzi a few questions in broken English and made some notes. Then he stapled the papers together. Coming from behind the counter, he led Powers to a heavy metal door.

"You're making a mistake, Capizzi," Powers said.

Capizzi and the policeman were walking out the door.

The attendant took Powers down a hallway to a small interview room. He sat him down on a bench jutting from the wall and picked up an open handcuff attached to a chain bolted to the floor. He affixed the cuff to the chain joining Powers's leg shackles. Then, without a word, he lumbered out of the room.

A few minutes later, a middle-aged man wearing a white nylon doctor's smock came into the room. His face was thin and he had an extremely sharp nose and graying goatee. He was holding an unlit stubby pipe. Obviously, he was the intake officer.

"I'm Dr. Porkolab," he said in broken English. "I understand you've been having some disturbing thoughts."

"I'm not mentally ill, doctor."

"Do you know where you are?"

"I've committed scores of people here myself. I was a special agent of the United States Secret Service until three weeks ago."

"Why do you think you've been brought here?" Porkolab interrupted.

"They said I made a threat against the President, but that's a lie. So help me God, it is a lie."

Porkolab nodded. "I see."

"There is absolutely nothing wrong with me. I am asking you to give me any test to determine I am sane. I shouldn't be here."

Porkolab licked the stem of the pipe. "Why do you think all this is happening to you?"

"I know this will sound illogical and unbelievable, but I have been sent here as part of a political plot. Someone wants to keep me from telling the President what I know."

Porkolab's teeth clacked on the pipe. "What is the valuable information you want to share with the President?"

"I can't tell you, because the information is secret and you aren't cleared."

Porkolab shrugged. Powers could tell by his vacant expression that nothing he was saying was having any effect.

"I understand you struck Mr. Capizzi."

"Mr. Capizzi is an asshole and arrested me illegally."

"Do you still feel angry?"

"No," Powers said after a long pause, realizing nothing he could say was going to free him.

"Would you like some medicine to calm you down?"

"No. And if you try to shove pills down my throat like you do the rest of the lunatics in here I'll bite your fingers off. Now I'm asking you, man-to-man, to believe me and take off this straitjacket."

Pipe jutting, Porkolab met Powers eye-to-eye as if, by virtue of his training and experience in dealing with the insane, he could predict whether Powers would become violent when unrestrained. Then, with Powers still shackled to the bench, he stood up.

Powers came to his feet, turned, and allowed Porkolab to carefully unfasten the straps on the straitjacket—which was no real risk because, even if Powers had been a lunatic and became violent, he was still shackled to the bench. All Porkolab had to do was step back out of arm's reach and stand there, he could summon the asylum's goon squad to choke Powers into unconsciousness.

"I'd like to speak with an attorney."

"I will relay your wishes to the Administrator."

"May I make a telephone call?"

"Maybe later."

"I insist on making a call at once."

Porkolab extended a key from a rollback chain attached to his waist and unlocked the door. He sucked his pipe loudly and walked out the door.

"Where are you going?" Powers shouted. "I want out of here!"

*   *   *

Powers spent the remaining hours of darkness in his bare-floored cell, sleeping intermittently, pacing, and sitting on the edge of the bunk considering the possibilities of escape. By morning, his options seemed clear. He could feign illness and try to overpower a guard, but even if it worked, his chances of making his way out of the institution were nil. Besides, he might end up killing the guard and, after all, the guard—or Porkolab, for that matter—was just doing his job. On the other hand, he had to warn the President . . . and what if Susan left her hotel room to look for him, and was spotted by surveillants?

He decided to try to escape.

Powers started at the sound of a key entering the door lock. He came to his feet, his fingers tingling with anticipation, telling himself this was as good a time as any. He would tell whoever it was he was sick. At the infirmary, which he knew was closer to the building's only exit, he would make his move.

It was Porkolab. "There is an attorney here to speak with you."

Porkolab led him out of the cell and down a long hallway toward the reception area. He stopped, unlocked a door, and held it open. Powers entered a room containing a sofa and chair. Porkolab told him to take a seat on the sofa. He complied.

Porkolab moved to a door on the facing wall and unlocked it.

Susan walked in, wearing a stern expression that told him not to say a word. "I'd like to interview Mr. Powers in private, if I may."

"I will stay in the room while you conduct your interview. This is the rule," Porkolab said.

"I understand," she said curtly.

"I'm Susan Fisher," she said, offering her hand to Powers.

Powers shook hands, feeling slightly weak at the knees.

"Please sit down," she said. "We can't really speak freely with this doctor here, but perhaps we can figure out the best way to have you released."

"Can you get me out of here?" he said, searching her eyes for signals.

"I'm afraid we can't do that, but we can notify your relatives if you so desire."

"I'd appreciate that."

Her thumb undid the fastener on her purse. She reached in and took out a pen and notebook. "May I have the name of the person you want notified?"

"Mr. Mattix. Mr. Otto Mattix," he said.

She swallowed. "Yes," she said. "And the address?"

"In D.C. Four-two-three Flee Street."

"Is there any message I should give him?"

"Ask him for transportation when I'm released."

"My law firm can provide for that," she said, glancing down at her purse. She got to her feet. "That should be about it," she said. As if to replace the pen and pad, she opened the purse with one hand and allowed him to see the butt of the automatic inside.

Porkolab moved to the door and inserted his key in the lock. Catlike, Powers grabbed the gun and swung toward Porkolab. "Keep your mouth shut and I won't have to kill you," he said, touching the automatic to the back of Porkolab's head. "You're walking us out of here."

"You will never get out. The others will see."

"Then this nuthouse will be looking for a new shrink."

"Please don't kill me."

"Where's the car?" Powers said.

"In the parking lot beyond the front gate," Susan said.

"Lead us there," Powers said to Porkolab.

Porkolab opened the door carefully. There was no one in sight. He stepped out of the room. As he moved down the hallway Powers was next to him, his hand holding the gun inside his jacket pocket. Susan feigned friendly chatter with him as they passed two nurses walking in their direction. Porkolab, his voice thick, greeted them and they kept walking.

At the end of the hallway they stopped by a glass window. A middle-aged man was seated behind the window in a small office. Porkolab motioned to him. The man leaned close to a speaking port in the glass and said something which, though unintelligible, Powers construed as being an objection to opening the door because Powers was an inmate.

"He's being released on a writ," Porkolab said.

"He's a White House case."

"Are you disputing my authority?" Porkolab said.

The man picked up the phone receiver and dialed a number. "I have to get authorization," the man said sheepishly.

"Please don't hurt me," Porkolab whispered. "It's not my fault if he won't open the door."

Powers studied the edge of the glass window separating him from the man on the phone. It wasn't bulletproof.

Powers pulled the gun from his pocket and shoved the barrel through the glass. Eyes wide with fear, the guard raised his hands. Using his free hand, Powers reached inside and pulled the guard's gun from its holster.

"Open the gate!" Powers shouted.

The guard stood frozen.

Porkolab reached through the broken window and hit the switch. The tall metal gate, creaking loudly, began to recede.

Powers grabbed Susan by the arm and ran with her through the reception area and out the front door.

There was a blue Volkswagen in the lot. They jumped in and Powers was thrust back in the seat as Susan accelerated out of the parking lot and into the street.

"How did you find me?" Powers asked.

"I went to the Ramada, and the desk clerk told me agents had been there to search your room. Then I just made some calls."

"Every agent and every cop in D.C. will be looking for us."

"What are we going to do?" she said.

"Talk to the President."

****
****

28

At the Decatur Hotel, Powers and Susan hurried across the lobby to the elevator to avoid contact with the desk clerk.

In their room, Powers opened the dresser drawer and took out a pencil and some hotel stationery. He asked Susan to write a one-page statement detailing how she'd been sent to impersonate Marilyn Kasindorf.

"What are you going to do with this?"

"I'm going to need something to show the President."

Susan gave him a puzzled look, but then began to write.

Sitting down on the bed with writing materials, Powers began sketching: first, a box representing Camp David; then, inside the box, a circle for the Camp David presidential residence itself. Outside and above the box he drew two curving lines representing the Cavetown River, an outlet of Maryland's Blue Ridge Lake touching the easternmost edge of the Camp David grounds: the river the President fished whenever he was in residence there.

Having participated in the last security inspection, Powers knew Camp David was as secure as any military facility in the world. Getting inside, into the President's quarters, would be a risky, perhaps suicidal task. He also knew it was his only chance to get to speak to the President in person. Sneaking into the White House was, for all intents and purposes, an impossibility. At least at Camp David he'd have a chance. The river would allow him an opportunity to get past the two security fences, and if he could make it to the inner perimeter he believed his insider's knowledge of the compound's maze of alarm systems and guard posts would give him a chance to get into the President's quarters.

Like any Secret Service agent who'd spent time at the Camp, Powers knew its entire layout by heart. From the hundreds of working shifts he'd spent standing outside and inside the presidential quarters there, he knew he could find his way around the place blindfolded.

The first line of security at Camp David was made up of a contingent of U.S. Marines, armed with M-16 rifles, posted at the outside perimeter. As with all of the other places the U.S. President lived, the inside or "close-in" security was left to Secret Service agents of the White House Detail. Armed with submachine guns, they would be stationed both inside and outside the front and rear doors of the President's house.

Powers considered trying to trick some young Marine posted at the perimeter into believing he was, for instance, an agent coming on-duty from D.C. He might be able to convince him he'd inadvertently left his identification pin inside the camp during the last shift of duty. But by now he assumed Capizzi must have notified everyone that Powers was wanted, and had probably even distributed his photograph to every post.

Recalling his knowledge of the construction blueprints of the ranch-style house where the President stayed at the Camp, Powers drew a heavy line to it from a point about two hundred yards along the riverside. This represented the path of a storm drain leading from the northern edge of the conference facility construction site to the edge of the river.

As explained to Powers by members of the navy construction team, the drain had been installed after a heavy rain had flooded the northern edge of the compound. The mouth of the drain had been installed at a low point on the property at the rear of a storage shed—about fifty yards from the presidential quarters.

The Secret Service, using its theory of studying security systems from the point of view of an intruder, had considered the drain a security problem and neutralized it by having a portable motion-detection alarm installed inside the drain.

"What are you sketching?" Susan asked.

"Camp David."

"What are you going to do?"

"I have to get in there to tell the President about all this."

Susan sat down next to him. "It's too dangerous," she said, her voice cracking.

"I think I can get inside."

"You'll never make it!" she cried.

"There's no other way."

"You can talk to someone else in the administration, the Attorney General or the Secretary of State."

"Someone has put my name on the threat list. No one in the administration will talk to me. Look: Ken Landry is dead, and someone is trying to destroy the President. The only way to get to the bottom of all this is to tell him."

"You were a Secret Service agent! You, better than anyone, should realize you can't get through presidential security! They'll kill you!" she said angrily.

"I wrote the last security report for Camp David," Powers said quietly. "I know I can get inside."

Susan sat next to him on the bed. She put her head on his shoulder.

"I have to do it," Powers said. With his rough sketch of the area having been completed to refresh his memory, he now decided how he'd attempt to breach the security and gain entry. He made a list of the equipment he would need for the operation. It read as follows:

1. Scuba gear
2. BB gun
3. Bolt-cutters
4. Screwdriver
5. Wire-cutters

After some telephone calls to determine where to purchase scuba gear, he and Susan spent the day shopping at sporting goods and hardware stores. Powers used his credit card to purchase the needed gear.

With the equipment he'd purchased in the trunk of his car, he drove to Fort McNair, a nearby D.C. army post. As Susan waited in the car, Powers entered the post recreation office carrying the scuba gear and informed the sergeant on duty that the post commander had made arrangements for him to test some scuba equipment in the post's swimming pool. At first the sergeant questioned him, but when Powers bluffed and suggested he call the post commander, the sergeant considered it too much trouble and relented, as Powers had hoped.

In the dressing room, Powers changed into the black wet suit he'd purchased and carried the equipment into the pool area. He strapped the air tank onto the back plate and hooked up the valve, console, and harness straps.

With the backpack in place, he stepped into the shallow end of the pool and moved slowly toward the deep water. Having tested the regulator mouthpiece and the purge valve, he pulled the face mask into place and submerged. Underwater, he tightened his mask and adjusted his weight belt. Satisfied that the equipment was in working order, he climbed out of the pool and doffed the gear. He was ready.

Darkness fell as Powers drove north on Highway 279 out of D.C. He was consumed by his thoughts—his plan. Neither he nor Susan had spoken much since leaving the hotel. Because of heavy traffic, it took nearly two hours to reach the Catoctin Mountains. By the time they arrived, darkness had fallen. On the wooded Highway 15 near Thurmont, Maryland, Powers pointed out Camp David as they cruised past. A security light illuminated two fully armed uniformed Marines standing at the front gate. The interior as well as an exterior security fence were well lighted, each lined on top with a curl of razor-sharp concertina wire.

Camp David was a U.S. Navy installation, complete with military barracks used by a permanently assigned contingent of U.S. Marines and sailors, and the White House Detail Secret Service agents when the President was in residence. At Camp David, the President stayed in a rambling California ranch-style house in the middle of the compound. Out of sight of the military barracks, the building was situated toward the rear of the compound, near guest cottages used for foreign leaders and other presidential guests. The guard booths and posts in and around the camp were situated so that if an intruder was able to shoot his way past any one sentinel, he would, as if entering a flytrap, be in the fire zone of two more.

A mile or so down the road, Powers swerved off the highway and followed a dirt road along the bank of the winding Cavetown River into the forest.

Though he'd been lucky enough to survive Vietnam and two presidential assassination attempts while in the Secret Service, he knew breaking into Camp David would be the most dangerous thing he'd ever done. The White House Detail agents posted in and around the Palace, as the President's house was called, would believe he was a threat to the President, and shoot him on sight.

At a spot where the dirt road jogged right, Powers pulled over. He made a U-turn and pulled the car behind some trees at the edge of the river to park. When he turned off the headlights they were immersed in blackness. The only sound was the *whiz-hum* of cars careening past on the highway.

Powers opened his door and climbed out of the car. He opened the rear door and pulled the tank and the other scuba gear from the backseat. Susan got out and came to his side.

"Return to the Decatur," he said. "You should still be safe there. If something happens to me, get in touch with David Broder at the *Washington Post*. Tell him everything. Once you're on record with him you'll be safe. No matter what is going on in the White House, no one will risk coming under the spotlight by harming you. Tell Broder everything."

"Do I know everything, Jack?"

"Everything except the fact that Marilyn Kasindorf was having an affair with the President. That's why I was asked to conduct a discreet investigation rather than turn the matter over to the FBI. I was protecting the President from embarrassment."

"Now I understand."

"I'm asking you to keep that secret forever—unless you find yourself still in danger. But it's something you should know. It could provide a valuable piece of the puzzle later."

"I don't want you to do this," she said, her voice cracking. "Please. I love you, Jack."

"I love you too, Susan. And I want to spend the rest of my life with you. But I have to go through with this."

"No, damn it. You don't. There has to be another way."

She threw her arms around him, and he hugged her tightly.

"After I left Kassel I thought about you every day," she said. "I swore I was never going to take another government assignment. Now I'm afraid I'll never see you again."

He tried to escape from her embrace but she held him. He grasped her arms firmly and pulled them from around his neck. "Don't put your lights on until you reach the highway." Though he had the urge to kiss her again, tell her he loved her, get back in the car, and drive away, he turned and walked to the river's edge.

He heard the car start, and she drove off. Powers stopped and turned. As the shadow of the sedan moved past some trees along the roadway and disappeared, Powers suddenly felt empty and alone, more alone than at any other time in his life.

Dropping to his knees at the muddy edge of the water, he donned the scuba backpack, weight belt, and other gear. With these items fitting snugly, he slipped into swim fins and waded into the black water. Before going under, he shoved the BB gun and screwdriver inside his wet suit and tied the bolt-cutters to his left wrist with a nylon cord. Rubbing spittle on his face mask to keep it from fogging later, he checked the regulator hose.

He slipped underwater for a moment to test the equipment and sensed the dull, aching cold of the water surrounding his wet suit. When he was sure his breathing equipment was operating, he worked his fins and moved into the middle of the river. For more than a mile he traveled slowly downriver without going underwater. Then, at some jutting rocks, he realized he was within the one-mile security perimeter of Camp David. Already his arms and legs were aching from the cold.

Per the Secret Service Camp David Security Manual, Marines on roving posts were responsible for patrolling the river and the woods for one mile outside of Camp David. All were equipped with night-vision glasses allowing them to see clearly in darkness, two-way radios, and a body alarm that activated an emergency radio frequency in the event someone was lying down for more than five seconds rather than standing. Any guard killed or knocked unconscious by an intruder would alert everyone at Camp David.

Powers submerged.

Underwater, with his limbs aching from the cold, he moved by treading with his fins. Careful to remain along the edge of the river nearest to Camp David, now and then he would become disoriented and flail about to get his bearings until he touched the shallow riverbed. After what he guessed was about twenty minutes, he came to the surface. Camp David, security lights illuminating its perimeter fences, was about two hundred yards away. Praying the sentries hadn't seen him, Powers submerged again.

Swimming close to the right bank with his right hand guiding him, he made his way along the river until his hand hit an obstruction: a chain-link fence extending across the bed of the river. It had been installed about five years ago at Landry's suggestion. Wedging himself close to the fence, he tugged the cord on his wrist and drew in the bolt-cutters. Guiding the blades of the tool to a strand of chain link, he laboriously clipped through an approximately four-foot-square section and swam through. Continuing toward Camp David he surfaced frequently, searching for the storm drain opening along the river bank.

Traveling as fast as he could manage with the fins and other equipment, Powers moved himself to the drain opening. He unzipped his wet suit and pulled out the BB pistol. Pulling the slide to charge the cylinder with air, he aimed the pistol into the mouth of the drain opening and fired. With the knowledge that the BB alone was enough to set off the motion alarm installed inside the drain, he shoved the gun back into the wet suit and submerged.

Confident that in the darkness he would be invisible to Marines probing the water with flashlights, he headed for the bottom of the river. If his oxygen ran out and he had to come to the surface, he might be shot. Though the standing orders for those assigned to the perimeter were not to fire unless they spotted a weapon or believed the intruder was engaged in an activity designed to result in either loss of life or property damage, in the eyes of a nineteen-year-old combat-trained Marine what else would a frogman be doing in the hours of darkness near the temporary residence of the President of the United States?

Finally, after hiding on the bottom for what he guessed was about twenty minutes, he came back to the surface. In the distance, near the Palace, two figures were kneeling on the ground shining flashlights into the drain opening. After a while the men got to their feet, and there was the metallic echo of the grating cover being dropped into place over the drain mouth.

His plan was working.

As he'd expected, the motion alarm had been activated and two agents from the Camp David Secret Service command post had been sent to investigate. Seeing nothing, they would notify the command post of the false alarm via radio and return to their assigned posts.

Powers used the breaststroke to make his way to shore. He unzipped, took out the BB pistol, pulled the slide back, and fired into the drain opening again. He shoved the gun back into his wet suit and dove underwater.

A minute or so later, a spotlight moved across the top of the water. Remaining on the river bottom, Powers turned the switch to activate his auxiliary oxygen tank. Later, with the sentries gone, Powers returned to shore for the third time and shot BBs into the drain opening. Again, he waited until the guards had gone.

The fourth time Powers fired the air pistol into the drain opening, nothing happened. Whoever was on duty in the Camp David command post had, as Powers planned, come to believe the alarm was defective and disabled it by turning off its power switch.

Heartened by the absence of activity, Powers paddled to the storm drain. Making his way to the opening, he shrugged out of the scuba backpack and removed the swim fins. Having unfastened the weight belt, he tossed it into the water. Because the fins and air tanks would float and might be observed by one of the Marines on patrol, he pulled them inside with him, after crawling into the opening of the drain pipe on his back and head-first.

With barely enough room to crawl in the pipe, he inched his way along, holding one swim fin in each hand and with the scuba backpack scissored between his shins. About forty feet in, figuring the items would be safe from a probing spotlight at the drain opening, he dropped them and continued to crawl.

Suddenly, there was an electric *slap-crack* of thunder. Powers started. Echoing through the pipe was the sound of rain hitting the lake. "Sonofabitch," Powers said out loud. He crawled faster in the darkness but was stopped by an impediment, a lump of something wet and pungent, which he hoped was nothing more than just a mixture of earth and mown grass that had washed into the drain. Holding his breath, he pushed his way through the soggy mass. About fifty yards away, up the grade at the end of the pipe, was a faint gleam of light: the drain opening.

Water coming from that direction hit him fully in the face and mouth. He gagged and, panicking for a moment, rose up involuntarily and bumped his head on the cement pipe. At that moment, he imagined, if he was killed, his drowned corpse would float out the opening of the drainpipe and plop into the Cavetown River: Jack Powers as flotsam. Susan, whom he would never see again, would probably be standing on the shore downriver watching as agents and marines dragged his swollen remains to shore.

With rainwater running steadily through the pipe, he found himself losing ground and being taken down the pipe toward the opening. Simultaneously arching his back, spreading his feet for traction, and scraping his fingers along the sides of the pipe above the water line, he continued his agonizingly slow forward progress. Nearing the drain reservoir, he reached the motion alarm. Attached with a cement screw to the top of the pipe, it looked like an aluminum speaker— and it occurred to him that, since the rain probably would have activated the alarm anyway, he had wasted his earlier effort. On the other hand, he hadn't known it was going to rain.

By the time he'd reached the three-foot-square drain reservoir at the mouth of the pipe, he was exhausted and his fingers were raw. Rainwater was rushing into the drain and splashing on the cement. He spread his arms to keep himself from being washed down the pipe.

As he pulled himself fully into the cramped cement reservoir, it occurred to him that the scuba equipment he'd abandoned inside the storm drain might have been washed all the way back down the pipe. The oxygen tanks would float and be seen by some agent on post near the river after all. He had to hurry.

On his knees, he reached up and pushed the heavy steel grate. It wouldn't budge. Water was filling the reservoir. Had someone welded the drain shut?

Coming to a squat position with a steady stream of water rushing into his face, Powers held his breath and maneuvered himself into position so that his back was flat against the underside of the grating. Powers knew the grate was in the field of responsibility for the agent manning Post Twelve. From having spent hundreds of hours manning Twelve over the years, he knew that the area around the grate itself, though not illuminated as well as the area around the presidential residence, could be seen clearly. If, when he lifted the grate and crawled out, the agent happened to be looking away, he would have enough time to crawl to a shadowed area next to the residence itself. However, if the agent happened to be staring in the direction of the grate as Powers emerged, Powers figured it would take him only two seconds to grab either a shotgun or submachine gun from the post gun box and open fire. Because the residence was so close, there would be no chance for Powers to surrender. In another scenario, there was a good chance that all the agents, having been notified of Powers's escape, might be holding their shoulder weapons while on post. In that case, Powers might simply push open the drain and be shot in the face.

Powers shut his eyes and gritted his teeth. With all his might, he pushed upward.

He could feel the grating, seemingly immovable, dig heavily into his back. Nothing. He pushed again . . .

and again. Had it moved? Coughing and gasping for air as the water continued to rush in, he gave one last mighty shove.

The grating came free.

Powers edged forward to unseat it a few inches from the top of the reservoir. Using all his strength, he slid it from the opening and poked his head out. He was less than fifty yards from the President's quarters.

He crawled out of the reservoir and low-crawled frantically, following a shadow extending from the President's quarters to a spot he knew was just a few feet out of range of the command-post surveillance cameras. Waiting there to catch his breath, he low-crawled in the grass and mud to the wall of the President's house. Lying hidden in a thick bed of ice plant next to the building, he unzipped his wet suit and took out the wire-cutters. Then he moved forward to a crawl-space opening. Working as quickly as possible, he snipped a body-sized V in the screen covering and slid into the crawl space under the house. On his hands and knees he made his way slowly and quietly, in the total darkness, to the opposite side of the house, where he knew the wine cellar to be. Feeling a ridge of cement, he lowered himself into the basement and stopped for a moment. He could hear himself breathing.

Crawling again to avoid falling in the darkness, he located the bottom of the steps. Making his way up the steps to the door on all fours, he leaned close to the keyhole. The door across the hall was to the office used by the President. Powers was in luck again. If the President had been in the room, a Secret Service agent would have been posted in front of the door.

Using the screwdriver, Powers worked to remove the door handle without making a noise. Finally he pulled, and the handle came away from the door.

There was no sound coming from the hallway, so

he pushed the door gently. It came open. He closed the door behind him and checked that the outside door handle had remained in place. Across the hall, the door to the President's office was open. Powers entered.

Crawling to avoid being seen by agents posted outside, Powers moved through a spacious study lined with tall bookcases. A gold-leaf table, the focal point of the room, was surrounded by three overstuffed sofas. The President's desk was in the corner. In the bedroom, where he knew he was safe from being spotted by any of the outside posts, Powers came to his feet. On the table next to the President's bed were three White House telephones, installed by a select inter-agency military communications team who worked twenty-four hours each day to ensure that the President, no matter where he was in the world, had the ability to communicate. The three instruments, which Powers knew had been hand-carried under lock and key from Washington, were red-striped.

Powers looked in the mirror. His entire body was covered with mud.

There was the sound of footsteps in the hallway . . . those of more than one person. The footsteps came into the study. A door closed and there was the sound of rustling papers, as if the President might have set them down on the desk.

Powers took a deep breath and let it out. He turned the handle slowly and opened the door.

The President, a tall, sixty-three-year-old man with a full head of gray hair and the ruddy features of an outdoorsman, was sitting at the desk with his feet up. He was reading a blue Top Secret briefing book. As was his habit when reading, he ran a finger quickly down the middle of the page and then, with a snapping sound, flipped the page. Once, at the presidential vacation residence in Key West, Florida, Powers had watched him plow through a full box of books and briefing papers in less than three hours.

The window facing the President was within binocular view of the Secret Service command post. The security floodlights gave the trees and shrubbery outside the look of a movie-set forest.

Powers, his heart beating wildly, stepped into the room. Staying out of view of the window, and with the thick carpeting muffling his footsteps, he tiptoed to the right side of the desk close to the President.

29

★★★★★★★★★★★★★
★★★★★★★★★★★★★

Mr. President?"

The President started and turned. His eyes widened with fear, and he reached for a small red dictionary on the desk, a disguised alarm button that, if activated, would transmit a danger signal throughout the Secret Service radio net. Upon hearing the sound, response team agents, per the *Secret Service Manual of Protective Operations* would, within seconds, burst into the room with guns at the ready. Powers figured he probably would be shot by the first agent through the door.

Powers grabbed the President's hand firmly.

"Please don't activate the crash alarm, Mr. President. I'm not here to harm you. I know you've been told that I'm crazy, that I've made threats against you, but those are lies. I know I look strange in this wet suit, but there was no other way I could get to talk to you. As God is my witness, I'm here to inform you of a matter affecting the national security."

The President, who, the press had agreed, owed his political success to an uncanny ability to read people, studied Powers eye-to-eye. He didn't try to move his hand.

Powers took his hand slowly away and, holding his own hands away from his sides, stepped back slowly.

"You can see I'm not armed, sir. All I'm asking is that you listen to me for a few minutes. Then, if you still think I'm crazy, you can sound the alarm."

After a while, the President moved his hand away from the dictionary. He rose slowly from his chair and took off his half-frame reading glasses.

"Sir, I'd like you to step to the window and close the drapes," Powers said.

"Why do you want me to do that?"

"The agents on the outside posts use binoculars and can see you clearly through the window. If they see you talking with someone in here and there's no visitor signed in on the log, they'll come to investigate."

"Are you armed, Jack?"

Powers unzipped his wet suit, raised his arms, and turned around slowly.

The President walked the few steps to the window and tugged a cord. The drapes closed.

"Sit down, Jack."

Powers, his temples throbbing, sat down lightly on the edge of a sofa.

The President sat down on a sofa opposite him. "How did you get in here, through the sewer?" the President said.

"I've done the security advance here, Mr. President. It still wasn't easy. I mean, it shouldn't reflect badly on the Secret Service."

"I was sorry to hear you'd resigned. The government is infested with so much dead wood it's a shame to see a hard worker like yourself leave the federal service," the President said, studying Powers.

"I thought you asked that I resign."

"Why would I do that?"

"I guess I'd better start at the beginning. . . ."

"Jack, I'm in the middle of preparing for the first

election debate. If I lose, I'm out of business. I'm going to let you have three minutes to tell me about this matter of national security. Starting now."

"It all started when Peter Sullivan called me in and asked me to follow Marilyn Kasindorf."

The President, whom *Time* magazine referred to as "The Velvet Hammer" because of his ability to wield Machiavellian power while maintaining a smile, did not avert his eyes at the mention of Marilyn's name, nor did he blink.

In careful detail, Powers recounted the surveillance in Washington and in Kassel and the apparent defection. He explained the circumstances causing his resignation, and Landry's telling him about finding the listening device in Marilyn's desk. Step by step he detailed the events arousing his suspicion that Landry's murder hadn't been a street robbery gone bad but an assassination. He related how he'd located Susan and what she'd told him, his call to Sullivan, the events at The Rustic Inn, and his escape from St. Elizabeth's. As he spoke the President, his mouth a straight line, nodded and made notes. Finally, Powers was finished. The President set his pen down.

"You're telling me the defection of Marilyn Kasindorf was staged?"

"I'm not sure. But I know the person I followed to Germany wasn't her."

"How do you know this?"

The President fidgeted as Powers reached into his back pocket, took out Susan's written statement, and handed it to him. The President unfolded it, put on his eyeglasses, and read for what must have been half a minute or more. He removed his eyeglasses and stared at Powers.

"Susan Brewster was activated from the Inter-Agency Source Index. She resembles Kasindorf and posed as her," Powers said.

"What is your theory on all this, Jack?" the President said, giving himself time to think.

"I'm not sure. But I think someone is out to finish you politically."

The President leaned back on the sofa. "Why should the defection of Marilyn Kasindorf ruin me politically?"

"If everything came out . . ."

"What do you mean?"

Powers throat felt dry. He swallowed. "Her . . . connection with you, Mr. President."

"Your three minutes are just about up, Jack. What the hell are you talking about?"

"I don't know exactly how to say this, sir. . . ."

"Just say it."

"The affair you and she were having."

"And what exactly have you heard about this so-called affair?"

"I was told you were secretly meeting with her here at Camp David. That she was your . . . girlfriend."

"If I was having such an affair with her, it would mean I'd been compromised by a spy. And the concern would be that this fact would come out and ruin me politically?"

"Yes, Mr. President."

"You say your assignment to follow Kasindorf came from the Chief of Staff?"

"Through Pete Sullivan. He briefed me and asked me to follow her."

"I see."

The telephone rang.

Powers's stomach muscles tightened. It rang again. On the third ring the President, without taking his eyes off Powers, leaned to the coffee table and picked up the receiver.

Powers stepped forward. "Sir . . ."

"It's okay, Jack. Relax."

"I'm busy now," the President said after a moment. "Reschedule the meeting." He set the receiver back on the cradle.

The President glanced at Susan's statement again and came to his feet. At the liquor cabinet, he picked up a bottle of Jack Daniel's and filled two cocktail glasses. He sauntered across the room to Powers. "You look like you could use this," he said, holding out a drink.

"Thanks."

The President sipped his drink, then set the glass down on the table. "Jack, I've never had an affair with Marilyn Kasindorf. And I didn't authorize anyone to initiate a surveillance on her."

Powers felt a chill, as if all his pores had suddenly opened. His skin felt clammy. "It's none of my business anyway, sir, even if—"

The President met him eye-to-eye. "Jack, you've just broken into my house, dressed like the Creature from the Black Lagoon, but I believe you. And I expect you to believe me."

"Yes, sir."

The President went to his desk. He sat down and picked up a fountain pen and a yellow legal tablet. "Pull a chair over here to the desk," the President said.

Powers complied.

"Jack, the election debate is tomorrow afternoon. That means every minute between now and then is important. There is no time for anything but frankness and honesty. Right now, I want you to start from the beginning and, again, tell me everything—leaving out no detail."

During this telling Powers spared nothing, giving dates and times as best as he could remember. The President, like a prosecutor interviewing a witness, nodded, interrupted him with brief questions, and took copious notes. Finally, Powers had completed his story.

The President set his pen down and left his desk. "After the Lebanon crisis, I detected that the Syrians were anticipating my moves," he said softly. "During secret negotiations they would hold to positions in areas where I'd planned to give way . . . and give up too quickly on positions I'd planned to hold firm. It was always very subtle. But there was no doubt in my mind they had a pipeline. There was a group of pro-Western Syrian army officers, a second front, who had begun providing my predecessor with valuable intelligence information during the heat of Operation Desert Journey. One by one they were killed by the Syrian Intelligence Service. We established that the leak wasn't in the CIA; the info was getting out of the White House itself. So I had Patterson limit access at CIA, and he assigned Marilyn Kasindorf as liaison to me. Even other CIA employees didn't know she was my briefer. Things worked fine for a while like that, and I thought the White House leak had been plugged. Then more Syrian officers began to disappear." The President picked up his drink and sipped. "The woman who posed as Marilyn Kasindorf—who is she?"

"Susan Brewster, an airlines flight attendant recruited by the Agency a few years ago to service dead drops. A CIA helpmate."

"How was she activated?" the President said.

"She received her assignments by a telephone cutout."

The President rubbed his eyes for a moment and leaned forward in his chair. "What do you think of all this?"

Powers didn't respond. He couldn't bring himself to say what he thought. The President went on.

"If what Sullivan told you was true, the White

House Chief of Staff, who sits in on every strategy session I have and has access to ninety percent of our top-secret information, may be an agent of a foreign power. Any suggestions as to how to proceed?"

"I'm just an ex post-stander, Mr. President. This is a little out of my league."

The President rubbed his chin, then ran his hands through his hair. "I need a moment to think. If you'd like to change and clean up, you'll find clothes in there," he said, motioning to the bedroom.

By the gesture Powers knew that the President believed him. Beyond needing a few minutes to think about his next move, he'd want Powers, his key witness, to be dressed in something other than a frogman costume for the investigation that was about to begin.

Powers went into the bedroom and closed the door behind him. From the closet, he took a pair of slacks and a jacket and set them on the bed. In the bathroom, he showered quickly and dried off. Less than ten minutes later, dressed in presidential gray slacks and a blue jacket (both slightly too big), and a gray silk necktie with a Windsor knot, Powers returned to the study. He realized he was out of breath.

The President, head in hands and looking gray, was sitting at the desk. "As a Senator and a Congressman things were a lot easier, Jack. Even the knottiest of problems could be shared with my staff, my political allies. But things are different now. We're living in the age of narcissism. It looks like you and I will have to wade into this one alone."

"Yes, sir," Powers said, feeling like a hundred-pound weight had just been lifted from the top of his head.

The President came to his feet, picked up the telephone receiver, and dialed. "Get David Morgan. I need to go over tomorrow's itinerary with him. Thank you, Mary." He set the receiver down.

Moments later, there was a knock on the door. The President told him to enter. Morgan came in, closing the door behind him. Seeing Powers, he stopped abruptly, his expression shocked.

"Mr. President, Jack Powers is on the watch list. He threatened your life."

"I've determined he's not a threat."

"But Mr. President . . ."

"I said he's not a threat, David. Jack's brought me some information concerning the defection of Marilyn Kasindorf. I'll come right to the point. Did you order him to surveil her?"

"No," Morgan said, in a tone of subdued astonishment.

"Did you tell Powers or Peter Sullivan or anyone else I was having an affair with Miss Kasindorf?"

"Absolutely not. Why—"

"Did you tell anyone you'd been sneaking Miss Kasindorf into Camp David to visit me?" the President interrupted.

"No," Morgan said, glaring at Powers. "Mr. President, the Secret Service believes Powers is insane, and if he's given you some story . . ."

"I've resolved all that, David," the President said, picking up the legal tablet and referring to his notes. "Did you activate a CIA helpmate named Susan Brewster to impersonate Marilyn Kasindorf?"

"No, sir."

The President coughed dryly. "Do you have any knowledge concerning the death of Ken Landry?"

"None. I don't understand what this is all about, Mr. President," Morgan went on. "But if there is some question as to my loyalty I'm willing to submit to a lie detector test."

"I'm the lie detector in this administration," the President said. He picked up Susan's statement and handed it to Morgan.

Morgan pulled a pair of eyeglasses without temples from his vest pocket and put them on. As he read, his jaw dropped. "Holy shit."

"How is it that Peter Sullivan took over the duties of bringing me CIA briefing papers after Marilyn Kasindorf defected?" the President said.

"After her defection, someone suggested that the Secret Service pick up the papers from the CIA and hand-deliver them to the President."

"Do you remember *who* suggested that?" the President asked grimly.

"Peter Sullivan."

Powers felt a tinge of nausea . . . nausea and anger.

"And did you take his suggestion?" the President said.

"Sullivan said the Secret Service had never been compromised, and he would personally guarantee that the papers would be secure. For the last three weeks he's been driving to Langley every morning and getting the briefing papers from Director Patterson himself."

There was a long silence in the room. Powers thought Morgan looked ill.

"Jack, give me the names of two detail agents, men you trust."

"Tomsic and Harrington."

The President turned to Morgan. "Phone the Secret Service command post and ask those agents to meet you here."

Morgan picked up the receiver and complied. When Tomsic, a former Denver police officer and army ranger, arrived a few minutes later, he was wearing a tailored blue suit and shiny black shoes. In his right hand, he was holding a walkie-talkie. Harrington and Capizzi followed him in the door.

"I thought I'd come along too," Capizzi said obsequiously. "Can I be of help, sir?"

Tomsic and Harrington looked astonished as they turned and saw Powers.

Capizzi turned toward him. "Mr. President . . ."

"Agents, Mr. Powers is on a special assignment for me. He isn't a threat to me in any way."

The President picked up the telephone receiver. "Send Deputy Director Sullivan in." He set the receiver down. Capizzi avoided looking Powers in the eye.

There was a knock. The President nodded and Morgan opened the door. Sullivan, dressed in a tailored dark suit and tie, entered the room. Seeing Powers, he stopped suddenly.

"How did he get in?"

"Mr. Powers has my permission to be here," the President said smoothly.

"Are you aware he's on the watch list, Mr. President?"

Powers felt a chill creep along his spine. *Was it Sullivan?*

"Yes. But I've learned some things that lead me to believe that perhaps he's not the one who should be watched," the President said.

"I don't understand, sir."

"Did you tell Agent Powers I was having an affair with Marilyn Kasindorf?"

"Sir," Sullivan said, looking to the others, "Powers has threatened your life. He is insane, and you are in danger just being near him."

"I asked you a question."

"No," Sullivan said. "I never told him any such thing."

"But you did ask Agent Powers to surveil Miss Kasindorf?"

Up to that moment, Sullivan hadn't shown any sign. But suddenly, with the distinctive "look" that overtook him, Powers knew. He'd seen that look cross the faces of hundreds of people he'd arrested over the years. It was not so much a single expression as a combination of facial aspect, body movement, and a rapid loss of color that, occurring simultaneously, gave the lie to any pretense of innocence. It was the-cards-have-been-dealt, back-to-the-wall, on-the-ropes-in-the-corner, down-on-the-mat-and-being-counted-out-look: the trapped look of those caught in the very act of crime.

"I was only relaying orders I received from Mr. Morgan."

The President turned. "Mr. Morgan?"

Morgan glared. "He's lying. So help me God, he's lying."

"Pete," Powers heard himself saying, "you son of a bitch."

"Tomsic, take Director Sullivan's weapon," the President said. Tomsic stepped forward, reached inside Sullivan's suit coat, and pulled out Sullivan's revolver. Capizzi, seeing an opportunity to look good, stepped in to take the gun from Tomsic as Tomsic frisked Sullivan for other weapons.

"Mr. Sullivan, you are hereby relieved of duty pending a formal investigation," the President said. "Chief of Staff Morgan and Mr. Powers are, at this time, detaining you for the crime of espionage until the arrival of the Attorney General of the United States." The President reached for the phone.

With a quick karate motion, Sullivan punched Capizzi in the stomach, grabbed the gun from his hand, and aimed it at the President.

Powers, like Tomsic and Harrington, froze rather than move toward Sullivan and endanger the President. Capizzi writhed on the carpet, trying to catch his breath.

"Put the phone down," Sullivan said, aiming the gun at the President. His hand was shaking.

"Pete, don't do this," Powers said.

"Shut up."

"There's no need to harm anyone," Morgan said.

"And after I walk out of the room you sound the alarm?" Sullivan said. "No." He moved to the table and grabbed the phone. "Sullivan here. The President wants to take a drive. He doesn't want any other shift agents along. I'll accompany him alone." He set the receiver down for a moment, then picked it up again. "Give me a local number, 265–4291. . . . Is Mr. Keller available for the concert? Thank you." He set the phone down.

"Letting the Syrians know where to pick you up, eh, Pete?" Powers said.

"That's right. And the man is going to get me there."

Powers eyed the President.

"I'm not going to jail, Jack," Sullivan said. "If you try to take me, you'll be responsible for killing the man. I'll shoot him first."

"Do as he says, Jack," the President said. "There is no need for anyone to be hurt."

Powers recalled standing in front of San Francisco's Fairmont Hotel near President Ford when shots rang out, and at the Washington Hilton when President Reagan had been wounded by an armed lunatic. In both places everything had occurred in the flash of a second. Both times his instinct had been to protect the President.

Was he going to be pegged as the agent who failed? He'd decided then that he would rather be killed. Now he was facing the same question. Was he going to be known as the man who allowed a White House mole to kidnap the President and force him to help in his escape? There'd be no explaining that one away over drinks at Blackie's.

Powers stepped between Sullivan and the President. Following his lead, Tomsic and Harrington moved close to the President in a protective formation. He could hear the others breathing.

"You killed Marilyn Kasindorf," Powers said to Sullivan. "And to make the murder look like a defection, you went to the Special Projects Office and forged her name on a request for annual leave. Stryker caught you in the act and you had to kill him too. To cover up, you had Nassiri sent here to blame Stryker and set the stage for the phony defection."

"Shut up."

"The CIA was nosing around, so you had the Syrians hire some freelancers to kill Miller and me. I hope they paid you well." Powers felt a tingling sensation in the tips of his fingers.

There was a shot as Powers dove for Sullivan's gun arm. Powers felt his right side spasm with the powerful shock of a bullet and suddenly he was on the carpet, wondering whether he'd been killed. Tomsic and Harrington were struggling, punching and kicking Sullivan. Then Tomsic had Sullivan in a choke hold. He thrashed like a snared animal as Harrington snapped handcuffs on his wrists.

Powers, charged by adrenaline and ignoring the burning pain of his wound, came to his feet. Then, overcome by a wave of nauseating pain, he sank to his knees.

"I got him!" Capizzi shouted, aiming his gun at the handcuffed Sullivan.

At the Camp David medical office, Powers phoned Susan at the Decatur Hotel and told her she would be picked up by Tomsic and Harrington. Then he was lifted onto a long aluminum table. Admiral Hollis, the

White House doctor, administered intravenous fluid and drugs and Powers's pain moderated. Susan arrived while he was being treated and held his hand. Finally, with Susan describing the procedure for Powers, Hollis placed tiny plastic drains in both the entrance and the exit wounds in his side.

From the sound of voices, doors opening and closing, and cars arriving and departing outside, Powers knew the President was calling in his most trusted advisers and explaining what had happened. He would listen to their advice and then make a decision.

"This wound is through-and-through, Jack," Hollis said. "You have nothing to worry about."

A few minutes later the President, his sleeves rolled up and his eyeglasses pushed back on his forehead, came into the office.

"How are you feeling, Jack?"

"A little weak, Mr. President."

He looked at Susan. "You have a good nurse."

"Yes, sir."

"What happened tonight has been classified Top Secret," the President said. "I'd like you to stay at Camp David until everything is sorted out. You can take as long as you like to recuperate. And Susan, I'd appreciate it if you'd accompany Jack. There will be a lot of necessary debriefings, and Camp David is a good place to conduct them. You two will be staying in my quarters."

"Yes, sir," Powers said.

"Yes, Mr. President," Susan said.

The President strode out of the room.

30

★★★★★★★★★★★★★★
★★★★★★★★★★★★★★

Camp David was a beehive of activity for the next two weeks. Powers and Susan, at the insistence of the President, remained as guests while being debriefed by CIA Agent Green. Powers and Susan took most of their meals in Cabin 18, which had a beautiful view of the grounds. The evenings were spent in front of the fireplace chatting quietly and making love, even though his wound still caused Powers some pain.

During the debriefing sessions Powers learned that the CIA, by monitoring Syrian secret communications, had learned it was Syrian agents who'd killed Landry and had followed Powers in San Francisco. The Syrian mission had been to preserve Sullivan's unique access to the White House at all costs. In the opinion of CIA analysts, Sullivan had been the most valuable agent ever directed against the United States.

A lengthy investigation of Peter Sullivan conducted by the FBI determined that Marilyn Kasindorf had unwittingly been used by Sullivan and killed at her apartment by him, probably on August 12, when she had discovered he was a spy and confronted him. After disposing of her body, Sullivan realized he had to cover her absence from the White House and hurried there to submit an annual leave request in her name. He discovered Stryker in her office and had to kill him too. Leaving his weapon to be discovered, he then switched the serial numbers of his gun and Stryker's in official Secret Service records and planted Marilyn's pocketbook on Stryker's nightstand.

In going over the evidence, Powers discovered that on August 12 Sullivan had signed the Camp David Secret Service's daily log for the listed purpose of examining the security features of the conference facility currently under construction. On that day, there was only a skeleton security crew manning Camp David. Sullivan, because of his rank, would not have been stopped from cruising into the compound and parking his car in the facility's partially covered first level. And what better place to dispose of a body than in a remote, highly secure area? Acting on a hunch, Powers directed a team of hand-picked Navy Seabees to examine the portion of the building under construction on the twelfth with an X-ray machine.

They found the outline of a body embedded in the cement lining the basement and spent more than four hours extricating it. As Marilyn Kasindorf was ready to be lifted from her resting place by a Navy crane, Powers notified the President.

The President summoned the off-duty shift of Secret Service agents, Press Secretary Eggleston, David Morgan, CIA Director Patterson, and other trusted members of the White House staff whom the President had allowed to be at the camp when the sensitive work was being undertaken, as well as Clint Howard, the Secret Service chaplain, whom the President had ordered to stand by.

As a Navy crane lifted the body out of the excavation pit, Howard recited a brief prayer. Susan cried openly, and the President and Powers and a number of others present found themselves wiping their eyes. The body was placed in a Navy ambulance and CIA

Agent Green, driving a Mitsubishi sedan, followed it out the front gate.

Though the President and the other members of the White House Staff returned to the White House that evening, Powers and Susan remained at Camp David. That evening, lounging around the cabin, they watched the television as the President's press conference was broadcast live from the White House briefing room. In it he announced his decision, without qualification, to support an isolated Israel against her enemies in the Middle East. In a news conference post mortem, CBS anchorman Dan Rather characterized the President's decision as "courageous." During the next five days, they were debriefed by representatives of the State Department's Office of Research and Intelligence, the National Security Agency, and the staffs of the Senate Intelligence Committee and the National Security Council—all asking the same questions as Green.

After two weeks, and with Powers nearly recovered from his wound, the President summoned Powers and Susan to the White House. Harrington, posted outside the Oval Office, winked at Powers as if he knew a secret, then opened the door. The President was at his desk with David Morgan. Morgan stood up as Powers and Susan entered. He was smiling.

"How are you feeling, Jack?" the President said.

"Just fine, sir."

"I'll get right to the point. Would you like to return to duty in the Secret Service?"

"Yes, sir. Thank you, sir."

"I wouldn't ask you to reenter the lists without offering you an incentive."

"That's not necessary."

"So I'm promoting you to be Agent-in-Charge of the White House Detail," the President went on. "Assuming you'd accept, I've notified Director Fogarty. And just between those of us in this room, he's not far away from retirement. I'm going to wait just long enough that the press won't put Sullivan's arrest and Fogarty's resignation together, and then you'll be offered the Directorship."

"I don't know what to say."

"David, administer the oath to Agent-in-Charge Powers."

Morgan pulled a piece of paper from his inside jacket pocket and raised his right hand. Powers did the same, and Morgan administered the same oath Powers had taken upon graduation from Secret Service School. The last sentence was: "And, bearing in mind my personal honor and the glorious tradition of the United States Secret Service, I swear I will, without hesitation, forfeit my life to protect the person of the President of the United States."

Powers shook hands with both Morgan and the President. Susan kissed Powers on the cheek.

Leaving the White House, Powers was congratulated by the members of the Secret Service working shift, including Tomsic, Harrington, and Capizzi— whom he planned to transfer to Training Division his first day on the job. In keeping with Secret Service tradition, Powers invited everyone for drinks at Blackie's.

Powers and Susan walked out the front door of the White House and under the hanging lantern on the portico. The manicured grounds were green and lush, and the sky had been cleared by a warm breeze. Walking along the path under the tall elm trees arching over the wide lawn, Powers suggested renting an apartment at the Georgetown Arms while looking for an affordable condominium to purchase. Susan agreed.

At the East Gate, Powers stopped for a moment

and looked back at the White House. His mind finally emptied of anger and frustration, he thought sadly of Stryker and of his pal Ken Landry. Then he nodded at the uniformed guard, and the gate opened to a bustling Pennsylvania Avenue.

Powers took Susan's arm in his and they strolled along the wide sidewalk, past the spiked fence at the foot of the White House lawn.

Exciting SIGNET Fiction For Your Library

New from the #1 bestselling author of *Communion*—
a novel of psychological terror and demonic possession. . . .
"A triumph."—Peter Straub

UNHOLY
FIRE
Whitley Strieber

Father John Rafferty is a dedicated priest with only one
temptation—the beautiful young woman he has been coun-
seling, and who is found brutally murdered in his Green-
wich Village church. He is forced to face his greatest test
of faith when the NYPD uncovers her sexually twisted
hidden life, and the church becomes the site for increas-
ingly violent acts. Father Rafferty knows he must overcome his personal horror to unmask a murderer who
wears an angel's face. This chilling novel will hold you in
thrall as it explores the powerful forces of evil lurking
where we least expect them. "Gyrates with evil energy
. . . fascinating church intrigue."—*Kirkus Reviews*

There's an epidemic with 27 million victims. And no visible symptoms.

It's an epidemic of people who can't read.

Believe it or not, 27 million Americans are functionally illiterate, about one adult in five.

The solution to this problem is you... when you join the fight against illiteracy. So call the Coalition for Literacy at toll-free **1-800-228-8813** and volunteer.

Volunteer Against Illiteracy. The only degree you need is a degree of caring.